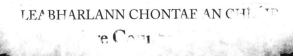

KEEPING THE WORLD AWAY

FICTION

Dame's Delight
Georgy Girl
The Bogeyman
The Travels of Maudie Tipstaff
The Park
Miss Owen-Owen is At Home
Fenella Phizackerley
Mr Bone's Retreat
The Seduction of Mrs Pendlebury
Mother Can You Hear Me?
The Bride of Lowther Fell
Marital Rites
Private Papers
Have the Men Had Enough?
Lady's Maid
The Battle for Christabel
Mothers' Boys
Shadow Baby
The Memory Box
Diary of an Ordinary Woman
Is There Anything You Want?

NON-FICTION

The Rash Adventurer:
The Rise and Fall of Charles Edward Stuart
William Makepeace Thackeray:
Memoirs of a Victorian Gentleman
Significant Sisters:
The Grassroots of Active Feminism 1838–1939
Elizabeth Barrett Browning
Daphne du Maurier
Hidden Lives
Rich Desserts & Captain's Thin:
A Family & Their Times 1831–1931
Precious Lives
Good Wives?
Mary, Fanny, Jennie and Me, 1845–2001

POETRY

Selected Poems of Elizabeth Barrett Browning (Editor)

KEEPING THE WORLD AWAY

Margaret Forster

Chatto & Windus
LONDON

Whilst some of the characters portrayed in this novel actually
existed, the events described therein are entirely imaginary.

Published by Chatto & Windus 2006

2 4 6 8 10 9 7 5 3 1

First published in Great Britain in 2006 by
Chatto & Windus
Random House, 20 Vauxhall Bridge Road,
London SW1V 2SA

Random House Australia (Pty) Limited
20 Alfred Street, Milsons Point, Sydney,
New South Wales 2061, Australia

Random House New Zealand Limited
18 Poland Road, Glenfield,
Auckland 10, New Zealand

Random House (Pty) Limited
Isle of Houghton, Corner of Boundary Road & Carse O'Gowrie,
Houghton 2198, South Africa

The Random House Group Limited Reg. No. 954009
www.randomhouse.co.uk

A CIP catalogue record for this book
is available from the British Library

ISBN 9780701179821 (from Jan 07)

ISBN 0701179821

Papers used by Random House are natural,
recyclable products made from wood grown in sustainable forests;
the manufacturing processes conform to the environmental
regulations of the country of origin

Typeset in Bembo by Palimpsest Book Production Limited,
Polmont, Stirlingshire

Printed and bound in Great Britain by
Mackays of Chatham plc, Chatham, Kent

FOR MY DAUGHTER–IN–LAW
ROSA MAGGIORA

'Rules to Keep the World away: Do not listen to people (more than is necessary); Do not look at people (ditto); Have as little intercourse with people as possible; When you come into contact with people, talk as little as possible . . .'

3 March 1912, Gwen John Papers, National Library of Wales

'As to being happy, you know, don't you, that when a picture is done, whatever it is, it might as well not be as far as the artist is concerned – and in all the time he has taken to do it, it has only given him a few seconds pleasure . . . People are like shadows to me and I am like a shadow.'

[?] March 1902, Gwen John to Michael Salaman

Prologue

T HE COACH, caught in the heavy traffic along the embankment, barely moved. Plenty of time to look out of the window, plenty of time to daydream. Gillian could see Westminster Bridge coming up, but it didn't seem touched by any of the majesty that Wordsworth saw there, according to the sonnet they'd been reading in class the day before. Big Ben was satisfyingly impressive, though. She enjoyed the chance, as the coach crawled along, really to look at these landmarks, and at the same time she was trying to frame what she saw, to separate the images and make pictures of them in her mind.

Nobody else in the coach appeared to be looking at anything. They were having a party, the other girls laughing and shouting, and two of them dancing in the aisle, in spite of Miss Leach's order to sit down and behave. Everyone was excited about being in London, and the art exhibition they were going to seemed just an excuse. Plans to sneak off to Oxford Street during the lunch break were well under way – Miss Leach was easily fooled. Gillian felt sorry for the poor woman. She was a good teacher but otherwise hopeless, with her straggly hair and nervous twitches and desperate desire to be liked. All the way here she'd been bleating for silence, her thin face tight with apprehension, flushed with indignation that no one showed her the slightest respect.

Eventually, the coach stopped outside the Tate Gallery and a spontaneous cheer went up. Miss Leach stood up and clapped her hands, shouting for them all to be quiet. Immediately, the girls at the back clapped back and stamped their feet, but then, sensing their teacher near to tears – they were not cruel girls, just high-spirited today – they calmed down. Miss Leach told them to get off quickly, because the coach had to go off to park, and not to forget to take all their belongings with them. Gillian was first off the coach. She waited while the others tumbled out, with their jackets and backpacks and carrier bags and the bottles of mineral water everyone had to have at the moment. Her own friends weren't among this group – they didn't do A-level art – so she felt a little apart. It made her sympathetic to Miss Leach, who was leading the way up the steps and through the doors into the gallery, where she stood in the lobby, her finger to her lips, looking ridiculous and being ignored. The giggling and chatting created such a hubbub that Gillian could tell their teacher would never impose order, so she decided to act herself. Standing with her back to Miss Leach, she put her fingers in her mouth and gave a sharp, short whistle. There was suddenly a shocked silence, and then a burst of laughter, and when Gillian turned to her teacher and said, 'Shall we go, Miss Leach?' everyone fell into line, perfectly obedient.

In the exhibition itself, the girls' behaviour was exemplary. A little whispering among themselves, but that was all. They moved from painting to painting in groups of three and four, dutifully consulting the notes Miss Leach had given them as they went. Gillian had read them on the bus. She found, looking at the paintings, that they seemed irrelevant. Did she need to know where the artist was born, or trained? All that mattered now, surely, were the paintings themselves and what she could see in them. The artist's intention didn't matter, did it? If a painting didn't speak for itself, what use was it? She was convinced that art should be looked at in a *pure* way, uninfluenced by any knowledge either of the artist or the circumstances in which it had been painted.

But then, in front of one painting in particular, she began to have her doubts. She stared and stared at it, becoming more and more puzzled, and also, in an odd way, disturbed. Something was there which she couldn't quite grasp. The effort to understand made her feel agitated, and she found herself biting her lip so hard it began to hurt. She lingered so long that Miss Leach came to see why she was not in the second room yet, and she moved on hurriedly, afraid she would be asked to explain. She took care, after that, not to separate herself. They spent over an hour at the exhibition and then the coach picked them up and took them to Hyde Park for their picnic lunch. Gillian wandered off, to sit on a bench in front of the Serpentine, in peace. She felt light-headed, the painting which had intrigued her flashing over and over before her eyes until she felt dizzy. After she'd finished eating her sandwiches, she opened her notebook, and sat with pencil hovering over the blank page. A new thought had occurred to her, but she wrote nothing. Her mind was full of simple but unanswerable questions.

Miss Leach was approaching, a silly, hesitant smile on her face. Hastily, Gillian closed the notebook, and braced herself. She knew she was one of Miss Leach's favourites. She knew, too, that she ought to be grateful to her – at the last parents' meeting the teacher had defended her right to study art when her father said it was a waste of her abilities and that she ought instead to go to university. But Miss Leach was creepy, it took an effort to be polite and friendly. She couldn't stop the woman from sitting down beside her, though. 'Well, Gillian,' she said, 'wasn't it wonderful, to see all those paintings brought together, almost a lifetime's work?' Gillian nodded. 'And what did you think of them, dear? I know you'll tell me in due course, in your essay, but in general, what was your impression? I'm curious.'

Gillian surprised herself. She realised what had been bothering her. 'I thought about their lives,' she said, looking down at the water to avoid seeing her teacher's face. 'Whose life?' Miss Leach said. 'His, or hers?' 'Neither,' Gillian said, beginning to feel embarrassed. 'I meant *their* lives, the lives of the actual paintings, especially one of hers. I was wondering where it had been, who had owned it, who had looked at it. And other things – I mean, what effect did it have on the people who have looked at it? What has it meant to them, *how* have they looked at it, did they feel the same as I did, did they see what I saw, and . . .' Her voice tailed off.

Miss Leach was silent for several moments and then, in a voice quite unlike her usual plaintive tone, said that where paintings had been since they left an artist's hand was of no consequence whatsoever. A painting took its chance. It was as simple as that.

But Gillian thought that somehow it was of consequence.

GWEN

I

THE WIND pushed and forced them along, great savage gusts
of it, stinging their ears, penetrating their scarves, whipping
their uncovered hair into fierce tangles, slicing through their coats
and chilling their small bodies so completely they were crying
and gasping for breath before ever they reached the steps. Gwen
fell. She tried to take the steps two at a time but the wind unbal-
anced her and she tripped, clutching in vain at the iron handrail.
Thornton hauled her up, half dragging her to the door where
Winifred, lifted up there by Gus, already cowered. Gus had set
her down, and stood with his back to the door, his eyes closed,
his arms spread wide to welcome the wind, and a smile on his
face.

All four of them, gathered together at last, hammered on the
big solid door, thumping it with their fists, rattling the letter-box
and yelling to be let in. The door swung violently back, the weight
of the wood for once unequal to the powerful thrust of the gale
force wind. Closing it, as soon as they were safely inside the hall,
took their combined strength. Eluned had not stayed to help. The
children collapsed on the tiled floor, pulling at their outdoor
garments, removing their boots, which were still thickly caked
with mud and under no circumstances to be worn in the rest of
the house. Winifred lined the boots up, taking pleasure in the
task. On stockinged feet, they pattered down the stairs into the
kitchen, eager for the hot milk awaiting them. Thornton and Gus
drank greedily, and even Winifred sipped hers quickly. Gwen held
her mug tightly, wanting its outer warmth on her hands, but not
its contents. One mouthful was enough. The rest she would give
to the cat, taking care that Eluned (who would report this to her
father) did not see.

Slowly, mug carried carefully, she left the others and went back up the stairs to the hall, and then up the next flight and into her room, where Mudge awaited her, expecting the milk. She emptied her mug into his dish, and he lapped the milk up without looking at her. Closing the door, and sitting on the floor with her back to it, she watched him. He was said to be an ugly cat, the runt of the last litter, but she saw in the dull grey of his coat and the white-lined sharpness of his ears something unusual that stirred her. He was her cat, unloved by others and all the more precious because of it. But he did not like to be fondled or petted. They communicated through staring, at a distance, into each other's eyes, and by listening for each other's slightest movement. They did this now, when he'd finished the milk. There were sounds outside the room, of feet approaching. Gwen braced herself. It was Winifred's room too, but if she pushed back hard enough against the door, Winifred would not, three years younger than she was, be able to open it. She would run complaining to their mother, and Gwen would gain more time.

But the footsteps ran past the door, heavy and hurried. Not Winifred's, then, but Gus's. She was safe a while yet. She smiled at Mudge, who turned disdainfully and jumped onto the window seat. She did not join him. Here, on the floor, against the door, the room looked different. The window loomed above the window seat, seeming twice the size she knew it to be. Interested, she followed the shape of it with her eye, measuring it for length and breadth. She wished there were no curtains framing it. The curtains were of dark red plush, thick and heavy, hanging from a brass rail all the way to the floor. She hated them, detested too the cushions covered with the same material on the window seat. Underneath there was wood which she loved to touch, the raised grain of it satisfying to her fingers. She was sitting on wood now. There was a patterned carpet on the floor but it left surrounds of wood on each side. These floorboards, stained dark, were full of splinters but she liked the feel of them and never chose to sit on the carpet. Its swirls of colour and its cloying woolly thickness offended her. So did the wardrobe, gigantic from where she

4

was sitting, seeing herself reflected in its oval mirror. It dwarfed everything in the room. At night-time, waking from dreams, it sometimes seemed to her that its mahogany sides ran with blood.

I am here, but not here, she thought, staring at herself. There is my head, and my hair, untidy as a rag doll's, and there is my body in its green dress, limp and still, and there are my legs, sticking rudely out. It is me, but not me. And this room is not mine, it has nothing to do with me. I do not inhabit it. It is just a place in which I have been put. I can rise out of it whenever I want. So she rose, first just a little way, enough to hover over the head she had just left, and then higher, until she broke through the ceiling and was in Gus's room, and then higher still and saw their house below, its roof gleaming in the rain. Then she came back down, satisfied. For the moment. Mudge turned and looked at her. He knew what she had been doing.

Reluctantly, she got up and went over to the window seat, where he allowed her to join him. It still poured with rain, the wind still howled. It was a mad March storm, sweeping in from the sea. They should not have been out in it. Their father, when he came home, and was told by Eluned about their escapade, would be angry. No one was to cause trouble in the house. Trouble, of any sort, upset their mother, and she must not be upset, ever. Mother's legs hurt, and so did her neck, and her back. She moaned when she moved, and bit her lip. She had stopped drawing and painting and playing the piano, and now she had to have her meat cut up for her because her fingers had no strength. Gwen stared at them at mealtimes. Her mother's fingers appeared bent and there were strange lumps on the knuckles. She had tried to draw them but they did not look right. Gus had tried too, and was more successful, but he had hidden his drawing, not wanting their mother to see. He showed her instead a drawing of her face, sweet and smiling when she was at rest on the chaise longue. Hands were hard to do and attaching them to arms harder still.

Her mother was upstairs, in bed, though it was only three in the afternoon. Winifred would have crept up to be with her. She

5

would have crawled under the eiderdown and snuggled up close, and Mother would be cuddling her and stroking her hair and kissing it. Whenever Gwen went into her mother's bedroom, she stood at the end of the bed, silent and anxious. 'Come to me!' her mother would say, and hold out her arms, but though Gwen obediently moved from the foot to the side of the bed, she could not do what Winifred did. She perched on top of the covers, and her mother put her arm round her waist and squeezed her. It felt awkward, and soon she was released. Inside, there would be a swelling of something she feared, a rising pressure of panic which made her hurry out of the room before something happened which she would be unable to control. She did not know what she would do. She might scream or cry or shake so hard that she would frighten her mother. So she left the room.

It was always a relief. The bedroom stifled her and she disliked it even more than she disliked her own. It was so packed with furniture, so overcrowded, and there was a smell which made her feel peculiar, a mixture of the scent her mother used, stephan-otis, and the embrocation she rubbed into her limbs. The window was rarely opened, the room rarely aired. She had tried to draw this bedroom but the paper was not large enough to fit in more than half. She had drawn the window, liking the way it sloped inwards, and the view through it of the slate rooftops, but could not work out how to draw the bed and the chest of drawers and the linen box and the dressing table and the wardrobe and the nursing chair – it was too much, it made her dizzy. Her mother had looked at it and smiled and said the wallpaper was well done and the carving on the bedposts excellently rendered. She had said Gwen was ambitious but must learn to walk before she ran, and she had set her to colour in outlines of children playing on the beach, which she had drawn herself, for Gwen and Gus.

Her mother's paintings hung in the drawing room. They were admired by all who saw them for the first time. 'Oh, how pretty!' people said, especially of 'Oranges and Lemons', a picture of chil-dren playing that game. Gwen could see this was true. Her mother drew figures well. The colours were vivid. There was life in the painting and yet it did not stay in her head. She had stood staring at it for a long time when no one else was in the room and then turned her back and all that was in her mind's eye was a vague impression of dresses and arms. Something was missing but she did not know what it was. She had asked Gus. He had said he did not know what she meant. She knew that he did but that either he could not say or he did not want to tell her.

Below, she heard the front door open and close. Their father was home from his office. The house seemed to breathe differently. Still sitting on the window seat, Gwen listened, raising her head like Mudge, stretching her neck as he stretched his. She must not move, must not betray her presence. The light, never strong on such a day, was fading. She liked the dimness, it made the room friendlier, as its bulging furniture was half lost in the gloom. She heard her father's voice below, and the striking of the grandfather clock, and then his footsteps, slow and measured on the stairs. He was going to see her mother. He would send Winifred away and spend half an hour with his wife, alone, and then they would be called to high tea where they would sit silently, eating and drinking. Their father would ask only the occasional question, and Thornton would reply. If their walk had been reported, there would be a lecture. Gus would have to say where they had been, and why. He would tell the truth. So long as he did not mention the Gypsies, it would not matter. They would all say they were sorry.

Winifred looked round the door. 'Why are you in the dark, Gwen?' she whispered. Gwen did not reply. She got up from from the window seat and followed Winifred down the stairs to the nursery where Gus was sprawled on the floor in front of the fire, drawing, and Thornton was turning over the pages of his atlas. 'Mama is going away,' Winifred said, 'I heard Papa say so.' They all looked at her. She was pleased to be important and smiled at them. 'Nothing to smile about,' Gus said, 'the aunts will come again.' Thornton groaned and slammed his atlas shut. Gwen said nothing. It was always happening. Their mother would be too ill to get out of bed and then, when she seemed a little better, and had come downstairs sometimes, she went away and the aunts came and everything changed, and there was nothing that could be done about it.

They waited at the table for their father to tell them what Winifred had already told them but he said nothing until the meal was over and then he cleared his throat. 'Two pieces of information for you to digest while you digest your food,' he said. 'One, your Mama is going away for the sake of her health. Two, Aunt Rosina and Aunt Leah will come to be with you. You must all be obedient.' None of them said anything. Gwen wanted to cry but if she wept in front of her father he would want to know why and he would keep her at the table to explain what she felt did not need to be explained. She bent her head and concentrated on her plate, tracing the flowery design over and over, forcing her eyes to follow the outline of the pink roses and up the green stems and round and round the prettily painted leaves decorating the rim. Her father was saying something else. 'When your Mama returns, we will go to Broad Haven.'

This news helped. Gwen saw herself at once in her own tiny room there, at the very top of the house, bare except for its truckle bed and the mat on the floor and the stool in the corner. Her mother had wanted her to share with Winifred, as she did at home in Victoria Place, but she had begged and pleaded to be allowed to be by herself at Broad Haven. The room was like a cell, Thornton said, and neither he nor Gus envied her it. She had never been in a cell. But a prison cell would surely have little or no light and her attic room was full of it. She could lie on the bed at night and look up at the moon and the stars through the uncovered skylight, and in the morning the racing clouds, flashes of white, woke her. Winifred's room, and the boys' room, had views of the sea, but she did not care. Views of the sky excited her. She had tried to draw the sky, seen through the skylight, but nothing came of it.

★

Yesterday had been market day in Haverfordwest. The streets and squares of the town had been full of activity, thronged with cattle

8

and pigs herded by the drovers and with strong, tall Welsh women carrying creels of oysters on their broad backs. But what had fascinated Gwen and Gus were the Gypsies, great gangs of them, taking the town over, acting like kings and queens in spite of their raggedness. Their encampment was outside the town but Gus had vowed he knew the way to it and she had agreed to let him take her there, though she had not quite believed he would want to do something so dangerous when the time came. But he was determined, and had woken her, and she could not let him go alone. They stole out of the house soon after dawn, using the side door which was the easiest to open, with no big bolts on it like the front and back doors. The single key turned smoothly, and was never taken out of the lock. It led into a narrow, covered passage which they crept along, knowing that the window above was Eluned's and that she was a light sleeper (or so she claimed). Another door opened into the garden, and then they could run through the bushes down to the hedge and the wooden gate in the middle of it. This was locked, but it was easy to climb over. Gwen tore her dress slightly on a nail, but cheerful Aunt Leah (whom the children called Lily) did not fuss about such things, and Aunt Rosina (known by them as Rose) who did, would never notice because her eyesight was not so good.

Gus knew where to go. They had an hour. If they were back by six, they could slip in the way they had slipped out and neither Eluned nor the aunts would ever know. Even if discovered, they could claim to have wanted to see if there were mushrooms ready in the field opposite. Gus was so very young but his daring astonished her. Gwen was not afraid of the Gypsies but she would never have approached an encampment, or been bold enough to talk to them. It worried her that she was older than Gus and ought to be more responsible and that she should have forbidden him to go where he went instead of agreeing to accompany him. She knew that their father feared that they might be kidnapped by the Gypsies, especially Winifred, though Gus had no fear. He said he would like to be kidnapped and live the life of a Gypsy.

She did not think that she would like it. There was no order, so far as she could tell from spying on them with Gus, and no privacy. But she longed to look inside a caravan, though she did not see how this could be safely managed. She would never go near to one, and would not allow Gus to do so. She had told him she would scream if he left her side. All they were going to do this morning, all she would permit, was to observe the Gypsies from a distance, securely hidden in the long grass. There would be much to see. Today the Gypsies would move on. They would hitch their carts and caravans to their ponies and horses and move away. Their fires would be put out, and their pots and pans packed up and all this would be entertaining enough. It was their clothes that fascinated Gwen most, the startling colours, the voluminous skirts, the rich mixture of textures, so many fabrics thrown carelessly, triumphantly, together. She longed to dress like them, despairing of her sensible attire. Aunt Rose said the dress of Gypsies was vulgar and loud. When Gwen ventured to express the opinion that, on the contrary, it was colourful, and cheerful, a half-hour lecture on the sin of vanity followed.

The sun had risen, a red glow spreading low on the horizon, and the mist, though still dense elsewhere, was lifting from the fields outside the town. They hurried along the lanes, making for the woods on the slope of the hill. For a small boy, Gus had an unerring sense of direction. The path by the River Cleddau was narrow and often muddy but today, after the long hot spell, it was dry most of the way. She could see the dark bulk of the castle looming out of the rising mist across the grey tidal flats on the other side of the river. Gus did not pause to check that she was following but rushed along, his footsteps loud slaps in the silence. The path ended abruptly. To enter the wood they had to ford the river over stepping stones. Gwen skipped from one stone to another without wetting her feet, but Gus slipped and soaked his right boot, another thing that would have to be explained later. In the wood the undergrowth was thick with bramble bushes, but Gus knew the path. She followed him closely, glad that he now kept stopping and turning, finger to his lips. He was being cautions, and it struck her that in spite of his bravado he was as frightened as she was. Then they saw and smelled smoke. Gus halted, gesturing that she should turn with him to the right, and take another half-overgrown track. She wondered how he had come to find it, so far from the walks they had all taken together with their father. But now they had emerged on top of a small hill, and below them was the Gypsy encampment. The noise rising up from all the activity was tremendous, the shouting and yelling, the cries of the horses, the screams of babies, the clattering and crashing of goods being loaded onto carts. They lay on their stomachs and watched without speaking. The biggest, most decorated caravan was directly in line with Gwen's vision. She was looking down on to the top of it, but the window at the side was propped open with a cane, and she could just see into the caravan's bottom. There was a blanket, red and white, thrown over something, and yellow cushions with tassels, and a glimpse of a table top with a blue teapot on it. She imagined the rest and tried to draw herself into that space, but she was baffled – she could not fit herself into it.

They were off. Mounted horses led the procession of carts and caravans, pulled slowly by older, heavier horses. Children ran alongside and so did the dogs, howling and barking and jumping. The silence they left behind was eerie. Suddenly, Gwen could hear birds singing and the cracking of twigs all around. She got up. 'Come on,' she said, touching Gus gently with her foot. He still lay prone. She prodded him again, and he rose, his face a scowl. This time, she led the way, remembering it perfectly, but he was slow, and he dawdled. She had no means of knowing the time but she feared it must be nearly time for Eluned to go into the kitchen and she did not want to have to face her. But Gus did not care. He was in a dream, away with the Gypsies. The thought of home made him miserable. Their mother had been away a long time. Gwen was miserable, too, but she would not care to show it. It did not do to show her feelings. Crying brought unwelcome attention. She wanted to hide, to find her room at Broad Haven and lock herself into it.

At the gate in the hedge, she waited for Gus. His head was

down, but he was coming along a little more quickly. They tiptoed through the garden. Gwen noticed her father's curtains were still drawn. So were all the others in the house so it could not be six o'clock yet. On the stairs, she paused, waiting for Gus, and squeezed his hand. He squeezed back. Softly, she crept into the bedroom she shared with Winifred and got into bed, fully clothed. In a short while, the household would come to life. She knew all the sounds off by heart, though the order varied. Sometimes Aunt Rose sang her hymns as she got up, sometimes she did not. Sometimes both aunts waited until Father had breakfasted and left for the office before emerging themselves. Today, none of the sounds were right. A faint click downstairs told her Eluned was up, but none of the other usual sounds followed. She lay there, alert. There was whispering on the landing above. Who? The aunts never whispered. Her father, to one of the aunts? He never whispered either, never. She sat up. More whispers, this time passing her door. Then a gentle knock. 'Gwendoline? You are to dress, and dress Winifred, and come downstairs. Your father wishes to see everyone.'

She got up and drew open the curtains on the bright August day. She helped her sister to dress and brushed her hair as best she could. She heard her brothers jumping down the stairs and a loud 'Sssh!' from Aunt Lily. Her heart began to beat a little rapidly. She put her hand over the place where the beating was and held it there. Winifred looked up at her anxiously, and she tried to smile. Hand in hand they descended. Eluned and Gwenda and Josiah were standing in the hall, side by side. Aunt Lily emerged from the morning room and beckoned to them. Thornton and Gus were already there, standing awkwardly in front of their father, who had his back to the fireplace. He stood very still and erect, gazing far off over the heads of the boys. Then he told them. Afterwards, barely pausing, but touching Winifred's hair as he passed, he walked into the hall and repeated the news. Then he went up the stairs, steadily, not holding on to the banister. They heard his bedroom door close. Winifred was weeping and Aunt Rose went to her and tried to embrace her but she wanted only Gwen. Gwen let out a loud 'Oh!', almost a shout, and Gus echoed it louder, and called out, 'Mama! Mama is dead!' and began to run round the room hitting things, and Aunt Rose could not stop him. He ran out into the hall and the other children followed him, crying and laughing at the same time, and he yelled over and over that Mama was dead and they laughed hysterically and sobbed and clutched each other. The aunts and the servants did not know what to do.

All day, curtains and blinds were pulled tight shut, and the aunts sorted out sombre clothing for them. Mama was dead. How? Gwen wanted to know. When? Where? And did this mean they would not go to Broad Haven? Gus drew, all day. He covered white page after white page with mysterious crosses drawn in thick black charcoal. Gwen longed to be outside, anywhere. Inside, the walls pressed in on her and the ceilings lowered towards her and the doors came to meet her. She felt she would burst. She had to shut her eyes tight and rise out of the house and hover above. It was so exhausting and frightening.

'Gwendoline has not wept a single tear,' she heard Aunt Lily say to their father.

*

They were going to leave Haverfordwest and move to Tenby. No reason was given. Eluned was going with them, and Gwenda, who helped her. Gwen heard Eluned tell Aunt Rose that she would give it a try but did not know if she would take to Tenby. Gwen felt superior. She had been to Tenby many times, with her mother. She remembered the bay, and the beach with the bathing huts on it, and the palm trees. She felt glad to be going there, away from the house to which Mother would never return. It hurt so much to look into her bedroom and see Mother lying there and know she was not really there at all, that it was only her imagination. The room was empty. Her father had moved out of it. He had taken his clothes and moved to the bedroom next to the boys', and no one went into that other room any more. Except for Gwen. She did not put the light on, or open the curtains, but stood with her back to the door, and looked.

The room was all shadows, merging into each other, streaming across the quilt on the bed, an army of them. Half-closing her eyes, she made sinister figures out of them. They were frightening but that suited her mood. Being frightened was preferable to aching with misery.

They all had to help to pack. The aunts had tried to organise the packing before they themselves left, but they were too distressed, and too concerned with their own departure, to succeed in getting the children to empty their drawers and cupboards and put the contents in trunks. Gwen had been surprised the aunts were not coming to Tenby, and had not understood why. It was, she thought, something to do with her father. Did he dislike his sisters-in-law? It was impossible to tell who or what her father liked. He did not talk to them, unless to give orders, and he had said nothing about the aunts, except that they had done their duty and he was grateful. Aunt Rose's face, when he said that, in front of them all, was strange. Gwen did not know whether she had seen anger or contempt there, or perhaps only pain. There was no point in thinking about it. There was no point in thinking about a great many things, but she could not help brooding.

It was exciting taking the Tenby road out of Haverfordwest. They had all wondered if they would cry when the door of No. 7 was shut for the last time, but nobody did, and nobody looked back. 'Where are we going?' Winifred whispered. Tenby meant nothing to her. She was only five, and had never been there. 'Beside the sea,' Gwen said, feeling that was all she needed to know. Beside the sea. But when they got to Tenby, glimpsing the tawny sails of the fishing smacks, they found that their new home was not exactly beside the sea. It was not one of the tall yellow houses above the harbour but was up a dreary side street off the Esplanade, one in a row. The paint was peeling off the window frames and it had a shuttered, dingy look. No one said anything. They were afraid to offend their father by expressing their dismay. Silently, they entered the house which seemed dark and crowded with mahogany furniture. It was a tall house, with a basement and three floors and attics above. 'Soon we will be settled,' their father announced, but there seemed no comfort in his words. Gwen hardly dared to climb the stairs behind her father. On and on he went, never turning to look at her and Winifred, never speaking. 'Wait,' was all he said, when they reached the top landing. He opened the doors to the three attics, looked in them, and then gestured that the girls should enter the middle one.

There was a lot to be thankful for. Gwen kept telling herself that. For a start, there was light, two skylights without blinds. And the walls, though papered, had bland, creamy-coloured flowers wandering across a pale yellow background. There was cracked and horrid linoleum on the floor, but the two rag rugs, one beside each bed, were pretty. There was a small chest of drawers, and above it a painting in a gilt frame. It was of a boy wearing a red velvet suit. He was standing with his hands in his pockets, one foot resting on a dog. Gwen shuddered. Her father noticed, and to her surprise said, 'You may take it down.' He took it down for her and carried it away. The nail it had hung on looked odd above the blank square below. She would draw something herself to hang there.

The first night was hard. Nothing felt right, and they all longed for the morning when their father would go to the office and they could escape onto the beach. But he did not go. When Gus asked at what time he would be leaving he said he would not be going to an office again, ever. He would work at home. The news appalled them. They stared at him. They could not work it out. Father always went to the office. He had impressed upon them many times how hard he worked, how necessary it was for him to work to cater for their many needs. What would happen now? 'You will go to school,' he told them. 'It is being arranged. Until then, we will take walks.' So they put coats on and followed him out, and he walked ahead, as he always did, his carriage rigidly upright, his nose in the air, and they half-ran to keep up. At least they were outside and nothing was so bad. The sun shone, the sky was nearly all blue. Once they got to the Esplanade the sight of the sea lifted their spirits. 'Breathe deeply, in, out,' their father said, and they stood in a line and did what he said, in, out, many times. Down on the beach, where they were then permitted to go, they ran away from him, Gus leading, shouting and yelling and chasing the seagulls. The tide was out and there were patches of hard sand where Gus drew pictures with a stick he picked up. Gwen and Winifred looked for shells, collecting them to take home, and Thornton gathered up seaweed and popped it. All this time, their father stood where they had left him, watching, but there was something unusually patient about him. He did not bother them.

★

There were caves under the crumbling town walls, dangerous places where the boys went. Gus had told Gwen about them, how dark they were, how damp to the touch the rocky sides felt, how strange the smell of putrid sea water. The boys took candles into the caves and lit them and frightened each other with the shadows they cast. Gus said he would take her one day, but not Winifred, who would be sure to scream. Gwen did not think she wished to go with him though she was curious to see what the caves were like. She wondered if she could live in a cave, if she had to, if some peculiar set of circumstances made it imperative. She imagined herself running away and having nowhere to go and no money to obtain shelter. She imagined what she would need to take with her to make a cave into a home. A blanket to sit on, a paraffin lamp to see by, a wooden crate to put her clothes in. She would cower there and no one would know where to find her. It would be quiet, so quiet, and she would hear drips of water falling from the rock above and her own breath going in and out. She would be alone, huddled into a ball, almost invisible in the gloom.

She tried to draw the cave as she imagined it. She put nothing in it except some stones, some shells. She used pastels, dark brown and grey melded together and a lighter brown for the ground. It was hard to draw the entrance. Could the sea be glimpsed? Would the sun strike through it? She needed help but Miss Wilson did not teach drawing beyond tracing outlines of flowers. Gwen would get no help from her. Gus, who could help, was now away at school, and her mother was dead. She imagined that the grave her mother lay in was a kind of earth-cave, but it would be alive with insects and worms weaving their way through the heaving soil. Her head was spinning, thinking of it, and she had to stop. Drawing Winifred settled her dizziness. Winifred wearing a hat, or Winifred with a ribbon in her hair, or herself, looking straight into the mirror.

It was disturbing, staring at herself, but she grew used to it. After a while, she saw a person who was not familiar but a stranger and then she could begin to draw. This person in front of her had such a cold, haughty look, as though proud of herself but unlikely to say why. She was not pretty. Her face was too flat, none of its features had any charm. The lips were thin, the chin receded, the eyebrows were too marked. The expression in the eyes bothered her and would not translate to paper. Only the clothes were easy. She liked clothes. She and Winifred had very few and none that were fashionable but with no mother and no aunts in the house they were allowed to choose material and instruct the dressmaker themselves. They spent hours hunting for fabrics beautiful to the touch but serviceable, knowing that the dresses must last a long time. They liked subtle colours, dark reds, deep greens, nothing too light or bright. Their mother's clothes had mysteriously disappeared but they had her jewellery and wore her brooches and some of her necklaces and bracelets and cameos. When they were older, they would try the earrings, especially the pearls.

They had special skirts made for cycling, in black worsted material, but the waists had white ribbons sewn into them which streamed behind as they pedalled. They had jackets made with tight sleeves, and cut into the waist so that the wind would not ride up them. Clothes were a comfort. Clothes were something they had control over and they could make their own even if they could not dress like the Gypsies. Their dressmaker said they had good figures. Even though they had yet to fill out, she commented, rather impertinently, that for their age (Gwen fifteen, Winifred twelve) they were developing nicely. Gwen was pleased, though she did not show it. Her body was easier to look at in the mirror than her face. Having no eyes, her body did not challenge her. She could look at it and try to draw it and not feel irritated. Breasts were interesting to draw. Hers were not large, or not yet, but she liked their shape, round and high with brown nipples, pert and almost sharp. Pubic hair was difficult. She had seen Gwenda's bush, when they had changed together on the beach at Broad Haven, and it had made her draw in her breath and want to touch the auburn fuzz, so springy-looking and plentiful, and spreading high and wide on Gwenda's lower belly. Touching her own was disappointing. It was dark and sparse and she would rather it had not grown at all.

She was too old now to run naked on the beach, or so people would say. It made her curl her lip in contempt when she saw the bathing cabins being taken out to sea so that the modesty of the female bathers might be preserved. It was not the way to bathe. She longed still to stand on the beach and disrobe and walk naked into the waves but she could not face her father's fury when such a scandal was reported to him, as it surely would be. He would call her wanton and say she tempted men to sin. He was the one tempted to sin, she knew that. He hung pictures of naked women in his bedroom. He humiliated her and Winifred with his attempts at courting women. They knew why he wanted another wife and his need disgusted them. She had tried to draw the male body but her attempts were unsatisfactory. There was something ridiculous about the genitals which her pencil exaggerated and she had torn these drawings up, but not before Gus had seen them. He had shaken his head and asked did she want to draw him. He would pose for her, and she could pose for him. Why not? She did not know why not, but she had shaken her head, said no. But when Gus was sent away to boarding school, she regretted her refusal.

It made her shiver to think of what she had missed.

★

'Sit,' their father said, and the girls sat, smoothing their skirts down and folding their hands demurely on their laps. Their eyes were lowered, ready for him to begin. Gwen stared at his feet, encased in black slippers, side by side, absolutely flat on the carpet. He kept them so very still all the time he was reading, and his knees too, firmly pressed neatly together, never one leg restless or flung over the other. 'The red room,' he read, 'was a spare chamber, very seldom slept in; I might say never, indeed, unless when a chance influx of visitors at Gateshead Hall rendered it necessary to turn to account all the accommodation it contained; and yet it was one of the largest and stateliest chambers in the mansion. A bed supported on massive pillars of mahogany, hung with curtains of deep red damask, stood out like a tabernacle in the centre; the two large windows, with their blinds always drawn down, were shrouded in festoons and falls of similar drapery; the carpet was red; the table at the foot of the bed was covered with a crimson cloth; the walls were a soft fawn colour, with a blush of pink in it . . .' He read on, but Gwen heard no more, only the rise and fall of his voice. She was in the room with Jane Eyre, oppressed by the mahogany and stifled by the red drapes. She fought for breath and there was a hissing in her head. It was the room of her nightmares. Her father noticed nothing. He loved to read to them and paid little attention to the effect of the words he read out. Should he look up from the book, he had Winifred to be gratified by. She sat, rapt, her mouth slightly open and her expression one of utter concentration.

It was after tea, on Sunday. This was part of the Sunday ritual and it was not unpleasant. The fire burned brightly in the drawing room and they were full of plum cake. That morning they had been to St Mary's where their father had played the organ for the service. They had walked there, as usual, even though it was raining and there was a bitter wind. Without the boys, both long since away at boarding school, it seemed a dismal and embarrassing walk. They were too old now to be led through the streets by their father, stalking ahead in his top hat. It would have been more bearable, and more fitting for their ages, that he should walk *with* them, side by side, he in the middle, in a dignified way. As it was, they felt they were scurrying after him. Anger burned in

Gwen at this enforced humiliation and she could only manage her rage by projecting herself into a future where she would walk by herself and never have to follow anyone.

On the walk back from church, they had passed a woman to whom their father had doffed his hat. He stopped and exchanged greetings, and they had been obliged to stop too, though they took care to stand some way off. He had not introduced them, though in fact they knew her by sight. She was called Mrs Thomas and had a little girl, Stella, who had red hair and was pretty. They might have been servants, but for once Gwen was glad of the insult. She did not want to have to speak to Mrs Thomas. There were other women to whom their father made tentative advances. His manner was always proper but his intentions, Gwen was quite convinced, were not. The woman, today, had blushed. It was not, both girls afterwards reckoned, a blush of pleasure at a compliment but rather a colouring caused by unease. Mrs Thomas, they knew, was a widow. She had not wanted his attentions. But he failed to appreciate this. Afterwards, when they had walked on, there had been a spring in his step and a foolish smile on his normally unsmiling face. They hated his complacency.

'I will continue next Sunday,' their father said.

★

Gwenda left, to be married. She went back to Haverfordwest and she was not replaced. Then Eluned went home to nurse her mother though their father made it clear that he thought her first loyalty should be to them. There were tears when her brother came to take her home, her tears, not Gwen's, though Winifred managed a few. Unlike Gwenda, Eluned would have to be replaced so an advertisement was put in the paper. A series of what their father described as highly unsuitable women applied for the post before someone was found. 'You are old enough, Gwendoline,' her father said, 'to take your place as head of my household. You must learn how to manage the servants and see that it runs smoothly.' Gwen stared at him in disbelief. Eluned had never been 'managed'. Not even Aunt Rose had managed her. She had done what she thought needed to be done and her word had been law. Their father did not seem to realise this. His notion of how their household was run was founded on a myth to which he had clung in the face of all the evidence. Gwen kept quiet. She had no intention of learning how to manage any running of the household. It could continue to jerk along as it had always done, though without Eluned and Gwenda it was difficult to see how.

The new cook was a Mrs Ellis, who came in daily, and therefore breakfast was half an hour beyond the usual time, which did not suit Father at all. But Mrs Ellis could not arrive before seven in the morning, for reasons so long-winded and tedious that Father did not hear them out, but was obliged to accept the change in his timetable. Gwen was forced to speak to Mrs Ellis on her first day. 'You may cook what you think fitting,' she told her, 'as long as it is within your budget.' Fortunately, Eluned had left a list of their preferences and dislikes, and Mrs Ellis seemed content to work from that. Gwen had added a few dishes to the list of family dislikes. Rice pudding was one. She loathed it with a passion, but in the past her father had made her eat every last slithery spoonful. She wondered how long it would be before her father enquired of her why Mrs Ellis never gave them rice pudding.

Mrs Ellis expressed surprise at the meagreness of the budget. Gwen told her that her master liked plain food and had no desire for luxuries at his table. But she felt ashamed on her father's behalf. There was no need, she was sure, for them to live on boiled mutton and scrag-end beef and have every last scrap of inferior meat turned into rissoles. Food did not matter to her unless it was fatty or stringy. She preferred to eat bread and cheese and fruit, and had vowed that when she left home and lived by herself that is all her diet would consist of. Winifred ventured the opinion that without meat Gwen might not grow, but Gwen replied that by the time this happy day came she would already be fully grown. 'Then you might faint,' Winifred argued. 'Your blood would not be rich enough without meat.' Gwen did not believe it. Meat was disgusting. She could not bear the sight of it. She had tried to explain this to her father as she sat, tearful, with lumps of meat in a stew before her, but he had said she was too squeamish. 'You cannot go through life squeamish,' he had said. 'It is not possible. Eat.' He told her that she was too pale, too thin and that it was her duty to eat what was good for her or she would become ill. Once, he began a sentence, or what seemed likely to be about to be a sentence, with the words, 'Your mother became ill . . .' and then stopped abruptly and played with his silver napkin ring. He bowed his head, and Gwen waited. Had he intended to blame her mother for her own illness? Had he meant to go on to say that if she did not eat what was put before her she, too, would become ill? 'Eat,' he repeated, but his tone was soft.

★

The journey was long, but they were glad to make it. Hours and hours they sat in the train, straight-backed, silent enough to please their father, books open on their knees. Gwen was reading *Far from the Madding Crowd* and did not know what to make of it. They had neither food nor drink with them. Their father thought it ridiculous not to be able to endure six hours without sustenance. They would eat and drink when they arrived in London. He knew a teashop near the National Gallery which was modest and gave good value. There they would refresh themselves before proceeding to the pictures.

Once inside the galleries, it did not matter that their father ignored them. Gwen was glad of it. Within minutes she had lost him and could stop and look at whatever she wished. It would have been better to have had Gus with her but really she had no need of anyone. Even Winifred was a distraction, soon whispering that she would like to sit down. Gwen left her in front of a picture of a winter scene with skaters and went to find Vermeer's *A Young Woman Standing at a Virginal*, which she very much wanted to see. She was annoyed to come upon a small crowd in front of the painting and she hung around the doorway until it had dispersed somewhat. First she viewed the picture from the other side of the room and then slowly moved forwards. She admired it more from a distance, and this seemed curious to her. She thought it meant that the artist was outside the painting and not condensed within it. She herself was *in* what she drew and painted. She knew she was.

Winifred fell asleep in the theatre. They were in the circle, front row (about some things their father could be startlingly generous). Red plush, comfortable seats, proper arm-rests with tiny binoculars inset, which they were allowed to use, their father willingly providing the coins for both of them. But Winifred dozed, exhausted by the travelling and the walking round the galleries and streets, her head nodding forward after the first half-hour. It was a stupid play but Gwen was happy. She had her sketchbook and worked rapidly, drawing the costumes one after the other, and then started on the set. The action of the play was in a drawing room. It was boring to draw the furniture but there was a spiral staircase in one corner which was a challenge and she drew it in minute detail, using the little binoculars to scrutinise the ivy embellishments on the wrought-iron banisters.

Their father was absorbed. He kept lifting his binoculars again and again to study the leading actress, whose voice Gwen thought shrill. She had already made two sketches of the actress, for no other reason than that her costume was ravishing. She wore a dress of striped silk, with gorgeous panels of purple and gold in the skirt, its sleeves, wide and full, in shimmering gold. Gwen thought that the sleeves, cunningly devised so that again and again the actress's perfect white arms were displayed, were of a different, heavier, material from the skirt. Satin, probably. She spent a great deal of time shading the sleeves to convey this difference. There was plenty of bosom on display too. The top of the dress was tightly corseted, pushing up the actress's breasts. Gwen, staring critically, found she was not envious. She did not wish either to have such breasts or to flaunt them. But she thought how, stripped of the dress and the corset underneath, the actress's body would be interesting to draw.

Coming out into the Haymarket, they were confused by the commotion, by the many carriages waiting for the theatregoers and by the press of people pouring out of the theatre. Their father seemed to hesitate, unsure which way to go, unused to crowds. Gwen was happy to stand there with him, taking in bits of over-heard conversation and watching the expressions in the faces around her. At last their father decided where they would go. For once, he held both of them, one either side, clutching them just above the elbow and squeezing hard enough almost to hurt, and led them round to the left where the crowd was not so dense. There was no question of a cab. They walked again, quickly, and were soon at their lodgings in Covent Garden.

Winifred slept the moment she got into bed but Gwen sat awhile, looking at her sketches. Some she thought good, worth keeping, but most she tore up, upset that she had wasted the special paper. She never liked to tear up paper, and tried hard to concentrate and think carefully before making any mark in her precious sketchbooks. She did not like to rub out, it was messy, so once she had made her drawing it had to stand or be destroyed. Painting was less wasteful. She had learned already that paint was amenable to alteration, oils especially. She could paint in layers and rectify mistakes. She wished she could learn more of the subtleties involved in the use of paint about which she felt she knew so little. It was no good trying to teach herself these prac-tical things. She needed a teacher, and access to materials which she did not have. Her hunger to learn was ferocious.

Gus was going to learn. It had been agreed. Their father, aston-ishingly, was willing to pay for him to enrol at the Slade School of Art, and he was to begin soon. Gwen's envy was violent; she could hardly bear to think of what lay ahead for Gus, and she had said so. She had told their father that she wanted to follow Gus. 'Do not think of such a thing,' he had said.

But he had not said no.

II

THE NOISE, the dirt, the grey gaunt buildings, the filthy front door, the knocker all greasy, the smell in the dark hallway (of cabbage cooking), the broken light, the worn-into-shreds stair-carpet, the missing banisters – and then her room. At the back, overlooking the dustbins. The net curtain a grimy veil which she tore away at once and bundled into a corner, not caring what the landlord would say. A little more light came in, but not much. The dirt on the window panes was both inside and out. Gwen rubbed at it. Interesting. The smears were yellow, like a darkened egg-yolk. Smoke, someone had smoked heavily in this dungeon.

She smiled. Everything looked dingy and dreary, but, for the time being, it was hers. She had come to this room a stranger (only seventeen and away from home for the first time), but she would make it familiar and not be afraid of it. The noise of the trains shunting in and out of Euston was loud, but only the piercing whistles of the guards alarmed her. The noise of the trains themselves, of the wheels on the rails, was a rhythm she could get used to. She would have to. There was no money for a better place and she did not want to go out to St Albans, as Gus at first had done, to stay with their aunt. She wanted to be close to the Slade, able to get there and back with ease every day. Gower Street, she had already established, was a mere ten minutes' walk away.

A dull walk. No greenery, only pavements and tall houses cutting out the light except on the brightest days. And so many people, hurrying along from Euston Road all the way down to Bloomsbury. She had not expected beauty here, she had known there would be no exhilarating sights to match those of the sea at home, but the grimness of her surroundings was a shock. She had had to hold herself together very firmly, tell herself to wait. What she had come to this part of London for would soon be made known to her and nothing else would matter.

She surveyed her room, hands on hips, and decided to change nothing. The bed would be better turned the other way, but she would leave it. Sitting on its edge, she felt the mattress sag. She must find a board and slip it between the springs and the old mattress. But the linen was clean: it gave off a fresh smell when she sniffed it. There was no mirror in the room, either on the wardrobe door or over the mantel. No wonder – this room did not want to reflect itself in any particular. There were no ornaments either, which was a relief. The surfaces of the chest of drawers and dressing table were bare, not even a cloth to cover the scratched tops. Too much furniture, though, in too small a space. She had to edge sideways to get from the bed to the door. Where was she to wash? There was a washstand with a jug and basin upon it but no water in the jug. Would someone bring it each day, or would she have to fetch it herself?

She unpacked quickly. The narrow wardrobe seemed to receive her clothes reluctantly. There was no rail inside it, only a row of hooks. She had brought four dresses only, and two skirts, and six blouses that she would wear to the Slade. Two pairs of boots, one pair of galoshes. Her stockings and underclothes went into the drawers of the chest, leaving plenty of room. Her nightdress and robe she spread out on the bed. They looked vaguely indecent sprawled there, the white cotton startling against the brown counterpane, too pure for its old face. The problem was her drawing equipment. There was nowhere to put her sketchbooks and charcoals, her rubbers and brushes. Gus had told her not to bring anything but she had disobeyed him. She put them in the long bottom drawer of the chest, and her valise under the bed.

It was late. She had not eaten since she left the Bayswater establishment, Miss Philpot's, where she had previously stayed, but hunger did not plague her. She was too excited, by the thought of the morning and making her way to the Slade, and *beginning*, at last. Getting undressed and into bed, after the adventure of finding the water closet down the passage, she lay with her arms behind her head and stared at the wallpaper. Maroon and brown with an inexplicable green that appeared every foot or so. What was the green? She concentrated. The pattern made no sense. She had left the curtains open and the lamps outside, shining in the street above, gave only a murky glow. The green, she decided, was meant to represent stems of flowers, but flowers of a sort she had never seen. It was enough to give anyone nightmares, but she slept well.

★

Oh, the size of it! Gwen had never been in such a large room, the ceiling so high that the space seemed to diminish her. Not an empty room – in fact it was crowded with busts and statues and easels – but there was a feeling of emptiness that thrilled her. The air was cold, the light harsh. She stood, solemn and hesitant, in the doorway, unsure where she should go. A girl, with long wavy hair, worn loose, turned from her easel and saw her. She stood up and came towards Gwen, smiling, welcoming, her arms outstretched in an extravagant intention of a greeting to follow. Gwen quickly held out a hand to forestall an embrace. The girl laughed, took her hand. She said she was Edna Waugh and that Gwen should come and sit by her. Gus had told her of his sister's arrival and they were all eager to meet her. Gwen sat, as directed. She had no desire to talk. She was impatient to start, and picked up her charcoal at once. There seemed to be no teacher to tell her what she should do, so she did as Edna was doing and drew what was in front of her. Everyone began in the Antiques room, men and women. She had her box of charcoals with her, and her sheets of papier Ingres, and a chunk of bread, as instructed. She set herself to toil over the casts of Greek, Roman and Renaissance heads, and waited to be corrected.

Correction did not come that day. Henry Tonks, the teacher, duly arrived but he was much engaged with others in the vast room and beyond a polite greeting to his new student said nothing, though he stood and watched her for a moment. This did not make her as nervous as she had anticipated. She knew, from Gus, who had been through this a year ago, what Tonks expected: his students' taste must be formed by studying sculpture before they proceeded to Life drawing. Simply to be sitting in this room drawing all day was a privilege, and one she did not need to be told to value, so there were no complaints from her about what others, sighing over the repetitive drawing, considered tedious. Five o'clock came too early for her, and she was last to leave, a sheaf of drawings in her folder but none of them, in her own estimation, good enough. Tomorrow she would try harder, and the day after that harder still, and she would not be deflected from her purpose.

There were those who wished to deflect her, though. Sirens everywhere, singing of the pleasures of gathering in cafés and going to boxes at the theatre and meeting in each other's homes. Temptations all around, to which Gus was always ready to succumb. She was not sure that she could resist entirely, or that she should.

★

'Come home with me,' Ida said, 'it isn't far.' They crossed Tottenham Court Road, Ida talking all the while and Gwen with head bent, not looking at her new friend but listening intently, and carried on along Goodge Street – she was noting the names, memorising them – and so into Wigmore Street, where Ida lived. The house was intimidatingly tall. It spoke of grandeur and wealth to Gwen but, once through the front door, that impression disappeared. The hall was cluttered with what seemed to be bales of material, and large sealed cardboard boxes. But Ida was leading the way up the stairs, rushing up them, beckoning Gwen to follow, and laughingly repeating, 'Not far now, not far now.' On the fourth floor, she flung open a door and said, 'Here we are, now sit, do, catch your breath.' Gwen had no need to, she was not out of breath, but she sat on the nearest chair to the door, an odd, straight-backed chair painted gold.

She caught the room's life instantly. Crowded, friendly, dimly lit, full of colour and texture, messy, somewhat shabby, worn and faded fabrics everywhere. Ida brought tea, and behind her came a fat, soft-looking woman moving slowly, like a ball rolling across the floor. 'My mother,' Ida said, and, to her mother, 'Gus's sister.' Gwen thought she saw Mrs Nettleship's eyes harden. 'His sister,' Mrs Nettleship said. 'I see.' It was not an approving comment. Bells rang somewhere in the house, and Mrs Nettleship sighed and said she must go, she was needed. As she left the room, a girl came running in. 'Ethel,' Ida said, 'this is Gwen, Gus's sister.' Ethel smiled and was friendly, offering to bring more tea, but Gwen felt vaguely insulted. She did not want to go through her new life as Gus's sister. She was herself, people must see that.

Leaving the Nettleship household an hour later, she felt relieved, and then immediately guilty. The Nettleship girls were charming and had exerted themselves to make her feel wanted and at home. But that was where the problem lay. No. 58 Wigmore Street *was* a home. It breathed 'home', though in fact, as she had already learned, it was three-quarters a place of work, with Mrs Nettleship running a dressmaking business on two floors and Mr Nettleship painting on another. But there was a closeness and comfort that had been entirely lacking in Tenby. Walking back to Euston Square, Gwen wondered if her disturbed feelings while she was with the Nettleships were to do with envy. Did she want what Ida had?

★

'Let us have lunch,' Edna said. She had found Gwen wandering down a corridor in the Slade, seeming lost. Gwen did not want lunch, she never ate lunch, she had no money for lunch, but she went with the irresistible Edna, pausing only to put on her hat. 'Your hat!' Edna said. Was she laughing? 'Oh yes,' Edna said, 'wear your pretty hat and I will wear mine, though I was not thinking of a lunch where hats are needed. We will look very smart, very proper, nobody at Bella's will recognise me.' There was a joke somewhere, Gwen knew. Bella's was a café in Charlotte Street, a tiny place squashed between two other grander restaurants. There were four small circular tables and round each table four stools upon which the clientele could perch (uncomfortably). Gwen saw that the two young men already seated in the café could not take their eyes off Edna. She was not surprised. Edna was lovely, she radiated brightness, as though sparks were coming off her hair and clothes. But she was not flirtatious or frivolous. Gwen wanted to tell these ogling men that Edna was a serious student of art and that they must not mistake her prettiness for a coquette's. She knew no one would doubt her own seriousness. Everything about her spoke of it – her dark, restrained clothing, her solemn expression, her aloof, detached demeanour. But there again they would be wrong. Her mind raced with millions of violent and spectacular thoughts and ideas, and in the centre of herself she stored a passion which might terrify people if they suspected it. It lay coiled inside, powerful, making the occasional twist and thrust through her veins to remind her that it was there, waiting, but still dormant. Edna bought her coffee, and a boiled egg, and toast, and invited her to come home with her, to St Albans, at the weekend.

★

It was Grilda who asked her, which was strange because she had been thinking of asking Grilda, and not Ida or Edna. Grilda, whose real name was Maude, seemed the most like her. She flitted in and out of rooms, never quite settled, and this had made Gwen notice her. She drew well. Gwen had watched her in the Antiques room and had seen how careful she was, how she took pains to understand the anatomy of a head or body. Now that at last they had progressed to the Life room Grilda showed the same scrupulous attention to detail.

They had not exactly become intimate friends, but that was another mark in Grilda's favour. She moved among the young women students easily, included in their gatherings, but she was not close to any particular girl, she did not pair off with any of them. Gwen had hardly spoken to her. They sat next to each other in the Life class and it was not till almost five o'clock in the afternoon, and time to pack up, that Grilda asked her, in an offhand way, making nothing of her request, whether she would serve as a model for her. Gwen nodded, giving the suggestion no thought. She wanted someone to model for her, too, but had delayed asking anyone because she did not think she could draw them in her room and she had no other place to take them.

Grilda, she heard, had two rooms, which were spacious and attractive. Gwen had already thought of offering herself as a model, hoping that the modelling could take place at Grilda's and the arrangement would become mutual.

But Grilda asked first. That evening, Gwen went home with her, neither of them speaking. Grilda was tall, with long arms and legs, and a chest Gwen assumed flat until she saw her naked and realised that Grilda hid her breasts. There was no embarrassment on either side. As soon as they were in her rooms and the curtains had been drawn, and the fire lit, Grilda sat down with her sketchbook on her knee and said, 'There, I think, to the right of the fire, near the lamp.' Gwen undressed rapidly, draping her clothes neatly over the back of a chair. She had not been told how to pose so she sat as the model they had been drawing that day had sat, knees together, hands resting on them, head slightly raised. The room was not yet warm and her nipples were erect. Grilda drew in silence, studying her more than sketching. There was a jug of lilies on the round table near which Grilda sat, waxy white flowers with orange stamens. Their scent filled the room and made Gwen feel slightly nauseous.

'Thank you,' Grilda said, closing her sketchbook. Gwen did not ask to see her drawings. She hesitated, wanting Grilda to offer to pose for her. It was her room, it might seem impertinent to ask. 'This light is bad,' Grilda said, 'we should wait until the summer.' And then, at last, 'Are you rushing? Do you want to draw me?' She took Gwen's place, throwing her clothes on the floor, but her pose was different. She perched on the very edge of the chair, arms behind her back, legs stretched out. Gwen did not like this pose but there was an impatience about Grilda which made her reluctant to say anything. She drew badly, unable to capture the quality of Grilda's awkwardness. Her body split into two distinct halves, the torso rounded and in proportion, the limbs almost jagged and too long, too heavy. She didn't look at Grilda's face at all, leaving it blank.

The evening was not a success.

★

She allowed herself to be taken, just sometimes, to one of the Tottenham Court Road cafés. Ida pleaded with her to come, at the end of the day, and it was hard to resist Ida. But when she went, the first time, Ida had company with her. 'This is Ursula,' she said, 'back from Paris, fancy!' Ursula was elegant and rather beautiful, and Gwen was drawn to her at once, knowing that this was the girl Gus had been infatuated with in his first year. Ursula did not mention Gus. She talked of Paris and Gwen listened carefully. Did Ursula have money, to have been able to afford this visit, she wondered. Ursula was quiet beside the animated, talkative Ida, but Gwen read into her reserve a sensitivity which she felt might match her own. She needed a friend and it could not be Ida, or not in the way she wanted, much though she liked her. Ursula, she thought, might be the one. She would see.

★

She wrote to Winifred often, but could not seem to catch in words what she could catch in drawings and in the end, as writing became ever more stilted and laborious, she resorted to sending sketches upon the back of which she scribbled other information. She drew her fellow student Ambrose McEvoy with his flat, straight black hair, his monocle, his immaculate clothes, and on the back of her drawing she wrote that his voice was strange, it had a cracked sound, and that she was learning a great deal from him about building up colour in painting and how to emphasise light and dark. This did not tell the whole story, of course, but she lacked the language to do that. A tiny trickle of feeling had been cautiously running through her from that deep hidden well she knew was there, but she was afraid of its turning into a torrent, and of being engulfed by it before she was ready. So she dammed it up and set her face against it. There was so much to learn and nothing must get in the way. She knew she was born to love, but not when or whom. There was safety in numbers and she kept to them for the most part. She did not care for groups, but within a group, she felt secure.

★

Winifred was coming. Their father had agreed that she might come to London and study music. She was to live with Gwen and Gus and another friend, Grace, in Fitzroy Street. It had been kept from their father that the house, No. 21, had once been a brothel, and that the woman who owned it was an extraordinary character of whom he would not have approved. Gwen had not yet met Mrs Everett, but she had seen her, dressed in her widow's weeds and men's boots, and carrying a large bag in which were rumoured to repose a Bible, a dagger, a saucepan and a loaf of bread. One of the students at the Slade, William Orpen, who lived in the basement of her house, had been to a session of what she called her 'Sunday School', where religious songs were sung and there was much clapping and swaying in time. William found it hilarious, and so did Gus when he was taken along, but Gwen shuddered. She knew her father would be furious.

She did not know how it would be, the four of them living together, but the financial and other advantages were too obvious to overlook. The lack of space and light at Euston Square meant she could not work there – and she had always known that in her second year she must move. For a while, she shared with Gus when he moved to Montague Place, but this was not a success. They needed someone between them who could keep them apart but also connect them. Winifred was that person, their own sister, intimately acquainted with both of them but like neither of them. She would provide the balance and, being joined by Grace, the burden would not become too great.

She arrived in January, on a bitterly cold day. It had snowed the night before and the blackened buildings of Fitzroy Street had been prettified. Gwen had bought flowers to welcome her, at great expense, six Christmas roses which she stuck in a green glass carafe and put on the washstand in Winifred's room. They'd given Winifred the room overlooking the street, the best room, though this was not as generous as it seemed since she and Gus both preferred the back rooms where the light was stronger and from the north. Grace was to have the smaller front room, connected by a door to Winifred's. The rooms gave the impression of being larger than they were (but also, it was true, colder).

Mrs Everett did not care what was done to them and so Gwen and Gus had rearranged things considerably and thrown lengths of old velvet, purchased cheaply in a street market, over any especially hideous item. Winifred and Grace were charmed.

In her own room, Gwen had rolled the carpet up and pushed it under the window, leaving the floorboards bare. She liked the feel of them on her feet. There was space for her easel, and she could pretend this was her studio and not her bedroom. But this had a curious result. By placing her easel and her paints, and all that went with them, so prominently, she did something to the room which made her uneasy. The bed was still there, the other pieces of furniture were still prominent, and she felt threatened by them, she wanted to be rid of them. They had no place in an artist's room; they did not fit.

Winifred was admired by the art students who came to Fitzroy Street but she made no attachments. Gwen watched her being watched, and wondered at her lack of response. It was not, she thought, the same kind of withholding which she employed herself. Winifred was not suppressing passion. She was simply not interested in any of the students. Rather they mystified her with their flamboyance and noise, their apparent lack of seriousness. She was mistaken, of course. Gwen knew how deadly serious they all were about art if not life, but her sister could not discern their strength of purpose. She saw only the drinking, the smoking, the laughter and fooling about and the disregard for convention. It puzzled her that Gwen belonged to this crowd, that she did not spurn it but appeared as involved as Gus in all its activities. She wished sometimes that she could see them all at work in their precious Slade School of Art. It was like a secret society to which they all belonged. Gwen, she decided, was a reluctant member, and not as happy as Winifred had expected to find her.

There were sudden storms of tears which were bewildering. Winifred would come back in the evening to Fitzroy Street and find Gwen prostrate on her bed, fists clenched, body rigid in some kind of sustained grief too awful to speak of. Once, the name Ambrose McEvoy was mentioned when Winifred asked what was

34

the matter, but no explanation followed the muffled reference to him. It was all rather frightening.

★

Climbing the steps of the National Gallery made Gwen feel important. She was not a tourist, she was not an ignoramus, she had not come merely to gape. This was her work. Tonks had had no need to urge her to make this gallery her second home, to visit it often and learn from all it held. The very stones of the building felt sacred to her and when she was settled in front of a painting that she had come to study, she lost herself completely for hours. She sat on her folding stool perfectly composed, staring, seeking the internal structure of one picture before her. She looked for the muscles beneath the sleeves, the bones beneath the skin and the sinews of the neck, the veins in the eye. Then she opened her sketchbook and copied the line, leaving aside all colour and texture.

She had finished with Gabriel Metsu's *A Woman Seated at a Table and a Man Tuning a Violin*. Today she had come to look at Rembrandt's *Self-Portrait*, aged thirty-four. Young, but fourteen years older than she herself was now. She had fourteen years to reach Rembrandt's standard, a thought which made her shiver. She wished he had looked straight at himself but his gaze was slightly off-centre. Why? How? Where was his mirror? And was he left-handed? If not, why was his right hand folded across his body? He was leaning on something, a banister perhaps, or a shelf. The clothes, the hat, were striking, but she was more interested in the face, especially the chin and the sparse growth of hair around it. Her own chin made her despair. Gus hid his chin, which like hers receded slightly, with his beard, and she almost wished that she could do the same. Always, she drew herself full-face, and then the chin did not bother her as much. Full-face and, increasingly, one hand on her hip. She liked the feeling this gave her, of defiance, even arrogance. She hoped it suggested that she was in control and able to face herself without shame. It was a lie, but she wanted it to be a successful lie, one that would not be questioned.

35

Last night, they had all gone to the Café Royal, she and Gus, and Ida and Ambrose and Grilda. (She would rather have been with Ursula, but Ursula had gone home to her father's vicarage in Essex.) They had eaten sandwiches and drunk lager, and watched what was going on around them though none of them sketched. Winifred would not go with them; she had said she would be out of place and feel uncomfortable, and this had made Gwen realise that she herself felt perfectly at ease. To be part of a group, a gang, was not a situation she had either wanted or anticipated – surely, she was a solitary being, more solitary than her sister. It was Gus who needed people around him and liked to be at the centre of activity, not she. And yet there she had been, as she now often was, sitting with friends, drinking and eating and talking, quite comfortable. She had caught sight of herself in a huge mirror fixed along the wall opposite and she could not credit it was herself. Ida on one side, Ambrose on the other, squashed up together on the banquette, smoke wreathing their heads and the light from candles casting their faces into shadow. She looked so small and demure beside Ida who was dressed in crimson and wore a flower Gus had given her in her hair. Nondescript, that was the word that had come to her as she looked at herself. Dark dress, plain hairstyle, pale unpainted face. Only her necklace sparkled, her mother's diamonds brilliant against her black velvet dress. She hadn't known whether she should wear them or not: they looked out of place on her and might draw attention in a way she did not want. But wear them she did.

It was the beer, she supposed, but towards the end of last evening she had become convinced that Ambrose was singling her out for meaningful attention. So often he evaded her eyes but then suddenly he looked into them and his expression changed. It was exhilarating and yet tantalising. She wanted him to take her hand, or put his arm round her, as Gus had his round Ida. And then she could lay her head on his shoulder and close her eyes and feel him embrace her . . . But he went no further than a look and it made her want to cry. What did she have to do? Ida needed to do nothing, Gus did it all. And Ambrose had not come back to Fitzroy Street with them afterwards, as he usually did. They had parted in the street. He and Grilda walked in one direction, she and Gus and Ida in the other. She had felt bereft and cold, and once home had flung herself onto her bed and bitten her pillow in fury.

It was all gone now, the anger, the frustration. So long as she was here, in the gallery, in front of Rembrandt she was safe from unseemly emotion. It was people, people who were alive, who caused disturbance in her. What she must do was cut herself off from them, and yet to do so would be perverse. She loved her group, all women artist friends. They had taken her to their hearts and enriched her life immeasurably – what folly to discard them. Men, then. They were the disturbance, even Gus – especially Gus. Look at Edna, only nineteen and about to be married and already her dedication was wavering. Was it, then, to be a choice? Was Ida going to make this choice?

Gwen stared at Rembrandt. She would paint herself and try to bring into her portrait all this seething beneath the surface and with it the determination to save herself.

★

The summer vacation came and her money did not stretch to staying on in London, so she was obliged to go to Tenby, though she no longer thought of it as home. Agony to take the train back to Tenby, knowing that Ida and another Gwen, Gwen Salmond, were going to Paris where she had never been and longed to go. They were to try to study at the Académie Julien, where Bonnard and Vuillard had studied, and were in a state of excitement so extreme that it came off them like heat. It was quite unbearable. Is this jealousy, raw and ugly? Gwen asked herself, and the answer came quickly enough – yes, she was jealous to the point of angry tears.

Her father had no patience with tears. She knew that. They only irritated him. But tears trickled down her pale cheeks every time she confronted him in his cold, dull house and she could not seem to stop them. 'Please,' she said. She would do anything, she would go without anything. For long enough she had existed merely on

37

bread and nuts and a little fruit and could exist on bread and water entirely if only he would finance a brief trip to Paris. Her begging – and she had held her hands out, like a beggar – maddened him. Why, he asked, was she not content? Once, London, the Slade School, had been all she craved. He had given it to her, and now – he was reading *Oliver Twist* again – she wanted *more*.

So for three days, Gwen ate nothing. She drank water and weak tea but closed her lips firmly against food. She sat at the table with her father and Winifred and refused all sustenance. On the fourth day, she fainted. It was no ploy. She rose from the table as her father rose, at the end of the meal, and she could not get to the door. Silently, gracefully, she slid to the floor, her skirt crumpling around her, rustling as it settled. Winifred told her how alarmed their father had been, how he had rushed to Gwen's side and anxiously felt her pulse and – Winifred vowed it was true – kissed her forehead. But she knew nothing of that. When she came to, her father was not in the room. Winifred was kneeling beside her, pressing a damp cloth to her face. 'You must eat,' her sister said. 'You must eat, or you will not be strong enough to travel to Paris.'

★

She had only enough money to travel third class but this suited her perfectly. It was September and sunny, and being out on deck was exhilarating. No one noticed her, and she was able to lean on the rail and watch the white cliffs fade. Only the thought of arriving in Calais, and having to get herself on the train to Paris, made her apprehensive. No one seemed to understand her French and the speed with which the French themselves spoke meant that she understood little of what they said. But, though she felt nervous, she was also aware of a kind of relief to be so isolated. The hubbub was great, and in the midst of it she was speechless and deaf and turned in on herself, which thrilled her. There was a sense of containment that she had never experienced before, and when, at the Gare du Nord, she was met by Ida she was almost sorry. Ida laughed and talked and hugged her, and that sense of being remote, untouchable, disappeared.

The apartment thrilled her. Three large rooms, *empty*. Wooden floors, long windows, dazzling light. They did not need beds. Mattresses would do, and cushions were preferable to chairs and stools. Gwen felt giddy with excitement. In no time the three of them had been to the market and bought the very minimum they needed, and then Ida and the other Gwen went off to Boulogne for the weekend leaving her alone. When the door closed, Gwen let out one of her loud exclamations. 'Oh!' she cried with delight. Round and round the rooms she paraded, arms flung wide, dancing in the space. At one and the same time she never wanted to leave the apartment but longed to explore Montparnasse. Out she went in the end, not caring if she got lost, and wandered the streets, the boulevards, feeling carefree and eager. When she returned to her room, she began painting immediately, her easel set up near the window so that she could see the scene below.

But street scenes were not what she wanted. The only reason she wanted Ida and Gwen Salmond to return was so that they could pose for her, so that she could attempt an interior with figures in it. They were obliging when they arrived, understanding her feverish impatience. The other Gwen donned a white muslin dress and Ida a flounced skirt with a pink shawl draped round her upper body, and she posed them standing together, Gwen reading a book, Ida peering at it over her shoulder. Though it was not the figures she had difficulty with – the composition was simple – but the room around them. She struggled to capture the spirit of the room but felt it slipping from her. The eye was drawn to the window in the background but tripped up on its way there by the fireplace and a picture framed on the wall above it. And the plaster rose in the ceiling. There was something not right. She needed a teacher. The teacher she wanted was Whistler, but his fees, for lessons in his Académie Carmen, were double those of other schools. What was to be done?

She borrowed money. It was against everything her father had preached – neither a borrower nor a lender be – and he would be furious if he found out. But his allowance would not pay for lessons at the Académie Carmen and so she took the money

Gwen Salmond offered. The moment she stepped into Whistler's presence, she was happy. He was small and neat, with curly grey hair; she noted his bright inquisitive eyes and his exquisite hands, which were rarely still. There was a passion about him which appealed to her immediately. He was different from Henry Tonks and his ideals not those of the Slade. Art, he believed, was about poetry, about bringing forth the spirit of things and expressing beauty of every sort – line, form, but most important of all, emotion. Art was about speaking from the soul.

She did not want to return to London and the Slade. Paris was right for her, she decided, it was where she must stay. So she wrote to her father, an impassioned letter, trying to make him understand the vital importance to her of Paris and Whistler and the Académie Carmen. Never had she anticipated that he would come to inspect where she was living – 'Oh!' she cried out as she read his letter. The others could not understand her dismay. Her father, they said, could not fail to see how happy she was and how her work had improved. But they did not know him. He was not interested in happiness, only in obedience and decorum. He would find fault even with her appearance. The girls said they would help. If she designed a new dress, they would make it up for her. So she tried to make herself look pretty and girlish, abandoning her usual dark colours and choosing a lustrous blue taffeta material and a style she copied from a painting by Manet, a dress with a full skirt and billowing sleeves and a neck with lace round it that showed some bosom.

The stare he gave her . . . was chilling. Disgust was in it, and horror. He told her that she looked like a prostitute. She was tempted to ask how he knew but instead snatched a cloak off a peg and swathed herself in it. 'Is that better?' she challenged. He turned and walked out of the apartment and she did not follow him. Watching him from the window she saw him march back to his hotel, upright, swinging his cane, not caring that he had insulted her, confident that she would have to come crawling to him for money. But she would not. She would never ask him again for money.

Rather than plead for money from her father she would readily have become what he had accused her of being. To stay in Paris it would be worth becoming a prostitute – if necessary.

★

How long had it been? On the train, she counted the months – only five, and yet they had stretched and stretched to fill her life. To be leaving Paris now was pitiful, but loans from the other Gwen, and income from modelling, was not enough. She would have to return and learn to paint by herself without expensive lessons. Ida's company helped, but not enough. Ida was going home to Wigmore Street, but where would she herself go? She did not know. Perhaps Gus would help, not with money – he was as poor as she was – but to find a room.

In fact she found one herself, in Howland Street, round the corner from their old apartment in Fitzroy Street. A basement, dank and ugly, but which suited her mood. The steps down to it were made of iron and her boots clattered upon them unpleasantly. No light, of course. The window looked out onto a wall streaming with damp, its bricks all mossy. She did not bother to take the net curtain down, it would make no difference. She did not bother to unpack either, leaving most things in her two bags and hanging up only her best red blouse. Then she sat, bolt upright, on the bed and tried to think. How was she to return to Paris? It seemed impossible. Gus was to have an exhibition of his paintings at the Carfax Gallery and hoped to sell them, which he probably would. Could she earn money to get back to Paris, by doing the same? The idea was absurd. She had nothing to exhibit. She knew no gallery owners.

In Tenby, before she went to Paris, she had worked on a self-portrait in oils that she thought might have a future. It was, for her, quite a large canvas, twenty-four inches by fourteen, oblong in shape, and she had laboured over it, staring so fixedly into the wardrobe mirror between brushstrokes that she had felt disembodied – the woman staring arrogantly back was not she but some other demanding taskmaster of whom she was a little afraid. She had left this unfinished painting in her father's house, and

41

did not wish to go there to complete it and bring it to London. What, after all, would she do with it? Show it to Gus, see if he had any ideas? He always showed interest in her work and had already expressed dismay that in this basement she could not paint. He'd told her she must get away, into the air, into the light. He himself would go mad confined to such a dungeon.

In the spring, he took her away himself. Arriving one afternoon to find her crouched beside her grimy window sketching a stray cat which had perched on the sill, he said she must come with him to Dorset and walk among the primroses and swim in the sea and restore her spirits. The invitation to stay in a boarding house in Swanage had come from their old landlady, Mrs Everett. So she went, wishing only that one of her women friends could go with her (though not voicing this to Gus). It was, as he'd promised, a lovely, wild place and she revelled in the freedom to walk and swim and be outside all the time but the odd thing was that, though she relished the solitude and appreciated the beauty of the landscape, it did not make her want to paint. She did no work while Gus sketched madly. Instead, thoughts of people and rooms, and people *in* rooms, haunted her. It was as though the wide open skies of Dorset and the vast stretch of the sea inhibited instead of releasing her – she wanted to draw herself in, concentrate on the essence of someone or something containable. She became restless and jumpy, and Gus became irritated.

But he was kind to her. It was his friend who, back in London, let them have his house in Kensington, a whole cottage to herself. She left her basement and once in the cottage began to work again, getting Winifred to bring her self-portrait from Tenby. It was the hand she had to work on, the way it rested on her hip in that deliberate way, the hand and the belt, cinching her waist tightly. It was finished before Gus's friend returned, and she moved again, this time to Gower Street, on her own, but not for long. Gus was going to France and asked if she would go with him, and because she could not resist the lure of France, anywhere in France, she agreed. There was another factor that lured her. Ambrose was to join them at Le Puy-en-Velay in the Auvergne where they were to stay with another friend, Michel Salaman. Surely something would happen between them? Her yearning had gone on so long now and nothing had come of it.

They began well, travelling to Le Puy together, Ambrose delighted to be leaving London and telling her without embarrassment that Michel had sent him a cheque to pay for his fare. They were united in their poverty and their inability, it seemed, to earn money. But once they reached Le Puy, where Gus awaited them as well as Michel, the ease between them began to disappear. Ambrose wanted to be with Gus more than with her. They were absinthe friends, sitting in cafés listening to an alluring girl singing songs. Gwen was left alone, her arms wrapped round herself, pacing the floor until they returned. When they did, they were most often drunk, but not drunk enough not to want to go on drinking. Ambrose drank even more than Gus did, and then fell asleep and stayed asleep until the middle of the next day. Then, he'd seem a little ashamed, and go off with her picking flowers, though hardly talking. Instead, she talked. She overcame her reticence and she told him of all the feeling that raged inside her and for which she could find no outlet. 'I am born to love,' she said, and watched him closely. He turned away.

Her tears were wearying. They exhausted her and yet she could not stem them. 'Gwen!' Gus said, and sighed. He never asked her what she was crying about. He knew, and could do nothing about it. There he was, with all his girlfriends and his whores, not for one moment having to control his passion. And there she was, just as passionate, driven mad with frustration. It was not only the sexual adventures she envied but the general unfettered nature of his life. She felt imprisoned and no one, least of all Ambrose, would turn the key and let her out.

★

The fog was thick and yellow, swirling round the blackened bricks of St Pancras Register Office as Gus and Ida came out, married. It was a secret marriage. Back in Wigmore Street, Ida's unsuspecting parents had yet to be told and she both shivered and laughed at the thought. It was, Gwen reflected, how she herself

43

would wish to marry, should the occasion ever arise (though there was no suggestion that it might). No pomp, no ceremony, simply a quiet pledging of themselves to each other in the eyes of the law. The eyes of the law that day of 12 January 1901, were set in the narrow face of a thin, weasly man, eyes so very small it was difficult to ascertain their colour. Ida and Gus looked all the more beautiful in contrast to him.

Ida would probably never paint again to any effect. Did it matter? Gwen could not decide. She had never felt that Ida burned with ambition, or that within her was a raging urge to express herself through art. Gus had the need, and marriage and fatherhood would not stop his art. But about herself Gwen saw difficulties. She could not say that she did not want love in her life, and intimacy with the one she loved, but that was not the same as wanting to be a wife and mother. She hoped she would be brave, and take, and give, the love without allowing herself to be bound in any way. It ought, surely, to be possible. She intended that it should be.

Ambrose was engaged. Two months after they returned from Le Puy, he had become engaged to Mary Edwards, nine years older than himself, a woman she did not know and was sure Ambrose hardly knew. It was inexplicable, cruel. Gwen gathered from Gus that Mary had declared her love to Ambrose and that he had immediately succumbed. Well, she, Gwen, had declared her love for him, had she not? And he had not succumbed. He had turned away, run away, and now she had to tell herself she was better off without him. But the hurt was there, raw and bitter inside her, and she had to work hard to conceal it. Looking at herself in mirrors, using herself more and more as a model, she had seen the sore place seeping through her flesh, staining her skin, tightening the muscles of her face. She tried not to paint this but increasingly her brush told the tale.

Thankfully, her self-portrait, begun in Tenby, had preceded the damage and did not reveal her suffering. She had completed it before the news of Ambrose's engagement and was able to exhibit it at the New English Art Club, the first painting she had ever publicly exhibited, confident that the impression it gave was the one she had striven for. She had wanted to show herself as calm and collected, aware of her own strength, a little superior and extremely serious. This was to be a portrait of a woman who was no adornment of the fair sex but a member of a new generation that intended its work to be important. There was no proof in the picture that she was an artist – no paintbrushes or palette, such as Elisabeth Vigée-Lebrun had used, or a hand on a painting beside her, as in Mary Beale's self-portrait. The viewer did not need to know she was an artist. It was enough that her skill should be appreciated. Sometimes, she felt she was a mere shadow of a person. Her portrait reassured her that she was not.

★

She was an aunt. A boy, David, born 6 January, in Liverpool of all places, where Gus was holding a temporary post at the art school. Gus thought Liverpool 'gorgeous', but when Gwen arrived there to see her nephew, she could not share his opinion, not that she saw much of the city, being too occupied with the baby, who truly *was* gorgeous. He was said to look like her, a nonsense of course. She studied him for hours, stripping off his coverings and examining him in minute detail. Was he not a work of art? She marvelled at his structure, the perfection of his limbs and the contours of his skull. Through her mind went all the paintings of babies she had seen and not one of them, not even by Michelangelo or Raphael, had captured this. It was a shame to cover him up at all, but she did, and took him out in his big black pram to get the air. She walked miles, pushing forcefully, stopping now and again to rest in doorways, squatting down on the steps and rocking the pram when the baby whimpered.

Ida looked beautiful nursing him. Gus drew and drew her, lightning quick sketches, but Gwen merely looked, noting the swell of the breasts lessening as the baby sucked, and the way his nose was flattened against them. She stored the images in her head and thought one day she might make use of them, but not now. Now, she was finishing another and much better self-portrait and it had drained her. She needed this break, it gave her time to stand back and gain some objectivity before she returned to work. It was strange, she could not help thinking, that seeing Ida's child made her own work more important, not less so. She did not look at their baby and pine for one of her own, nor did the baby make her work seem irrelevant. On the contrary, he made it seem vital. She herself was not going to create a baby. All her creative talents had to go into her painting, all her feelings and emotions, all her ideas and plans, all her hopes and fears, all the turmoil within her, everything that was precious.

She could see now how life, her life, had turned out.

★

Another baby, another boy, Caspar, born in March 1903, barely fifteen months after David. This time, Gwen saw the baby at once, living as she was in Howland Street, with Ida and Gus back in Fitzroy Street. A newborn infant, she suddenly realised, was more alarmingly fragile than beautiful and she contemplated him with awe, wondering how he could survive and grow into the sturdy toddler David had become. Ida was distracted and not nearly as glowing with motherhood. Her radiance was dimmed and Gwen felt concern for her. Was she eating enough, was she sleeping? Ida laughed at both questions. She ate when she could and she snatched sleep when she could. All was chaos in her household, and Gus nowhere to be seen. Mrs Nettleship was outraged at her son-in-law's neglect of her daughter, but Ida defended him. She did not want him to be bored. Let him go to the Café Royal, let him mix with his friends. He had a new friend, she told Gwen. He was painting her. It was so convenient since this new friend and model lived in the basement of a house in their street.

Gwen met her coming into the house. She had seen her some-where before, at a party, given by an artist friend of Gus's. She stopped, stood stock-still, and said, 'Dorelia?' Dorelia McNeill, only twenty-two, sultry and beautiful, with high, prominent cheek-bones, slanting eyes and an air of detachment about her.

No wonder Gus was painting her. Who could resist?

III

A GLORIOUS AUGUST DAY, the dirty Thames for once a sparkling silver and the sky as blue and cloudless as ever it could be in France. But the steamer was not what they had expected. Their cabin was hardly worthy of the name – so tiny, the door without a lock, the single porthole covered in salt and impossible to clean from inside. Their painting equipment filled most of the space. They were going to have to climb over the wrapped-up easels every time they went in or out, like climbing over rocks. Each had a cloth bag of clothes which went on their bunks, under the thin pillows. If they were seasick, this would be a dreadful place to suffer.

But they were not seasick, not once. They spent most of their time on deck, leaning on the rails, eyes closed, smiling into the wind. Away! They were away, from London, from Fitzroy Street, from poor Ida and her noisy babies, from Gus and his demands. Hardly anything had been decided. 'Come with me,' Gwen had urged, 'walk with me to Rome.' And Dorelia had stared at her, and raised her eyebrows, and put her hands on her hips, and her head on one side, and then she nodded. She left all the preparation to Gwen, who launched herself immediately into a flurry of time-tables and tickets and maps. They would sail to Bordeaux and walk the rest of the way along the Garonne and then to the Mediterranean coast and so into Italy. It was mad, quite mad. Everyone said so. 'Walk?' people exclaimed, and they lifted their long skirts and showed off their strong, laced walking boots. They were prepared.

On the steamer, they went barefoot, to the consternation of the only other passengers, a single elderly gentleman on his way to visit a relative, and a couple from Yorkshire who were prim and proper and changed for dinner. Gwen and Dorelia never changed. It was a nonsense in such circumstances, and 'dinner' the most basic of meals. They wore the same dresses all the time, Gwen's a dark brown, Dorelia's a vivid blue. They washed only hands and faces and, of course, their bare feet (twice a day). When they reached Bordeaux – even the Bay of Biscay was calm – they had to put on their boots before taking a single step on French soil, and it was a painful business. The delicious freedom had made their feet spread, or so it seemed. Their feet resisted being confined in thick woollen socks, purchased with such pride – they were so sensible – before the journey, and once the socks were forced on, the feet would not fit comfortably into the boots. 'What are we to do?' Gwen wailed. Dorelia sat on the edge of her bunk, quite still. She thought. Carefully, she undid the laces in her boots and spread the opening wide. Then she removed the woollen socks, rolled them into a ball and put them aside before finding and donning her thin stockings. She stood up and tried the boots, saying nothing. Gwen followed suit. She looked down at her flapping boots and took a step forward. They stayed on. Dorelia did the same. They looked at each other and laughed and laughed.

The laughter faded on the quayside. They had so much to carry and their feet weighed them down. To get out of Bordeaux, which they were in a hurry to do, they were obliged to hire a cart and its driver, a surly fellow who did not seem to understand their French and whose face was one tight mask of complaint. But he took them to the outskirts of the town, as they had requested, and dumped them by the River Gironde near Podensac. It was late afternoon, the light beginning to fade from a dazzling blaze to a shimmering glow. They stood beside their heap of equipment and sighed, stretching their arms out wide and throwing their heads back to feel the sun on their faces. Then they took off their boots, and moved into the grass beside the road, taking up their bundles and walking slowly along the river-bank. Where to? They did not know. They had taken the precaution of buying bread before they left Bordeaux, and had filled their water bottles. When they were tired, they would lie down and sleep under a hedge, if need be.

That first night, it was what they did.

★

One night was spent in a barn, empty except for straw, the perfect place to bed down, though the straw had a yeasty smell; another night under a cart, left in the corner of a field, the ground under it dry when all around it was wet; several nights in ferny hollows, the moon bathing them in white light and making the thought of sleep absurd. But every third or fourth night they paid to stay in a house, glad to be able to wash and attend to their hair. Gwen was more particular about her hair than Dorelia, though her hair was finer and not so prone to pick up bits of grass and twigs from the ground they lay on. They were both particular about their clothes, not wishing to appear vagabonds even if they were living like tramps. They regularly washed and pressed their dresses and cleaned their boots and made sure they were presentable. They needed to look respectable and attractive when they set up in village streets to offer themselves as portrait painters, or if, as sometimes happened, they had earned nothing from portraits and must sing for their supper.

At La Réole, thirty miles from Bordeaux, they met another artist. He came to stare at them, with other men, as they slept in a stable. His name was Leonard Broucke. Gwen did not like him – she thought him arrogant, with his offer to give them a lesson – but Dorelia stared at him, and Gwen wondered if she saw something of Gus in him. They left La Réole poorer than when they arrived, earning only 1.50 francs there and spending 2. Next night it was cold and they slept under a haystack, waking very early, shivering, and rolling together, Gwen on top of Dorelia, to try to warm themselves. When they got up, Dorelia said she had not slept at all but Gwen had done so, her arms loosely round Dorelia's neck and her body burrowing into the folds of Dorelia's dress and cloak. She felt entirely happy, in spite of the cold and lack of comforts. For breakfast, they picked grapes, but the fruit was not yet quite ripe and tasted sour. Every day, their portfolios and equipment seemed to grow heavier and they prayed for a cart to come along and relieve them of their burden.

Carts did stop, quite often, attracted by the sight of Dorelia whose attractions were obvious. Twice they were followed, after they had sung in an inn, by men eager to give them money for other services. The men were not frightening, not rough or threatening in manner, but they were persistent and once the two women had to seek refuge in a church (where the verger took pity on them and gave them a bed in his own house for the night). But on they went, mile after mile, walking or riding in carts (and once in a motor car, unimaginable luxury), the weather glorious except for a few isolated heavy showers which they rather enjoyed though the rain made them look bedraggled. How far had they travelled when, towards the end of October, they felt the first cold wind? They did not know. Not far, for sure. Gwen was aware of a change in herself, not just in the weather. She wanted to be inside, she wanted an *interior* to make her own. Four walls, and a floor. To be enclosed again, and have order and certainty, to shut out distraction. Dorelia, though she said nothing, looked astonished, even perhaps alarmed, when Gwen remarked that they should look for a room in the next village and stay there for a while. She was happy, in the open all day, as happy as Gus always was. She liked not knowing where they would lay their heads. She liked having the sky for a roof and trees for walls.

They came to Toulouse in November, on a grey, misty day, and Gwen said, 'Enough.' Toulouse was nowhere near Rome, it wasn't even Italy, but she could wander no further, or not for the moment. Dorelia shrugged, and let Gwen knock on doors and make enquiries about cheap lodgings until they were directed up a hill, up a cobbled street, to a house where a tiny woman in black glared fiercely at them and asked to see their money before she showed them a room. The room was small but clean and practically empty. It had a bed (only one bed, but quite wide, room enough for two) a table, and two chairs. 'Perfect,' said Gwen. The window looked out on to a stream and had heavy wooden shutters which kept the east wind from blowing in. On the table was a lamp, quite a large oil lamp which once lit gave a steady yellow light. The moment it was lit, Gwen reached for her paintbrush. This was what she had wanted: this sense of containment, of calm. All around the edges of the glow from the lamp it was dark, the light fading gently as it reached outwards, making the walls mysterious and shadowy. She held her breath.

★

Dorelia studied. The book was difficult, her French uncertain, but the intensity with which she studied it pleased Gwen. The heightened sensibility gave to Dorelia's face a touching and unusual solemnity. She had asked Dorelia to wear her grey dress today, grey but with black threads drawn through it, a black belt tied at the side, and black trimming round the high neck. A sombre dress against which Dorelia's skin looked peach-like. A demure dress, chaste, the sleeves long, her body hidden beneath it. Gus dressed her flamboyantly in vivid colours but Gwen wanted nothing to detract from Dorelia's loveliness. Her portrait was not about clothes.

She asked Dorelia to stand, and to raise her eyes from the book – but a direct stare ruined the atmosphere. She told her to drop her gaze again, back down to the book on the table, but to remain standing, one hand on the back of a chair. There was a bird singing outside, very close to the window, and the rushing of the stream was loud, yet within the room the silence was intense. Gwen could hear her own brushstrokes, the faint, light sweep of them, and the rustle of Dorelia's dress as from time to time she shifted her weight. The lamp was lit. She had given up trying to paint in daylight. There was not enough of it in the room, and during the day they were busy. By four o'clock these winter nights they were inside with many hours to pass so she had accepted the challenge of painting by artificial light. It had its own problems, its own excitements. Shadows came and went and could not be depended upon.

There had been letters earlier that day, each of them read a dozen times. Gus wrote to say he had opened a school of painting in Chelsea, with William Orpen. There was a letter from Ida too, from the new home in Essex, a house with the lilting name of Matching Green. She was there with the babies. Gus came and went. She longed for Dorelia to return, and said so with unmistakable emphasis. They could all live together and be happy.

Dorelia's reaction to Gus's letter was strange. Used as she was to her friend's inscrutable expressions, Gwen wondered at the blankness in her face while she was reading. Did she not see why Ida pleaded? Did she not understand that Ida was prepared to share Gus with her? If so, she did not appreciate Ida's generosity, or the self-sacrifice involved. Gus had written that he longed to look upon Dorelia's 'fat' again, and that had made Dorelia smile. For Ida's words, written, Gwen was sure, in a great pain, there had been neither smile nor frown. 'You write to Ida,' she said to Gwen. Gwen did not need to be told. She wrote to Ida and Gus, and Ursula, all the time. 'What shall I tell her?' she asked. The famous Dorelia shrug . . . But then, 'Tell her we are not going on to Rome.'

It was true, of course, but neither of them had stated it out loud, as a fact. They had just stopped thinking about it. They were going nowhere in this cold and damp, it did not encourage travelling. Holed up in their room, living on bread and cheese and figs, they had lost their adventurous spirit. To Gwen, it did not matter so much because she was teaching herself to paint in a new way, but for Dorelia it did. She was not a painter like Gwen, she could not paint all the time. 'Does Dorelia take two hours to do an eye?' Ida had joked in a letter to Gwen. Yes. She did. And after two hours' struggling with one eye she was bored and had no desire to go on to the other. Like Gus, she wanted to be outside, sketching in fields or by the river, not toiling in one room to get some minute detail right. And she wanted company other than Gwen's, even the girl they had found to sit for them. She was young, only fifteen, but pretty in a disordered sort of way, her hair unbrushed and wild, her nails far from clean. Nothing would persuade her to take her clothes off – she had squealed at the request and had had to be hurriedly reassured that there was no absolute need. She was a fidgety sitter and exasperated Gwen, but Dorelia was amused. She rather enjoyed the girl's bounciness. The sitter brought some spirit into the room. Gwen would not let her talk. She thought her thick red lips bad enough without having to watch them move. After the girl had gone, she shuddered and told Dorelia that the mouth made her feel ill, it was so fleshy, so greedy, so wet-looking.

Had Gwen known passion? Dorelia did not think so. She had

felt it, for Ambrose — everyone knew and it had been terrifying to witness, or so Gus had said — but had she known it? Dorelia saw that it was all there in Gwen, it boiled within her, but that while she was painting it did not plague her. Had she even been kissed, a real kiss? They did not ask each other such things. Dorelia had watched Gwen naked, posing for herself, and had seen how easy she was with her own body. It was a good body, lithe and firm but feminine in its gracefulness, not just in the breasts and genitals. It had a delicacy, Dorelia realised, which her own more voluptuous body did not. But had any man known it? She thought it unlikely. Mirrors had known it, other artists had known it, but never a man, surely.

In February, the sun came out again. Blossom appeared on the trees and once more they could work outside if they wished. But Gwen did not wish. She had learned more in their room and did not want to leave it for the open road. Their landlady put the rent up. It appeared they had been enjoying special winter rates. And that decided them.

★

A long day searching, and then to come to this . . . A dismal room, none too clean and far too crowded, but they were exhausted and had to lay their heads somewhere. Gwen would rather have slept in the Luxembourg Gardens, but Dorelia, usually so phlegmatic, had protested that she could not bear to be soaked and that they must find shelter somewhere inside. The room in the Hôtel Mont Blanc was inside, and that was all that could be said for it. Dorelia went to sleep immediately, fully clothed. Gwen sat and sketched her sleeping, but the light was harsh. Already she missed the lamp in Toulouse, and the sound of the birds, and the stream when it was in full spate. Coming to Paris from London, she had marvelled at the difference but now she despaired. The grime in the street outside, the infernal clatter of carts on cobbles, the shouting — all threatened to depress her.

When she woke up next morning, she was astonished to find that Dorelia was gone. There was no note. Her bag was still packed and lay on the floor next to the bed. Had she gone in search of food? Gwen doubted it. She could see that it was still raining and that the sky was grey and that Dorelia would be getting wet wherever she was. She had been strange ever since they left Toulouse and started for Paris, constantly turning her head away and staring into the far distance as though she could see something that Gwen would not be able to see. Normally patient, she had become impatient, and this was alarming, curiously hurtful. It was not Dorelia's place to be irritated by small things. 'You are vain,' she had said one day, and had told Gwen, 'You are admiring yourself in that mirror. You are not studying your body to paint it.' It was rather shocking to be accused of vanity, and by Dorelia. Did they love each other still? Gwen was not so sure. She could not talk of love, as Ida could. She could not ask Dorelia this, and she had never needed to until now. Their love was there, and of a special kind, and it did not need reassurance. But lately it had felt weaker. It might, Gwen thought, be due to Leonard Broucke, the artist they had met on the road, and she did not like that thought. Dorelia had seemed too smitten with him, and he had given her his address in Paris.

When, by midday, Dorelia still had not returned, she went out herself and bought bread and cheese and some grapes. If Dorelia came back with the same, no matter. The rain had stopped and a faint glimmer of sunshine defused the thin mist hanging in the air. She found a café and, though the seats were damp, she sat outside and ordered coffee and a roll. It was not pleasant sitting there – the trams passed very near and their roar shook the little tables – but she did not want to go inside and face people. Here, nobody bothered her. Everyone was too busy dashing past. Several dogs came up to her but she ignored them and they took the hint. Then, at the corner of the untidy street, where the tram turned, she saw Dorelia walking along. How she stood out in these drab surroundings! In the red skirt, given to her by Gus, and her yellow embroidered blouse and the brown velvet coat, open all the way down the front, Gwen could not take her eyes off her friend as she came towards the café, lighting up the street with her progress.

She was not at all surprised to see Gwen. Sitting down beside her, she broke off a piece of roll and popped it into her mouth. Gwen did not ask where she had been — they never asked such banal questions of each other — and Dorelia did not tell her, but Gwen could see that she had a letter sticking out of her pocket. From Gus? From Leonard Broucke? Sent poste restante? There were secrets now between them. The waiter came out again, would Dorelia require anything? Dorelia looked at Gwen. 'I have no more money,' she said. Gwen felt in her pocket: enough for coffee or a roll, but not both. The waiter brought a roll (larger than Gwen's had been) and a glass of water in which he had kindly put a slice of lemon. 'Well,' Dorelia said, 'Paris.' And she looked about her with an air of incredulity.

★

It was not difficult to find modelling work. There were artists' studios everywhere and it was only a matter of knocking at doors and announcing oneself. The women were safest, the German painter Miss Gerhardie, the Swiss painter Ottilie Roederstein, and others. They were pleased to see Gwen, even more pleased when she was willing to strip to the waist. For hours and hours she posed, easily adopting the poses they requested, never uttering a word, even when invited to converse. At the end of these sessions, she collected her money and left as quickly as possible, never pausing to look at how the artists had portrayed her. But she did not then go back to her room in the Hôtel Mont Blanc. Instead, she roamed Paris, walking miles along the Seine, watching the boats, or around the public gardens, her sketchbook always with her. The weather was good now, and she could sit in comfort on benches and draw whatever took her fancy. Scores of drawings, but no paintings. She had nowhere to paint. She could not paint in that dreary room and as yet she could not afford anywhere else. Leaving Toulouse had, for her, been a mistake. A bigger one might be to return to England, but the inevitability of this was beginning to worry her.

Dorelia had been gone weeks now. She had joined Leonard Broucke, who was in Bruges. Gwen's face, when she realised what had happened, felt hot and clammy. Dorelia had gone to Leonard, not to Gus, with whom she belonged, without consulting her, without a word. It was not being alone that troubled Gwen – she was not alone, she had a cat now – but the shock of realising that Dorelia had not trusted her. Maybe, as Ida suggested in a letter, she had been afraid. Am I so fierce? Gwen thought about it. She imagined that she was kind, a good listener, someone whom those she loved could confide in and find support from, but it seemed this was not true. She was too strong, too firm in her opinions, or at least Dorelia must have thought so. And that hurt.

The room in the Hôtel Mont Blanc was no more sympathetic but she could not afford to move out of it. With Dorelia gone, she had more space but she could not work there, still she was obliged to sketch outdoors and now that the winter was coming she was often so cold her hands could hardly hold a pencil. One day, she took the yellow tram to the end of the Rue de l'Université, to the Dépôt des Marbres. 'Rodin likes English ladies,' Gus had said in a letter, and she needed more work, so why should she not be brave and seek out Rodin? But she was nervous as she walked through the huge, mossy, paved courtyard, its corners over-grown with grass, where great blocks of marble – oblong, upstanding, flat – stood waiting to be claimed by the sculptors in the workshops surrounding it. She did not know which work-shops were his, only that he had two of them. Hesitant, she stood awhile, listening, then moved towards the door from which she judged the noise was coming. She knocked, once, twice, and a third time, louder still.

A woman opened the door at last. A woman wearing a white apron and white cap pulled down almost to her eyes. A woman whose hands were covered in a fine dust and who had a chisel in one of them. 'Yes?' she said, abrupt, frowning. Gwen gave her name. She said she was a model, an experienced model, an artist herself, and that she had been told that Monsieur Rodin might consider employing her services. She spoke in French but the woman replied in English, inviting her to step inside. Monsieur Rodin was in his studio, working, and could not, at the moment, be disturbed, but she could wait. Humbly, Gwen followed her. She was led through a vast room, where three men were hacking away at blocks of stone in a frenzied manner, chips of stone flying dangerously everywhere, to an arch at the other end. Here her guide paused, and beckoned her to come close. She pointed through the arch at a man who seemed to be caressing a half-finished statue, smoothing it over and over again and staring intently at the surface he was smoothing. 'Monsieur Rodin,' the women said, quietly. 'He will break soon, and then you may introduce yourself.'

Alone, Gwen stood and waited. Waiting and watching felt comfortable, natural. Rodin, she saw, was short, but powerfully built, with huge hands and a massive head, out of proportion with his body. His beard was reddish-blond, streaked heavily with grey. He was dressed like a workman, in an old knitted vest and blue trousers with a smock over the top. She thought, from the way he peered so closely at his work, that he must be short-sighted. As she watched, he took a mouthful of water from a jug on the floor and to her amazement spat it over the clay. She saw he was in the grip of some intense emotion, his face calm but concentrated, not a muscle moving. It was as though he were listening for the statue to speak, to hear its voice and obey its commands whatever they might be. She went on staring, thinking that he looked like an ancient patriarch, coolly assessing his physical qualities, and reminding herself of his reputation. She did not feel awed exactly. There was the excitement of anticipation, but of what? It was hard to tell. She wanted to stand there for ever, watching a master at work. But at last he stopped. He stood back and looked at the statue, appraising it, his head first on one side then the other. He shut his eyes, kept them shut for several minutes, then opened them wide again. This time, he looked beyond his statue. He looked past it straight at Gwen.

They seemed to stay still, eyes locked together, for a long time. The heat crept up Gwen's face. She remembered his erotic sculptures which she had seen at the Exposition Universelle, the lovers entwined together . . . But she was resolute, she would not drop her gaze and yet she feared that she might be considered impudent. She tried to put into her stare a pleading expression. What, she wondered, was Rodin putting into his scrutiny? I am not striking, Gwen thought; he is not looking at me with wonder or astonishment, but is he curious? When he called out, 'Come here, if you wish to speak to me,' she moved slowly, mouth dry, and could not manage more than a whisper when she reached him. 'Sir,' she said, 'I am a model. I would like to model for you.' She said nothing about being an artist herself, did not mention her brother. He smiled slightly, a mere twitch of the lips. His lips, she saw, were fleshy, his eyes a clear grey. He looked at her differently, she thought, quite challengingly, while he asked if she had experience. She named names. He nodded. Turning away from her to wipe his hands, he said she should go into the corner of his studio where she would find a peg to hang her clothes, which she should remove, and then he would look at her.

Many times she had taken her clothes off for other artists, over many years now, but she could not do it easily that day. Her fingers fumbled with the buttons on her boots, which she took off first, and again with the hooks and eyes on her blouse. She was wearing a white cotton chemise under her blouse but no corset, which was a mercy. She hung up her skirt and her blouse on the thick wooden peg sticking out of the wall and folded her chemise and knickers, putting them in a bundle on top of her boots and stockings. Once naked, she felt less nervous. She heard footsteps and knew Rodin was walking across the room towards her, so she began to turn round to face him but he stopped her with 'No! Just as you are, if you please, for a moment.' She stood straight, her feet slightly apart, arms hanging at her side. 'A good back,' he said. 'Now turn.' His eyes were looking at her feet. She looked down at them herself. She had, she thought, pretty feet, the toes almost all the same length, and not a corn or bunion to be seen. Slowly, his eyes moved up her body, pausing at her breasts, which she knew were small but believed to be nicely rounded, and finally they were looking into each other's eyes again. 'Raise your arms,' he said. She did. She did not shave under her arms but was not very hairy. He frowned, disapproving of the hair, she imagined. 'Hands on hips,' he said. She liked that pose and adopted it confidently. He asked her to assume several other positions and then he nodded. 'Very well,' he said, 'tomorrow, at ten.'

Elated, she dressed rapidly and left the studio. All the way back to the hotel she found herself humming odd refrains from songs she hardly knew and had only heard sung in snatches. She bought some violets from a woman in the street and held them tightly, wanting immediately to paint them, to capture the trembling blue delicacy of the flowers. With a sense of surprise she registered her happiness and thought it could not merely be because Rodin was going to let her model for him – it must be more than that, surely. *He* had been responsible for this new buoyancy she felt, he himself, not what he had offered her in the way of work. She would earn no more than she had earned from other sculptors (though money had not been discussed). It was the man who invigorated her, the very sight of him. She warned herself to be careful but immediately scorned her own warning. Rodin was as old as her father, perhaps even older, she did not know. She knew he had a wife, or a woman who had been with him so long that she was regarded as his wife, and that he had mistresses, so she must not entertain fantasies in which he did more than notice her and use her as a model. She was not a schoolgirl, not a student, but a grown woman of almost thirty years. She must be sensible.

But all sense left her in the months that followed. She felt herself bewitched, enchanted, changed utterly from the lonely young woman she had been. Almost every day she made her way to Rodin's studio and posed for him, and soon he was calling her his little Marie, which pleased her and strengthened the conviction that she was now someone else entirely. She had thought he would work in silence but no, he liked to talk: he asked her questions and listened and then asked more. Of course, she told him of her work, and that her brother was Augustus (of whom he had heard), and he took such interest in her. Soon she was showing him sketches of her cat and he appeared impressed, though there was no false flattery. How many hours a week did she work, he wanted to know, what was her routine, where did she buy her paints, her canvases – he wanted to know everything about her from the trivial to the more important. He told her how he himself worked. He rose at seven in the morning, was in his studio by eight, had a short lunch break at noon, worked on until eight, or even later, in the evening. He worked standing, or perched on a stool, and had no electric or gas light in his studio – candles, lanterns, sufficed. He told her he had always been 'wild' about working, and she said so had she, but circumstances sometimes curbed her passion. He did not like hearing that she lived in a lodging house in such an undesirable area. He frowned and said it was not *comme il faut*. She agreed, but was reluctant to plead poverty so could not explain why she lingered there. But he guessed, and went on to offer her other work apart from modelling. He needed, he said, someone other than his secretary to deal with his correspondence and to translate articles from English to French. She could be that person. She could get herself out of that miserable hotel room.

One day he began on a statue, for which she was to be the sole model. This statue was to be a monument to Whistler (who had died some two years ago) and was to be put on a site on the Chelsea embankment. She was, he told her, ideal to be the Muse to Whistler, English as she was (though she had told him that she was Welsh) and a one-time student of the artist. Days were spent choosing the position she should stand in, or rather appear to move in, and days more draping fabric first round her waist and then her hips. One leg, her left, was bent at the knee, the foot resting awkwardly on a plinth. It was not an easy position to hold, but she settled into it and he was pleased. His concern for her comfort was, she thought, unusual and surprising – most sculptors, and indeed most artists, in her experience hardly considered the aches and tiredness of their models. And at the end of the sessions, he helped her down from the platform and undid the drapes. That was when it began.

She was ready and eager, though at first he mistook her trembling for apprehension and began to withdraw his hands, but she took hold of them and placed them where they had been, on her naked breasts. To be enfolded in his strong arms gave her such relief and she sighed with the pleasure of it. Her body responded to his as she had known it would. There was nothing awkward or shy about it. The thrill made her heart race and she instinctively put a hand to her breast to calm it, which made him look anxiously at her. Did he see how willing and hungry she was? Did he see at last that she was no demure English girl? She thought she saw some sense of astonishment in his expression, and she smiled. She was not in the least astonished. This capacity to love had always been there, waiting. At last it had been found and used.

★

He wanted her to have a proper home, somewhere where she could work, somewhere he could visit and be with her, and she wanted this too, but lack of money was still the stumbling block. She had less money now, not more, because she had spent some on herself. She had been to Bon Marché and bought a new dress, and combs for her hair, and a ruinously expensive shawl which delighted her. 'It is wonderful,' she wrote to Ursula, 'the influence upon the mind clothes have.' Renting a better room was not possible. But it grieved him to visit her and find she lived in what he thought of as squalor; he looked disdainfully at the mess of clothes and paints around her. An artist, he said, must have order and calmness in his surroundings, and she lacked both. How could she produce good work in those conditions? But, suddenly, alarmingly, she had no desire to produce any work at all. She no longer wanted to paint. Why should she? She was happy and fulfilled without striving to convey emotion and feelings to canvas. It was enough to pose for her master – she liked to call him that, *mon maître* – and make love with him afterwards.

Sometimes they were not alone. Rodin watched her carefully as he said there was something he needed help with and wondered if she would provide it. She was at once eager, he only had to ask. What he requested was that she should pose naked with another woman, the sculptress Hilda Flodin, one of his assistants. Gwen knew her already, she had earned money posing for her, and it was easy to agree. But she had not understood precisely what she was agreeing to. Rodin wanted them to embrace, to touch each other, to adopt extraordinarily erotic positions while he sketched them, and though she obeyed and held and touched Hilda as instructed she could hardly restrain herself from calling out to him to take Hilda's place. The tension exhausted her but it inflamed him and in front of Hilda he came and took hold of her and made love to her, both of them worked into a state of desire ravenous enough to seem almost ugly in its ferocity. How Hilda could bear to watch, Gwen did not know.

He was her secret. Others in the Dépôt des Marbres knew, but outside it she told no one, not even Gus, or Dorelia who had gone back to him, the Leonard adventure over, and was living with him and Ida in Essex. Then they came, all of them, the children too (and now Dorelia had a baby boy to add to Ida's four) to Paris. They visited her, but still she kept silent as she entertained them, telling only of her work for Rodin and not her love. She did not want to share him with them – they all had each other, she had only him, and even then she did not have him completely and never would. Within the joy he brought her there was a kernel of bitterness because he already had a wife. She had seen Rose. Unable to resist the temptation, she had gone to Meudon, to find her master's house. It was on a hillside, sloping down towards the Seine, with a landing stage at the foot of the hill from where Rodin could catch a boat into Paris. It was quite a grand house, bigger than she had expected, three storeys and with a large garden. She had seen Rose in the garden; she had spied on her. There seemed nothing remarkable about her, but Gwen knew that Rodin had been with her many years and would never leave her. It was foolish to make herself wretched over this but the tiny hard bit of wretchedness was there.

Rodin felt it and was disturbed by it. He tried to teach her to be tranquil and let all distressing thoughts go. She must strive for harmony in her life, and begin with the small, unimportant details, like her diet and her routine. It was laughable how his advice contradicted everything she had thought an artist's life should be, but she tried to please him by adapting herself to his standards. When she woke up now, she lay for a few moments taking deep breaths, telling herself to relax, not to rush, not to roll out of bed and stare vacantly out of the window, then reach for an apple to eat, but instead to rise in a deliberate fashion and walk to the sink and wash herself, and dress carefully (clean clothes) and brush her hair and pin it back and then sit down properly at the table and eat a breakfast of bread and fruit. It was true, it made her feel better, not so constantly distraught, but the effort to keep to these rules was gigantic. She began to draw again, only a little, but her sketches of her cat pleased him. Outwardly, she was more composed and serene, as he wished her to be, but inwardly she felt volcanic, as though burning lava filled her and would explode with the force of what was beneath it, her overwhelming passion for him.

Rodin was, he said, going to pay her rent, for the first three months at least. All she had to do was find the room: it was an order. She obeyed, searching daily until she found a place in the appropriately named Rue St Placide. He was away from Paris when she found it but she wrote and described the beauty of it, with its red tiled floor and pretty wallpaper and the courtyard outside where her cat could play. It was clean, but she cleaned it again, down on her knees to scrub the floor, the window flung open to air it. She bought a wickerwork chair and made a cushion for the seat, and a simple wooden table with a drawer in it, and a bed. Coming back to the room each day filled her with pride as well as pleasure – who would have thought she could be such a good housewife? Rodin, when he visited, was satisfied. He could see how she had absorbed the lessons he had tried to teach her, and now he expected to see other results. But she could not paint yet, so intense was her longing for him. Every day she waited for him to come to her and when he did not she could hardly contain her impatience. All her energy went into making love when he was with her and yearning for him when he was not. The hand that stroked him could not hold a paintbrush, and her eyes were so concentrated on images of him, they could see nothing else. She was helpless, in thrall to him. He began to tell that he was tired and that she must not expect him to make public their liaison. He had his own life to lead, the life he had before she came into it, and she had hers. But he was mistaken. She had *no* life without him. She did not want one. He was her life, he had given her life.

The room in the Rue St Placide, much as she loved it and kept it spotless and adorned it with flowers, was a lie. She stood in the doorway, looking, admiring it, yet thinking that its harmony was a clever exercise in deception. It was not her, this room. It was an image of how her lover wished her to be, and how she had tried to be. All the violent tumult in her was supposedly stilled here. But the struggle went on, and no one, not even Rodin, knew how she was losing the battle. Sometimes, she was afraid of the power of the room she had created. She loved it, but it could make her want to scream and wreck it, hurl the chair out of the window, tear the curtains to pieces, smash the flower pots, and then say to Rodin, Look, behold, *this* is me.

But she never did. She went on straining to match herself to the room and make herself a true reflection of it. Gradually, this led her to paint it, the room on the courtyard, the room as he would have her be.

The lie.

*

But coming home to her new room could be a delight. She stood in the doorway, with the door pushed as wide as it would go, and she stared and stared into it until she felt dizzy and had to lean on the wall. She always left the window overlooking the courtyard slightly open so that the lace curtain blew inwards, a froth of mist in front of her, and the thicker material of the other curtain billowed like a cloud. The wickerwork chair, positioned near the window, with its cushion of apricot silk, took on its own beauty in the light that filtered through, seeming fragile (though it was sturdy) and its criss-cross pattern looked like a cobweb which might at any moment be blown away. She hardly dared to enter the room. The minute she did so, the feelings of inadequacy rushed out of her and fought with what had been total harmony before she stepped into it. She could barely breathe for fearing she was contaminating the peace. She tiptoed across the

64

red-tiled floor and laid her coat on the chair and then at once removed it because it ruined the grace of the chair. To paint this room she would have to empty it of herself.

But then she found she could not do this. She or a version of herself had to be in the picture. She needed to show the tension she felt. She painted a woman in black in front of the window, sewing. The dense black of her long frock told its own tale when everything else was lightness and colour. When Rodin came, she hid what she was working on, fearing that he would see how unworthy she was, not just of her room. He was so pleased with her progress. He smiled and nodded his satisfaction, admiring the cleanliness and order of her new surroundings. He did not like her to be wild in thought, he did not like her to be tempestuous in gesture, and he did not like her to make her need of his love so blatant. She must be composed and calm and let his own tranquillity enter her soul. Only then, he told her, would she do good work. She listened humbly to him and did not argue, but when they made love she wondered how he could hold composure in such esteem. Their love-making was neither calm nor composed. It was frantic and overpowering, the physical sensations transporting her to a kind of ecstasy and drawing from her cries of what to her own ears sounded like anguish, but which was a pleasure so thrilling she felt half mad. He did not tell her to be tranquil then. On the contrary, he appeared to marvel at her passion and even to be nervous of it. It was he who was the experienced lover, but she would never have known. He seemed almost shy, and was hesitant when he touched her. There was even an air of embarrassment about his undressing whereas she had none and tore off any clothes she was wearing, when he arrived, with great haste. She was proud of her body, but he was not proud of his. His belly was big and he was not happy for her to see him naked. Their love-making, though, was vigorous and his awkwardness disappeared during the sexual act itself. Afterwards, she often found she was bleeding but this neither frightened nor disgusted her – she was ready to begin again, when he was ready. He called her voracious and begged her, with a smile, to remember his age – he was sixty-four, an old man, he said. She put her hand over his mouth, silencing him.

He came to her room only once a week, never for more than an hour. Again and again she waited for him, and he did not come even when he had led her to believe he would. She tried to paint, but could not continue, her senses too alert for his foot on the stairs. Often, he was at home with Rose in Meudon, and her envy of Rose grew and grew until she could not contain it and had to go and spy on her again. That was how she felt, like a spy, a sneak, taking the train to Meudon, walking with head lowered to his house, and then looking through the hedge into his garden, watching for Rose to come out. When she did so, the woman moved very slowly round the garden, hands clasped in front of her, head held high, an expression of deep thought on her face. Gwen had not expected such dignity. It was humiliating to see at once that this woman was what Rodin wanted and would never let go. She had borne him a son, she had lived with him more than twenty years. How could she, Gwen, compete?

She could have a child, his child. Her cat had had kittens that summer. It struck her that she ran the risk herself of becoming pregnant, though Rodin had, from the first, said he would take care that she did not, and he was more reliable than Gus was with Ida and Dorelia. She did not want a baby (and she drowned the kittens), but she might end up with one and then she would have a hold over Rodin. This crossed her feverish mind but she dismissed the thought. What would she do with a child? All around she saw women artists whose work seemed stopped by giving birth – look at Ida, look at Edna, look at Dorelia. None of them producing anything now except sketches. A child would be a disaster, and would not help her keep Rodin. Nothing would. He had his own life which he intended to preserve, and besides she wearied him. He reminded her that he was old, and could not match her energy. The energy he had he reserved, for the most part, for his work. She must, he said, let him rest.

But when he did not come to her, it did not always mean he was resting. That, she could have borne. More hurtful was to hear that he was seeing other women. Sometimes, after yearning for him over several empty days, she would go to his studio and find him holding court. He liked sophisticated women who were the very opposite of herself. She felt dowdy and shabby beside them, though she bought new clothes and had thought herself elegant in them. She would stand on the fringe of these gatherings not knowing whether she was about to burst into tears or howl with rage, and he told her later that her very presence made him uneasy. Once, he paid her for her to model in front of these other women and she was humiliated. He said she should not demand so much of him. She should stay in her home and wait for him and paint while she did so. But she could not. She could not keep away from him. When she tried to stay in her room and paint, misery slowed her brush and she had to abandon yet another canvas, and start again.

Then he told her to leave her room. There was not enough sunshine in it, he said, and it was too stuffy. She should give notice, and move.

★

Another room, another beginning, and, at first that same sense of dismay which always filled her before she took possession. How was she to make this space, these four walls and window and door, her own? It was too much, she had been happy eventually in the Rue St Placide and had finally succeeded in owning her room there. She had painted it well, it had grown on her and by leaving it she was afraid that she was abandoning part of herself.

The new attic room she found was in a rather grand house and stood on a boulevard that was wide and impressive. There were five floors, reached by a spiral staircase, and her room was at the top, on the left. Getting her furniture up there was an almost impossible task which stretched over a whole day, from seven in the morning until ten-thirty at night, and before it ended she was in a state of collapse. The removal men were drunk and at first would not even try to get her wardrobe beyond the second floor. If it had not been for the other tenants in the house, who emerged to see what the commotion was about, they would never have been forced to persist. She carried her paintings up herself, and then her hats, not trusting the men, hating them for their boorish behaviour and wishing she could have managed on her own. And then, the furniture was at last in the room but looked all wrong. She was so tired. She could not bear to start moving things to better positions and instead suddenly went out, fleeing down the staircase back to her old room in the Rue St Placide where she had left her cat. They went together, she and the cat, to a café, where she had a glass of wine and some lamb and green beans, and felt better. She prayed that she would never have to move again. That night, she stood in her nightdress at the window, listening to a nightingale, and weeping for the beauty of its song.

In the morning, waking up, she felt strange. Keeping perfectly still, her eyes closed, she tried to analyse this feeling. It was the light, surely, and the air. She opened her eyes and yes, the dawn light was rising through her window, which she had left slightly open, and now the cool air was filling the room. She shivered deliciously, wrapping the coverlet round and round her body. She saw where the wardrobe Rodin had given her should go, and where the chair should stand, and the wooden table. It would not take so long. She would buy some material and make a new cushion for the chair – apricot was the wrong colour for this room, she needed white or cream, some linen or cotton stuff. Her plants would flourish on the table if she put it in front of the window. Slowly, she began to hope. She would put this new room to rights, and her *maître* would love it and be pleased with her. She would bring out from herself all that he believed precious in her.

And then she would paint her room.

★

Gus and Ida and Dorelia and all their babies were still in Paris, but Gwen did not tell them about Rodin. Perhaps they knew without being told – she felt herself so transformed by love that surely it shone out of her – but they made no reference to it. Ida was near her time again, with her fifth child. Her body was distorted with the weight of it, her eyes lacklustre and her skin without its usual bloom. Gwen felt for her, and shuddered a little at the sight of her, feeling suddenly apprehensive in case by some unlucky chance she herself should suffer such gross interference with her own body.

The likelihood of this had lessened. Rodin came to her new room, admired it, and made love to her, but he did not come even once a week now, and he did not always promise to come again. There was a change in him and she sensed it and grieved. She wrote to Ursula, telling her that she felt Rodin liked to make her furious and then take her in the middle of her rage. He kept her waiting for a visit for days, because he said he was so busy, and then when he did come he accused her of being lazy and not trying either to work herself or find other work modelling, though all the time he was the cause of her inertia. How could she paint, how could she leave her room and go to pose for others, when she was ever waiting for him? She knew that his excuses were not always true. He was at home in Meudon more and more, with Rose, and he travelled to England and to Germany, but that was not the whole reason for his absences. But she was posing for him again, naked, willingly adopting the erotic poses he required – to prove, she hoped, that he still had need of her – and she tried to silence the resentment that was building up within her towards him. She worked, too, producing portraits she was not ashamed to show him, though it was not his artistic, professional praise she yearned for but a greater share in his life. When she did not see him she could not contain her love, it was too huge, it swamped all other feeling, and so she wrote to him, pleading with him to come to her and accept more fully what she had to offer. But it seemed more and more that what she did have to offer was not what he wanted. He told her he liked her 'anonymously', as a body, as a woman, but she appeared not to be able to supply what he wanted emotionally and intellectually. He gave her books to read – Richardson's novels, *Pamela* and *Clarissa* – and she did so but could not see why he wanted her to read them. Increasingly, he made her feel stupid and she knew she was not stupid. It hurt when she found he had told his concierge that she was not to be let into his apartment unless she had a letter from him arranging a visit. It was cruel, humiliating, but she could not do without him. She only had to see him to feel her body on fire.

Yet Ida called her 'reserved'. She did not know how lacking in the smallest scrap of reserve she had become when she was with her *maître*. Ida would have been shocked to see how brazen she could be, utterly without inhibition. But then Ida knew about a love like this. She loved Gus, but her devotion to him had not kept him by her side. Aware of this, Gwen wondered if there might be a lesson she ought to learn from Ida's position, and apply to herself. She did not like to think so – could not bear to imagine that by keeping nothing back, by exposing herself so completely to Rodin, laying before him all her love, she might have made him wary. Calm, calm, he was always advising, compose yourself, be tranquil, he urged, and what was that but a warning? A warning which she could not heed, and which made her angry. She saw herself as a blue flower growing high in the Alps, refusing to be found and cut and killed.

She voiced none of this to Ida, who had her own troubles, but she thought about doing so. She trusted Ida, and needed a confidante. But then, suddenly, it was too late. In the first week in March 1907, Ida felt her labour pains begin, mild enough to permit her to walk from her apartment to the Hôpital de la Maternité, where she gave birth to yet another boy. Gwen, when she received the message, said out loud, though there was no one with her, 'Oh dear!' Ida had so wanted a girl, every time. Mrs Nettleship arrived and, Gwen knew, would be in charge, so she would wait until later to visit Ida. There never was a later. On the 14 March another message came: Ida was dead, and Gus was drunk.

★

The studio was enormous. Gus had told her it would be magnificent when the workmen had finished, and she could see what he meant. But standing in the doorway that day she thought how its echoing emptiness, its disarray, the chill in the air were like a form of grief itself. Gus wandered about, still drunk, sometimes singing, sometimes whistling, a look of what anyone who did not know him might interpret as contentment on his face. Silently, Gwen moved about, clearing away some of the builders' debris, lifting bits of plasterboard very, very carefully and stacking them neatly. Gus should not really be here at all but she had guided him here, encouraging him to believe that it was perfectly proper for him to try to work. He was no good to his crying children and he antagonised Mrs Nettleship who, with Dorelia, was looking after them.

There was to be a cremation. Gus would not attend and neither would she. What was the point? They did not want to see a row of weeping mourners when their own distress was so savage. Work, that was the only thing. Work, try to put into their art all that they felt, and so keep Ida alive and warm within them. They did not talk about her. Neither of them mentioned her, not since the first moment when she went to collect Gus (she felt that is what she had done, scooped him up, taken him away from Mrs Nettleship). He had told her then how beautiful Ida had been just before she died. 'Here's to love!' Ida had said, and the two of them had drunk a toast in Vichy water. Gwen could hardly bear to hear this and had put her finger to his lips. She wondered if she should embrace him but instead she led him to his easel, and put a paintbrush in his hand. After staring at the canvas for a long time, he began to paint.

And she drew him. Sitting to his right, she positioned herself on a stool, sketchbook on her knee, and drew him, and while she drew she thought of her lover. Rodin would hear about Ida's death, everyone would, and when he returned to Paris he was sure to come to her, knowing how shocked she would be. She had left a note with the concierge and he would read it and come to the studio, but delicacy would prevent his entering, so she had left another note with the concierge here, saying when and where she would meet him. She needed his comfort. He would hold her, and stroke her hair, and do for her what she could not do for Gus. But instead, on the third day, when Gus had slept as though in a coma, and she had not slept at all, a telegram was brought round by her own concierge. Rodin was not coming to her. He expressed his condolences but said nothing more. And he had been in Paris all this time.

Anger began to mix with grief as she stayed close to her brother. Death was so near, time so limited, and her lover did not seem to appreciate this. He could die, like Ida. He was more likely to die than Ida had ever been. She developed a hissing noise again in her head and felt she might explode with the frustration of it all. Gus, awake at last, properly awake after days of stumbling about and drinking heavily, when she could not persuade him to paint, was unaware of her state of mind. He wanted his children back. Mrs Nettleship had taken the three eldest back to Wigmore Street with her, and he had had to let her do this, leaving the two babies with a nurse and Dorelia. Now he wanted them all reunited. Gwen could not begin to comprehend how this could be managed and was no help in making plans. But Gus was full of schemes, and the energy needed to explore all the alternatives began to come to him, so Gwen went home, back to her attic room, feeling that she was not needed so much any more. She could return to her own life.

Back in her room, soothed by its peaceful air, she wondered about her life. Did it have meaning without her master at the centre of it? But he was not at the centre now, perhaps never had been. He was on the edge, and ever threatening to slip off it. Dying would solve everything – if she were to die, like Ida, not him. She could kill herself and have done with him. What, after all, was there to live for if she had lost his love? She had no children to mourn her, no dependants she would be deserting. More and more it seemed attractive to end her own life. Wicked, but attractive. Lying on her bed, watching the tops of trees tremble in the wind outside her window, she thought how easy it would be to drift off for ever, fall into a deep, deep sleep, toasting not love, as Ida had done, but death itself.

Then he wrote to her, a letter full of concern, saying that he did love her and that he wanted her to be happy. He would come to her soon, and wanted to find her tranquil and working well. One last chance, she promised herself.

IV

QUIETLY, URSULA TYRWHITT climbed the stairs, pausing every now and again not because she found them steep but to listen. She could hear nothing from above. It might mean that Gwen was out but she did not think so. She hoped her friend was painting, and that the intense silence was a sign of creativity. A new painting had begun. Ursula had seen it the week before. It was different from anything Gwen had ever attempted, a painting in which there were no people, only objects. She had said this to Gwen – 'No figure? There is to be no figure?' – and Gwen had shaken her head. 'It is not about people,' she had said, and shrugged, a gesture Ursula knew well. It meant 'do not press me'.

She was carrying some primroses, bought that morning from a woman selling them in the street. They were fresh, newly picked, drops of moisture still on the delicate petals. Ursula was holding them in her gloved hands, conscious of their fragility. The stems were tied with a thin wisp of straw and would come apart any minute. Cautiously, approaching the top of the staircase, she raised the posy to her face to see if the primroses still carried their scent. They did, but only faintly, only a trace of the woodland where they had been picked remaining. Gwen's door was slightly open. Ursula hesitated. The gap was just wide enough for her to peer round. Gwen was standing motionless in front of her easel, paintbrush in hand but not poised to touch the canvas. She was staring at it as though she did not recognise it, and was bewildered by what she saw. 'Gwen?' Ursula whispered, fearing to break whatever spell her friend seemed to be under. Mutely she held out the primroses.

In a sudden swift movement, Gwen put down her paintbrush and crossed the room to take the flowers. Without speaking, she

73

took them from Ursula and turned and seized a glass tumbler which she filled with water from her sink and placed on the little wooden table in front of the window. She pushed the primroses into the tumbler, not seeking to arrange them, and stepped back. There was an open book on the table but now she removed it. The window was open, but she closed it and drew across it the fine lace curtain. Again she stepped back, and this time nodded. Ursula was afraid to speak and wondered if she ought simply to turn and tiptoe away, but Gwen spoke first. 'Good,' she said, 'the flowers are just right. They say the right things.' Ursula wondered what these right things were, but Gwen was asking if she would like tea and did not seem to want her to go.

They sat at the back of the room, on the bed. Around the window there seemed to be an aura which could not be touched. The table, and the wickerwork chair, were clearly arranged for a purpose, and so was the parasol leaning against the chair. Ursula said she hoped she had not come at an inconvenient time and spoiled Gwen's reverie, but was assured she had not. 'It is too late now,' Gwen said, 'the light has changed, the shadows are wrong.' They sipped their tea. It felt companionable, sitting perched on the bed, but Ursula sensed the tension in Gwen. She would not insult her by stooping to pleasantries. Instead, she waited. Gwen's question came at last: had Ursula been to Rodin's studio that day? Yes, she had. She had continued to work on the head Rodin had thought promising. And had the *maître* been there? No, he had not. 'He has not visited me for five weeks,' Gwen said. 'He no longer replies to my letters. What am I to think, Ursula? What am I to do?'

There was no honest answer possible to that. Gwen trembled slightly as she spoke, but whether with distress or anger Ursula did not know. Carefully, she placed a hand on Gwen's knee, the lightest of touches, merely to acknowledge that she knew how painful any mention of Rodin had become. 'May I look at your painting,' she whispered, 'or is it too soon?' 'Much too soon,' Gwen said, 'but look if you will. It is nothing yet.' Ursula, standing in front of the canvas, saw this was true. A vague impression of the window and the wall beside it and that was all. So far as her

74

friend could see, Gwen had not progressed beyond what she had done the week before, and yet a strange, hypnotic quality was starting to emerge. 'I love this room,' Gwen suddenly said. 'It *is* me, you know, at last.' 'But you said "no figure",' Ursula reminded her, 'so where are you in this room that is you? You are invisible to me.' Gwen pointed. 'There,' she said, 'coming home, leaving home. It is what I see. That corner. It is what I know, finally.'

Ursula took her teacup to the sink and set it down there, not wanting to turn on the tap and make even the slightest noise. Gwen was struggling to tell her something and she wanted to understand. It seemed to her that Gwen must be mistaken – there was nothing about that corner, with its window and table and chair, that could possibly be her. The corner was all peace and calm and serenity, whereas her friend radiated energy, the air around her crackled with it and there was always the feeling that there might be an eruption. Gwen must mean something else. 'It is a pretty room,' Ursula murmured, 'but you are more than a corner in it, Gwen. It is only a tiny part of you, surely, dear? You yourself are so much more.' Gwen shook her head violently and then put her hands up to her face. 'No,' she said, 'without him, I am *less* than that corner.'

The rumours had hardened recently into definite information. Ursula had heard about Rodin's new mistress but feared that Gwen had not. Should she tell her? It was not something a friend would wish to do. But Gwen would hear of it, it would come to her ears in the end and hurt all the more for her realising that her friend must have known. Hesitantly, Ursula went over to Gwen and took hold of her hands. 'Gwen,' she began, and then stopped. Gwen's hands were cold, yet her face was flushed. It was not the right time to tell her. She was happy with her conviction that this corner of her room, which she was painting, signified herself – calm, peaceful, content. To tell her about Rodin would be like smashing the window, throwing the primroses to the ground, upturning the table and chair. The painting would never happen.

'I must go,' Ursula said, and kissed Gwen lightly on the cheek.

★

75

All night she lay there, her body tortured by desire for him, his eyes locking onto hers, his hands everywhere, his body a weight upon hers which crushed her, and in her head a delirium of feeling she could not release. The dawn light creeping cautiously through the window found her exhausted and weeping, every bone in her poor body aching and her throat raw and dry, her head rigid with pain. It was hard to rise from her bed at all, and she staggered when she did so, clutching on to the rail of the headboard until it bent and creaked and threatened to come loose. Slowly, she steadied herself. The light grew stronger, it was changing in colour and she had to hurry. She went to the sink and splashed her face with water and then filled a cup and drank some of it. No time, no need, to dress. She shivered, but with apprehension not cold. Suppose it was not there this morning? Suppose what she had seen had vanished?

She settled herself in front of her easel and waited. The sun was up, the flood of light now tinged with gold, bathing that corner of her room so softly. The sunlight touched the primroses and made them shine, it stroked the top of the table until the solid wood seemed to become smooth and liquid. The wall was defined strongly, a wedge near the window, sharp and pointed at the end, and then a great shadow beyond it where no colour was visible. The chair was too near the table. She crossed the room and moved it an inch or two to the left. Yesterday she had put her coat over the chair, beneath the parasol, but then removed it. She had tried, last week, a different painting, with only her coat over the chair and the curtain open, as well as the window itself. She had put an open book on the table, pleased with what this would signify. But that had been another person, one full of hope still, cheerful, confident her *maître* would soon knock on the door and be welcomed in. That reading of herself was finished. She saw now how far away she had been from achieving the state of mind her lover wished her to attain. *This* picture, this was what he wanted. It even occurred to her that his absence was deliberate. He knew she would suffer, and would have to control this suffering, and through doing so would reach a level of serenity she had not yet come near.

Two hours after dawn and the light exactly right. She painted. Carefully, slowly, building up the layers of paint, catching the strengthening radiance diffused through the lace curtain. She could hear her own heart beating, her own breath escaping. Her hand was not quite steady and she had to support her left arm, the arm she painted with, with her right. She would have to go in search of more primroses herself – Ursula's would not last beyond another day. The flowers had become crucial to the painting, giving the corner of her room the touch of colour it needed. Without them, the scene was barren. It struck her, as she went on painting, that she could give this painting to Ursula. It was not for exhibiting, or for sale. She would keep it or give it away to someone who would understand it and treasure it for what it was – see its significance.

It was over for another day. She cleaned her brush, pulled back the curtain and opened the window. The air was still cool and she breathed it in deeply, and thought that she must eat, but to eat she would have to go and find food, which meant leaving her room. She dreaded doing so, fearing that Rodin might come and find her gone and not trouble to come again. Here, she pined for him but he would not know that if the room was empty. She doubted if he could read the scene with her eyes and see how she had striven to please him. He must see her there. She wanted to be standing in the middle of her room, looking towards the window, proud of what it conveyed about her.

But she had to eat. She had allowed herself to exist on grapes and nuts and raisins and bread but now there was nothing at all left. Yesterday, she had drunk tea and now the tea was finished too. There was a pain in her belly and she felt light-headed, hardly trusting herself to dress and descend all those stairs. The noise of the street would overwhelm her but she must face it. Gathering her things together – her coat, her new black hat with its bright green ribbon, her purse, her key – she left her room and paused a moment on the landing. She looked at the shut door, the blankness of the wooden panels, and could hardly believe what lay behind it. It seemed urgent to get herself back inside as quickly as possible, and she began to run down the stairs so fast that at the bottom she almost fainted. She knew where to buy bread and cheese and more grapes, and where to get the tea she liked, but it was an ordeal to go through the necessary transactions. All the time she was peering up her street to check that Rodin was not alighting from a cab and entering her building. When she was back at the street door, she felt such relief, and yet also such disappointment. She had hoped, in an absurdly superstitious way, that by leaving her room she would be sure to make Rodin come.

She could hardly drag herself back up the stairs. Halfway up, she stopped and sat down, and broke off a piece of bread. It was newly baked, still warm, the crust golden, but in her mouth it tasted dry and threatened to choke her. A grape was better, the sharp bite of it delicious, the juice comforting. She took another, holding it for a moment on her tongue. The pleasure of the taste, when she crushed the grape this time, made her want to weep – there was so little pleasure, so little joy, in her life without her lover. Her senses were dulled and she had begun to feel all emotion extinguished. She stood up, climbed the remaining stairs, and then paused again on her landing. She wondered what she would see when she opened the door. The room might merely look sad. The corner, which she had turned into a representation of how Rodin wanted her to be, might be a mirage. Everything depended on that flash of recognition she ought to experience as she looked at her room with the eyes, for a mere second, of a stranger.

She had only been out of the room twenty minutes, but it was her first outing for a week. She had broken the spell it held her in. Taking a deep breath, she pushed the door open vigorously, wanting to take in the room all at once. The shock was profound – it *was* there! She felt dizzy with relief and had to sit down and put her head on the table. It was not an illusion. The corner of her room spoke loud and clear. It only needed her *maître* to come and hear its voice.

★

Winifred had written. When the concierge said that there was a letter for her, Gwen had hoped it was from Rodin and she had almost snatched it from the woman's hand. But she saw at once the foreign stamps and recognised Winifred's writing. It shamed her to feel such disappointment and she punished herself by not opening the letter at once. Winifred's life seemed to her extraordinary – to take herself off like that to join Thornton in his strange wanderings through Canada, and then to go on to America, was quite bizarre. It could never have been predicted. Where was her sister's music in all this? Once, it had seemed to drive her, as art drove Gus and Gwen, but now there was no mention of hours of devoted practice. Music was not her god.

It was a cheerful letter, amusing, full of lively descriptions of people and places. Winifred sounded happy, and Gwen was glad of it. She wondered, in this letter, if Gwen was once more working or whether she was still 'in thrall' to her lover. Only Winifred and Ursula knew about Rodin and sometimes Gwen regretted confessing to either of them, but there had been a great need in her to burst out to someone, to tell them what was filling her heart and her life. They had been kind, and respectful. They had not cast doubt on her passion, or uttered dire warnings of what might happen. They had, she thought, both been glad for her. She loved them for it.

But Winifred now upset her by asking if she was still 'in thrall' to Rodin. Of course she was, yet she did not like her feelings for him described thus. Someone 'in thrall' was surely blinded to reality, and on the brink of being silly. It made her sound weak and feeble, and she was neither. She tried to think how she could honestly respond to her sister's enquiry. The attempt stopped her painting. She sat at her easel, facing the beautiful corner of her room, and she did not touch the canvas all day. Slowly, seeping through her brain, was the terrifying knowledge that she was no longer 'in thrall'. She wanted to be, but doubt had begun to break the spell and she did not like what she glimpsed behind it. She loved her *maître* every bit as fiercely, but she needed him to love her as she loved him. His absences spoke for him. She had transformed herself for him, and had become his willing slave, but now he was wary of her hunger for him. He had said he was merely tired, he'd pleaded his great age, but she had seen in his eyes that it was more than that. It was like watching the moon wane, the full glory of its light weakening, the great roundness fading round the rim, and she could not bear it.

The next morning found her back behind her easel, still staring at the corner of her room but seeing it differently. It was a cheat. It was full of hope, yet she was losing hope. But instead of discouraging her, instead of breaking her heart, this revelation strengthened her sense of purpose. She knew what she saw in the corner of her room and she had to make sure that others saw it too. She wanted to record how things might have been and so nearly were. Contentment, peace, a life lived sweetly and quietly. No mess, no trouble, no agonising. The person who lived in this room was in perfect control of her emotions. She had been out for a walk and picked the flowers and had come home to it well satisfied. She might seem invisible, but she was across the room, pouring a glass of wine, putting bread and grapes for her supper on a plate. Soon, she would come to the chair and sit down, and put her glass and her plate on the table, and perhaps draw the curtain back and look out of the window. She wanted for nothing.

But I, thought Gwen, still want so much. I may not be quite 'in thrall' to my lover, but I am not free and I do not think I can bear to be free.

★

She had worked long enough on the painting. Day after day she had gone out and bought primroses and when primroses were no longer obtainable any other small flowers she could find. Sometimes, in order to get a posy of the matching size, she had to accept some tiny pink primulas too, and a few blue ones, though it meant changing what she had already painted. But now, on her thirty-first birthday, she had done as much as she could and it was not enough. She took the small canvas off the easel and turned it to the wall. She would try again, and meanwhile give this one to Ursula. Already she had the version with the open window and the book hidden away. It worked better but still did not say what she wanted it to say. She would keep that one.

The 22nd June, her birthday, was a lovely sunny day, but she was not happy. How could she be? No letter, no card, from her *maître*, and she had no hope that he was about to surprise her with a sudden visit. She went out in the afternoon and walked first by the river and then took a tram to Rodin's studio. She would confront him. She would remind him that it was her birthday and hope to witness his guilt at having forgotten. She wanted him to take her in his arms and see him contrite and concerned and eager to make up for his neglect. Her heart beat more quickly as she neared the studio but she did not falter – she was tired of waiting, of being humble. A birthday was a good day to make a stand. But his studio was empty of people. No one at all working there, only half-completed works shrouded in sheets. She had an insane desire to slip the sheets off and smash to bits what was underneath but instead she went into the adjoining studio in search of Hilda Flodin, who would know where Rodin was.

He was in Oxford, it seemed, attending a ceremony admitting him to the university. Hilda smiled when she gave this information, an annoying smile, malicious. 'He did not tell you?' she asked Gwen. Gwen did not reply. Why would she be asking if she already knew? And she would not pretend that she had been told and had forgotten. She turned, without saying anything to Hilda, though Hilda was saying something else, and left the studios. It was unendurable to think that Rodin had actually left the country and had not thought to tell her. Tears blinded her as she stumbled home and when she got back to her room she flung herself on her bed and wept and wept. Eventually, through sheer exhaustion, she fell into a half-sleep in which she was calling out to Rodin to come to her but was conscious enough to realise this was not a dream but a hallucination. She could see him coming towards her, arms outstretched, and she tried to rouse herself enough to stand up and embrace him. The effort was too much. She sank back onto the bed, and this time truly slept.

The light, when she woke, had changed. It was late evening, she knew. No need to consult a clock when the setting sun told the time so obligingly. She rolled onto her side, her head throbbing, her eyes hurting from all the tears. How sad the empty chair looked, how pathetic the little posy of flowers wilting on the plain wooden table. They spoke of loneliness and blankness. There was no life there, or no life worth having. The parasol did not fool her. It had not been opened, had not been taken on a walk. Why had she been so proud of this corner? Why had she been so sure her *maître* would approve of what it represented? It was an interior like any other. The props were universal – the cheap chair, the cheap table, the poverty of it all. And she had wanted it to prove her own triumph. She had wanted to show Rodin that this was evidence of her transformation. She had imagined him walking into her room and being transfixed, overcome with admiration for what she had achieved.

But now she doubted if she had achieved anything. Was the painting good? She did not know. She wanted to be rid of that first version, the one painted with such joy. The next she would complete in a different mood, and then hide. Then she would be done with trying to make herself into what her lover wanted.

★

This time, Ursula came by arrangement, to say goodbye. How her friend could leave Paris, Gwen did not know, but the answer was simple: Ursula's father wanted her home. 'You listen to your father?' Gwen asked. 'Still?' Ursula smiled, but felt her face flush. She loved both her parents but especially her father, who had always championed her cause. If it had not been for him, she would never have gone to the Slade. Were it not for his indulgence, she could not have come to Paris at all. Like Gwen, she was in her thirties and unmarried – she had no means of support other than her clergyman father's allowance. 'I did without any allowance from my father,' Gwen told her, 'and so could you.' Ursula shook her head. It seemed unnecessary to point out the difference to her friend, who knew perfectly well that she loved her father and would not for the world disobey or offend him.

Art was not important enough to contemplate a rupture with her parents.

Gwen was ready for her. She had bought delicious pastries and had the table set with pretty pink teacups and teapot. They sat by the window, listening to the canary singing in its cage on the balcony below and watching the tree-tops shiver in the breeze. 'I love your room,' Ursula said. Gwen nodded, and said that she loved it too, but that lately she had experienced a yearning for the country. 'The country?' Ursula queried, surprised. 'Meudon,' Gwen said. 'Oh, Gwen,' Ursula said, 'is that wise?' Gwen shrugged. They sat in silence for a while. A child laughed somewhere below them and they could hear a ball bouncing against a wall. 'Come and live with me,' Gwen said. 'We will take a cottage together. It will not cost much.' Did she mean it? Ursula was not sure. Her friend could be impulsive and then regret it. And she did not know if she could live harmoniously with Gwen. Often, after a mere hour in her company she felt drained by the emotional demands made on her, that urgent need for constant sympathy which was so exhausting to give. And Gwen, in that respect, gave little in return.

They ate the pastries and drank the tea and it felt comfortable and companionable, so much so that Ursula wondered what had happened to make Gwen seem relaxed and cheerful when for the last few months she had been tense and depressed. Had Rodin come to her? From what she had heard said in and around the studios of the Dépôt des Marbres, she did not think so. Or was this change of mood in Gwen due to her acceptance that Rodin had found someone new? Again, Ursula did not think so. Gwen did not accept unpalatable truths – she denied them, fought them and could only be bludgeoned into defeat. Then it occurred to Ursula that there could be another reason for her friend's apparent contentment. Perhaps her work was giving her pleasure again? Perhaps she had completed a painting, or even more than one, to her satisfaction? That would be something.

'I have a present to give you,' Gwen said, rising and brushing crumbs off her skirt. 'Take it, look at it when you reach home, and think of me.' She handed Ursula a package, clearly a small canvas, framed, already wrapped in calico and tied with string. She made to undo the knots but Gwen stopped her. 'No,' she said, 'don't look at it now. Wait. Look at it when you are home, alone, in your own room.' Ursula felt overwhelmed. She clutched the package to her, embraced it tightly, feeling the sharp corners of the frame with her fingers. 'Is it this room, this corner?' Gwen nodded. 'Your primroses,' she said. 'But Gwen . . .' Ursula began, and was stopped. Gwen put a finger to her lips. 'Say nothing,' she commanded. 'I want you to have it. It was the first. I have another, which will be better. But this one has your primroses. Show it to no one, promise?' Ursula rose, and kissed her on the cheek. They held each other for a moment. 'Thank you,' Ursula whispered. 'I shall treasure it.' 'There is treasure there, for you to find,' Gwen said, but smiling, laughing at herself.

All the way down the staircase Ursula puzzled over what such an odd statement could mean.

★

The temptation was too strong. Before she left Paris, Ursula looked at the painting Gwen had given her, justifying this dis-obedience by persuading herself that to open the package in absolute privacy fulfilled the spirit of her friend's command. And, besides, she needed to wrap it more securely for it to be better protected during the Channel crossing. She carried the package over to the window where a small desk stood, and searched in one of the cubbyholes for scissors. Outside, it was raining slightly but the sky was not completely grey. There were patches of blue visible and the clouds were white, not black. It was just a shower which would soon stop.

The calico was just the outer wrapping. Underneath, the painting was swathed in several layers of cotton muslin and she removed each one with exquisite care, folding them as she went to prolong the delicious anticipation. She guessed that the canvas underneath was about twelve inches by ten, small indeed, like most of Gwen's paintings. Every single one she had seen could hang comfortably in an ordinary-sized room – there would be no difficulty in hanging it. At home she had a dressing room opening off her bedroom and no one went into it except Mary, the maid, who, if she noticed a new painting on the wall would hardly remark on it. After all, Gwen would not have expected her to keep her gift literally hidden – it was to be enjoyed, gazed upon often, but not shown off, that was the difference.

No figure. She remembered saying that to Gwen. An empty room, a mere corner of an empty room, with no one in it, and yet Gwen's presence so powerfully there. Ursula held the unwrapped painting in her hands and stared at it. There was such longing there, she thought. For the quiet pleasures of a walk in the sun and the picking of primroses. A life outside which had been brought inside and held there? But then she held the small canvas at arm's length and looked again. It was in fact the opposite: a life *inside* which had been brought outside. The empty chair, the parasol leaning against it, the table bare except for the flowers – they were all disguises. But what lay underneath? She seemed to see the parasol trembling in Gwen's hands as she walked to Rodin's studio and found him absent, and then it would be furled up and held tightly to stop the rage this absence provoked. The empty chair would not be empty long – she saw Gwen hurl herself into it, slump down against its uncomfortable back and weep. The corner of the room was soon invaded by the real Gwen, the distraught Gwen longing for her *maître* who no longer deigned to visit her. He would not be fooled. Indeed, Ursula found herself thinking, in all probability he had never been fooled. Gwen had intrigued him, and he had undoubtedly felt passion for her, but he had always been wary of being consumed by her, and when that became too great a danger he had extricated himself. Ursula felt such pain for her friend. She walked around the room, cradling the painting in her arms, and there were tears in her eyes.

The frame was old and cracked and did not fit the canvas exactly. Ursula hesitated. She knew that Gwen searched out used frames, preferring them, and that this one would not have cost much. It seemed wicked to discard it but if she did so the painting would fit into the special compartment in her largest valise and be very well protected during the journey. This compartment was like a second case within the valise and she had used it to transport her own work. Carefully, she detached the battered frame and wrapped the canvas in a length of gauze she had bought that day, intending to make a veil for a hat, and then in the layers of cotton muslin Gwen had provided. She put the parcel between two sheets of cardboard and wrapped the whole thing in a woollen scarf. There was still plenty of room in the compartment so she further padded the package all round with her silk underwear before closing it. The valise was clearly labelled with the Pimlico address where she would stay before going on to her father's vicarage. Once there, she would take the painting out of its hiding place and carry it in her bag the rest of the way. The painting would be quite safe. The valise, purchased at Harrod's some years ago, was strong and had good locks.

At the last minute, she almost took it out and put it in her travelling bag there and then, but stopped herself with the memory of having mislaid two such bags on other travels through sheer carelessness – she was always putting her bag down and forgetting it and moving away only to realise, far too late, that she did not have it with her and could not remember when she last had it. She did the same with her purse, and her clasp bag, and had had to teach herself always to wear some garment with capacious pockets so that her money and passport could be kept within them. If only Gwen's little canvas had been just an inch or two smaller then, even well wrapped, it could have gone into such a pocket on the inside of her long coat. But it stayed in the big, secure valise.

Ursula was to regret this for the rest of her life.

CHARLOTTE

I

THE HOUSE was full. Every bedroom taken, and even the better rooms among the servants' attics commandeered for the weekend. Where the evicted servants would sleep nobody had the slightest interest. Charlotte should not have been up on that floor at all, she was in the way, but she wanted to see what was going on, and her mother was much too agitated to care where her youngest daughter had got to. It was Jessie who snapped at her instead. 'If you please, Miss Charlotte!' she shouted, as she staggered up the last flight of stairs, carrying bed linen, and Charlotte, pressed against the staircase wall, knocked a pair of pillowcases off the pile – 'If you please!' Charlotte apologised, picked up the pillowcases and followed Jessie into the end attic.

'Oh, what a sweet room!' she exclaimed. Jessie snorted. 'Freezing in the winter, sweltering in the summer, very sweet, I must say. Now move over while I make this bed.' Charlotte was not listening. She was standing looking up at the sky through the windows in the sloping roof. How wonderful to lie in bed and gaze up at the stars, or glimpse a crescent moon floating by. The room was so tiny, so intimate. There was hardly space for the narrow iron bedstead and otherwise there was only a stool and a wooden washstand, crammed to the right of the door. 'Out!' Jessie shouted. 'Out!' But Charlotte sat down on the newly made bed. 'Do you think, after the wedding, Mother would let me have this room, Jessie?' Jessie did not reply. Her expression was meant to say everything, and it did. Martha came in with a rug, and behind her John, carrying a jug and a bowl. 'Who are they shoving in here? Someone must've gone down in the world,' John said. 'How should I know?' Jessie said. 'As if I cared.' 'They're lucky,' Charlotte murmured. 'Miss, *will* you get off that bed and go downstairs. I've enough to bother me, thank you.' 'No,' Charlotte said. 'I will not. You can tell Mother if you like.' 'Out!' Jessie yelled, but this time at Martha and John, who were laughing. She followed them, slamming the door shut.

Charlotte lay down and closed her eyes. The bed was hard, much harder than her own, but she felt comfortable. She moved about a little, experimentally, judging how easy it would be to fall off. She felt like one of those knights whose sarcophagi she had stared at in Westminster Abbey, lying, as she was, all straight, with their feet crossed at the ankles and their arms folded. She might lie here and sleep for a hundred years. But she was not sleepy. She felt alert, and curious. What would it be like, to live in this room? If she were poor, this is where she would have to live, or at least sleep. There were three hooks on the back of the door and on one of them, overlooked by Jessie, there still hung a garment. Charlotte could not make out what it was. Cautiously, she lowered herself off the bed and went to examine it. It was a shift, that was all, a poor thing, the cloth worn, the buttons missing. Thrilled with her own daring, Charlotte took her clothes off, all but her knickers, and slipped the shift on. She shivered. There was no looking-glass in the room so she could not see herself, but she felt she knew how she looked: poor. Quickly, she dressed again and hung the shift back where it had been. She would have to go downstairs soon. The guests would be arriving and she had been detailed to look after several cousins and to behave herself. To anger her mother at this stage would be unwise. But she wanted to know about this attic, who slept here, or who used to sleep here, and who was going to be put here for the weekend. If it was a young cousin she had a plan. She would sleep here and give them her bed. She would wear the shift over her naked body and sleep a whole night here and pretend she was different.

★

The presents were laid out in the drawing room. They covered every available surface and it had taken a whole day for the maids to display everything to the satisfaction of the bride's mother. Lady Falconer's fear was that offence would be caused if undue prominence were given to a present of little value from a person of great

90

importance – people were odd – or to a gift of obvious expense donated by a person who was lucky to be invited at all. It had made Lady Falconer's head ache. But, finally, she hoped to have solved this delicate problem by having only close family gifts displayed on the centre table and everyone else's on smaller tables, brought in from all over the house, arranged right round the edges of the room.

Now that it was done, it all looked very splendid. The crystal glittered, the silver sparkled and the china offerings gleamed. So much stuff, such a magnificent show. The cards were discreetly laid flat in front of each gift so that to identify who had given what entailed a good deal of peering (which anyone with manners would not do). Priscilla would start married life in the style to which she had always been accustomed, and that was most satisfactory. Caroline had not been so fortunate, but then it was the girl's own fault, and she was doomed to pay the penalty. She did not worry about her sons as yet. They were young, both of them, still at school with no thoughts of romance or marriage in their heads. Then there was Charlotte. Best not to think about Charlotte, who was clever and peculiar, or perhaps peculiar because clever. How could one tell?

Cabs were still arriving at the door, blocking the road. The horses were having difficulty turning round in the narrow space in front of the house and there was barely room for those leaving to pass those still approaching from East Heath Road. Lady Falconer thanked God that she had reliable staff – from her house-keeper, Jessie Martin, downwards, they were utterly loyal and immensely hard-working. She had family and friends who regularly mourned the passing of the last century and the demise, or so they alleged, of devoted, unselfish servants, but Lady Falconer did not. Her servants stayed. She paid them well and treated them well, or so she believed. And she was understanding. Servants were servants, in her view, and expectations of impeccable moral behaviour should not be set too high. No servant girl was thrown out of her house if, as occasionally happened, she found herself (as these girls put it) 'in the family way'. If marriage was possible, it was arranged, and sometimes the girl was even allowed back, in due course, though in a lowly capacity. Lady Falconer believed her magnanimity was held to be astonishing and she was proud of it. Stealing, she handled differently. Pilfering, she could tolerate, in moderation, reckoning it to be inevitable, but if it went too far she faced the challenge and dealt with it. Stealing on a grander scale, however, she reacted to ferociously. If jewellery or silver went missing the police were called instantly, and the whole household suffered until the culprit was found. Oh, she ran a tight ship, did Lady Falconer, and was known for it.

Charlotte was standing on the stairs, staring vacantly into space in that unattractive way of hers. The hall was like Euston Station (Lady Falconer had only been there once but she was extravagantly fond of making comparisons to it), packed full of arriving guests, all calling out to each other, all falling over each other's luggage which the harassed servants could not get out of the way quickly enough. 'Hettie!' cried Lady Falconer's sister Philomena, rushing forward to embrace her. Lady Falconer endured the embrace stoically but returned it with a mere pat on her annoying sister's broad back. Sometimes she thought there had been some kind of strange accident and that Charlotte was really Philomena's daughter. It was not just that this sister of hers looked physically like her daughter – both tall, broad-shouldered, both rather heavy, with almost unmanageable thick black hair – but that they shared the same distinctly odd characteristics. And yet they did not take to one another, each seeming wary of the other. This, in Lady Falconer's opinion, was a pity. She would have liked to pack Charlotte off for long periods to Philomena, who lived in the country, in Hampshire, but had not been able to. 'I will not go,' Charlotte had said, and, when told that she would go where she was sent, 'I will run away and cause a scandal, you know I will.' Alas, her mother did know it. Charlotte, at fourteen, an age when she ought to have grown out of tantrums, was capable of quite appalling behaviour – one wondered, constantly, where she got her ideas from. Books, most probably, but she could not be banned from reading. Her father would not allow it.

Sir Edward loved his library. So did Charlotte. She was the only one of his five children who ever went into it for the reasons one ought to enter a library: to read, in peace and quiet, and to study.

At first it had been amusing – even his wife had been mildly amused – to see the tiny girl reaching up to turn the rather heavy knob on the library door and then totter into the room and climb up onto a chair to reach the shelf her father kept especially for her. She would select a picture book and then sit on the floor solemnly 'reading' it, long before she could read (though she could read fluently soon after her fourth birthday). Sir Edward was delighted. He encouraged her, sat for hours with her on his knee and read to her. She was his favourite, and he did not seem to notice her oddness. 'She has a fine mind, a keen intellect,' he pronounced with pride, and when his wife pointed out that she also was rude and strong-willed and had no social graces whatsoever, he shrugged. 'Leave her alone,' he said, 'she will do well in the end.' He had married his wife for her beauty and she was well aware of this. He had, in fact, hardly known her when he proposed – he had simply been mesmerised by her exquisite face, heart-shaped, the eyes violet, framed with an abundance of golden – yes, golden – hair. Sexually, she was the most desirable woman he had ever encountered and he had had to have her. But it was, in any case, a good match, which both families approved. Henrietta was a good wife, in the accepted sense. A superb hostess, a tremendous organiser, and looks that graced any occasion. It was possible for Sir Edward to do whatever he wanted, knowing that his children, his household, his very life, were in excellent hands. He was aware of how other men envied him, as who would not. Only he knew what was lacking, and he would have been a fool to make it public.

Turning away from her sister, Lady Falconer saw that Charlotte had disappeared just as the cousins she had been deputed to take charge of arrived. There was no mystery as to where she would have gone: the library, locking herself in, no doubt. But now Priscilla had come down and the noise was overwhelming, the screams of recognition, the fervent cries of admiration drowning any instructions to go and get Miss Charlotte which Lady Falconer might have attempted to give one of the servants. Instead, she stood watching the bride-to-be being mobbed by her relations, and she could not help smiling. The tension in her eased a little. Priscilla was a darling. Sweet, gentle, and devastatingly lovely. The gentleness had been a worry — she was much too easily influenced and could have been taken advantage of — and her father found her 'not bright', but now she was to be married to Robert Charlesworth all was well. She was a credit to her family and her wedding at St Margaret's, Westminster, would be the wedding of the 1908 season. 'Does the fellow *know* her?' Sir Edward had asked, after Robert had proposed. 'Do you think he knows the girl?'

Such a pointless question, or so his wife thought. What was this 'knowing' he was so keen on? Over and over again he asked it, as though it had some obvious and yet profound meaning. Well, it was quite beyond her. 'If I had truly known you . . .' Edward had once said to her, and then stopped. It was in a fit of rare anger, while they were going to bed. She had ignored him. She had said she wished to sleep alone that night, and he had left the room, slamming the door, saying, 'If I had truly known you . . .' Nonsensical. He had known all he had needed to know, surely, and yet in those peevish words had been the unmistakable suggestion that he had been tricked. On another occasion, during an argument about Charlotte's education, he had stared at her and said, 'If I had known . . .' and, again, stopped. She could very well have riposted to his 'If I had known' with 'If *I* had known', said with greater emphasis. She had known he was rich, handsome, from a good family, and said to be clever. It was his cleverness that had needed more attention on her part. Nothing wrong with a man being clever, but being bookish turned out to be intensely irritating. And then there was the painting. She hadn't known Edward had artistic leanings, and that if his nose was not in a book when he was at home he would be absorbed in front of an easel, painting unrecognisable portraits.

Lady Falconer put a hand to her forehead and pulled herself together. The gong had sounded, the hall had emptied and it was time for the 'light' luncheon she had ordered. Cold chicken, cold salmon, cold beef, all temptingly displayed on great oval platters and surrounded by bowls of salads of varying kinds together with tiny crystal goblets of strawberry mousse and lemon syllabub.

There was a sumptuous cheese board – all the French cheeses as well as good old English Cheddar and Stilton – and jugs of celery beside the biscuits. Guests, only family today, were invited to help themselves and then be seated round the big table, draped with a starched white cloth overlaid with another embroidered cloth. Very pretty, she thought, as she went into the dining room. Priscilla was already seated, a mere cream cracker and sliver of cheese on her plate, next to her Aunt Philomena, who had helped herself to all the meats and very little of the salad. Someone asked Priscilla where her honeymoon was to be spent. She shook her head, lowered her eyes, and blushed.

Lady Falconer knew. She had been flattered when Robert consulted her as to where he and his bride should stay in Paris. Her answer had been swift – the Crillon, of course, where else? That was where she and Edward had spent the first night of their honeymoon some twenty-one years ago, on their way south to Nice. Robert and Priscilla, too, were to go on to Nice. Nothing had changed, the pattern was being followed. Robert had not needed to ask Lady Falconer to keep the secret. The only danger was that Charlotte might tell because, unfortunately, she had over-heard. The girl was so rarely seen in the drawing room, where Lady Falconer was arranging flowers as Robert approached her, that it had been a shock when she sprang up from the sofa where she had been lying (hidden from view by its high back) and expressed the opinion that to go to Paris for one's honeymoon was terribly boring, and that Robert ought to be thinking about a trip up the Amazon or a boat to China.

She had promised, lip curled in exaggerated scorn, not to say a word to her sister. But one never knew with Charlotte. However, she and Priscilla were not intimate sisters and had not much to do with each other, so Charlotte was unlikely to be tempted to tell all. She had helped Priscilla pack her trunk, though. It was one of the many weird things about Charlotte: she had a passion for packing. Packing anything. A maid's talent, if ever there was one. She said she enjoyed fitting things into confined spaces and found it an agreeable, almost intellectual, exercise. Edward, when she came out with this, had roared with laughter and said, 'That's my girl!' So Charlotte had packed Priscilla's trunk, taking hours over it. Priscilla had sat on her bed and watched in awe, and her maid had sulked at being displaced like this. Charlotte had set everything out first, on the floor and on the bed beside Priscilla, and then she had counted all the items, enumerating the shoes (six pairs), the coats (four), the jackets (six), the dresses (ten), the skirts (four), the blouses (four) and then the nightdresses and under-wear. The nightdresses had astonished her. She held them up and exclaimed over the lace trimmings – 'It is as if you will be going out to a party, not to bed!' Charlotte cried, and 'What a waste, when Robert will just rip them off you!' Enough to make Priscilla burst into tears, and rush from her own bedroom.

As well as the trunk, there was a large valise. Charlotte frowned as she inspected the two pieces of luggage. If Priscilla was to spend a mere night in Paris, then the valise could be used for the smarter clothes, a selection only, and the rest could go in the trunk. She relished choosing what she judged would be appropriate garb for Paris, dressing her sister in her mind as she did so. People thought that a girl who was large and plain would have no idea about clothes but Charlotte knew herself to have good taste whereas Priscilla, small and beautiful, had none. She wore what her mother and her dressmaker chose for her and would be completely hope-less on her own. Kindly, Charlotte even wrote little notes – 'Wear this with red skirt' – and pinned them neatly to the garments. Priscilla would obey these helpful hints, she knew. She placed tissue paper into the folds of the clothes and laid them into the valise. It was new and had a delicious, leathery smell which Charlotte inhaled deeply. A few old labels still were stuck on the lid of the trunk, but Charlotte had been told not to remove them, and had judged (correctly) that this must mean they were indications of smart trav-elling. It was her job, though, to put new labels on the valise, with Priscilla's married name plain to see. She couldn't put them on now, or Priscilla would see and the secret would be out, but she had them prepared, ready to attach at the appropriate time. She would give them to John, who would do it.

The job done, Charlotte closed the lids and turned the little keys in the locks. Poor Priscilla. There was no envy in Charlotte's heart for her sister whereas when Caroline eloped she had been eaten up with a raw and painful jealousy. 'A lamb to the slaughter,' her father had said of Priscilla, and sighed. Her mother had been furious and had shocked his daughters by reprimanding him in their presence. 'A good marriage,' she fumed, 'is no kind of *slaughter!*' 'It is interesting that you say so,' her father had said, and stood up, dropped his napkin onto his plate, and left the room before pudding appeared.

Charlotte had pondered long and hard over what her father's words could have meant – not 'a lamb to the slaughter', she understood that well enough, and in her opinion it was an entirely appropriate description, but 'It is interesting that you say so', to her mother. Had he meant that her mother should see that a good marriage *was* a kind of slaughter, including therefore her own? If so, who or what had been slaughtered? Certainly not her mother. But perhaps her father's words had had a more abstract meaning. Perhaps he saw hopes and expectations being slaughtered. In that case, Priscilla was unlikely to suffer the doom he had prophesied. So far as Charlotte knew, and she felt she did know everything there was to know about her sister, Priscilla had perfectly ordinary hopes and expectations which would take little fulfilling.

The luncheon over, the older family members went to their bedrooms to rest and the others spilled out into the garden and lolled around. Some of the cousins started playing croquet but soon collapsed in giggles, swearing it was too hot to do anything. Charlotte watched them from the french windows. She never joined in games, despising all sport. Her eye was on Maud, a child of twelve, who she had discovered was to be billeted in the little attic. She had heard her mother apologising to Maud's mother, Clara (a second cousin of Edward's, a woman of no account), saying the house was so full that no other room was available, and she had heard Clara fall over herself to say that Maud would be perfectly happy in the sweet little attic. But Maud had cried. Charlotte heard her, and heard Clara being very cross with her. Maud hiccuped, and dried her eyes, but she was still in a sulk and Charlotte had her targeted. She waited until Maud came in for a glass of lemonade and then she pounced. She led the startled Maud into the library and shut the door. 'Now, Maud, dear,' she said, 'I have a proposition to put to you.' 'A what?' said Maud, anxiety creasing her broad forehead (a fringe would've been merciful, Charlotte had often thought). 'A proposition, a plan.' 'I do not care for plans,' Maud said. Quite idiotic, but Charlotte kept her temper. 'You have not heard it yet,' she said. 'Listen.'

Maud listened (she had little alternative, since Charlotte was standing with her back against the door). When the plan had been explained to her, in all its glorious simplicity, she only said, 'Why? Why should you give me your room?' 'Because *I* want to sleep in the attic,' Charlotte said, 'and Mother would never agree.' 'Why?' Maud said again. 'I just want to,' Charlotte repeated. She was not going to waste time trying to make stupid Maud see the attraction of the attic. 'Do not argue,' she said, and said it so forcibly that Maud hung her head and agreed.

★

She took a candle up with her, but there was one already there, beside the bed. Maud had been taken up to the attic after dinner – she had dined with the younger children but had been allowed to stay up another hour – by her mother, and left with instructions to be a good girl and not fuss. It was eight o'clock, and still light. All the adults were now dining and would be safely in the dining room for at least two more hours. Charlotte waited another half-hour, and then went up to the attic, wearing her nightdress and carrying her book. Maud was out of the room instantly – Charlotte hardly had time to remind her to be quiet, and to burrow down under the bedclothes when she got to Charlotte's bed and on no account say a word should anyone look in to say goodnight. She was to feign sleep if she was awake and not be tempted to risk replying.

The swap was achieved smoothly. Charlotte smiled with contentment. There was no lock on the door, but she wedged her slippers underneath, making it more difficult to open, though she doubted that anyone, least of all Clara, would check up on Maud.

So here she was, alone in this bare room, able to think without the distraction of furniture or belongings. It was like being in a nunnery. She had thought, once, of becoming a nun, but she had been unable to stand the thought of all the praying and the restrictions on conversation and, possibly, reading what she wanted to read. Privacy and independence would have to be gained some other way. Instead she had decided to become an artist. Her father had said he might consider letting her apply to study at the Slade School of Art, a notion her mother would label outlandish, and therefore not a word must be said to her as yet. It was a secret between them, one Charlotte clung on to desperately. There was another secret too. Her father had promised to take her on a tour to Paris and then to Florence and Rome, to see the art treasures. Her mother was not interested in art, and would not want to go with him, and Caroline, who was, had eloped and therefore missed her chance. Charlotte was to be the lucky one, but not yet.

She could see herself so clearly as an artist. She could wear whatever she wished and no one would remark upon it because artists were expected, were they not, to look a little peculiar. She would, of course, have to live in a garret, but she would not mind. It was true that she had never been in a garret – it was, she thought, different from a mere attic, though she could not have said in what way – but that did not matter. Whatever it was like, she would accept it, however cold and dismal, because she would be entirely wrapped up in her art. All day long she would draw and paint, and only her father would be allowed to visit her. How she would go about selling her paintings she was not at all sure but a true artist did not care about money. Being without money would be exciting. She had once unwisely said this aloud, to her mother, but in the hearing of Jessie, and had been more bothered by the look of contempt on their housekeeper's face than her mother's furious order not to be so stupid. She had rephrased the remark: being without money would be challenging. Exactly what would be challenged she had not stopped to think.

She did not put the maid's shift on but stayed in her own nightdress after all. It was a plain garment, modest and worn enough really to have been a maid's. Charlotte hated new clothes and had clung on to this old thing in spite of being given new ones. It felt comfortable, and she did not mind the tear in the hem or the missing ribbon which had once slotted through the holes in the neck. She got into bed, and pulled the bedclothes up to her chin and blew out the candle. It was dark now, and there was no moon. Staring upwards, she could only just make out the rim of the window in the ceiling and within it a blackness different in depth from the darkness in the room. It must be cloudy because not only was there no moon but no stars either. Maud would have been frightened. It pleased Charlotte that she was not in the least frightened but was excited instead. She had got what she wanted, a night alone in a strange, empty room. She wanted now to feel herself change, become another person, turn into the artist she was going to be. Closing her eyes, she concentrated on emptying her mind of trivia, but to her annoyance the trivia would not budge. Her head was full of the ridiculous wedding the next day, it raced away with visions of the whole charade in the church and then it was on to the feast and galloping towards the farewells to the bride and groom. Then afterwards. The trivia here was grotesque. She saw Priscilla in the hotel bedroom and pictured what would happen to her. She had read the books and knew. The library held books her father appeared to have forgotten she would have access to and which her mother would have burned if she knew of their existence. Charlotte knew. She had the anatomical detail correct even though it appalled her and she could not understand how what happened could be endured.

'This will not do,' she said out loud, sitting up in bed. She did not want to think of Priscilla or her wedding. She wanted to think about herself and art, and what she was on this earth for, and the meaning of life and other important, frightening questions. The purity of this small room was meant to help her. She had thought its bareness and simplicity would strip her mind of inconsequential clutter, that the room itself would have some sort of power. But again, Pricilla came into her thoughts. Priscilla was to live near Oxford, in the country, in what had been described as an attractive manor house. Charlotte had asked her what that meant. What exactly was a manor house? What was attractive about it? Priscilla did not know. She had not seen it. Charlotte could not believe it when her sister said, 'What does it matter what it looks like? I am sure it will be very nice.' Not to care what one's house looked like! Not to mind what its rooms were like! Whereas to Charlotte the power of place was everything (further proof, if she had needed it, of her artistic temperament). She felt ill in ugly rooms and could be rendered speechless by a room's furniture. All her dreams of the future were set in empty rooms, attic rooms full of light with magnificent views, rooms with only a bed, a desk, a chair in them. She had never yet in all her existence seen such a room.

She lay down again. The trouble with her mind was that it jumped about so and would not be disciplined. This was maddening but also fascinating – why and how were the leaps and jumps made? She could not keep track of them or account for them. She looked at other people and thought how extraordinary it was that something as thin as the skin of a face could hide as magnificently mysterious an organ as the brain. 'Let me look into your brain,' she wanted to say to people, and knew it would never be possible. She visualised her own brain as a series of tiny, tiny boxes and drawers constantly being opened and shut. But how did what was in one compartment get into another? That was the puzzle. Such an aggravating puzzle that she was exhausted grappling with it and fell asleep, a frown on her face, long before she wanted to.

★

Sir Edward was the last to go to bed. He sat in the library until three in the morning, worrying. The amount he had drunk ought to have taken the edge off his worries but it did not. Through a haze of his own making problems loomed none the less large. And he felt sad. A man, on the eve of his daughter's wedding, was perhaps entitled to be sad, in a sentimental sort of way, but his was not that sort of sadness. 'I am sad, Papa,' Charlotte sometimes used to say, 'and I do not know why, there is no reason.' Well, he had reasons. Hettie, for one. She would never bar him from her bedroom (that would be against her understanding of a wife's duty), but he no longer wished to go there. That was sad. It was also not true. He did wish to go there, but afterwards regretted his visits and what happened during them. At the time, there was a certain sort of pleasure but it was not the sort he wanted. He wanted Hettie to love him as he loved her. Another lie. He did not love her, and she did not love him. They were ill-suited. Faithful to each other − and God knew, it would have been easy enough for him to be unfaithful without Hettie ever knowing − but sharing no interests except the children.

Ah, the children. Slumped in his chair, Sir Edward reviewed them in his mind and the weight of worry increased. The children were Hettie's business. She'd made them her business from the beginning, expecting little from him in the way of participation in their upbringing. He was there to pay for them and that was about all. There was Priscilla, only eighteen and about to be married to the most boring young man in England. He hardly knew her. She was pretty, he liked to be seen with her on his arm, and he liked painting her. Caroline he'd known better: a wild card, Caroline, a redhead, high-spirited, pretty too, but it had turned out he had not had the foggiest idea what made her tick − the shock when she ran off! And now where was she, with his grandson? They did not know. He had nightmares in which Caroline was wandering the streets, begging for food, dressed in rags, her baby howling, clasped to her breast . . .

The boys were young. They were at school, out of harm's way, doing well, according to their reports. He did not worry so much about them. Which left Charlotte. 'The cuckoo in the nest', he had heard an unkind aunt remark when Charlotte was about seven. Dark, where the others were fair; very tall, when her sisters were average height; short-sighted, when no one else in the family needed spectacles; and clever, so clever. He'd taught her himself after she'd run rings round the governesses who had been perfectly adequate for her sisters. He had wanted to send her to that place in Harley Street, an excellent establishment (or so he had heard) for educating young women, but Hettie would not hear of it. She claimed that

Charlotte would only be encouraged in her oddness there. He had not yet dared to mention the Slade. He was not sure himself if to send Charlotte there would be the right decision. She had some talent, but her vision of herself as an artist was perhaps romantic rather than realistic. But he was proud of his youngest daughter's ability, he didn't want her to be stifled at home learning all those dreary accomplishments her mother set so much store by. Who said men only wanted their daughters to be dutiful and look pretty? He had high hopes for Charlotte and did not care who knew it. He would champion her whatever she wanted to do.

Sighing, he heaved himself out of his chair and made his way to bed. Life would be hard for Charlotte. Hettie was right. To be so very clever and so very plain and so very odd was not a recipe for a happy life if you were a woman. He could see already that people did not take to Charlotte. He feared that in the future few men would look past the unattractive exterior – he was not blind – and see the sensitive, original, deep-thinking girl he knew, one who, to him, was so full of interest. He would rather talk to Charlotte than anyone he knew. She constantly surprised him with her insight into areas of knowledge he had barely thought about, pondering problems he was ashamed not to have considered in his whole life. What would happen to such a girl? He found himself groaning aloud as he climbed the stairs.

★

Priscilla did not know how to repack her valise. Charlotte had always packed her things, wherever she was going and, though she had watched, and tried to pay attention, she had learned nothing. There had never been any need to learn how to do such a mundane job when, if Charlotte was not to hand, ever eager and willing, there were maids available. But at the Hôtel Crillon the maid she had asked for did not come and she had brought no maid of her own – 'Quite unnecessary,' her husband-to-be had said, in the excellent and expensive hotels in which they would be staying. So Priscilla sat on the bed, trying not to catch sight of the appalling stain on the sheets, and wondered what she should do. But her new husband was impatient. The cab to take them to the station was ordered for two o'clock and they must be ready, there was no time to await the elusive maid. Feeling dizzy – she had hardly slept, and had wept surreptitiously a good deal – Priscilla began shoving clothes into the valise any old how. 'Take the old labels off,' Robert instructed her, 'and put this new one on, firmly.' Priscilla stared at him as though he had asked her to do something requiring Herculean strength. Robert ripped the old labels off himself. Quickly, he scribbled their next destination on new labels, and handed them to his wife. He knew he should be tolerant, but he was finding it hard, and he, too, had no servant with him. A gentleman could travel without one these days, and he always had an eye on expense.

He left the bedroom and went to complain in person about the maid's not appearing. Priscilla could not get the lid of her valise closed. In tears, she pushed and pushed, and tried to sit on the lid, but it was no good. Something would have to come out. She pulled out her nightdress (hateful garment it suddenly seemed, and now torn) and thrust it down to the bottom of the rumpled bedclothes. Extracting it made little difference. Her bed jacket would have to be sacrificed too, and her robe, which grieved her – it was very pretty, embroidered with pink rosebuds – but she would get Robert to buy her a new one in Nice. With difficulty, she could now push down the lid. At that moment, a bellboy came to collect the luggage and she thrust the valise at him, glad to be rid of it.

The maid, finally arriving, found the new labels lying on the bed. She was far more interested in the beautiful robe and bed jacket, and wondered how she could smuggle them out of the hotel. Perhaps she would hand in one of them, together with the nightdress she later rescued.

★

A month later, when he had returned from his far from satisfactory honeymoon (if only he'd *known* Priscilla), Robert Charlesworth launched a determined investigation into how his wife's valise could just have disappeared. Since Priscilla had never confessed that she had not attached the clearly written labels he had given her – she was already afraid of his temper – he was at a distinct disadvantage and was soon aware of this. The manager of the Hôtel Crillon was emphatic: the bellboy had collected the Charlesworths' luggage and the porter had taken it to the waiting cab. Had Mr Charlesworth counted the pieces put into the cab before departure? No? It was not his job? It was not the job of the porter either. Perhaps the missing valise had gone in another cab, or to the wrong station? With respect, *profound* respect, Mr Charlesworth should make enquiries elsewhere.

But 'elsewhere' was a hopeless place. He was asked, by all he contacted, to describe the valise in precise terms. Priscilla could not. It was brown, she thought, but more of a yellow; it was square, or maybe more oblong in shape; it had two brass locks, or maybe three, or maybe four. Charlotte came to her aid in the end, giving an absolutely accurate description and remembering, as indeed Lady Falconer did, that it had been purchased at Harrod's. Harrod's were pleased to supply a catalogue, in which there was a photograph of the said valise, and this was sent off to the police in Paris (who, naturally, were not in the least interested). Then someone suggested that the valise might somehow have been sent back to Victoria Station, mixed up with someone else's luggage. Robert promptly charged off to Victoria's Lost Property office, picture of the valise in hand (though why he should go to so much trouble no one could understand, least of all Priscilla).

He was aware, when he took it, that the valise he had claimed as his wife's might very well not be hers. Harrod's had sold a great many of these things and besides the one offered for his inspection looked far more battered than Priscilla's had any right to be. He had been asked if he could identify any belongings inside (it had been forced open) and thought the nightdress on top was his wife's (it was white, wasn't it, with lace at the neck?). He signed a chit, and took the valise not immediately to Priscilla in Oxfordshire but to her family home in London. He asked Lady Falconer and Charlotte to examine it before he restored it to its owner. 'It is the same *sort* of valise but much more used,' Charlotte said, 'anyone can see that, but it is what is inside that will prove it is not Priscilla's.' As soon as it was opened, she flung the nightdress on the top aside – '*That* is not Priscilla's,' she declared, and, after a quick rummage through, 'nothing here is Priscilla's. It is not her valise.'

Robert refused to take it back to Victoria Station. Lady Falconer was rather taken aback at the vehemence of his refusal – 'But it is dishonest, Robert, to keep someone else's property.' 'Someone has kept my wife's,' Robert said, to which Charlotte riposted, 'That is illogical. There may be clues somewhere,' she went on, 'as to whose it is. We should search for them – think how grateful the owner might be.' Lady Falconer thought rifling through another person's belongings most distasteful, but Sir Edward, when brought into the frame, said Charlotte's idea was sensible. It was agreed that he would stand by while his daughter did the detective work and that if no identification proved possible he would see that the valise was returned to Victoria Station's Lost Property department.

Charlotte was thrilled. The mysterious piece of luggage was placed on the morning-room table and, watched by her amused father, she began. Carefully, almost respectfully, she took out item after item and laid them beside the case. The clothes were not in the least like Priscilla's trousseau. They were plain, though of good materials, and the colours were strong – deep blues, vivid greens, and a great deal of bright red. Charlotte was forming an image of their owner as she unpacked. Someone, she speculated, who was artistic, who had a love of colour and knew how to match it. Someone who walked wherever she went (three pairs of almost workmanlike boots and only one pair of light shoes). Knowing the structure of this particular valise as she did, from packing Priscilla's so recently, she saved the compartment in the lid until the last. 'Now, here,' she said to her father, smiling, 'is where we might expect to find a letter or a book with a name in, or some such.'

What she found was a painting. 'Oh!' whispered Charlotte, looking at it. 'Oh! It's lovely!'

★

The valise and its contents, including the painting, went back to the Lost Property at Victoria Station. It broke Charlotte's heart, but there was no honest alternative. Her father consoled her with the news that if, after three months, nobody claimed the valise, and could prove it was theirs, then she could buy it from the appropriate authority. Not much would be asked for it, he thought, since there was nothing special about its contents. 'The painting is special,' Charlotte said. 'I doubt if anyone will have the wit to see that,' Sir Edward said, 'and it is not signed, which would reduce any value it might have.' 'Someone,' said Charlotte, 'will be missing it dreadfully, someone will be frantic.' 'We will see,' her father said. 'They may search in the wrong place, or something may have happened to the owner. One never knows. The people at Victoria Lost Property are incompetent, the place is chaotic. Have patience.'

Patience was a virtue, however, which his daughter did not possess. The three months was an eternity, one during which she yearned and prayed for the painting to return to her, investing it with mythical powers impossible to explain. Her hunger for it was passionate, and even her father thought it a little ridiculous, considering she had hardly seen the painting before it was returned. He did not say, as her mother did, 'For heaven's sake, it is only a picture.' He could see that it was a very skilful picture, painted, he guessed, in tiny brushstrokes, the range of colours narrow, and the lack of any figure giving it a sense of mystery. But he expressed some exasperation with Charlotte's endless nagging about bothering the Lost Property people to see what was happening. He also hurt her by suggesting that she was being a little affected, and that he deplored affectation of any kind. And when she burst into tears and maintained she felt about the painting in the valise the way he felt about his Pieter de Hoogh he was angry with her. He said that all his teaching had been in vain if she could not see the difference between a masterpiece and what was almost certainly the work of a talented amateur.

'Papa,' Charlotte said, 'I am in love with it. It was love at first sight, and love may have made me blind.'

'For heaven's sake, child!' her father said, and refused to have the painting mentioned again.

II

CHARLOTTE AND her father dined together every evening, sitting not at the large table in the dining room but at the round table in the breakfast room, something Lady Falconer would never have countenanced, but she had gone to be with Priscilla. Nor would she have approved of the menus. Charlotte was allowed to order the meals and took full advantage of being able to choose her favourite dishes and eliminate those she detested. They had chocolate steam pudding every single night, served with thin, ice-cold cream (Charlotte was very particular about the runniness and the temperature of the cream, aping without realising it, her mother's exacting standards). They had no red meat – about which Sir Edward did voice a complaint, so he was permitted roast beef one night during the second week, though Charlotte did not touch it – and absolutely no offal. Chicken and fish dishes were included, and there were plenty of vegetables (but no cabbage or cauliflower). The cook did not care. Money was saved in a way she knew would be noticed and approved of by Lady Falconer when she returned.

There was not a great deal of conversation between father and daughter at the table, but there was a pleasant atmosphere of which they were both aware. Frequently, they exchanged smiles and little nods and raising of the eyebrows – they were so agreeably comfortable. But Sir Edward was worried. He hid his anxiety well, but it was there, and he recognised it as causing his headaches. 'You are frowning dreadfully, Papa,' Charlotte said. 'Is the chicken too spicy?'

'The chicken is delicious, just how I like it.'

'Good. So?'

Sir Edward sighed. 'Money,' he said, 'nothing for you to worry about.'

'Money?' echoed Charlotte. 'Lack of it, you mean?'

'No, thank God. What to do with it, how to be wise with it.'

'What is wrong with putting it in the bank?'

'Quite a lot, at the moment.'

'Spend it then. I'm sure Mama could spend it easily.'

'I am sure she could. She does very well as it is.'

Charlotte heard the sarcasm. 'I should hate to have my head full of worry about how to spend money.'

'My head is not full of how to spend money,' Sir Edward said, quite sharply. 'It was you who advised spending it. It is my job to conserve it, not spend it.'

'For what? Why must it be conserved?'

'Charlotte, you are an intelligent girl. Do not ask silly questions. For a moment you sounded like . . .' He stopped.

'. . . Like Priscilla,' Charlotte finished. 'I know. I am sorry. I know we need money to live on, especially in these' (she paused) 'uncertain' (she paused again, hoping to make her father smile) 'times.'

Why times were uncertain she had no idea, but she had heard the phrase repeated by adults frequently. But there seemed nothing uncertain in her own dull life. Everything went on in exactly the same way, nothing as exciting as uncertainty ruffled its surface. Priscilla's wedding had been the last time there had been any upheaval and that was months ago. 'Explain,' she said to her father. 'Tell me about *why* times are uncertain.'

'It is too complicated.'

'You mean I am too stupid to understand?'

'No. I am too stupid to be able to explain properly what I fail entirely to understand myself.'

'But, Papa, you are so clever, everyone knows that.'

'Am I? Well, everyone, in this instance, is mistaken.'

Sir Edward leaned back in his chair, declining pudding. He was not allowed to smoke at table when his wife was present, and he quite agreed that to do so was bad manners, but he took a cigarette out and lit it, taking care to blow the smoke away from Charlotte devouring the chocolate pudding. The window was open (another thing his wife would have disagreed with) and the room was airy. The view was of Hampstead Heath, stretching away down the hill, and through the trees he could just see the sun glinting on the ponds. He might go for a walk later, when Charlotte was in bed. Walking helped him to think about what to do not just about investments but about Charlotte. He had promised her that they would go to Paris and then Florence and Rome to study the art, and he intended to keep his promise, but now his wife wished to accompany them, though not of course with any intention of looking at paintings and statues. He had not yet told Charlotte this. She was still under the impression that it was to be only the two of them, and had looked forward to this adventure for so long. If he was clever, he would see a way to solve the problem but so far he had not done so.

He stubbed out his cigarette as Charlotte finished his share of the pudding as well as her own. She was getting fat. He could see the fat settling upon her frame. Her mother endlessly pointed it out, appalled that her daughter's waist was confirmed by her dressmaker as twenty-eight inches, and her hips as forty, though she was not yet sixteen. And she refused – Sir Edward did not think he ought to know this but he had been made to hear it – to be corseted. Even if he had not been told, he would have been aware of this. Charlotte bounced as she walked. Her mother felt she should not be allowed out of the house in such an unrestrained state but as she rarely went anywhere, and insisted on wearing a long black cape whatever the weather, it did not really matter. In her darkest moments, his wife had said to Sir Edward that they would be stuck with her for ever.

It had pained him to hear the sheer dislike in Hettie's voice, but he had told himself it was due to distress at their daughter's prospects. He himself had begun to share this distress. Once amused by Charlotte, and always proud of her originality, he was more and more aware how difficult her life was going to be. She was now a young woman, not a child, and must surely have a young woman's instincts even if these did not include a love of parties and fashion and shopping. And young men. The words 'flirting' and 'Charlotte' simply were unthinkable. Caroline and Priscilla had flirted furiously, but Charlotte, if she was in the presence of any man, looked them straight in the eye without a glimmer of interest in anything except what they had to say. Men were already alarmed by her, he could see that. She did not attract them, she was neither girlish nor womanly in the accepted way, and they turned away. Sir Edward felt it his duty to equip Charlotte to face a life alone.

Well, she would have money. That would help. He had already set up a trust for her, which she would come into at twenty-one. She would have independent means and never need to humble herself either by working – though God knew what work she could do in any case – or by submitting to a marriage of convenience. On the other hand, her wealth would undoubtedly attract suitors who would not otherwise have glanced at her. How to guard against that? Look at Caroline, and what had happened to her. But Charlotte was not Caroline. She would never be taken in by some bounder after her money. Flattery would never fool her – she would see through it at once. Yet he went on worrying about her, hardly comforted by these observations. It often occurred to him that Charlotte was not of her own time. Sometimes, when he read of Mrs Pankhurst's doings, he was made nervous – her influence on his youngest daughter would be pernicious, should she ever come near her. But, thankfully, Charlotte seemed to know little of what Mrs Pankhurst and her friends were attempting to do. Charlotte was in her own little world and showed no signs of breaking out of it.

He had said she could draw him before she went to bed. They sat together in his study, Sir Edward settled in his armchair, looking out of the window, and Charlotte on a stool opposite, sketch pad on her knee and a fine array of pencils in a box at her feet. Although he could draw well himself, he had discovered that drawing was something he could not teach her. Painting was different. He felt competent to teach her about colour, and how to achieve certain effects, and she was now quite skilled in the use of oils as well as water-colours. But as to drawing, she had

had to try to learn through practice and he could see she was not entirely successful though she tried hard. It moved him to witness how she struggled, how it upset her not to be able to draw well. She needed a teacher and he ought to find one for her. Or else face his wife's wrath and send her to the Slade, if they would have her.

'Charlotte,' he said, 'enough, time for you to retire.'

★

The painting hung on the wall beside her bed, where it had been for the last six months, as close to her pillow as it could be. Every night it was the last thing she saw, every morning the first. Her ideas about it changed all the time. Sometimes, it made her tearful, she would feel the tears seeping out of the corners of her eyes – the empty chair, the poor little table with its pitiful posy of flowers, the bare window draped with that misty net. The painting spoke of loneliness and despair, and emotion choked her throat. But at other times it made her feel cheerful – everything so neat, so simple, so clean, so calm. The parasol and the coat told of their owner – a woman, of course – and her walk in the woods, where she had delighted in picking the primroses. And what was she doing now? Preparing her supper, humming to herself, rejoicing in the serenity of her room.

Charlotte and her father had examined the painting minutely for any signature or indications of ownership, but there were none. The two of them had gone together to claim it and had been shocked at how casual the people at the Lost Property office were. They thought nothing of the painting but a great deal of respect was shown to the clothes and the valise itself. Sir Edward did not want the valise or any of its contents save for the painting, which was thought odd, as though it might be a trick to divert attention. He told them that he was sure some lady would in due course claim the valise and left his card so that, if anyone did so, the painting could be restored to the owner. Charlotte noted that his card was not put safely away but left lying on the counter from which she was sure it would soon be swept away to join the detritus on the floor. The prospect made her glad.

112

Sir Edward had thought the painting should be properly framed and had chosen a frame himself. Charlotte, from the beginning, was not sure that his choice was right – she preferred it unframed. Gilt did not look appropriate, but she thought it ungrateful to say so. A gilt frame contradicted everything the painting was about and she could not understand why her father, of all people, did not see this. But at least it was a narrow frame, which did not dominate the canvas, and in certain lights it did not look like gilt. Lying on her side, Charlotte began to live in the painting, narrowing her eyes and hypnotising herself. She felt herself to be twenty, or twenty-five, an artist at last. She must, she thought, be a successful artist because this room of hers was no garret. It was pretty, if simple, no sense of deprivation about it. She wondered what was hidden from view – this was only a corner of the room after all. A bed, of course. Somewhere to keep clothes, perhaps. And was she living in a house? She must be, and high up, from the vague outline of rooftops through the lace curtain. Did she have other artists around her? Charlotte thought not. No, she was quite alone, and content.

She did not understand why, but the painting looked best in the morning light. Waking, she would turn on her side and through half-closed eyes, still bleary with sleep, the painting would seem to shine before her. It had a radiance so gentle and soft that it made her smile. She would snuggle down under the bedclothes, keeping her eyes fixed on the scene before her, and there would come over her a feeling of expectation. Someone would come into her life and change it – perhaps that was what the painting promised. She had told her father how the painting made her feel and he had been a little irritated. He had told her to study the painting properly, as any art student should (Charlotte was flattered to hear that he deemed her worthy of such a title as 'art student'). Had she noted the use of Naples yellow in the colour of the chair, the handle of the parasol, the flowers and the trian- gular slice of wall? And what about the brushstrokes? Had she seen that they were tiny, that very small brushes had been used? These were the things, her father said, which she should be observing instead of being carried away by romantic flights of fancy. It was foolish, he said, to talk about 'loving' a painting if one had not taken the trouble to understand how it had been executed. It was, he finished, insulting to the artist.

But Charlotte knew that none of her thoughts insulted the artist. She was quite sure that she had interpreted the artist's intention.

★

Lady Falconer, arriving home, was not pleased. She could tell, the moment she walked through her front door, that things were not as they should be. The servants had become slack. They had not known, of course, that she would return on Friday instead of Monday, but that was no excuse. There were boots lying any old how in the hall, muddy footprints on the tiles, a coat tossed on a chair, still dripping rain onto the cushion. Instead of the smell of polish there was a most unpleasant aroma of onions. Exasperated, she stalked through the hall and stood at the top of the stairs leading to the kitchen. 'Jessie!' she called. There was no reply. Furious, Lady Falconer was obliged to descend to the kitchen, which she found perfectly clean and tidy but quite empty. There appeared to be no servants in the house at all, and if she wanted tea, and she wanted it very badly, she would have to fend for herself. But she was not quite ready to do so.

Back upstairs, she called again, this time for Charlotte. Again, no reply, but in Charlotte's case this was not necessarily significant, it did not mean either that she was not at home or that she had not heard. She would have to be searched for, every room looked into, and the thought of this made Lady Falconer weak with temper. She took off her travelling clothes and her corset and changed into a loose gown. She was very, very tired and wanted nothing more than some refreshing tea and then a bath drawn for her. Her energies seemed to be deserting her and she suddenly felt like one of those women she despised, forever complaining that their households were falling about their ears. Lying on her bed, though promising herself this was only for a few moments, she tried to relax, but her mind was full of annoying

114

images. Priscilla, for one. A Priscilla apparently hysterical at the not surprising news that she was to have a baby. What on earth had the girl imagined would be likely to happen? The fuss she was making was perfectly ridiculous.

There was a sound downstairs. She raised herself up, and listened intently. Someone had come in through the front door – therefore not one of the servants she so badly needed. It was either Edward or Charlotte. The steady footsteps on the stairs told her that it was her husband. She heard him pause on the landing. 'Henrietta?' he called, sounding both surprised and alarmed, which was hardly flattering. She kept silent, playing Charlotte's game. He rapped on her bedroom door and then opened it slightly. She did not open her eyes. The door was gently closed. She heard him descend the stairs again and go out of the front door. She knew she ought to be grateful that her rest had been respected, but she was not. Once upon a time, he would have tiptoed over to her bed and kissed her. Once upon a time, she would have laughed and kissed him back. Once upon a very long time ago.

Sadness swilled around the room and she struggled to dispel it. She was forty, Edward was forty-five, they had been married over twenty years, what could one expect. Again and again recently she had had the impression that he did not like her or feel anything for her and that he resented his own compulsion to come to her bed. Why he did, she could not fathom. They never discussed it. Only very rarely did she turn him away and when she did so he left at once. It made her head ache, thinking of this state of affairs, and ache even more when in some queer way it led her to remember Priscilla's distressed outburst that she hated what Robert 'did'. Her mother had stopped her at once. She wanted no such confidences, nor was she willing to provide any herself. Marriage was marriage. Each woman had to make of it what she could.

★

Mother was back, and Charlotte could not stay in her bedroom much longer. She hated the room and had no wish to linger, except that it held her painting. She had discussed with her father hanging it in the library, which only the two of them frequented, but they

115

had both decided it would not look right. There was no suitable wall upon which to hang it there, except the one where Sir Edward's most precious possession already hung. The two other walls were lined with bookshelves and the third had two large windows with only a narrow gap between. They had tried the little painting there and it looked utterly lost. In Charlotte's bedroom it looked not so much lost as drowned, smothered, but at least it was near her when she slept. The hideous wallpaper that she was obliged to endure could not have been a more unfortunate background for the painting – the huge red flowers, the brilliant green of leaves and stems connecting them, and the dark, dark blue of the spaces in between shrieked and howled at the tiny oil.

But then so did everything in the bedroom. The carpet was another horror, and the pink satin eiderdown and cover on the bed were hard to bear. No one had ever consulted Charlotte over how her bedroom should be decorated and furnished and now that she was nearly sixteen she resented this. Her mother said the wallpaper had cost a fortune, and would last many more years, and the carpet was valuable, with the dark blue in it matching the blue in the wallpaper *exactly*.

Charlotte felt rather proud of being susceptible to surroundings. It was a mark, she was sure, of great sensitivity. Coming into her bedroom, she could feel her skin prickle and her limbs tighten as everything crowded in upon her, the huge mahogany wardrobe, the chest of drawers, the bed itself. Conversely, when she walked into the morning room, so light and underfurnished, she felt her body relax and her spirits rise. The library was different again. There, she seemed not to be oppressed by the heavy bookshelves and the big oak table and chairs, even though the room was not especially light and the carpet was a dull brown. The atmosphere was somehow liberating, the privacy of the room generating not claustrophobia but security.

Her mother was calling for her. It was vulgar to shout, but she was shouting. Reluctantly, Charlotte answered the shout, made from the bottom of the stairs, with one of her own, from the landing outside her bedroom, and was instantly reprimanded. She descended the stairs slowly, thinking, as she saw her mother below, that she would like to slide down the banisters and land with a triumphant bump at her feet. Her mother, it was obvious, was angry about something and would be difficult to appease.

'Where is Jessie?' her mother asked.

Charlotte shrugged, knowing her mother would view this as an inflammatory gesture. 'Out,' she said.

'I am aware of that,' her mother said, 'and I am also aware that the entire staff seem to be out.'

'Yes,' said Charlotte. 'It was a half-day holiday.'

'For what? What is this holiday in celebration of?'

Charlotte risked raising her eyebrows and shaking her head.

'I go away, and all order disappears,' her mother said. 'Well, I should have known it. Your father lives in a dream and you are simply irresponsible.'

There was no point in defending herself. What had she done that was 'irresponsible'? Nothing, but then 'irresponsible' in her mother's opinion could cover a host of trivial misdemeanours. Already her mother was leading the way into the drawing room where a flustered Mabel was laying out tea-things. Charlotte followed, as she knew she was obliged to. Her mother waited until Mabel had gone, instructing her to close the door on her way out, and then she said, 'Tea, Charlotte?' her tone unexpectedly conciliatory. Tea was poured, a biscuit offered (and accepted). For a moment or two there was silence, during which Charlotte reflected how different it was being alone with her mother and not her father. She felt wary, ready for attack, and indeed she found her eyes narrowing over her teacup, as though she were preparing herself. Her mother did not like her, it was as simple as that. She had been a disappointment from the moment of her birth – a third girl! – and always would be.

'Priscilla is unwell,' Lady Falconer said.

'Oh?' said Charlotte, wondering what she was meant to assume by 'unwell'. Priscilla was often 'unwell'. It might mean anything, from having the curse, or toothache, to pneumonia.

'She is to have a child.'

'Oh!' cried Charlotte, in quite a different tone, so excited that she spilled tea on her dress, which in turn brought another exclamation from her mother, one of extreme irritation.

'Charlotte, *will* you be careful!'

'But it was a shock,' Charlotte said, 'a pleasant one, but such a shock.'

'I think you mean a surprise.'

'No, I do not, Mama, I mean *shock*. I was startled.'

'So was Priscilla,' Lady Falconer said, drily.

'When will the baby be born?'

'The spring. But do not mention this to anyone, it is far too soon.'

'I will be an aunt.'

'You will indeed, and a good one, I hope.'

'What is a good aunt?'

'Someone reliable and helpful, someone a child can depend on and look up to . . .'

'And have fun with.'

'Having fun is not high on a list of qualities needed to be a good aunt.'

'Then it should be. I wish I had an aunt I could have fun with.'

'At last,' said Lady Falconer, as her husband entered the room at that moment.

Sir Edward sighed. Told the news, he covered his eyes with his hands, and sighed again.

'Papa' said Charlotte, 'why are you not thrilled? You will be a grandfather, think of it.'

'I am thinking of it,' Sir Edward said, gloomily.

'I shall go to Priscilla for her lying-in,' his wife said. 'She has no idea how to manage a household. Even after a year, she appears to have learned nothing. She will need me. Arrangements will have to be made here.'

'Arrangements?' queried Sir Edward.

'For you, for Charlotte. I leave you for a mere week and come back to chaos. I cannot leave you for what is likely to be two months or so.'

There followed a squabble about the alleged 'chaos' in the house. Neither raised their voice but it was an unseemly display, one which they would not normally have given in front of their daughter (though she enjoyed it hugely, while taking care to keep her eyes on her feet and her expression blank). There was an antagonism between her parents with which she was all too familiar but which she did not understand.

'I shall make my own arrangements,' Sir Edward was saying, 'for myself and Charlotte. This house will be shut up. Two months, did you say? We will make it three.'

'Whatever do you mean?' his wife asked, frowning. 'There is no need to shut the house up, that is absurd, we will lose all the servants . . .'

'We will pay the servants to take a holiday.'

'Edward, do not be so ridiculous.' And then, remembering herself, appalled to have spoken to her husband in such a way in front of her daughter, Lady Falconer said, 'Charlotte, leave the room at once.'

'Charlotte,' Sir Edward barked, 'stay! What I have to say concerns you. We will go, you and I, on a tour while your mother is with Priscilla. It is an ideal opportunity. We will go to Paris and Florence and Rome, to continue your art education. It is settled.'

Charlotte shrieked with joy and, leaping up to fling her arms round her father's neck, sent the whole tea-tray crashing from the little table onto the carpet where the milk left in the jug formed a tiny puddle, and the tea seeped slowly into it. Nothing was broken but the mess looked worse than it turned out to be, and Charlotte made it worse still by scrabbling on the floor and crushing sugar into the carpet as she tried to mop up the tea. Lady Falconer was white, not red, with anger, and left the room before she lost control and said something to her husband which she would regret. Mabel, sent in to clear up the spillage, found Sir Edward and his daughter (Charlotte very dishevelled and pink, Sir Edward dazed) staring at each other, in some sort of trance. Quietly, she cleared things away and asked if fresh tea was required. They both shook their heads. 'Oh, Papa!' she heard

Miss Charlotte say, softly, and then again, so happily, 'Oh, Papa!' And Sir Edward smiled.

★

Charlotte announced the good news to the painting. She sat on the edge of her bed, hands clasped as though in prayer, and whispered. She did not feel in the least foolish – it felt natural to say out loud what she wanted the painting to hear. It was as she imagined it must be going to confession and seeing no one but knowing that behind the grille someone was there. Behind the painting someone still must be there, and though they might now be hundreds, even thousands, of miles away, painting other pictures, their presence hung in the empty room. Never once did Charlotte consider that the artist might be dead.

Lying in bed, much too excited to sleep, she blessed Priscilla. Without the wonderful opportunity given to him, she doubted whether her father would ever have fulfilled his promise to her. Every time she had reminded him, he looked uncomfortable, and she had begun to think the tour would never happen. And now they were to go to Paris and Florence and Rome and she felt giddy with the thrill of it. She would need a valise herself. Suddenly, she thought of using the valise, the wrong valise, in which the painting had been stowed. She could stow it away again, take it with her, have it by her side every night in strange places. She might even, without knowing it, take the painting to the place whence it had come – there had been labels of so many European cities all over the luggage. But then she thought of the risk. At home here it was safe, until her return, quietly waiting for her, unremarked by anyone, something to look forward to. It was not sensible to travel with it. There would be trains and boats and hotels and cabs and at every stage the dreadful possibility of the valise being lost in exactly the way it had been lost before. It was tempting fate to transport her picture.

'I will not tempt fate,' Charlotte promised, reaching out and touching the painting.

★

The enormity of what he had done at first overwhelmed Sir Edward. Much though he loved Charlotte and enjoyed her

120

company, he was daunted by the thought of being alone with her for three months and responsible for her in circumstances so different from home. The child had never travelled abroad. Indeed, she had hardly travelled in her own country. He would have to establish firm ground-rules from the beginning or she would exhaust him. Never once, with him, had she made the scenes his wife complained about, never once had she given him a moment's trouble, but then he had never been alone with her for more than a couple of hours at the most. She was not, he reminded himself, a child at all. She was a young woman, even if not dangerously pretty, and would need to be chaperoned at all times.

But then Sir Edward consoled himself with the realisation that Charlotte, too, liked to be by herself, and to read in peace. They would be staying in pleasant hotels where their rooms would be comfortable and Charlotte would not resent being sent to her room any more than he would regret going to his own. And she might make friends, of other young women with their mothers or aunts and who might welcome her company. It was unlikely, but always possible. Charlotte would become a different girl abroad. She would mature, become more sociable, acquire graces she did not have.

Paris first. Not the Hôtel Crillon. Such hotels were his wife's preference, not his. He knew of another, smaller, much less fashionable place in Montparnasse, the Hôtel de Nice. They would stay there a week and go every day to the Louvre. Perhaps not every day, but most days. Charlotte would want to see the obvious sights, he supposed, Notre Dame and so on, but this could be kept to a minimum – they were there for the art, after all, this was to be a serious pilgrimage, one she would remember all her life and gain much from.

The thought pleased him.

III

CLOSING UP the Hampstead house was quite a business. It was not, as Lady Falconer complained to her departing husband, as if one could merely walk out of the front door and pull it behind one. Three months was a long time. Time for dust to gather so thickly that precious furniture might be harmed. ('How?' Sir Edward had enquired. 'How does dust harm?') Every item needed to be covered with protective dust sheets ('Easy enough, I should have thought') and breakable valuables put away entirely ('Why? With no one in the place to break them?'). The beds needed stripping, the larder must be emptied of food, most of the servants dispersed. Jessie had agreed to accept half-pay and not take another situation. She would go home to Norfolk for the three months and return to get the house ready when called upon. But the maids, who had only been offered a quarter of their wage as a retainer, promptly found other places. It was against Lady Falconer's principles ('What principles?') to try to bribe them to return, and so she would be faced with having to hire new people at the end of June. The aggravation was immense.

But finally the deed was done and she was free to go to Priscilla, now very near her time and in a panic of terror about her confinement. It was not an attractive prospect. Priscilla lived in a muddle, and not a gloriously happy one. Lady Falconer felt that she had made a mistake: what she should have done was have her daughter come home, to her. Then the house need never have been so inconveniently shut up, and her own life could have carried on regardless. She berated herself all the way to Oxford for her own short-sightedness, but it was too late now. She was doomed to spend three months trying to organise Priscilla's household while her own husband gallivanted across Europe with Charlotte. She did at least have enough self-awareness to realise that she was, in effect, jealous. It was not that she had truly wanted to accompany them – she most certainly would not have wanted to travel with the excitable Charlotte – but that she could hardly bear the intense pleasure both husband and daughter seemed to be experiencing, even before they set off. The house had rung with Charlotte's laughter, and singing (tuneless), while she lumbered around getting ready to go, and each mealtime was an occasion for the endless discussion of itineraries and timetables. Sir Edward had grown more genial by the minute which, considering his usual morose state, was hard to bear. Only with Charlotte, it seemed, could he be good company – she herself was excluded.

They were such an odd-looking pair as they set off. Charlotte did not look as though she belonged to her father at all – he was so distinguished-looking, so tall and handsome, his clothes beautifully tailored and fitting to perfection, and Charlotte was, well, Charlotte. Lady Falconer had done her best. She had had new clothes bought for the child, and her friend Pamela (who chose them) had managed to turn Charlotte from being a frump into being just a tidy nonentity. Lady Falconer did not think she could have done much better herself and gave herself credit for knowing that if she had gone shopping with her daughter they would have had unpleasant scenes and returned with nothing. So there Charlotte was, large and lumpy, clothed in navy blue with white touches at the neck and wrists, looking like a governess next to her elegant papa. If she sensed the contrast – and Lady Falconer was well aware of Charlotte's sensitivity and intelligence – it did not depress her. Her face shone with happiness, her smile wider than any that had been seen on her face for years.

They had one rather affecting conversation together before Charlotte's departure. It was about the little painting. Charlotte asked what would happen to her bedroom while she was gone.

'Happen?' her mother had echoed. 'Why, nothing will happen to it. The house, as you very well know, is to be locked up.'

Charlotte's brow furrowed with anxiety. 'Do you think my painting could be placed in Papa's safe?'

'Whatever for?'

'In case the house is broken into and . . .'

'Charlotte! Please, it is enough trouble closing the house without imagining such disasters.'

'But *could* it go in the safe?'

Lady Falconer, out of sheer exasperation, said no, the safe was small and would be full of real valuables. 'No one,' she said, 'would think of stealing that daub,' so she assured her daughter. The child's passion for it was inexplicable to her, but she had to respect the fact that it was obviously genuine. She herself sat on Charlotte's bed and looked at it in complete bewilderment. She saw nothing moving or compelling there. The colours seemed drab and faded, the composition ordinary, and yet Charlotte acted as though it had some mystical force.

Years ago, very many years ago, Edward had tried to interest her in art and she had tried to respond. He had taken her to the National Gallery and stood in awe before several of his favourite masterpieces. She stood at his side, but not in awe. Sometimes, a face would strike her as beautiful, sometimes colours would appeal to her, but she felt nothing move within herself, and she soon grew bored. Edward talked to her about the paintings he revered, and about the artists who painted them (mostly the Dutch masters), and she absorbed the information, but it made no difference. And once she had confessed her indifference there seemed no point pretending. The art in their house had been chosen by Edward and she hardly noticed it. His prize was a 'masterpiece', a painting of a Dutch interior by Pieter de Hoogh. It was a pleasant enough picture, but when she saw Edward standing rapt in front of it, as he so often did, her puzzlement soon turned to a kind of frustration – why could not *she* be spellbound? – and then to resentment. She felt excluded, condemned for her lack of taste even, and in addition she had the irrational impression that she was being hoaxed. Edward was only doing it to annoy. When she found Charlotte, aged a mere six years old, standing staring at his beloved Pieter de Hoogh with him and showing evidence of also being smitten, she had felt somehow humiliated.

There was some lack in her which prevented her appreciating, and responding to, art. It was not lack of education – Edward had provided that – nor of any aesthetic qualities, she was sure. She could enjoy and be moved by music, and she knew that in her dress she showed great taste and style.

It did not matter. She told herself this frequently. Some people were tone-deaf and could not enjoy music – a far worse affliction. Let Edward and Charlotte trail round art galleries, going into ecstasies, doubtless, over pictures in which she would have been able to see nothing whatsoever beyond paint on canvas (and often not too carefully applied). People were what mattered, not paintings. But once, when she had said this to Edward in a moment of defiance, he had replied that paintings lasted, they spoke for ever. People did not. They were soon silenced.

That had made her cry, though he never knew.

★

Charlotte had never expected, among all the many things she did expect, to be tired. Tired? How could she be, when every day was exciting and so unlike her life at home? She felt, from the moment she awoke, as though an engine throbbed inside her head running at a merciless rate. Up she jumped and rushed to the window to gaze out on the roofs of Paris and convince herself that being in the city was not a dream she had made come true through the fearsome power of her imagination. But she could not have imagined this because it was all so different. Nothing she had read of Paris had adequately prepared her for the reality, for the sounds and aromas, as well as the sights. She stood for ages, the window (such an odd window) open, trying to analyse what seemed to be in the air – she could smell lemon somewhere, and coffee and smoke, and something baking, and heat, and it made her head whirl. Joining her father and going out to eat *petit déjeuner* was strangest of all – she loved the cafés they frequented, laughing at the thought of the dreary dining room at home.

But by the third day, she was exhausted, and simply could not keep up the momentum. Her feet hurt and her legs ached and

125

her head was sore. Miles she had walked, miles and miles along the galleries and around the city, having this, that and the other pointed out to her by a father who did not seem to tire at all but was more energetic than she had ever known him. She tried so hard to keep up with him not just by matching his pace but by responding to his enthusiasm. He took her to see Rodin's statue *The Thinker* and talked for a full half-hour to her of its brilliance, and for once she felt like her mother, unable to see more than a man in bronze slumped in thought. It was because she was tired, she was sure, that the power and magic her father found in it eluded her.

'Papa,' she ventured later, as they ate, 'do you think it matters how one is feeling when one views a work of art?'

'Well, of course.'

'But should it? Should responding to what the artist is saying be dependent on one's mood?'

Sir Edward paused in the eating of his perfectly delicious *boeuf en daube* and smiled. 'This is about the Rodin,' he said.

'I was tired,' Charlotte said. 'It seemed to me . . .'

'A lump of bronze, nothing more.'

'I could see it was very well done, but . . .'

'One cannot be ecstatic about *every* work of art, my dear.'

'But you said *The Thinker* is magnificent, you said . . .'

'Charlotte, I see what I see, you see what you see, the artist saw what he saw, and we can all see differently.'

'But what if someone, Mama even, sees nothing except bronze? How can that be? If it is magnificent?'

Sir Edward was half-amused, half-exasperated by the doggedness of his daughter's questions but he neither laughed nor sighed. He could see the child was exhausted and near to tears, turning her failure to be entranced by *The Thinker* into a sign that she lacked artistic appreciation. He had been too authoritative, making her doubt her own taste and feel at fault. And they had seen too much too quickly. Because Charlotte looked strong and was full of impatience to be shown all Paris had to offer he had forgotten her age and inexperience and demanded too much of her. At this rate, she would collapse before they reached Rome and grow to hate the mere prospect of a gallery.

'Tomorrow,' he said, 'we will look at nothing. We will take a boat and go on a trip down the Seine, and look at the scenery and think about what we have seen. It will be a rest day, and we will take our own sketch pads and idle away the time sitting on the boat with our feet up. Now, eat your dinner, and then we will retire very early and tomorrow rise disgracefully late and you will feel much better.'

★

The boat they took went from Montparnasse to Meudon. It was quite a large *bâteau*, with a covered deck on top where passengers sat on the shiny and uncomfortable slatted wooden benches. It moved slowly down the river and was soon passing through meadows grazed by black and white cows, which Charlotte tried to draw. Her father concentrated on the people in the boat, doing quick little caricatures of anyone who took his fancy. They were both watched intently by a small, slim woman, wearing a black hat with a bright green ribbon in it, who carried a portfolio of her own. Sir Edward shielded his sketch pad with his arm, but Charlotte, though knowing she was making a poor job of the cows, was unconcerned. Soon, she gave up entirely trying to draw. The sun was hot and she was not quite enough in the shade but the heat made her feel happy. With her sense of contentment went faint feelings of guilt – she knew she was enjoying this rest day more than the previous days spent looking at pictures and statues. It was pleasant to drift and have nothing asked of her.

'Shall we get off?' Sir Edward asked her, as the boat drew near to Meudon. 'Walk awhile, find somewhere to eat, return later? The woods are pretty, I'm told. Or we can stay on the boat and go back with it now.'

They got off, together with the woman in the black hat and carrying the portfolio. The landing stage was at the foot of a sloping hill which they walked up slowly, looking round at fields now empty, and down onto what looked like chalk pits. It was a relief to reach the woods, and they sat down to watch the boat

127

turn round for the six-kilometre journey back to Paris. Suddenly, everything was almost oppressively quiet, so quiet that a rabbit hopped close to Charlotte's foot and regarded her without any sign of alarm before lazily moving away. Sir Edward pointed to where he said Versailles lay, though it was too far away to be seen, and told Charlotte that the wood they were sitting on the edge of was really a forest which stretched for miles and had lakes in it. But they were not going to explore it. He was hungry and wanted to see the village and then sample the local fried fish, a speciality of the region. So they made their way round the edge of the wood, Sir Edward pointing out chestnut trees and oaks and wild cherry trees, and then they took a steep lane leading down towards houses. It wound round and round, passing a convent (which intrigued Charlotte) and a church, where little girls, wearing black dresses with little white collars and black hats with white ribbons round them, were coming through the doors. Charlotte stared at them but not one of them stared back. She felt conspicuous, but when people appeared, in what she thought must be the main street, they did not stare either, merely nodded their heads in an unspoken greeting. 'Imagine,' she whispered to her father, 'living here.'

'Very peaceful,' her father said. 'Very pretty. Would you not like it?'

'Perhaps. Perhaps not. It would depend.'

'On?'

'Who I was with, what my life was. I would never fit in, but then I do not fit in anywhere, that I can see.'

'Oh, come, Charlotte. What do you mean, "fit in"?'

'I mean, I would feel awkward here, foreign. I *am* foreign, of course, but being here would make me feel even more so.'

'Yet you say you like to be alone, you do not wish to mix. Being foreign you would be safeguarded from company.'

'But I want not to be noticed, to be comfortable alone, and if I were living here that could not be.'

They were back near the Seine, an hour later, where Sir Edward had seen the sign outside La Pêche Miraculeuse. The restaurant was nearly full, but a table was found for them near the window and they settled down at it, surrounded by a hubbub of French. Charlotte tried to listen to the conversations around her but could make out only individual words. But one of the words, she was sure, was 'Rodin'. She whispered as much to her father, who nodded, and appeared to be listening intently to the two men dining behind them, even though this transgressed, as Charlotte knew, good manners. They spoke little until, the meal over – it had taken a full two hours – they were outside the restaurant and on their way to the landing stage to catch the boat back to Paris. 'Rodin lives here,' Sir Edward said on, 'on that hillside.' And he gestured behind them. 'He travels each day to his studio in Montparnasse on this very boat.' Charlotte thought about this all the way to Paris, constantly looking round her to see if anyone bore a resemblance to the pictures she had seen of Rodin. It made her shiver to think of being in the presence of so famous a sculptor, perhaps even sitting next to him, brushing arms with him, the arms he had sculpted *The Thinker* with. But there was no likely candidate among the men on board. The boat was much less full on the return journey and they had a whole row of seats to themselves. 'Will you not sketch?' her father asked. She shook her head. 'Then I will draw you,' he said. 'Keep quite still, look straight ahead, at the bank. There.'

She was looking almost attractive today, the hideous navy blue costume discarded and her hair in a simple plait. She had asked him if he minded her hair not being up and he had said, truthfully, that he preferred it as she used to wear it. There was another truth, of course, but he kept quiet about it. It was her mother who had insisted it was time for Charlotte to put her hair up, like a proper young lady, and her maid had seen to it, skilfully coiling and braiding the girl's hair all round her head and securing it cunningly with unseen combs and clips. It had looked most flattering, but the child had been too self-conscious, turning her head awkwardly as though she found the weight of her hairstyle a burden, and one she might at any moment lose. Once in Paris, and trying to do her hair herself, the result had been disastrous.

His wife had instructed him to make sure he arranged for a maid in the hotel to attend to Charlotte, but he had ignored this instruction. Charlotte could manage a plait, just, and he told her she looked much more natural.

Drawing her, he smiled to himself, thinking how appalled Hettie would be to see what Charlotte was wearing. It was the first garment she had ever chosen for herself, the first shop she had ever entered on her own. At the end of the Rue St Placide, a short busy street, she had seen the Bon Marché department store and out of the doors there came a girl wearing a green-and-whited striped dress over which she had flung a lacy, white gossamer shawl. 'Oh!' Charlotte had said. 'Look, Papa, what a pretty dress.' It was the only time he had ever heard his daughter express the slightest interest in any garment and the temptation was too strong. The dress was, in fact, gaudy, but he had taken her inside and had a similar dress found for her – and now she would hardly be parted from it. It was rather low-cut, he conceded, but it fitted her perfectly and he had seen how aware it made her of her figure which usually she struggled to hide. She was in Paris, after all, and a different being, not ashamed of her breasts. She would not be able to wear it at home – she understood, he was sure, that there was no question of such a thing.

She had ribbons in her hair too, tied in a bow at the top and the bottom of her thick plait. Drawing her as he was doing, it was difficult to catch the angle of the bows and he thought about asking her to untie them but did not want to disturb her reverie. She was sitting, as instructed, so beautifully still. In profile, the squareness of her face was lost, and the heaviness of her eyebrows, and even her nose looked fine, if large. She had, he noticed, surprised he had never truly registered this before, good skin, pale but not pasty, and without a blemish. If only, he found himself thinking, men would look at his daughter as he was looking now they would see not a beauty but a young woman who repaid close attention and became more appealing the more she was looked at. He hoped such a man would come into her life one day, someone worthy of her who would match her intelligence and sensitivity, and understand what she had to offer. He only had one daughter left, his favourite, and could not bear to see her make the kind of disastrous alliances her sisters had made.

Walking from the boat to the hotel, Charlotte took his arm and squeezed it, telling him how she had loved the day. Passers-by saw her do this, saw her animated face looking up at him and her arm threaded so closely through the crook of his, and he realised how it might look. In her bright dress, and with her plait now coming asunder and her hair flying in the breeze round her head, she could quite easily be taken for something other than a daughter. He ought to have purchased a pretty shawl for her, too, but there had been none in the shop. She needed something to cover her exposed neck and the top of her bosom, and he suddenly began to feel embarrassed. He was, after all, responsible for her appearance. Clearing his throat, he said gently, 'Charlotte, tomorrow we will return to the Louvre. Your pretty dress will not be suit-able. Be sure to wear something more appropriate.' Surprisingly, she did not demur, nor did she seem in the least hurt. 'My black skirt and my white blouse?' she suggested. He nodded. 'Excellent.'

Entering the hotel, he saw a man looking at Charlotte. He caught his eye, and glared.

★

Priscilla's baby mercifully arrived early. Equally mercifully, the delivery was not the horrific, long-drawn-out affair that she had dreaded. Priscilla screamed and howled and behaved altogether badly, but she only had five hours to do it in. Lady Falconer had anticipated a whole day of drama, and so was immensely relieved. No forceps were needed, and no stitches. Remarkably, her daughter had proved made for childbirth (though when the doctor said this to her she took it as an insult and sobbed and declared she would never, never go through such an ordeal again). Even more gratifyingly, the baby was a fine, healthy boy, which delighted Robert, who apparently had let it be known that only a boy would do. He was to be named Jasper. Lady Falconer said that her father's Dalmatian had been called Jasper and that it would be unseemly, to say the least, for his great-grandson to share this name. But Robert was adamant. His father and his grandfather were both called Jasper, and Jasper it must be. There was nothing even Lady Falconer could do about it. She knew her husband and Charlotte would laugh but she did not find the coincidence in the least amusing.

The boy was born almost a month early, but was thriving, and within another month Priscilla had recovered sufficiently for her mother's presence not to be necessary. Within the time she had been in her daughter's house she had found a competent house-keeper and engaged two trustworthy other servants and, unless Priscilla was very foolish, her difficulties should be over. So Lady Falconer could go back to London and reopen the Hampstead house. She would stay with her friend Pamela in Kensington at first and open her house bit by bit. The arrangements she had made for her sons would still stand – no need for them to come home when the holidays began – and as for her husband and Charlotte, they would not care where she was. They hardly had the courtesy to keep her informed of where *they* were. Postcards were few and the total of letters was precisely one, and that not very satisfactory. They did not seem to have met anyone of interest, though she knew several people who had just returned from Paris, and no one she mentioned it to had ever heard of the Hôtel de Nice in Montparnasse where they were staying. 'Montparnasse?' they queried, looking vaguely horrified.

Lady Falconer herself was unacquainted with Montparnasse. Indeed, she could not claim to be familiar with any part of Paris except for the Hôtel Crillon. It grieved her a little that Charlotte would return able to say (as people did, after only one week) that she knew Paris quite well, though of course it would be the art of the city she would know and nothing much else. The effect of this experience might be startling. Charlotte might return transformed, able to socialise and be graceful in company, with all the rough edges of her personality smoothed over. But Lady Falconer doubted it. In all probability, she and her father would speak to no one and no one would care to speak to them, and no lessons would be learned. Charlotte would come back as gauche as ever.

She frowned heavily as she alighted from the cab in front of her house. The frown deepened and never left her face for the rest of the day.

★

On their last day in the Hôtel de Nice another Englishwoman came to stay. Charlotte spent a long time over dinner trying to fathom how she knew this woman was English and thought it something to do with her complexion, which was what she had once heard Priscilla's described as: 'peaches and cream'. It had not made sense to her at the time. She had looked at a peach, holding it in her hand and studying it carefully, and could not see any resemblance to Priscilla's skin. The cream part was easier but still not entirely fitting. But now she found herself looking at the woman's face and hearing 'peaches and cream' in her head. The women she had seen in Paris all week did not have this startlingly fresh complexion, the skin so pearly white and smooth with the faintest blush of pink in the cheeks which clearly was not rouge. Or perhaps her Englishness sprang from her hair, so golden, almost white-gold, piled neatly on top of her head. Most Parisian women seemed to be dark-haired and did not pile their hair up in this rather old-fashioned way.

It might, Charlotte allowed, be simply the clothes. She did not know how but Parisian women dressed differently. They simply did. She knew the word was 'chic' but wherein lay this chic-ness she did not know – it was something to do with *how* garments were worn and not what they were. The Englishwoman was dressed rather oddly. She wore a long blue skirt over which she had what Charlotte could only describe (to herself) as a high-necked shift in a lighter blue. It fell below her waist, where it was cinched with a silver brocade belt. On top of it she wore a velvet jacket with silver buttons. The jacket was purple which, with the blue, looked odd. Pretty, and unusual, but odd. The lady spoke French but it was, Charlotte could tell, the same sort of French as her father's, which is to say correct and fluent but with an unmistakable accent that was not French.

133

They were, that evening, the only three in the dining room. On other evenings Sir Edward had elected to go to restaurants but tonight preparations had to be made for an early departure and so it seemed sensible to stay in the hotel. The food on offer was limited but good – charcuterie, pâtés, grilled meat or fish, cheeses – and the new guest appeared to enjoy it as much as they did themselves. Charlotte saw her looking in their direction once or twice, and smiling, and she wished that her father would say something. Eventually, at the coffee stage, he did. He asked her – in English – if she would care to join them in the courtyard for coffee. 'It is very pleasant there,' he said, 'and much cooler.'

The courtyard was not large but there were flowers and greenery at the edges, and in the middle was a tree with a bench seat running round it. There was room for three to sit side by side, with Charlotte in the middle. Normally, this would have embarrassed her, but there was something so relaxed and friendly about the way they were all obliged to sit that she was not. A little table was brought out and set in front of them, and coffee brought and poured. Charlotte did not drink coffee but she inhaled the aroma enthusiastically. Her father began a polite conversation, offering the information that they were to leave for Florence in the morning, and that they had spent a delightful week looking at art. The woman asked if he were an artist himself, and when he said no Charlotte interrupted to say that indeed he was and that he could draw beautifully. Sir Edward, smiling, demurred, saying that their companion should not be misled by a daughter's loyalty, and that being able to draw tolerably well did not make one an artist. But Miss Tyrwhitt – by now they had exchanged names – disagreed. She said that on the contrary, drawing was essential to any artist and that at the Slade, where she had studied, her professor had valued drawing above all else. This led, inevitably, to a discussion about the Slade and its suitability for young women to study there. Miss Tyrwhitt vowed it was a perfectly proper establishment, where men and women were separated in the Life classes, and discipline was strict. 'Your daughter,' said Miss Tyrwhitt, 'would do very well there, I am sure.'

Charlotte longed to ask her why she was in Paris, but her father was already asking her if she was a painter and if so what was her subject matter. The answer was yes, she was, painting in both oils and water-colours, and that she painted flowers, not perhaps the sort of floral pictures he might imagine but bolder compositions. She had, she volunteered, exhibited at the New English Art Club the year before. Charlotte could tell that her father was impressed, and so was she. It seemed to her marvellous that this woman, who clearly was not afraid to travel, and to stay in hotels alone, actually had a profession and followed it seriously. Miss Tyrwhitt protested that she was not a particularly good artist, certainly not compared to her other women contemporaries at the Slade, one of whom was tremendously gifted. She mentioned names but they were meaningless to Sir Edward as well as to Charlotte. They learned that her father was a clergyman, and that he too had taken his daughter on a tour of Europe's art galleries just as Sir Edward was taking Charlotte. 'You will remember it all your life,' she told Charlotte, 'and get a great deal from it. It will entirely reshape how you think about life and what you are to do with yours.'

★

Ursula felt better after the little interlude with Sir Edward and his daughter – more relaxed, not so tense, not so worried about seeing Gwen the next day. She had never confessed to her friend that she had lost the valise and her painting with it, and it troubled her to be deceitful. Her distress had been awful – she had wept for days and been quite unable to sleep, going over and over in her mind the process of the packing and labelling and despatching of her luggage. The fault, she was sure, though, had not been hers. Nobody to whom she spoke in her search for the lost valise seemed the least surprised at its disappearance – rather, they said that it was amazing more pieces of luggage did not go astray.

She had thought of writing to Gwen and telling her what had happened but it seemed too cruel. Gwen might say she did not care, that the painting had been a first attempt and a failure, but on the other hand, in her present state of mind, it might depress her more. It was a risk Ursula did not wish to take. It was more than a year now since she'd seen her friend and she was supposed to be visiting to cheer her up in the new room she did not like, in the Rue de l'Ouest. Gwen knew, now, about Rodin's latest mistress and was suffering accordingly. Ursula did not want to tell her about lost valises. She would amuse her instead by describing Sir Edward and his daughter, with their solemn respect for art. The girl, Charlotte, adored her father, it was plain to see. Ursula had loved her boast that he was a fine artist himself. Maybe he was. He had not, she noticed, made any extravagant claims for Charlotte's talents. It was always a strangely touching sight, a father with a devoted, admiring daughter. She supposed that once upon a time she had felt the same about her own father.

Gwen had never felt that way about hers, she knew.

★

It had been a pity to bid goodnight to their new acquaintance and to know they would not see her the next day, or indeed, probably, ever again, just when the relationship seemed so very promising. Charlotte had never met anyone like her, and neither, she could tell, had her father. Miss Tyrwhitt was their main topic of conversation in the train all the way to Italy. 'I wonder why she is not married, Papa,' Charlotte could not help speculating, but her father would not be drawn beyond saying, 'Some story there, I imagine, death of a fiancé most likely' (which for him was quite indulgent). Charlotte promptly imagined it too, but though this gave her a pleasant few minutes she rejected the idea. 'No,' she suddenly said out loud, 'she has *chosen* not to marry, I am sure of it. She is married to her art. She prefers it.' Sir Edward smiled and murmured, 'Very well, she is married to her art, and it makes a much better husband for her, I am sure.'

'I should like to be married to art,' Charlotte said, 'but I am not worthy of it.'

'Dear me, Charlotte,' her father protested, 'why not worthy?'

'Not good enough at drawing or painting for it to be my whole world.'

'I should think not. I am sure it is not Miss Tyrwhitt's whole world either. It cannot be a woman's whole world.'

'Can it be a man's?'

Sir Edward hesitated. 'Perhaps. A man is better able to let art dominate his life and sweep aside interruptions.'

'Interruptions?'

'Distractions, breaks in concentration owing to other events.'

'Whatever do you mean, Papa?'

'A woman . . .' began Sir Edward, and then stopped. As so often with Charlotte, he found himself verging on the kind of philosophical conversation which led into questions from her that he had difficulty answering as straightforwardly as he would have wished.

'A woman?' prompted Charlotte.

'A woman has children to occupy her.'

'Not all women have children. If women are not married, there are no children to be a distraction. A woman then can be like a man and have the same dedication, can she not?'

'Perhaps,' Sir Edward said, weakly.

'Well then,' Charlotte said, satisfied. But then she recalled what had begun this dialogue and said, 'Still, I am not good enough. I could never dedicate myself to art. I need something else, but what?'

'You are barely sixteen, Charlotte, you cannot yet know what you want.'

'Caroline was . . .'

'We will not talk about Caroline, if you please.'

'But why not, Papa? Why can we never talk of her? Why is it so wrong even to mention her?'

'It is not wrong. It is distressing, and better left alone.'

'Well then, Priscilla. Priscilla is only twenty and was barely nineteen when she married . . .'

'Where on earth is this leading?'

'You said that I could not know what I want in life because I am only sixteen and my point is that my sisters were not much older when they knew what they wanted.'

'Did they?'

'Why, of course. Priscilla longed to be married . . .'

'She longed, I think, for a grand wedding and the status of wife.'

'Oh, Papa! That is cynical, is it not?'

'And the truth, I am afraid, a truth, Charlotte, not to be repeated outside this railway carriage.'

'I am discreet, Papa.' Her father smiled, so she repeated this. 'I am known for my discretion, I assure you.' He smiled even more broadly. 'At any rate, Priscilla chose to be married,' she carried on, 'and the unnamed one chose adventure and uncertainty and a wandering life.'

'Is that what you call it? How very romantic it sounds.'

'Now you are being horribly sarcastic.'

'You tempt me too far for me to resist.'

'If we could name names and talk freely I would explain what I mean about your eldest daughter, but as I am forbidden . . .'

'You are indeed forbidden, and your point is taken. You feel that sixteen ought to be quite old enough for you to know what you want from life. I accept that, madam, but nevertheless I suggest that it need not concern you unduly that you do not, in fact, know. The knowledge will come soon enough.'

'Good,' said Charlotte, and did not speak again until they arrived in Florence.

★

Jessie was waiting in the hall, her coat still on, her box at her feet. 'Oh, ma'am, oh milady!' she gasped, hand to mouth. Lady Falconer did not speak. It was all too obvious what had happened. The ornate mirror above the hall table had gone and so had the silver tray and the runner from the floor, brought back by Edward's father from Afghanistan. Calmly, she asked Jessie, 'We have been burgled?'

'Yes, milady.'

'Have you inspected all the rooms?'

'No, milady, fearing who might still be about, fearing . . .'

'Have you sent for the police?'

'No, milady, knowing you were about to arrive, and thinking it best that . . .'

'Very well, Jessie. We will telephone for the police and until they arrive we will have some tea and be sensible. There is no use in being agitated. The deed is done.'

And most thoroughly done. The opinion of the policeman who turned up with gratifying promptness was that the burglars had known what they wanted. Lady Falconer observed, drily, that this was most discerning of them. There was no real mess, apart from the glass broken in the pantry window and the lock forced off the kitchen door – the burglars had been tidy, smashing nothing else and opening but not emptying out any drawers ('unusual' the policeman said). The list of what had been taken consisted of small items of furniture, all of the silver and the safe, containing most of Lady Falconer's jewellery. Itemising these jewels proved trying. She remembered the pearls and the diamonds well enough, necklaces, bracelets and rings, but listing the gold chains and lockets and the various brooches, some amethyst, some rubies, proved more difficult. 'Thousands of pounds,' the policeman murmured. 'And of great sentimental value,' Lady Falconer sternly rebuked him.

She did not know what had been taken that belonged particularly to her husband. His bedroom and his study appeared untouched, but she could not be sure of this and said she would have to wait until he returned from abroad, which would not be for several weeks. The policeman was perturbed by this, but understanding, and most concerned that Lady Falconer would be alone in a now vandalised house. He advised that at least until the window and door had been repaired she ought not to stay in the house. Jessie was glad to hear this because she herself had no intention of staying a single night until new male servants were engaged and preferably not until the master himself was home. Lady Falconer's calmness – 'cool as a cucumber' as Jessie reported to everyone afterwards – alarmed her. It might mean her mistress was unafraid and about to ignore the policeman's advice. But she did not. 'As you say,' she said to the policeman, 'the house must be secured first, if it ever can seem secure again. I believe there are burglar alarm systems, am I correct?' The policeman said she was, but that they were expensive to install and liable to malfunction.

There was nothing else to do but wait for a locksmith and a glazier to arrive. It angered Lady Falconer that she was obliged to call for them herself when it was surely a man's job to make the arrangements. But there was no man available, and Jessie had already departed back to Norfolk, anxious to catch the last train. The policeman had toured the whole house, ascertaining that no one lurked in the attics or basement, so Lady Falconer felt able to look into each room herself in case she could recognise any disturbance. A rug had gone from the library – more Afghan loot – and so had some ornaments. Then she noticed that there was also a bare patch on the wall where Sir Edward's treasured Dutch painting had hung. He would be more upset about that than anything else, but it was his own fault for insisting on closing the house up for such a long time. She knew that to think such a thing was spiteful and petty but that was how she felt. In the dining room everything had gone from sideboard and table – all the silver, as she had told the policeman – but she now saw that there was another bare patch to account for. It was a larger patch than the one on the library wall and this one she did recall. It was a painting of fruit, a tureen heaped with fruit, and it had belonged once to Edward's aunt who had left it to him in her will some years ago. She had thought it ugly, almost vulgar, but Edward had been thrilled to inherit it. The frame, she remem-bered, was rather fine, quite the most attractive thing about it. Perhaps the 'discerning' burglars had taken it for the frame.

It was only in order to be thorough that she went into Charlotte's bedroom at all, since there was nothing in it that was of any real value, or at least nothing that could be moved. The wardrobe was a beautiful piece of furniture but would have taken four strong men to steal. Peering into the room she saw nothing untoward, and closed the door firmly. She did not go up to the attics. The policeman had been, and it did not seem necessary even in the interests of scrupulous checking. She had only once, in all the years in the house, been up to the attics and that was at least ten years ago during the unfortunate incident involving a maid who had given birth. She trusted Jessie to see that all was as it should be up there. As she descended the stairs again after her tour of inspection, the house was extraordinarily quiet. She paused midway, hand on banister, and listened. It was not that she was afraid, though she would have had every justification to be, but that she felt a sense of surprise. The house always seemed full of noise to her even when only her husband and younger daughter were at home with her. The memory of familiar noises, now shockingly absent, overwhelmed her suddenly. No doors banged, no servant clattered about on the tiled kitchen floor, no grandfather clock ticked (and how had the burglars managed to steal that?). The air felt heavy with dust and the unnatural silence was ominous, making her imagine a bomb about to explode.

Hurriedly, she swept down the rest of the stairs and picked up her coat. She could wait no longer for the locksmith and glazier. Instead, she would drop the key off on her way to Pamela's and trust them to see to the repairs – the house had been burgled, everything worth stealing had already gone. She had no intention of returning until both Edward and all the servants were in residence.

And she was certainly not returning to Priscilla's.

★

Charlotte felt a great leap of recognition. This, surely could be the room. The ceiling sloped, the wallpaper was yellow, the window had a lace curtain in front of it, there was a small wooden table and upon it a vase of flowers. But the chair was wrong. It was not a wickerwork chair but an uncomfortable wrought-iron chair. And the floor was not right. It was covered in rush matting. But still, the room spoke to her and she was delighted with it, rushing down to her father to urge him to come and see her quarters. He came willingly, and saw what she meant but said gently, 'There are many rooms such as this, Charlotte. I doubt if this could be the room itself.'

The villa was on a hillside outside Florence, near to Fiesole, and he had been directed to it by an old friend in London before he left. The landlady took English visitors and there was the atmosphere of a private home rather than an hotel which greatly appealed to her clientele, especially Sir Edward. He himself had been given a charming room with a superb view in the direction of Florence. Her view was, if anything, even better than his own and they stood for a moment, lace curtain drawn back, admiring it.

'I am going to try to draw it, Papa,' Charlotte said.

'What, the view?'

'No, no, this room. I will sit on the bed and try to draw it and perhaps paint it.'

'A good idea,' her father said. 'When will you begin?'

She began the next day, after they had returned from the Uffizi, and discovered at once how hard it was to capture what she wished to capture, and which had been captured for her in the little painting at home. Nothing came out right, either in pencil or charcoal or water-colours. All she produced was a corner of an undistinguished room, rather depressing in its flat ordinariness. Light was the problem. She could not convey the quality of the light, how it made the flowers glow and the table's surface shine and the wallpaper recede into shadows. There was no sense, either, of herself in this room, or of anyone else. It was empty, of feeling, of human presence, of everything.

She tore her attempts up day after day. It began to hang over her, this self-imposed task, which at first she had been eager to embrace. All she could think of was the painting back home, its perfection, its powerful simplicity, and she yearned to have it with her. But her failed efforts were not entirely in vain. Lying in bed at night, the window before her open and the stars shining in the dark sky, she thought she had learned something about herself on this trip. Art could not give her everything she needed. There was, for her, no real fulfilment in striving to draw or paint. She did not, after all, want to go to the Slade School. She could be moved by art, she could admire and value what artists produced.

She cared about great art passionately, but she was not an artist. At first, she felt distressed at this growing realisation, and almost panicked at the gap which now opened up in her young life: if not art, what? She felt troubled, trying to invent other ambitions. The romantic image she had been able to envisage for so long was being denied her – she would never, now, starve in a garret or succeed in expressing herself in art.

Emerging for breakfast on the terrace at the end of the week with red eyes, she presented a woeful sight.

'Why, Charlotte, whatever is the matter, child?' her father asked, dreading the answer (that Charlotte might fall ill was his greatest worry).

Charlotte sat down at the table and waited until the coffee and fruit and pastries had been brought, and then she shrugged. 'Nothing,' she said, and then, 'everything. I am not an artist, Papa, I am nothing.'

Sir Edward did not mean to, but he laughed. 'My dear,' he said, 'someone who is not an artist is not therefore nothing or no one. You did not manage to draw your room to your satisfaction, I take it?' Charlotte nodded. 'Well, that is not so surprising, and proves nothing. You are untaught, untrained, only sixteen, and yet you imagine you can match the best. Have some sense, do. And eat up, we must be off.'

'It is not about failing to paint my room,' Charlotte protested, a little sullenly.

'What are these red eyes about, then? They are not becoming.'

'I cried . . .'

'I can see that. And did not sleep, I am sure, very foolish when we have a long day ahead.'

'I cried out of despair, Papa.'

'Despair? With what, pray?'

'Myself, of course. Art is not the answer. I have just realised it.'

'Try, try, try again.'

'No. That is my point. I do not wish to try any longer. I think I hate trying.'

143

'Then give up, and be done with it. It is not a tragedy.'

'But it *is*, because now I have nothing to aim for, and I *must* have an aim, something to strive for.'

Sir Edward stared at her. Was there ever such an exasperating, infuriating child? Any other girl would be content to sit in a sunny garden in Florence and simply enjoy being where she was, with an exciting day to look forward to, being squired round the city's marvels. But not Charlotte. Ludicrous though her tragic face was, he could see her feelings were genuine. He thought back to himself at sixteen and was dismayed to be unable to recall any dissatisfaction with himself at that age. Life had seemed to stretch before him in a set pattern he was content to follow – he had no recollection of the kind of restless, all-consuming desire to know what he should and could make of himself. How old had he been before questioning what he was doing with his life? Thirty, at least. And now here was his youngest daughter driven endlessly to question her path in life – it did not seem right. This tour was not helping her in the least. If anything, the more she travelled, the more she saw, the more anxious about her future she became, and he did not know what to do with her.

'Charlotte,' he said, 'perhaps it is time to go home. Rome will keep for another day.'

★

A telegram had arrived from Florence, announcing the early return of the travellers, so Lady Falconer was there to greet them. The few servants who had been retained were summoned back and the process of engaging others had begun. But there was, as Jessie put it to John, 'an atmosphere'. How would the master react to the burglary? Lady Falconer herself had seemed hardly perturbed, even though all her jewellery had been taken. They were astonished by her evident composure. But the master? Hard to tell. 'She'll blame him,' Jessie said, 'for going off, you'll see. She never wanted him and Miss Charlotte to go. She never wanted the house shut up.'

It was early evening when the cab drew up. John rushed to

open the door and help Miss Charlotte out. He noticed straight-away that she looked different – thinner, but there was some other difference he could not discern. He took hold of some of the luggage and staggered into the house with it. Lady Falconer was standing in the hall, looking almost regal, hands clasped in front of her and back rigidly straight. Sir Edward walked up to her and kissed her cheek. 'Welcome home,' she said, but in a distinctly unwelcoming tone.

'What's wrong?' Sir Edward said, immediately. 'Is Priscilla well? And the baby?'

'Both well.'

'Good. And the boys? Yourself?'

'Perfectly well.'

'Why, then, the tone?'

At that point, Charlotte came in, setting down the bag she was carrying with a thump.

'Charlotte! Your hair!'

'Hello, Mama. My hair? Papa likes it like this.'

'That is hardly the point. You look quite wild, quite . . . you look disorderly.'

'We have been travelling a long time, Mama.'

'That is no excuse for slovenliness.'

'It was not meant to be an excuse, merely an explanation. I am so tired and hungry, I might faint at any moment.'

Sir Edward, meanwhile, was staring at the blank wall where the mirror had been. 'Are you redecorating, Hettie?' Then he turned and saw that the grandfather clock had gone, and at the same time peered down at the floor, where once the carpet runner had been.

'No, Edward. The redecorating was done for us.' Lady Falconer smiled, pleased with her own sarcasm. But her husband was quick. He looked at her sharply and read her expression. She nodded, though he had not asked her a question. Leaving her in the hall he strode off to the library, and she heard his 'Damn!' echo through the house.

There was an attempt to keep things calm and controlled, but

Sir Edward's fury and distress made this almost impossible. He did not want to hear about the jewellery or the silver or the items of furniture – his sole concern was the theft of his Dutch painting. He would never, he said, be able to replace it. He had been so fortunate, in the first place, to acquire it and would never have another opportunity. It was, his wife thought, though was not so crass as to remark, such a fuss to make about a missing painting. She did, however, venture to point out that no one was dead. And then Charlotte reappeared, to announce that her painting had also been taken. Lady Falconer noticed at once that she did not seem as extravagantly upset as would have been expected.

'A mistake,' Sir Edward said. 'They confused it, they thought it was another Dutch masterpiece, I dare say.'

'Are thieves so clever?' Charlotte asked. 'Do they *know* about art? And what is valuable?'

'The policeman said that our burglars were clearly discerning,' Lady Falconer volunteered. 'He even suggested that they may have stolen to order, as it were. Such thieves do, apparently, exist, taking only the best things.'

'And what do they do with them?' Charlotte asked.

'For heaven's sake, child,' snapped her father, 'what on earth do you suppose they do with them? They sell them, of course. They have buyers waiting. It is all a racket.'

'But if they took my painting mistaking it for something valuable and then find it is not, what will happen to it?'

'It will be discarded.'

There was no scream from Charlotte, her mother noticed, nor even any sign of either anger or misery. Instead, she sat quietly, gazing rather vacantly into space. Like John, Lady Falconer saw how Charlotte had changed but unlike him she was able to pinpoint the difference. It was simply a matter of having grown up, and the change was more striking in her case because they had not seen her for several months. If she had remained at home, the change might have happened imperceptibly. Studying her daughter, Lady Falconer even saw signs that in spite of her unkempt hair, the once ugly duckling might become, if not a swan, a far from hopelessly unattractive creature. Her voice softened as she said, 'I am sorry about your painting, Charlotte. I know how you cared for it.' Charlotte bowed her head and did not reply, but Sir Edward gave a little grunt which his wife could not interpret.

'Edward?' she said. There was no reply. He was slumped in his chair, his eyes closed. Smoothing her dress, Lady Falconer asked if they might move on from the unpleasantness of the burglary and she might hear something of their tour. Her husband sighed heavily. 'Charlotte?' Lady Falconer said.

'It was wonderful,' Charlotte said, with no wonder in her voice. Realising this herself, she tried again. 'Paris was beautiful,' she said. 'We saw so many works of art. And in Florence too,' she added lamely.

'The weather?'

'Perfect. It rained one day in Paris, but otherwise, perfect.'

'Did you meet interesting people?'

'Not really. We were engrossed in the art, Mama. Oh, we did make the acquaintance of one lady, but I forget her name . . .'

'Miss Tyrwhitt,' said Sir Edward, eyes still shut.

'Yes, Miss Tyrwhitt. She is an artist herself.'

Lady Falconer was instantly alert. 'How did you meet this lady, whose difficult name your father remembers so easily?'

'She was staying in our hotel, that's all.'

'She was attractive, I take it?'

'Charming,' Sir Edward said, 'very knowledgeable about art.'

'Quite to your taste, then.'

'We only talked to her once,' Charlotte said.

Supper was served, but though Charlotte ate heartily – in that respect she had not changed – Sir Edward picked at his food. There was virtually no conversation between the three of them. The minute Charlotte had finished, she begged to be excused, saying she wished to go to bed at once. When she had left the room, Lady Falconer said, 'She does not seem distraught about the loss of that painting she used to treasure so.'

'She is disillusioned,' Sir Edward muttered.

'About what, precisely?'

'Art, Hettie, art, of course. Taking her to see great art has revealed to her her own inadequacies. It has had quite the opposite effect from that which it ought to have had.'

'But how has this changed her view of her painting?'

'It does not mean the same to her.'

'I am lost, Edward.'

'And I am tired. Goodnight.'

The next day, while her husband spent his time haranguing police officers, Lady Falconer addressed herself to Charlotte in a way she had never quite done before. For the first time she felt intrigued by her daughter rather than irritated, and found herself wanting to understand what on earth Edward had meant by his bewildering remarks concerning Charlotte. It had always seemed rather ridiculous, the way she used to fawn over that little painting – Lady Falconer had wondered if she was quite right in the head – but now that it had been stolen, and Charlotte seemed unperturbed, there was a mystery her mother wanted to solve. How could a painting mean so much to its owner one day and apparently mean nothing some weeks later? Charlotte *ought* to be upset.

They chatted first about baby Jasper. Lady Falconer described him in predictable detail to Charlotte and said that he would be a joy for her to draw when she saw him. Charlotte shook her head. 'I have given up art,' she said.

'Oh, come, Charlotte, that is a little melodramatic.'

'Then it is. There is nothing I can do about it. I have lost all enthusiasm. I cannot do what the artist who painted the attic picture can do, let alone what the great artists can do.'

'But, Charlotte, you have not been trained. It is ridiculous to imagine that you cannot paint when so far no one has taught you except your father.'

'I thought you did not wish me to become an art student.'

'True, I did not, but as a hobby . . .'

'Art that is a hobby is useless, Mama.'

'Your father does not think so.'

'But I would. It is all or nothing with me. There.'

Still struggling, Lady Falconer said, 'Let me understand. The attic painting made you believe you could be an artist?'

'No.'

'What then? What did it do?'

'It made me want the life.'

'The *life*?'

'Mama, please, there is nothing to understand. I had foolish ideas. I imagined things, and now I do not. I am realistic.'

'And what form does this realism take?'

'I have no more ridiculous dreams about living in attics and being an artist.'

In spite of herself, Lady Falconer was touched. 'How sad, dear,' she said. But this was evidently not the right thing to say.

'It is not in the least sad,' said Charlotte. 'A painting deluded me into thinking I was something I clearly am not. That's all.'

'So now you do not care for art?'

'Mama! Of course I care for it, how could I not, seeing what I have seen. I will always "care" for art. But it pains me to know I can never be an artist, do you see? Am I plain enough?'

Lady Falconer did not see. Nothing was plain to her. It seemed to her that her daughter was in a muddle, and somehow she was blaming the stolen painting. How this could be, Lady Falconer could not fathom, but since she had never understood Charlotte she told herself this was to be expected. But at the same time she began to hope that, with all this art nonsense out of the way, her youngest daughter might yet turn into a young woman of whom she might be proud – graceful, sensible, well-mannered.

The tour, she thought, had done Charlotte good.

★

The bare patch on the wall was not so very noticeable. The painting had not, after all, been there long enough for the lurid wallpaper behind it to fade much. Nevertheless, Charlotte did not like to see it, and looked around for some other picture to cover it over. She found a harmless scene of Hampstead Heath and hung that up instead, but still she felt disturbed and guilty every time she looked in its direction and began trying to sleep on her other side so that she would always wake looking the other way.

It would be better if she went to Queen's College rather than to the Slade. If she had no artistic talent then she must use her brain. Perhaps, in the end, the stolen painting had taught her something. That, at any rate, was how she resolved to think of it, but the memory of it floated in her mind, the image of it, the atmosphere, the spell it had cast over her.

She could not bear the thought that it might have already been damaged or discarded or even destroyed.

STELLA

I

C OMING OUT of the hospital, Alan turned sharp left and began walking quickly, sticking to the kerb side of the crowded pavement. His sight was blurred, but he knew where he was going, there was no need for him to be able to see clearly in order to recognise signs. It was a stifling hot day, though there was no sun. London in August, an uncomfortable place to be, but soon he would be on the train and speeding – he hoped speeding, and not dragging – towards Cornwall. Once there, once home, he would feel better. Everything would settle down. A humdrum life, that was what he wanted now. A quiet, uncomplicated existence.

He loathed hospitals. He had been surprised to discover how many men found them safe, comforting places. He'd seen faces light up when the decision came – 'Hospital for him.' But he had no trust in doctors, not much respect for most nurses. It seemed to him that some of the medical staff in the hospitals where he had been didn't know what they were doing. Suspicion and scorn probably showed on his face, because he was not a popular patient. He asked too many questions, analysed closely too many answers. Before the war he'd been a civil servant, desk job, Trade & Industry, which had taught him to be meticulous. He liked to get things right, and couldn't stand bluster.

The city was packed. He saw lots of men like himself, obviously wounded in the war. A few were even in uniform though it was two years since the Armistice. He didn't like looking at them, and tried instead to concentrate on the traffic, a mixture of automobiles and horse-drawn vehicles which still struck him as strange. He thought he would like a car one day, if he could ever afford one. Moving less carefully among the rushing pedestrians, though his sight was clearing, he noticed a woman who looked a bit like Stella getting onto a bus. Odd. He hardly ever saw another woman who looked like her, whereas there were quite a few who reminded him of Charlotte. It was a question of colouring, obviously. Stella's bright red hair and disturbingly green eyes were not a common combination whereas Charlotte was a brunette, a tall, fairly ordinary-looking brunette. You had to look closely (as he had done) to see the sweetness in her face.

Tiring, and still nowhere near the underground station, he decided to stop at a café and have a drink. The café he turned into was more of a teashop, but his bad leg ached and he had to sit down. He ordered tea, and a scone. There were only two other people in the place, women, both with shingled hair, a style he hadn't yet got used to, deep in conversation. They paid not the slightest attention to him, which relieved him. His burns invited attention, and he hated being stared at. There were those who tried not to look but their furtive glimpses proved harder to bear even than stares. There was a paper lying on the table he'd chosen, *The Times*. He shoved it aside, not wanting to know any news. He'd finished with news. Politics, foreign affairs, share prices – they no longer had relevance to his life. He felt he didn't really belong to the world any more. 'Cutting yourself off, hiding away, won't help,' Charlotte had said. But she was wrong. It did.

He'd been with her for only six months, just before the war began. The future had been so bright, so full of every kind of promise. In 1916, remembering himself in the summer two years before produced a kind of tearful emotion in him harder to cope with than the misery he had had to endure ever since he was injured. All his images of his pre-war self were of a man over-whelmingly energetic, a man who had found it difficult to sit at a desk, though his job demanded that he should. He'd liked games – mainly cricket, and tennis – and had been good at them. His school reports had referred to his 'exuberance' and Charlotte had once said this was what had first attracted her to him. She liked exuberant men, men who glowed with vitality and physical well-being. She didn't play games herself but she was a great walker, and had taken up the new fad for cycling with enthusiasm. That was how he'd met her. She'd been coming too fast down East Heath Road and her skirt had caught in the wheel, sending her flying into his arms as he came off the heath after his swim in the pond. He'd been almost at the road when he saw her hurtling down and he'd sprinted into her path, seeing what was about to happen – and caught her as she crashed to a halt.

Neither of them was hurt. It could have been embarrassing, being thrown onto his back as she catapulted on top of him, but they both laughed, not at all shy. He'd helped her disentangle the offending skirt, and a slight scratch on her ankle, where something had cut through her stocking, gave him the opportunity to produce his handkerchief (luckily clean and unused) and tie it round. He pushed the bike back up the hill for her to the rather alarmingly grand house where she turned out to live. On the way, they chatted about cycling and bicycles. He told her that he loved to cycle, belonged to a cycling club, and went off most weekends on long rides, taking the train to various places outside London. She said she wished she could do the same. Then he offered to fit a guard to her back wheel so that her skirt could not catch in it again and, to his surprise, she accepted his offer. That was the beginning. They had never, of course, become lovers, though he had thought of himself as in love and he was sure Charlotte had felt the same. Who knew what might have happened, had it not been for the war starting just as they were really becoming close? But if it had not been for the war, he would not have met Stella.

It distressed him that Stella had never known him as he used to be. He'd been so dreadfully afraid at first that what attracted her to him in that wretched hospital was his helplessness, and that it was pity which drew her to him. She denied this, but it had taken him a long time to believe she could see anything at all to love about him. 'You're brave,' she said, and 'You *try* all the time,' and then, later, they discovered a shared taste for the same kind of music and the same sort of books, and she said no one she'd ever known could talk so intelligently about things. It didn't seem a lot, to him, to inspire love, especially when so much of why *he* loved *her* was to do with her looks. She was beautiful, as Charlotte had not been.

He'd met Charlotte again, briefly, after peace was declared, to tell her about Stella and to finish things properly, and he'd been shocked at the change in her. She'd written to him throughout the war, sisterly letters, but never mentioned how thin and worn she had become, though she'd told him how ill she had been after the death of her father. But then she'd been equally shocked by his appearance. They sat in the buffet at Victoria Station, a meeting which lasted twenty minutes but felt like twenty hours. He was ashamed of his prepared speech but also relieved to have made it, to get it over.

The scone was delicious – light, fluffy, with a hint of cheese in it. He ordered another. Thank God, his taste buds were unaffected. Food was so important now, and drink, wine in particular. He'd gone off to war thinking of food as just a kind of fuel to keep his body running smoothly, not caring much what he ate as long as his hunger was satisfied. He'd used to drink beer, and occasionally a whisky. Since he returned, food was of much greater interest to him. Stella was a good cook, and he had picked up a lot from her. The kitchen had become as much his as hers. It was small but compact and there was a view of the estuary from the window, the best view in the cottage. It faced west, so that in the evening, when he was in the kitchen, wonderful sunsets illuminated the room. Going into the other rooms afterwards was a little depressing. It was a metaphor for his life, he thought, from brightness to dreariness, to gloom.

But that was a lie. His life had not been particularly bright before the war. It was just that he had been thoughtless, or rather he had never thought about anything deeply. He went to the office, he did his not-very-demanding job carefully enough, he went home, he played tennis, he went cycling, he went to cricket matches, and was quite content to enjoy himself. These days, he couldn't stop thinking how breathtakingly unprepared he had been for war. And then four years of it, and months in hospital with not the slightest hope of regaining what he had once had, that unworried existence. Only four years, and every-thing about him and his circumstances was changed for ever. 'But you survived,' Charlotte had said to him. 'You're alive.' She meant he ought to be grateful. Her own life, and the lives of thousands of others, had also been dramatically altered, some-times far more than his had been.

There was sympathy in the eyes of the waitress when he paid for his tea, but he bore it stoically. He'd seen chaps in hospital smiling in spite of the most awful injuries just because someone was sitting holding their hand and being sympathetic. Sympathy hadn't helped Alan at all when it came his way. It just made him bad-tempered and determined to manage without. 'You are a surly fellow,' Stella had reproached him. It was true, he was now. Pain had made him surly, fear made him surlier. Today, he'd set off for his hospital appointment, afraid that he was going to be told he was losing his sight and that nothing could be done. But, as it turned out, the condition was entirely treatable. He had the drops in his pocket. Nothing more could be done about the burns, nothing further could be done about his leg or his shoulder, which would always pain him, but his eyes were safe.

He wanted to buy a present for Stella, something to make amends for his vile temper the last few days. There were no decent shops on this route between hospital and underground station. In fact, there were hardly any shops at all, only a few small grocery stores, and a couple of newsagents. He hadn't the energy to walk to Oxford Street before going on to Paddington. Flowers, he thought, he could buy her flowers, when he got to St Austell, but then he remembered how late he would arrive. There would be no flower stalls. It would have to be scent, but where the hell was he going to get that? Then, just ahead, he saw what looked like a market. It ran down a side street, both sides of the road, crammed with open stalls. The goods on sale were not new but second-hand, maybe with some genuine antiques hidden among the bric-a-brac. Slowly, he began searching, looking for jewellery. Stella liked cameos; perhaps he would find an old cameo which could be made into a brooch or have a velvet ribbon threaded through it. He noticed he was being closely observed by the stall-holder whose trays he was scrutinising. The man, who had been slouching against the wall at his back, was alert. 'Looking for something special, sir?' he asked. There was a slight emphasis on the 'sir'. Shouldn't it have been 'guv' or 'mister', Alan wondered. Did he look as though he had money and was worth a 'sir'? Or was it the war wounds? Shaking his head, he moved on.

There were several book stalls, which he paused to browse over, almost selecting a very pretty copy of *Gulliver's Travels*. Stella liked old books with decorative covers and this one looked Victorian, a deep turquoise colour with gold foil flowers embossed in it. There was a label pasted inside the cover, recording that the volume had been awarded to James W. Hayston for regular attendance at school, and proficiency in reading, in 1896. The man selling it wanted a shilling. But Alan decided he needed a more appropriate book, and passed on. The next stall was a mess. He almost didn't stop at all – it looked heaped with junk. But a box caught his eye, and he asked the stall-holder if he could examine it. She handed it over, pointing out that it was in perfect condition, not a scratch on it. It was a biscuit box, made for Queen Victoria's golden jubilee, the queen looking immaculate in her robes. But it was large, and awkward to carry. Handing it back, he watched as the woman moved her stuff about to make a space for it. 'What's that?' he asked, pointing at something that had caught his eye. She hauled out a small picture, and showed it to him. He stared, recognising something in it but he couldn't think what. Had he seen this room? Been in one like it? Was it a little like Charlotte's? Her rented room had been her secret from her family. She'd decorated it herself. He remembered that the wallpaper was yellow and she'd hung a white lace curtain in front of the window. They'd kissed and fondled each other there, nothing more, and then afterwards she'd gone back home. It had all felt very odd to him, he'd never been able to understand why Charlotte had this room at all when she hardly ever went there. She'd said it was an indulgence, and she could afford it. It was a dream she'd once had: it meant something to her. She couldn't explain more than that. The last time he'd been in her room she'd begun to tell him about a visit to Paris and then Florence which she'd made with her father.

Something stirred now in his memory but wouldn't come to the front. 'Do you know who painted this?' he asked. The woman shook her head. 'Where did you get it?' She seemed evasive, shrugged, said she couldn't remember, maybe her dad had picked it up somewhere – he had a cart, people gave him things. It had been in his shed for years and now he'd passed on she'd been left to clear everything out. He could have it for sixpence. The frame might be of some use.

She didn't have a bag, but she wrapped it for him in a piece of brown paper and obligingly tied it with string, making a little loop for him to hold it by. He thanked her profusely, feeling suddenly more cheerful, and gave her a shilling instead of sixpence. She was right, the frame might fit one of Stella's own canvases if she didn't care for the painting. It was a good-quality frame, dirty but easily cleaned. Shame he couldn't clean it before giving it to her, but all he had to do it with was a handkerchief. It occurred to him that he might say he had bought it in an art gallery but she would know he couldn't possibly have had time. He would have to tell the truth. Strange how telling the truth so often seemed unappealing these days. His brain was forever tempting him to embroider and enlarge, to make up stories where there were none. It wasn't that he sought to make drama out of the prosaic – quite the contrary. To have bought the little picture in an art gallery would have been ordinary, normal, whereas to find it among a heap of rubbish in a street market was, by contrast, exciting.

Paddington Station was chaotic and he had trouble making his way to the right platform. There was a group of people bang in the centre with great piles of luggage surrounding them and he had to step carefully over suitcases and cardboard boxes. The people were foreign. At first, all he registered was that they were not speaking English, and then he realised they were German. They were poor-looking people, not in the least threatening, their features drawn, their attitude one of exhaustion, but he started to sweat and had to stop to take deep breaths to steady himself. He remembered the Gare de Montparnasse, and lying on the stretcher, barely able to move, and the small, slight woman in black, wearing a hat with a green ribbon in it, who had bent over him and asked if he wanted water. He'd said yes, and she'd turned and asked, in French, one of the orderlies to pass her a beaker of water. He'd wondered what she was doing there. She didn't look like a nurse. No, she'd said, she was an artist, she lived in Paris, though she was Welsh. She had calmed him for a moment. Amid all the hubbub and confusion she was quiet. She'd touched his cheek lightly with her hand before she moved on.

The train was half-empty. He settled himself comfortably and unwrapped the painting, propping it up on the seat opposite so that he could study it. Stella would see things in it which he could not. He was used to that. She was always explaining to him what paintings were 'about' and he hardly bothered any more challenging her interpretations, though often he considered she spoke absolute twaddle. This particular painting would be a test. What did he think it was 'about'? Nothing much. It was a painting of a corner of a room, an attic room, with a small table and a wickerwork chair in it. No people, though he realised that the flowers on the table and the coat and parasol on the chair indicated a human presence, a woman probably. 'What does it *say* to you?' Stella was always asking him in that affected way she had where art was concerned. He didn't think it 'said' anything. It was restful, quiet, calm, that was all. If it said anything, it was speaking in whispers which he couldn't hear. Once the train passed Plymouth, he fell asleep. Not properly asleep, but into a doze. This was happening a lot lately. He didn't sleep well at night but instead went into a state of suspended animation which was not at all restful. He'd been like that in hospital, in France, always hazily aware of what was going on around him without being able to respond to anything they said to him. A nurse would ask if he were awake and he would be unable to reply that yes, he was, and in pain. She would pass on, convinced he was out for the count. It was how he imagined it would be to have had an anaesthetic which had only half-worked, leaving him conscious only to a dangerously limited extent. No good going to a doctor about it. He had too many other reasons to seek medical advice, all of them much more pressing.

The light in the carriage was now very dim. Opening his eyes, fighting against his feelings of lethargy, he found himself staring again at the painting. He could hardly make it out. It was just a matter of shadows, the curtained window now the only light patch. He'd never lived in an attic. The cottage had one, but it was tiny and they used it to store cases and suchlike. Stella intended to clear it out and turn it into another bedroom, but she hadn't got round to it, and he himself had seen no need to do so. What did she want another bedroom for? There were two, one each, and they had no children.

It was dark when he got off the train, deeply dark, no moon, no stars. Walking home, the painting under his arm, he felt pleased with himself.

★

Stella thought the rooms in the cottage were too small, a succession of three rooms leading from one to another. She longed to knock down walls and make a space in which she could move and breathe easily, but it was impossible to contemplate – these walls were almost as thick as the solid exterior walls. All she'd been able to do was get Alan to lift off the connecting doors, leaving each room open, so that at least from one corridor-like end to another there was now a sense of distance. And she'd put down a single dark-green runner, going the whole length of the stone floor. But she still felt confined. Only in her studio, the glorified shed, her hut in the garden, did she feel comfortable. It was an ugly hut but inside its flimsy walls the room was large and square and there was plenty of light from the windows all around.

But in the winter, it was too cold to work in it for long. Alan had fixed up a paraffin heater, and she wore thick jerseys and always had a scarf knotted round her neck, but eventually the cold would numb her hands. Today, though, it was summer, but she had worked in the cottage itself since Alan was not there to distract her. It wasn't that he was noisy – he was a quiet man – but that his very presence broke her concentration. Even when she could not see him, she could somehow feel him there.

She wished he could get a job that would take him out of the cottage in a regular way, a nine-to-five job, but there was no sign of that yet. He wasn't well enough. The doctor provided him with certificate after certificate, attesting to his poor health, and now of course there was the new worry, his eyesight. But she'd made her mind up: if he was going to lose his sight, as he feared, she was going to insist that they left this cottage. They would not be thrown together so absolutely. She envisaged a modern house with two rooms either side of a wide hall, his on one side, hers on the other, and some common ground at the back. He would be upset, loving the cottage as he did, but she would not care. It looked pretty from the outside, and its situation on the headland above Charlestown harbour was attractive, but once inside she felt stifled. She had said nothing to Alan at the time, not wanting to hurt him when he had been hurt quite enough. They were near the sea and she had told herself that was what she wanted.

Throughout the war, when she was living so far from the sea, she had yearned for the sight of it and vowed she would never move from the coast again. She walked most days on the beach here benefiting from the sea air and the invigorating winds. Place mattered in the end. She'd felt disorientated and adrift during her years in London.

She had been painting all day. The moment Alan had departed she set up her still life – a jug, flowers in it, a plate alongside with a single red apple on the edge. They were positioned on a small table underneath the window, a round occasional table covered with a piece of green silk. The jug, a milk jug which held a pint and a half, was white, the flowers – roses – pink and white, the pink blooms almost fully opened, the white ones still in bud. The plate was green, but a paler green than the cloth. The light coming through the leaded window was not strong but she wanted just

162

that faint touch of light. She painted in water-colours, though oils were her preferred medium, because they were easier to manage in the cottage and because this still life was meant to be quick and delicate. The result was better than she had expected. She'd caught the fragility of the pink petals about to fall, the tight strength of the white unopened flowers, the roundness of the apple. Eight hours' work and something to show for it. Maybe it would sell, if she framed it.

She'd given herself a year to see if she could make even a slender living out of painting, a year as a reward for getting through the war. Alan had encouraged her. He had his pension, he could support them, and he had bought this cottage, right away from it all, out of money left to him by his parents. But in that first year after the war was over, she had made no money and spent a good deal. The hut had cost money, humble though it was, and so had all the materials she needed: the easel and paints, and canvases and paper. Alan had said not to worry, she shouldn't expect success in a year. So a second year went by, in which she sold two paintings. She'd thought it might be the beginning of some modest success but it hadn't proved to be so. Alan said it didn't matter, but it mattered to her. Not the success itself but the encouragement it would have provided. She needed it: she had so little confidence, untrained as she was.

She heard him coming along the track leading from the road. He was whistling. She went to the door and opened it, and stood in the darkness waiting, hearing his whistling, hearing his feet crunch the stones beneath them. There was a hint of rain in the wind, soft gusts blowing into her face, and far off at sea the sound of a ship's horn. He stopped a few feet away from her and stared. She glanced behind her, to see what he might be looking at, and then felt his arms round her. 'Your hair,' he whispered, 'it looked on fire . . . with the light, behind.' His coat smelled of smoke and she had a sudden image of all the crowds he'd passed through during his day, their smells absorbed by the jacket he wore. 'Take your coat off,' she said, and helped him. It dropped to the floor and he would not let her pick it up. First, he had to embrace and kiss her, hugging her to him fiercely. All she did was yield, but it was enough. 'So?' she said, when at last they were sitting down. 'Good news, yes?'

'Good news,' he said, and repeated what they'd said at Moorfields. 'Nothing to worry about,' he finished. 'And look, I've brought you a present, to celebrate.'

She was surprised by the brown paper package. And then she felt bewildered. 'What is it?' she asked, stupidly. 'A painting. I thought you might like it, or if you don't, you could use the frame for one of your own.' Slowly, she took the wrapping off, and stared. It was so unusual, so odd of Alan to have been attracted to such a quiet picture. 'Well?' he asked. She went on staring, holding the painting first at arm's length and then closer. She asked him where he had got it, and listened carefully while he related his story, adding to it his theories about where the little painting had come from. 'The frame is expensive,' he said. 'Whoever framed it didn't paint it, I bet.' 'The frame is wrong,' she said, 'all wrong,' and she began to turn it over to remove it. Once the canvas was in her hands, she felt relieved – it was like taking off an ornate dress and finding a simple petticoat underneath, so pure in its cotton simplicity and lack of adornment. 'Thank you,' she said.

Alan was happy. This was such a rare event that it confused her. She knew how to comfort him when he was sad or in pain, she even knew how to lift his spirits a little when he was depressed, as he often was, but Alan happy was such a rare occurrence it was hard to adapt to. She suddenly saw him as he must have been before the war – carefree, eager, optimistic. Even the burn did not look so ugly, with his smile pushing it to one side and his suddenly bright eyes catching attention instead. He seemed no longer a damaged man and she no longer felt like his nurse. He wouldn't let her make him something to eat but insisted on going into the kitchen and banging about making them both scrambled eggs and toast. The toast was burned and the eggs overscrambled, but they were presented with a flourish and eaten with relish. Then he opened a precious bottle of malt whisky and they drank some of it in front of the fire.

How, she wondered, as she often did, had Alan and she ever come together?

★

The sun streamed through the windows of her hut, lighting up every dancing speck of dust as Stella swept the floor. She stopped to admire the swirling patterns in the air. The door was open while she cleaned and she could see the white horses riding on the sea. She was not going to try to paint today. Later she would walk with Alan, if he decided his leg was up to it. Her water-colour of the day before, her still life, was propped up on a chair. She was going to frame it herself, in a narrow, plain wooden frame, and then take it down to the pottery, to Conrad Jenkinson, who might sell it for her. He sold his own pots there and let other people display their artistic efforts at no charge. (It was he who had sold Stella's two paintings last year.) Conrad knew real artists, he was a friend of Dod Proctor, and would not have let her show her paintings in his place if they had been embarrassingly bad (or so Stella told herself).

There was nothing hanging on the hut's walls, which were not much thicker than plywood and shook alarmingly in any strong wind, but at one end Alan had built a broad shelf, right across, and here she displayed her work when it was finished until she decided whether it was worth taking to Conrad. She had four awaiting judgement, as well as the latest still life. Cleaning the shelf first, she put Alan's present up with the other paintings, and stepped back. She felt herself blushing, a slow heat spreading through her, and put her hands up to her face, unable to understand what was causing her discomfort. Slowly, her eyes went from left to right and back again, and each time she stopped at Alan's offering. Something was there, she could sense it. Something that made her own work instantly brash. Worse than that – shallow, empty, flat. There was no meaning in what she had done, no feeling. In despair, she rushed forward and laid her pictures face down and then retreated again to look at the unknown artist's work. To her relief, it did not look so powerful – it was the contrast with her own that had made it so dominant.

165

She longed to dash off and show it to Conrad, but there was Alan to think about. The day was dedicated to him, and he would be up by now. Quickly, she finished the floor and closed the door on the newly clean and tidy hut. Leaving it, she always felt reluctant, whether she had been working well or not. It was her place. Alan never came in unless invited, and then he seemed uncomfortable. Strange, she thought, how a room, and in this case just a makeshift room, could take on an atmosphere. There was little in it that was purely personal except for her paintings, no belongings or furnishings that reflected her own personality, and yet the hut felt like hers. It *was* her.

She said this to Alan as they set off on the jagged cliff path. 'How can a hut be me?' she wondered aloud.

'It isn't,' he said, 'you just like to think it is. Rooms aren't people. Anyone could walk into your hut and make it their own.'

'Then why do I feel it is me?'

'You're a romantic, you like the idea of it.' He stopped to pick up a stone and hurl it down to the sea. There was no splash that they could hear.

'Well then, why do I like the idea of it? What does it say about me that I want to believe the inside of a wooden hut is me?'

'You want something inanimate to belong to you. It's the thrill of ownership.'

'You're not serious!'

'No, I'm not. You are. I'm humouring you, can't you tell?' He was laughing, but she felt annoyed.

'Don't humour me, then. I don't like it. I'm trying to understand myself, and you're mocking me.'

'Oh, Stella, really.'

'I am. I want to sort myself out.'

'What on earth is there to sort? You're thirty years old, beautiful, healthy, loved by me, an artist . . .'

'But am I an artist?'

'So you don't question the rest?'

'I can't question being thirty and healthy and to say I'm beautiful is too silly.'

'You *are* beautiful, and loved. How can you ignore those facts?'

'I'm only beautiful to you.'

'Isn't that all that matters?'

'Alan, don't. You keep teasing me, don't.'

'I'm not teasing you. Look at me.' He stopped again, and turned her to face him, and held her face between his hands and stared into her eyes. 'You-are-beautiful,' he said, slowly, 'and-I-love-you. There. Is that teasing?'

She broke away, and walked ahead. The path dipped alarm-ingly, running very near the edge. They would have had to go in single file for this bit anyway. She could hear Alan behind her, not able to move so rapidly, and on the steep section ahead coming out of the dip he would be slower still. It was stupid and ungrateful to feel upset, she knew that. Alan would never let her try to trace why she always felt disorientated and anxious about where she was and what was going to happen. He just said it was normal, that everyone who'd gone through the war, as he and she had, felt the same – unsettled, suspicious. But she felt it was some-thing to do with her life before the war. She had never felt safe since she'd left Tenby. Alan wouldn't let her explore that. He hated her to dwell on her life before she was with him – it was as though he were jealous of it. She'd wanted to take him to Tenby, to show him her childhood haunts, but he refused to go with her, and would not come and meet her mother who still lived in Victoria Street. The past, her past, was to be a closed book, because he wanted to blot out his own past, the war and what it had done to him. She wanted to talk about Emlyn, too, but Alan couldn't even bear the sound of his name. She wanted to confess her shameful envy of Emlyn, of how she was consumed with jealousy, burning and horrible, when he went off to London, to paint. It was only twelve years ago but it seemed like a century. Emlyn's talent was so obvious that she'd known hers was not in the same league, but still, she hoped and longed for the same opportunity. They had had one year together in London, when she'd followed him and was nursing at St Bart's, the year before the war started, and then it was all over. Alan knew she was a widow, but he preferred to ignore the fact of her marriage entirely. In the same way, he rejected her own curiosity about his life before the war. She knew there had been someone else, but that was all. 'It is a New Year,' Alan had said at midnight on 31st December, 'and a new decade. Here's to the future. The past is not worth remembering.' But she wanted to remember it. Sometimes she wondered if her urge to paint was an act of remembrance, of Emlyn, of trying to hang on, however pathetically, to what he had been.

At the top of the incline, she sat down and waited, facing out to sea. It stretched, now sullen and grey, to the horizon, meeting a sky furiously busy with scudding clouds pushing across it. The early morning sun had almost gone, only flashes of it appearing hurriedly from behind clouds which grew bigger and darker every minute. The wind was coming from the west and would bring rain soon. They should go back. Alan would never manage to get round the headland. But he was stubborn. If she said that the path was proving too difficult and that they were going to get caught in the rain, he would insist on continuing. Turning back had to be his decision, and she would have to be cunning and help him make it.

She remembered seeing him for the first time in Netley's Royal Victoria Hospital. She should not have been in the main building at all – her place was in the Welsh hospital, a large hut in the grounds holding 200 beds – but she had been sent over to ask for some extra pillows. She was lost, totally confused by the crowded, enormously wide and long corridors, not knowing which way she should go. The light was poor – all the lights were covered in brown paper shades – and she could hardly get past the iron bedsteads now in the corridors as well as the wards. She'd come to a halt, wondering whom she could ask for directions, and something had made her look up. There was a landing above, and a man standing on it, poised to come down the stairs. He was on crutches, and as she watched she guessed what would happen. When the man fell she was already halfway up the staircase and reached him in time to stop his falling the full length. She bent over him, soothing him, telling him to lie still and she would get help. He didn't speak, but out of the corner of his right eye tears leaked onto the horrific burn covering his cheek. It had no dressing, and she could see it was as healed as it ever would be. Pity was what she felt. It was what all the nurses felt, all the time, pity, exhausting pity, the sort that drained them. Some of the soldiers hated it. Sympathy, concern, interest, yes – but not pity. It diminished them, made them feel less like men. But after the pity, when Alan had been carried back to the ward and she had gone to check he was recovered from his fall, pity was followed by admiration. He brushed aside her solicitous enquiries. 'My own stupid fault,' he said. That had been the beginning.

She made a point of smiling at him as he reached her so that he would not think she was offended by his dismissal of her wish to talk about herself. But still he asked if he was forgiven now, as he dropped down beside her.

'Bloody leg,' he sighed.

'It does well,' she said, patting the leg lightly on the knee, 'when you think what the poor old limb has been through.'

'Don't tell me that at least I've got a leg to moan about.'

'I wasn't going to, I wouldn't be so crass.'

'Of course you wouldn't, nurse.'

'Look at those clouds.'

'Rain.'

'Will we shelter, or go on?'

'Or go back?'

'If you like. We won't get so wet then.'

'Go slowly, though. I'm not ready yet.'

She waited with him, reclining on her side, chewing a piece of grass and looking at him, but he didn't return her gaze. He was looking out to sea, his chest rising and falling as he recovered his breath. 'You are tying yourself to an invalid,' her mother had said, though she had never met him. 'It's one thing working as a nurse, it's another having to take your work home with you.' She wasn't nursing any more anyway. She'd given it up, the moment the war ended, and her mother was scandalised. 'All that training, all that good you could do.' But Stella hadn't been able to throw off the knowledge she had. She was watching Alan now as a nurse, calculating what he was suffering, wondering if there was something she could do about it. When he began to get up, she helped him, and he said again, 'Thank you, nurse.'

'Don't call me that,' she said.

'All right, thank you, artist.'

'Alan!'

'Sorry.'

'I'm not an artist, you know that.'

'Then what, who, is an artist? Someone who draws, paints, no? So you are an artist, good, bad, or indifferent.'

'No. I play, I dabble, I try.'

'You play, dabble and try all day long, then. That sounds like an artist to me.'

'It's embarrassing. I feel a fraud.'

'I'm a fraud myself, I don't find the term insulting.'

She was silent. They'd reached the broader path, where they could walk together, but she was still ahead. She knew what he meant: he considered himself a fraud as a man. It was best not to pick up on that. No good assuring him that as far as she was concerned he was a man and that she loved him as he was. Hadn't she shown it? Hadn't they lived together happily these two years, ever since the war ended? Never once had his being 'a fraud' mattered. They had what they had, and it was enough. If she had wanted a child she could have had one with Emlyn.

Alan went to lie down when they reached home. She went to her hut. When she opened the door, the little painting greeted her and once more a strange yearning filled her for something unobtainable.

II

SHE CHOSE to walk, though her paintings would have fitted into the basket on the front of her bicycle. It was a long way, all of three miles, but walking calmed her. She wanted to arrive relaxed and betray no signs of the agitation she felt. Because of course it was wicked, what she proposed to do, and most likely she wouldn't be able to carry it off.

The pottery was at the top of a hill, up a track similar to their own leading from the road. Above it, to the west, loomed the tall ruined engine house of the Polgooth mine, which always made her shiver. She had to skirt the little town of St Austell to get to the pottery and the bag weighed heavier on the pavements than it seemed to on the grassy paths. But once she was clear of the town, she enjoyed the walk and took her time over it, sorting out in her head as she went along what she was going to say. Conrad Jenkinson was kind. If he suspected a lie, he would not accuse her outright. He would smile, and look at her searchingly, and she would have to be bold and hold his gaze. Alan thought Conrad (whom he had never actually met) liked her a little too much by the sound of it, and was, because of this 'liking' (said with sarcastic emphasis), a little too kind. But she had to believe he was wrong. Alan even suspected that Conrad had not sold her paintings at all but had bought them himself, to be 'kind' and make her grateful. She hated him when he suggested this, and said so, and then he had apologised and said he was just jealous.

The Jenkinsons, she knew, had been away. The last time she'd called, the girl who helped Mrs Jenkinson told her that they had gone to France and she didn't know when they would be back. She was keeping an eye on the place for them. But that had been some weeks ago and Stella was sure they must have returned by now. As she approached the pottery, she wondered what on earth the Jenkinsons had gone to France for, and how they'd managed to go at all.

★

Conrad had not wanted to go to France but Ginny, his wife, longed to go and look at the house she'd suddenly inherited. She'd been there once, when she was five or six, she thought, and had only vague memories of the house being near a much bigger building, a *château* with a tower and a round turret on the top which convinced her that the Sleeping Beauty must be inside. She had no idea, though, of its precise location. Conrad got a map out and they eventually found it, on the northern coast of Brittany, some kilometres from Lamballe. Ginny wanted to go and look at it immediately and they talked, wild talk, of leaving Cornwall and going to live there permanently.

Getting there, with two small boys, was hard, and when finally, exhausted, they reached Pléneuf they had trouble, in the dark, finding the house, and then gaining entry. There was a wind howling round it that night and the sea, very close by, was crashing furiously against rocks. But then, in the morning, when the wind had died down and the sun dazzled them as it came through the uncurtained windows, they were charmed. The house was dusty and neglected but it hardly mattered – they spent all day on the beach. There were rough paths from the house leading to the beach, where black rocks were strewn all along it. The light was beautiful. They found the *château* Ginny had remembered, the Château Vauclair, and it was as mysterious as she had recalled. The iron gate was locked and they could see that the gardens inside were overgrown and when they asked about the place in the village they were told it was for sale. There was a woman interested, it was said, an artist from Paris. She was staying with friends in a cottage nearby and had been to look at it.

Conrad wondered if he might have seen her, a small, very thin woman dressed in a blue serge coat and skirt, walking away from the *château* and carrying what he recognised as a sketch pad. He followed her, not quite knowing why. She went into the church and sat in front of the shrine to St Thérèse of Lisieux, and began to draw. He wanted to see what she produced but did not dare disturb her privacy and came out again, quickly, into the sunshine. He told Ginny about her and she gave him a sharp look. 'She wasn't young,' he said, though he hadn't seen her face. 'I was only curious because of her sketch pad.' Ginny envied the woman. She herself would like to be sitting quietly in church drawing instead of tied to the children. Conrad had told her she could go and draw any time she liked, but she did not trust him to watch the boys, especially Sam. He would let them drown, she was sure.

They put her uncle's house up for sale. It was a pity, but they needed the money and could not afford to own and maintain a house in Brittany. Living there no longer seemed an option. Establishing another pottery would be too difficult and then there was the language problem. It was an adventure that was over. After a month, Conrad was homesick. He felt disorientated, and he wanted to work; idleness did not suit him. It was Ginny who would have liked to stay. She could, she felt, have been happy there, starting again.

*

To her relief, Stella saw signs of life at the pottery. The two small boys were running up and down the path that led to it, trying to fly a kite and yelling at each other. She found Conrad on his own, emptying his kiln. He was a big man, bearded, beside him she always felt smaller than she was, more fragile. Sometimes, standing beside him, she imagined him picking her up with ease and the idea made her dizzy. Alan, when she had described Conrad to him, accused her of being attracted to him – 'Any girl would be, if he's as tall and strong as you say' – but she truly believed she was not, or not in the way he implied. And yet there was some kind of attraction: she did feel she was held within a powerful magnetic field when she visited him, but then she was sure everyone did. Conrad *was* powerful. Physically powerful, mentally powerful, able to radiate energy all around him. People locally spoke of him with awe and talked of genius and wondered how he came to be where he was, apparently unrecognised by the world. They expected fame to come for him at any time and then he would leave them. Stella hardly knew him; she was just an amateur artist who turned up from time to time, timidly showing her paintings to him and asking his opinion. He had only recently asked what the star she signed her paintings with signified. He had never asked her any personal questions, and, as far as she was aware, didn't know where she lived or with whom. She knew far more about him, just from the gossip around the town. He was reputed to be 'a ladies' man'.

He had his back to her, so she coughed nervously, and he turned round at once. He nodded. Encouraged, she put the bag down, leaning it against the wall. 'I've something to show you,' she said, 'it's different, I think, I hope.' She'd thought long and hard about how to do this, whether to show him the others first, or whether to show none of her work; whether to preface the showing with an explanation, or whether to say nothing. Deceit was involved either way. She wanted it over quickly, but he offered her tea, and she found herself accepting. He had a little iron stove in his studio, and now he opened its door, raked up the coals, and put a kettle on top. 'Takes a while,' he said. Two mugs appeared, a tin with tea in it and a brown teapot. Whistling, he stood staring at the kettle admiringly, as though it were a work of art, and she stared too.

Time, she had noticed, never seemed to matter to Conrad. He was always vague about judging it. His 'I'll be with you in a minute' could take an hour. But finally the kettle bounced with boiling water, the tea was made (neither milk nor sugar offered) and they sat companionably on the only two stools. The tea was so hot she couldn't even begin to sip it but sat nursing the mug in her hands while Conrad alternately blew on his and gulped. Carefully, she put the scalding tea down. 'Can I show you?' she asked. 'Of course. Show away.' The decision, now that the time had come, seemed made for her – absurd to have imagined she could show him the others. Reaching into the bag, she found the painting she wanted and unwrapped it. 'There,' she said, holding it up in front of her. Her heart was thudding. She could hardly bear to look at him. She supposed she was looking for a dramatic reaction, but none came. Conrad had put his tea down, and sat with his hands on his knees, studying the painting held up before him with interest but no great amazement. 'Good,' he said, finally, nodding his head. 'Can I see it?' and he held out his hands.

She gave it to him, and watched him as he scrutinised it. 'Cleverly done,' he murmured, and then, 'I wonder, is it applied in layers, the paint?' It was a question. She ought to reply that she didn't know, how could she when she hadn't painted it, but she was silent, unable to give up her hope that he would believe she had painted it. He hadn't said, 'Did *you* apply the paint in layers?' but nor had he said anything definite to show he knew she had not, and could not have done. 'You've never brought me anything like this before,' he said, and seemed to wait. 'Can you sell it, do you think?' she blurted out. He smiled. 'Oh yes, I can sell it.' 'How much for, do you think?' She hated herself for the eagerness in her voice. He shrugged his shoulders, raised his eyebrows. 'Who knows?' he said. 'It depends who comes along, who will be discerning enough to buy it for what it is worth. Maybe as much as £5.' He was still holding the painting, peering at it closely, but now Stella took it from him in one hurried movement, almost snatching it. 'Thank you,' she said, 'but it is not for sale. I don't wish to sell it.' She turned and picked up the wrapping paper and wrapped the painting again and put it back in the bag. 'And the others?' Conrad asked, indicating the bag, which he could see was full. 'Oh, the others,' Stella said, 'don't bother with the others.'

'But you've brought them, at least let me see them.'

Reluctantly, she took them out and handed them to him, leaving him to unwrap them himself. 'Pretty,' he said, 'you're coming on. These will sell, if you want to sell them.'

'Yes, I do, please, if possible.'

He was watching her face intently, she could see. 'And the other, the corner of the room? What will you do with it?'

'Keep it.' There didn't seem any point any more in pretending. 'It was a present.' She was blushing, and he would know why. 'I just wanted to see what you thought,' she said. 'I wasn't really

175

pretending I'd painted it. I knew you'd know I couldn't have done.'

'Being trained shows,' Conrad said. 'Technique tells.'

'Of course.'

'Have you ever thought of . . .'

'All the time. But it's never been possible.'

'Why not?'

'Money, opportunity.'

'Does painting make you happy?'

'Not really. Yes. Sometimes. But I know I'm playing, no more. There's nothing in these but playing, and trying. It frustrates me. I can't get into them what I want.'

'Which is?'

'Oh . . .' She was embarrassed. Conrad hadn't moved, was sitting in exactly the same position, scrutinising her, making her move about, backwards and forwards, in front of him as though rehearsing a part in a play.

'What do you want to get into your work?'

'That's the point, it isn't work, it's – I don't know what to call it.' Suddenly, she snatched the other painting from the bag and tore off the loose wrapping and held it up again. 'There,' she said, 'there's the difference, this *says* something!'

'But how do you know that it didn't fill its artist with the same sort of despair that you feel about your painting?'

'What?' She was startled.

'How do you know this wasn't discarded as a failure?'

'It couldn't have been.'

'Why not?'

'It's perfect.'

'To you, maybe. Not necessarily to the person who painted it.' Conrad got up at last and went through to the other part of his studio where he stored his finished pots. He returned carrying a bowl, a large shallow bowl. 'Look at this,' he said. 'What do you think?'

'It's beautiful,' Stella said. 'Perfect.'

'But not to me,' Conrad said. 'It isn't perfect. I thought it was going to be, but it isn't. The curve is a couple of millimetres too wide, the glaze is fractionally the wrong shade.'

'Nobody else will see that.'

'Probably not. I'll sell it easily. But I'll be glad to see it go because to me it's a failure. We all do it, striving, aiming high and falling low.'

'But it isn't the same for people like me. You're a real artist, I'm not. It's no good trying to persuade me you feel the same as I do. You know the difference.' She had begun to cry and yet hardly knew what she was crying about. 'Oh, I'm being ridiculous,' she sobbed. 'I'm sorry, I don't know what on earth is the matter with me. I must go.'

For a moment, she thought he was going to embrace her, but he only picked up the bag and put the painting back inside and handed it to her. She didn't look at him, dreading the pity, or maybe the exasperation, she would see in his eyes. She would never be able to come again – he would have her down as a silly little fool who entertained delusions of grandeur. From the beginning, his kindness had been just that; he'd never thought what she produced for him to sell was anything but chocolate-box stuff. She didn't know how she had ever had the nerve to show it to him. 'Thank you,' she said, more composed. 'I won't bother you again.'

'That would be a pity.'

She gave a derisive little laugh. 'Oh, I'm sure it would,' she said, 'you must think I'm quite mad.'

'Not mad, no. Distressed. I'm not sure why. Is it really about art? I don't think so, somehow.'

'Goodbye. Thank you. Sorry.' And she was gone.

★

Trying to describe the little painting later was hard. Conrad struggled to recall every detail of it, but he knew the details were not what mattered. The pine table, the wickerwork chair, were almost standard features of so many paintings, and the attic itself was a cliché of the artistic way of life. It was, he told his wife Ginny, more the atmosphere that had captured him. There had been an air of mystery in spite of the obvious props, a feeling that there was a life outside the painting which was being hinted at. Time, he said, seemed to be suspended, frozen almost, but why that should feel so significant he did not know. He wished he could show the painting to her, see if she could fathom the emotion he had felt there. Already, he was forgetting the nature of the bleached palette used, and the exact way in which the tiny brush-strokes – maybe a brush as fine as oo – had been applied. 'There was something vulnerable there,' he said. 'It was a calm, tranquil scene but there was something unsettling about it.'

'Same as that young woman,' Ginny commented, 'Stella, isn't it? The woman who brought it?'

Conrad nodded. He didn't really want to think about Stella.

'What's wrong with her?'

'Haven't the faintest idea. I hardly know her, you know that.'

'She's pretty but pathetic.'

'Yes, she is.'

They left it at that.

★

Stella didn't go straight home. She hung around in the town for an hour, lurking in Holy Trinity Church, looking aimlessly in shop-windows, reading the newspapers in the library. She bought an orange to eat. Passing the station, she went and sat on a bench, as though waiting for a train, and ate the orange, putting the peel neatly in her bag. She could get on a train, any train, see where it would take her, but if she didn't go home soon, Alan would start to worry. Alan, Alan, Alan. She was always putting him first. When she thought of him it was always as poor Alan, the man who had suffered so much and to whom she was devoted. But more and more this devotion made her resentful – she was devoted, but didn't want to be. Devotion was not love. What was love, then? Angrily, she got up from the bench as a train came in, and left the station. She'd tricked herself. Tricked herself twice. Tricked herself into believing that tenderness and compassion and admiration all swept into one equalled love. Tricked herself into thinking she could be an artist when she had neither the talent nor the dedication. What was it she had said to Conrad? That she couldn't get into her paintings what she was feeling. How pretentious. How lucky she couldn't get her feelings into them, because they were ugly, murderous. She didn't want to be with Alan. She didn't even want to be in Cornwall.

There, she'd said it to herself. The relief was instant but didn't last long. Leaving Alan was impossible, both emotionally and practically. He would never survive her desertion. He would kill himself. He'd said this often enough, and he'd meant it. And she had no money and nowhere to go. Except home, to her mother, to Tenby. What a mess she'd got herself into and must now get herself out of. Bit by bit. Start nursing again, earn money. Alan would accept that. All she needed to do was confess that she had deluded herself. Now and again she might like to try her hand at painting but two years of doing nothing else had shown her there was no real satisfaction there, only sometimes a fleeting pleasure. He'd understand that, maybe be glad. But he wouldn't like her returning to nursing. It would take her away from him, and he would worry that she might meet someone just as she had met him, and then worry some more that this would be a 'real' man.

Walking home, she allowed that he might very well be right. Looking after people was what she had always done. Perhaps what she needed was the life hinted at in the painting she was carrying home – a serene life, selfish, untroubled by having to consider others, and without passion. But then there was no passion in her life as it was. If, as Alan feared, a 'real' man were to come into her life, he would bring passion. What effect this would have on her she no longer knew. Her body felt dead. Did it need sex to make it feel alive? It was a frightening thought which she wanted to reject. No sex since Emlyn was killed. Years of nothing. But that was not true – some of those years had been full of love, Alan's love. He had held her tight, embraced her fiercely, put into his caresses and kisses his overpowering love for her but there had been no consummation of their love. She felt, all the time, on the brink of achieving an ecstasy and relief that never arrived, and it was painful. But she would never tell him so: she was ashamed of her longing, and that it should matter. Love, she had *love*.

He was waiting for her at the end of the track, leaning on his stick. 'Thought I'd go for a walk,' he said, as though apologising. 'Didn't get far.'

'You should rest the leg today after yesterday.'

'The leg? Sounds as if it has nothing to do with me, *the* leg.'

'You know what I mean.'

'Indeed, I do. So? What did the great Conrad think?'

'I've no idea.'

'Haven't you been to him?'

'Yes. I've no idea what he thought.'

He sighed heavily. 'I'll rephrase it then: did you show him your paintings and did he agree to try to sell them?'

'Yes, and yes.'

'Well then, good. He liked them.'

She didn't reply. Often, they had this kind of tennis-match dialogue – she played the game knowingly just as Alan did and yet both of them professed to hate it. She let him limp behind her, not bothering to slow to his pace. There was an odd smell in the cottage which it took her a moment or two to identify. As Alan came in, she said, quite sharply, 'Embrocation does no good, you know that.'

'It does if you massage it into my knee.'

'Alan, it does not, it can't. And when *you* put it on you just rub your knee, you don't even massage it.'

'But you weren't here, and it was damned painful. Will you do it now? Please. I've been waiting for you to do it . . . I soon gave up trying myself.'

'Get on the table, then,' she said, curtly, 'but I've told you, it does no good. It's a waste of your time and mine.'

'*Time* we've got,' he said, almost in a whisper.

She warmed her hands at the fire first while he clambered onto the kitchen table, a stout old pine table, too big for their needs, but it had been there when they bought the cottage and they'd liked it. He'd taken his trousers off and lay in his shirt, the tails of it covering his thighs.

'Bend the knee up slightly,' she ordered, and then, when he lifted it too far, 'No, only slightly. You know how to do it.' He had his eyes closed, to her relief, and lay with his arms folded behind his head, forming a pillow. Slowly, she began the massage, putting all her weight behind the movement, kneading the flesh just above the knee and just below it. She didn't even know the proper procedure, it was simply a technique she'd made up, but Alan had absolute faith in its beneficial effect, and it did no harm. It did not, though, have the other effect, the one he wanted. She knew perfectly well what this massage was about, and what he hoped for. His leg was warm, the flesh round his injured knee surprisingly lumpy. She pressed all over with the palms of her hands, trying to rotate the muscle. He asked her to go higher, saying the worst of the pain was above the knee, but she knew he was lying. She would not do what he wanted her to do. She couldn't. After a mere five minutes she said, 'There. Enough.'

'Will you do my neck and my back now?'

'No.'

'Please?'

'No.'

'Why not?'

'I don't know how to do it properly, and I don't feel like doing it.'

'Why? Can't you bear to touch me?'

'Oh, for heaven's sake.'

'That's it, isn't it? You can't bear to touch me. I repel you.'

'Alan, stop it. You're being childish. I can't be bothered with this.'

'That's obvious. You can't be bothered with me, you mean.'

'Not when you're in this mood.'

'It's you who is in a mood.'

'All right, maybe I am, so leave me alone.'

'But I want to know what's put you in this sulk . . .'

'Sulk? I'm not sulking, I didn't say I was *sulking*.'

'That's what it looks like. You should see your face, the minute I saw you, your face, set in an absolute sulk. I thought maybe boss Conrad hadn't taken your paintings.'

'Boss Conrad? Whatever do you mean?'

'Well, he is your boss, in a way.'

'He certainly is not. I don't work for him. I never have done, I'm not his employee.'

'You'd like to work for him, though, wouldn't you?'

'No.'

'Fibber.'

'Alan, *stop it*! Or else I'm going into the hut and I'll stay there.'

She should say it now, tell him that she wasn't just going to her studio but that she was leaving altogether. It was so tempting. Into her head flashed an image of herself packing a bag and storming out to the station with Alan weeping and shouting in the background. She stood still, relishing the vision, and then collected herself. The room was very quiet. Alan hadn't got down from the table or put his trousers back on. How ludicrous he looked. She found herself smiling without wanting to do so, and all the old affection she had for him came rushing back. She went over to him and slapped his foot lightly. 'Come on,' she said, 'get down, get dressed. I'll make some lunch.' But he didn't move, didn't open his eyes. She saw the tears seeping out from under his closed eyelids. She took a deep breath. 'Alan,' she said, 'Alan,' and kissed him on the cheek. There was no response. Turning away again, she went into the pantry and began heating some soup she'd made. The silence seemed appalling, she couldn't bear it. Going back through the kitchen into the next room, she put a record on the gramophone, not caring what it was, and when the jazz notes began she felt better. The music filled the cottage and none of her movements could now be heard. She stirred the soup, cut some bread and got ready the bowls and spoons, and was busy. They would eat. This scene would end. They would carry on as normal – they always did. 'Ready,' she called, taking the soup through.

He still hadn't moved, but she saw that his cheeks were dry, the tears had stopped. 'Here,' she said, and put his bowl down on the table. 'It's going to be very difficult to eat lying down and with your eyes shut, but it's up to you.' She took her own soup and walked through the cottage and out of the door and perched on the garden wall. It wasn't warm enough to sit there, and she had taken her coat off, but she was not going to stay in the same room as Alan while he lay there. It felt freer outside, she was glad to be in the open air and ate with enjoyment. The strains of jazz floated outside and she found herself humming. She would have liked to dance. Another picture came into her head, of Alan coming to join her and making her dance with him, his leg improbably better. But she had never danced with him or ever seen him dance, and this image faded quickly. With enormous reluctance she went to take her empty bowl into the kitchen, dreading the sight of Alan still lying prone, the soup uneaten at his side. But he had gone. So had the soup. Relieved, she went to do the washing-up. He must be in the little living room, sitting beside the gramophone, the music soothing him. She would make him some tea and take it to him, and then she would go and lie down, exhausted.

★

Alan, opening the door, had no idea who the man standing there could be, though afterwards he realised he should have identified him instantly. Tall, broad-shouldered, muscular, Conrad was the sort of man Alan hated and envied, and he was barely polite. 'Yes?' he said, expecting to be asked where the road to St Austell lay, so when Conrad said good afternoon and might he speak to Stella, Alan was thrown. They knew nobody. Neither he nor Stella had made any friends. They kept themselves to themselves, spoke only to the postman and the shopkeepers. 'Stella?' he queried. 'Stella,' Conrad repeated, and then, 'I sell her paintings.'

'Oh,' said Alan, furious to have been so slow and stupid, 'do you indeed?'

'I'm Conrad, Conrad Jenkinson, from the pottery.'

'I see. Well, I'm afraid Stella is asleep.' It was three in the after-noon. 'She was tired.' They were still standing at the door, with

Alan trying to close it as much as possible behind him, so that his voice would not carry to Stella upstairs. 'Can I help?'

'You are?'

Alan frowned. 'Her husband,' he said, the lie coming easily because the pretence had gone on so long.

'Ah,' Conrad said, 'I didn't know she was married, sorry.'

'She doesn't wear a ring.'

'Doesn't she? I never noticed.'

'Rings irritate her skin,' Alan improvised, 'give her eczema.'

'Right. Well, if you could tell her I called, and if she'd like to drop in some time I might have some news for her.'

'What news?'

'I think I'd like to tell her, if you don't mind.'

'Why?'

'Why? Well, just that . . . well, I'd just like to tell her.'

'Is it personal?'

'Not really, no.'

'Well then, give me the message. I'll tell her. She'll want to know why you came.'

He was making the man dislike him, Alan could see that, any fool could. He was being hostile and unfriendly and rude, but he couldn't help it. It was how he felt, confronted with someone in such glowing health, face unmarked, legs strong, a fine specimen of manhood. Conrad Jenkinson was just as he'd feared. Thank God, Stella hadn't answered the door. She would have invited him in, made him tea, and it would have been unbearable watching them together. But now the visitor was turning away, an odd superior smile on his face.

'What's the message?' Alan said. 'What shall I tell her?'

There was no reply. Conrad Jenkinson was at the gate, bending to open it, carefully shutting it. His motor-bike was parked on the grass verge. He got it started, with a struggle, and slowly rode down the track.

Angry, Alan went back inside just as Stella came down the stairs, yawning, her hair dishevelled and her cheeks rosy with sleep. 'Was that someone at the door?'

'No.'

'But I heard you talking.'

'Oh, that, yes, someone was lost, man on a motor-bike, asked the way. You know they haven't put the signposts back yet.'

'The way to where?'

'St Austell, of course.'

More yawns, some stretching. 'I'm going for a walk, wake myself up.'

'I'll come.'

'But your leg, you said . . .'

'I know what I said. I'll come, unless you'd rather I didn't.' He saw her hesitate.

'You'll make the pain worse.'

'I can stand the pain.'

'No point, though, making it worse.'

'I want to walk with you. That's the point. Unless you don't want me, which wouldn't surprise me.'

'Don't start again, Alan.'

'Start what?'

She turned round from looking out of the window so abruptly that he almost jumped. Her eyes met his and he saw how furious she suddenly was. 'No,' she said, 'since you've asked, I do not want company on my walk, thank you. I'd prefer to walk on my own.'

'I don't blame you. No fun walking with a cripple. Cripples are a drag, can't swing along, can't . . .'

'I'm not listening.'

'Of course you aren't, you never do.'

'What? How dare you! I've listened to you ever since I met you. Listened and listened, and now I don't like what I'm hearing, I'm tired of it, I want to go for a walk alone.' She was rushing about, getting her coat, hurling it on, hunting for her scarf, pulling on boots. Any minute she would be gone.

'Your Conrad man came,' he said. She stopped, one boot on, one lying on the floor. She was waiting. 'Don't know what he wanted . . .' he said, and before she could ask, '. . . just you. He wanted you. Don't we all.'

'You lied.'

'Yes, I lied. And I said I was your husband, another lie.'

'What on earth for?'

'I didn't want him to think you were a kept woman.'

'Don't be so stupid.'

'I'm afraid I was. Stupid, that's me.'

Would she still go for a walk? He watched her. She resumed getting ready, but he could see how disturbed she was, more by his lies, he thought, than by the news that Conrad Jenkinson had been. The anger had gone out of her and she looked worn and sad. 'Stella . . .' he began, but she shook her head, and, opening the door, stepped out. Anxiously, he stood in the doorway, to see which way she was going to turn. She turned right, towards the cliff path, and not left, towards the pottery beyond the town. Relieved, he put his own coat on and collected his stick. His leg was much too painful to follow her but he couldn't bear to be inside, waiting. He would limp to the end of the track and sit on the tree stump there, and when she reached the highest point on the path he would briefly be able to see her in the far distance. When she returned, he would be properly contrite. She would see his shame, and understand.

III

CONRAD WISHED he had not gone to call on Stella. She hadn't been difficult to find, or at least her cottage hadn't – everyone seemed to know where the lovely redhead lived. He'd asked about her in the post office and immediately two other people in the queue there, as well as the postmaster, had piped up with her address. Odd, though, that gossip hadn't extended to telling him about her husband, but perhaps he hadn't given his informants a chance. He hadn't wanted to reveal why he wanted to find her. They would all think he was 'after' her, had designs on Stella. It would fit with what they knew of him, and there was nothing he could do about that. A reputation here was a reputation. Once gained, never shed.

But he had no designs on Stella. Thin, neurotic women did not tempt him. Thin she most certainly was, much too thin, and neurotic he'd judged her from the moment she turned up with her pathetic daubs, almost trembling with anxiety. He was not running an art gallery, fortunately, or he couldn't have afforded to display them – they would have damaged any reputation he hoped to have – but as it was there was no harm in tucking them away in the shop together with the cards Ginny stocked, and his reject pots. Someone with no artistic sensibility would buy them one day, he thought, and someone duly did. He'd been glad to see them go and had hoped there would be no more. She'd come by his place every now and again, flitting in and out nervously, and he'd smiled and nodded but left any talking to her. Ginny chatted to her occasionally but didn't find out much about her except that she'd been a nurse, a surprising piece of information – she didn't look like their idea of a nurse, neither calm nor capable-looking, and she wouldn't have inspired confidence.

There were plenty of people in Cornwall these days who were like Stella, people escaping London, wanting to put the war behind them and change their lives for the better. The war had made them think both that they ought to do it and that they had the courage and nerve. A big rethinking had gone on and as a result would-be artists and writers were everywhere, most of them heading for disillusionment. Conrad didn't resent their presence. Why should he? He wasn't one of them. He had been to art college and, since giving up painting, had long been established in his own pottery. He didn't fear newcomers and he didn't despise them either. Let them spread their wings, let them try to fly.

Stella would never fly. She was doomed to be for ever grounded, a poor little sparrow with clipped wings, hopping feverishly about looking for crumbs. How long would it take for her to realise she was no good? Not much longer, surely. She'd switched to still lifes from landscape and, though she had some feeling for composition and colour, her technique was hopeless. He hadn't felt he needed to tell her this. She hadn't asked his opinion, only if he would try to sell them. And then she'd produced that other painting. One look was enough. Never in a million years could she have painted it, so it was just as well she hadn't actually claimed to have done so. She'd pretended, though. She would have liked him to assume it was hers: the intention to deceive had been there. Where on earth had she got it from? After she'd taken it away, he hadn't been able to recall what she'd said, or indeed whether she'd told him anything at all about who had painted the picture. Ginny needed to see it. 'Buy it from her, if you liked it so much,' Ginny had said. 'Offer her a fiver, she'll be thrilled.'

So he'd gone to offer her a fiver. He had been going to say it was to be a birthday present for his wife, for Ginny, forty next week. He'd been going to say Ginny was an artist herself, she'd had her work exhibited at the NEAC in London, and he was sure she would love the little painting, it was her sort of thing. But then that strange man had come to the door, looking so ill and acting in such a hostile way, and he hadn't wanted to tell him why he had come to find Stella. There wouldn't have been any harm in it, but for some reason he had felt immediately secretive. He hadn't trusted Stella's husband: he'd been sure that if he had said he'd come to buy a painting from her, then her husband would have told him it was not for sale.

But this left the problem of how to get hold of Stella and deal only with her over the painting. Did her husband work? Could he demean himself further and return to the post office and enquire? The man had looked too ill to work. He must have been wounded. Probably a hero. Conrad was not a hero. He had not even served in the war. Tall and strong though he looked, he had failed his medical spectacularly. No one ever gave him a white feather in Cornwall but he'd awarded himself one many times though he had shown no cowardice and could not help his TB. Six months in a sanatorium turned out to be infinitely preferable to the same time in the trenches and, finally, TB cured (or so it was hoped, if not guaranteed) he was grateful. When the surviving soldiers returned to civilian life he'd felt awkward and worried about how he would be regarded but, beyond being called a lucky blighter, he had never been asked to account for how he'd spent the war years.

Clearly, Stella's husband – who had not, it occurred to Conrad, had the courtesy to give his name – had not been lucky. The burn on his face told one story, his frail appearance another. The man had every right to be bitter. He might be suspicious – Stella was lovely, even if thin and nervous. He would want to keep her to himself. Conrad wondered what Stella's husband knew about him. He must know about the pottery and Stella bringing her paintings. She must have told him about Ginny and the children and the whole set-up, but of course if he was a jealous man that would not necessarily allay his fears. It had been a mistake after all not to be straightforward with him.

There was nothing he could do now except wait for her to come round to the pottery again. Since he now had three of her still lifes on show she would come eventually to see if he had sold them. Maybe in a month, maybe six weeks, she'd appear, shy and diffident but wanting to know if he had had any success.

All this went through Conrad's head on his way back to the pottery. What he didn't expect to find when he got there later was Stella herself.

★

She had to go somewhere. Wandering along the cliff path would not do for long, though at first it helped to calm her. She would have to leave Alan, there was no other solution. If she didn't, scenes such as the one which had just driven her out of the cottage would be repeated and their misery would deepen. He wanted her to be someone she was not, a person happy to subjugate herself to his greater need. And it was entirely her own fault. She had led him to believe that she would be happy to care for him, to help him recover, content to while away the days, the weeks, the months, the years, amusing herself with her attempts to paint. When Emlyn was killed, there had been such a quietening, then, of all her senses. She had only wanted to be still, to drift, not to feel. She had thought painting would help.

There was another faint path that led away from the cliff path at its highest point. It was barely visible, but she had taken it a couple of times, without Alan, and it had led to a broad track that in turn wound its way past a rubbish tip to the road. She took this path now, slipping a bit on the stones, her dress catching on the bushes, but soon she was on the track and walking rapidly to the road. She had no idea where she was going except that she wanted to be as far from Alan as possible and away from the cottage as long as she could. There were places in St Austell she could go, but she found herself avoiding the town, and going up the hill. The pottery came into view before she had thought about it, and then it seemed so natural, to call in on Conrad. Even if he was not there, someone would be, some other human being to whom she could talk, though she couldn't imagine what kind of conversation might result from her confusion.

Ginny, Conrad's wife, was in the shop at the entrance to the pottery, doing something at the till. She looked up as Stella came in and said good afternoon, and Stella responded. Then she didn't know what to say or do. Ginny intimidated her. She was a large woman, as tall and strong-looking as her husband, with something of the Gypsy about her — the black, long hair, the tanned skin, the dark eyes. She wore flamboyant clothes, brightly coloured skirts down to the ground, and had bangles on both wrists and long earrings dangling from her ears. She was quite unlike any woman Stella had ever seen — voluptuous, dramatic, sure of herself. Helplessly, Stella turned away from the sight of her own pathetic paintings and examined some cups and saucers arranged in a row on a shelf. She might buy some — they were pretty, pale green, not too big — but then realised she had no money with her. Ginny, she knew, was watching her closely. Her hands shook as she lifted one of the cups and it clattered slightly when she replaced it on its saucer.

'Sorry,' she said.

'They're seconds, don't worry,' Ginny said.

'I like them. I've no money with me but next time I'll buy two.'

'Take them now, pay later. I'll wrap them for you.'

Before Stella could stop her, Ginny had lifted two cups and saucers and was wrapping them. 'Conrad isn't here,' she said. 'Did you want to see him?'

'No.' She said it too quickly, too abruptly.

'Sure?'

'Sure. I was just wandering about, really, aimlessly . . .'

'And you found your feet leading you here,' Ginny said.

Stella heard the edge of sarcasm in her voice, and flushed. 'Yes, as a matter of fact. I don't know why. I was . . .' and then she stopped. She couldn't begin to tell this woman, with whom she had nothing more than a nodding acquaintance, how desperate she felt.

'Where did you come from?' Ginny suddenly asked.

Startled by the odd question, Stella said, 'Southampton.'

'But your accent is Welsh, no?'

'Yes. Tenby, originally. Then London. Then the war, and I ended up at the hospital there.'

'Quite a change, here, then.'

'Yes. I'll be leaving soon, though.'

She couldn't think why she said that. It could only lead to more questions, the sort she had no answers for. Silently, she held out her hands for the parcel Ginny had made. They were still shaking. Ginny noticed and instead of handing the package over put it to one side and, taking hold of Stella's arm, led her to the chair beside the till and gently pushed her down onto it. 'You can tell me,' she said, 'I'm used to it, it doesn't worry me.'

'What?'

'Well, you're obviously in a state. It's about Conrad, isn't it, whatever you say. You're not pregnant, are you?'

Horrified, Stella gasped. 'No!' she kept saying, shaking her head violently. 'No! It is not about your husband! I hardly know him, I've never even spoken to him outside this place. You're quite wrong, how can you think . . . ?'

'So what's this about, why are you so distraught? Why did you come here?'

'I told you, I don't know. I'd nowhere to go and wanted to go somewhere, anywhere.' Stella took deep breaths and dabbed frantically at her eyes.

'Have you been ill-treated? Have you been thrown out?'

'No!'

'Then I give up. Sit a while, get yourself together. I don't mind. I'll go and make you a cup of tea. Relax, don't upset yourself any more, for God's sake. Do you smoke, would you like a cigarette as well? Wait there. I won't be long.'

But Stella had no intention of waiting. The humiliation was enough without having to be grateful for a cup of tea. She waited until Ginny had gone across the yard to her house and then she got up and went over to the door leading to the workshop where she knew there was another exit. There was a sink in the corner of it, and she stopped and splashed her face with cold water, wiping it dry with the sleeve of her coat. The door at the other end was bolted and she had trouble forcing the bolts back, but at length she managed it and was outside. But then the door would not close properly, and she panicked. She could not leave it flapping open, but Ginny would be coming with the tea any minute. So she picked up a stone and, closing the door as far as she could, wedged the stone against it. It would do. Conrad would notice it as soon as he returned and, though it would puzzle him, he would simply bolt it again.

She heard his motor-bike coming up the hill before she saw it. To her right, there was a high wall, to her left, the house from which Ginny would emerge. There was nothing she could do, no possibility of slipping quietly away, unnoticed. And yet, instead of dreading the coming encounter with Conrad, she felt only a strange kind of relief. He would listen. She'd gone too far now to care about further embarrassment.

Taking another deep breath, she waited.

★

Conrad was startled to see Stella standing in front of the pottery. He thought that the unpleasant husband must have been lying, and that she hadn't been asleep in the cottage at all. But then he had stopped to call on Phoebe. It had been too good an opportunity to miss, with an alibi so handy, should Ginny be suspicious. A hurried meeting, no time to take her to bed, though he would have risked it and enjoyed the frantic haste – Phoebe had been furious at the idea. 'No,' she'd said, as he pressed her against the wall as soon as she let him in, 'I won't have it like this.' It was exactly how he liked to have it, urgent, sudden, answering his need, but Phoebe, like Ginny, like every woman he had ever known, no matter how passionate her nature, liked to set the scene. Speed insulted them. Perhaps at first, the first few times, they could match his impetuosity, but the longer an affair went on, the longer sex had to take. It was why he always moved on, except with Ginny.

Stella looked dishevelled and wild. Her hair was all over the place and it looked as though she had been crying – her complexion, usually so pale and smooth, was red and blotchy. She was standing with her hands clasped in front of her so tightly that the knuckles showed white, looking like a penitent schoolgirl. As he went towards her, she took a step back and gestured at the back door of the workroom.

'I'm sorry,' she said, 'I couldn't close it properly.' He shook his head, mystified, but told her it didn't matter. 'Your wife,' she said, 'she was being very kind, making me tea, and I . . . well, I wanted to leave, it was very rude of me . . .'

At that moment, the door was pushed open, sending the stone flying. Ginny appeared, a mug of tea in her hand. 'Why ever are you here?' she said, addressing Stella. 'I brought you tea. Take it.' Then she turned and went back into the workroom, ignoring her husband. They heard her bolt the door again, making a great deal of noise.

'I've offended her,' Stella whispered.

'I'm afraid you have,' Conrad said, but he smiled. 'Why don't we sit down while you drink your tea? Over here, in the sun. It's sheltered, the view's good.' Gently, he took her arm and guided her to the bench. She sipped the tea, and he waited. 'I called on you,' he said, eventually, when she hadn't spoken.

'Yes, I know.'

'Your husband said . . .'

'He isn't my husband. My husband was killed in the war. I'm a widow. Alan's my friend.'

'He was very unfriendly to me.'

'I'm sure. He isn't well, he was badly injured.'

'I guessed that. I should have shown more sympathy.'

'Oh no, he hates pity.'

'I didn't mean pity. I meant understanding, made allowances.'

'It wouldn't have made any difference.'

'Right.' Conrad paused. He wanted to ask why Alan had pretended to be her husband but decided it was a stupid question. Maybe he just wanted to protect her reputation. 'Anyway,' he continued after a while, 'I didn't want to give him a message for you. I wanted to explain, myself.'

'What?'

'The painting you showed me. I'd like to buy it, if you're willing to sell it.'

'It was a present, from Alan. He found it on a junk stall, in London.'

'Ah. Well, yes, I see, selling it might not be a good idea, I suppose. He would mind, would he?'

'Yes.'

'Does he care about art?'

'No.'

'So what he would mind is your giving, I mean selling, the painting to someone, to me?'

'Yes.'

'It would suddenly become precious, just because he'd bought it for you, not because he valued it for itself?'

'Yes.'

'Well, then, that's that. Forget what I said.'

'How much?'

'What?'

'How much would you pay for it?'

'You mean you would sell it? What about Alan?'

'I'm leaving him. He need never know.'

Conrad shifted uncomfortably on the bench. He had a sudden vision of a mad Alan arriving to accuse him of being the reason Stella had left him. He'd looked capable of such behaviour.

'I'm going now, today, tonight,' she was saying. 'I need money to get me back to Tenby. I'll sell you the painting. How much?'

'Five pounds?' It was a not inconsiderable amount to him. Only by giving the painting to Ginny as her birthday present could he justify such a sum and even then he wasn't absolutely sure it was worth it.

'Fine. I'll bring it to you this evening before I go. Will you have the money?'

'I think so, yes. But how will you manage to bring it? Won't Alan be suspicious? What will you say?'

'I don't know yet. But I'm going. I'm leaving. I haven't thought exactly how.'

The last thing he wanted to do was aid and abet her, so he kept silent. He wanted her to go. Sitting with her had become embarrassing. But she must have felt it, too, because she got up and said she would bring the painting when she'd worked out how best to leave, and she walked off down the hill looking purposeful, her arms swinging in an oddly military way. He watched her until she had disappeared from view, regretting that he had ever taken an interest in her. Ginny, coming round the corner from the house, was surprised to find him slumped in thought. 'Where's the girl?' she asked. 'You should be careful,' Ginny added. 'She's too highly strung, she's a bundle of nerves.'

'She's leaving her fellow, the man she lives with.'

'Not for you, I hope.'

'Don't be ridiculous. I hardly know her.'

'So why does she come here when she's upset? Tell me that.'

'Ginny, I swear on anything you like that I haven't so much as shaken that girl's hand. She brings me her little water-colours and no more.' But he had to tell Ginny that Stella would be back, and that he would be giving her money. He couldn't afford any misunderstandings. He explained that he was going to buy the painting for her. To his relief she was intrigued at the prospect and as eager as he was to have it in her possession. They went into the house arm in arm and sorted the cash out to have it ready and waiting.

It proved a long wait. Stella did not appear that night, nor the next day. By the following day they were convinced she never would come with the painting. They swapped theories: Ginny was sure that Stella had, after all, found it impossible to desert her man; Conrad reckoned Alan was preventing her from leaving, perhaps even to the extent of locking her in. 'He won't let her go,' he said to Ginny, 'he needs her too much. And she's not strong enough, in every way, to make the break. He'll watch her like a hawk, she won't get the chance.' Sometimes he wondered if he ought to go and rescue Stella, but quickly abandoned that idea. Then, in the early hours of the next morning, Stella appeared. Ginny heard the crunch of gravel on the path outside their bedroom window, then the knock on the door, and woke Conrad. When he opened the door, Stella was standing there, her bicycle leaning on the wall. She was shivering and holding out the painting, uncovered, so that he could see what it was. He told her to come in while he got the money but she wouldn't, only urged him to hurry. Once she had the cash in her hand, she turned away and set off on her bicycle without another word. Conrad heard later that the bike had been left at the station.

Afterwards, going over and over what had happened, Alan blamed the painting. It was irrational, but it seemed to him that something about what he'd seen as an innocuous little oil painting had started a change in Stella which had developed rapidly into a crisis. He had seen no sign of it. Again and again he went over their life before that day he went to London, and it had been, he was sure, harmonious, peaceful. They had been placidly chugging along, each recovering in their own way from what had happened to them. Were they happy? Neither of them ever used that word, it was too daring, too dangerous. But they had not been unhappy, had they? About Stella he didn't know, but for himself being with her made him as near to happy as he would be ever again.

He had waited a long, long time sitting on a boulder, watching her on the cliff path. He saw her reach the highest point, and then she was lost to view. The walk to the end of the headland would take her half an hour and then another half an hour until he would see her, at the same point, returning. But he never did see her. An hour went by, an hour and a half. He was cold and stiff, and finally, realising she must be going the long way back, by the road, he went home. Already he was anxious, with faint feelings of doom stirring in his mind, visions of accidents and attacks and all manner of catastrophes. They had no telephone, she couldn't ring him, nobody could, should there be any need. He kept expecting a policeman to arrive but nothing disturbed the intense silence. Mad ideas began to occur to him: could Stella somehow have returned without his having known? Could she be upstairs? Could she be in her hut? He searched, knowing he was being foolish, and ended up lurking in the hut, her studio.

There was little to see there. Everything was tidy. No work appeared to be in progress, but then she'd just taken her latest efforts to the man at the pottery. The place looked abandoned, as though she had left it not expecting to return, and this filled him with a dread so awful he began to feel dizzy and had to sit down. It wasn't possible, it couldn't be. Agitated, he tried to calm himself by walking up and down, searching for some evidence that he was wrong. Her things were still here, her paints, her easel, none of them cheap. She would never go without them. Then he saw the painting he'd bought her, hanging on its own on the only wall without windows or door. She'd said she loved it: she would never leave that behind. Relieved, he sat down again and stared at it.

That was how Stella found him. Opening the door quietly, intending to take the painting then and there and run away with it, she saw him hunched on the stool in front of it. He turned, and for a second the anguish showed in his face before the weight of worry lifted and he smiled so beautifully that she thought she could not do it, could not hurt him so cruelly. 'Thank God,' he said, and tried to get up, but sank back weakly. 'Thank God,' he repeated. 'I was imagining . . . all sorts of ghastly things.' She didn't reply. It seemed vital not to engage in conversation. What she must do was to take the painting and go, before he realised what was happening. But Alan wanted to talk. As though aware that he mustn't nag, mustn't ask her to account for her lengthy absence, he said, as she picked up the painting, 'I'm sorry. I can't even remember what I said, or why, but whatever it was that upset you I'm sorry, I'm sure I was wrong, let's just forget it, can we? It's been a bad day.'

Pathos, Stella thought, is his most powerful weapon. He doesn't have to pretend to be pathetic and in need, he really is. He expects my heart to melt at the sight of him, so frail, so contrite, so pleading. But this time it is not going to, it cannot afford to. She ignored his outstretched hand and went to pick up the painting.

'Aren't you going to say anything?' he asked. She shook her

head, picked up the painting, and prepared to leave the hut. But he barred her way. He stuck out his left leg, the bad one, and at the same time snatched at her coat. 'Please,' he said, 'at least say something. I don't care what it is.'

'Let me past, Alan.'

'Where are you going?'

'To pack a bag. I'm leaving.'

The shock, she saw, was genuine. The expression in his eyes was incredulous and he was biting his lip so hard it had drained of all colour. 'You can't,' he whispered. And then, 'Why? Why?'

'You should know why.'

'But I don't. We had a silly row, I can't remember what . . .'

'The row doesn't matter.'

'Then what does? What happened?'

'I don't want to talk about it. I can't stay, I can't. I have to get away, let me past, Alan.'

'I won't let you go. You must be ill, or mad. This is ridiculous, it's all out of proportion . . .'

'Maybe.' And then, weakly, she added, 'Maybe I'll come back, maybe I just need to be by myself for a while.'

'Exactly,' he said. 'You just need to calm down, but you don't need to go away to do that.'

'I do.'

'Where will you go?'

'I don't know. Tenby, I suppose.'

He hesitated. 'Not today, though, don't go today, please, go tomorrow if you must, let me get used to it, but don't go now, after a day like this, with both of us upset. Go tomorrow, I won't fuss, I promise.'

It wasn't that she gave in, more that all the energy drained out of her and a great weariness swept through her. She could barely follow him into the cottage. His arm went round her, and she let it be. The two of them wandered slowly across the garden, relieved to reach the cottage door. Once inside, she sank onto a chair and put her head down onto her arms, folded on top of the table. Quietly, Alan put the kettle on. She heard the tinkle of a teaspoon, the clink of the teapot lid being lifted off. She stayed where she was, feeling the steam from the mug of tea warm her hands. Mercifully, Alan said no more. He left her alone. She heard him locking the doors, front and back, and climbing the stairs to his bedroom. She couldn't leave now. He would hear her opening the door, and there would be a scene. She hadn't the strength for it, for anything.

She wished that Alan had someone to turn to – knowing he had not made leaving him so much harder. She had no knowledge of any friends he might have had before the war because he wouldn't talk about those days. The only person he had mentioned, just once, was a girlfriend called Charlotte. Nothing serious, he'd said, it wasn't a real romance. He'd had no contact with her since they'd been in Cornwall, she was sure of that. Charlotte, whoever she was, had long since faded from his life, and apart from her he had never referred to any friend or relative. His parents were dead, he had no siblings. He would be absolutely alone after she had gone, which, in his present state, was almost too awful to contemplate.

Going to her own room, she packed a bag and put the painting on the top before fastening it securely. With luck, she would waken before Alan and make her escape. But luck was not with her. She slept heavily, and when she did wake up she heard Alan downstairs, whistling. Never before had he gone downstairs before she took his tea to him. She could smell bacon frying. He had never before cooked breakfast. It was all she could do to dress. What should she do with her bag? If she walked into the kitchen with it, determined to leave at once, he would block her way and there would be an ugly fight – he had no intention of letting her go home even for a while. His agreement had been a ploy, to get her to stay the night, and it had worked. Going to the window, she opened it as wide as it would go and looked down. Her room was at the front, the kitchen at the back. Below her window was a flower bed with lavateras flourishing against the wall. The drop was not long. She couldn't jump out herself but she could lower her bag. It was easy. Knowing that it now nestled, hidden among the shrubs, made her braver when she went downstairs.

They spent another strained day together, with Alan reading and watching her, and Stella staring out of the window. By the evening she was desperate. He always had a hot, milky drink to help him sleep, Ovaltine usually. She had his sleeping pills in her hand. It was absurdly easy to drop two into the mug when he turned to get the sugar – done in a flash. She was sure that he had not taken any the last two nights or he could never have been up so early, and now all she had to do was stay awake all night herself, which was not so easy, and leave just before dawn. It seemed an age before he said goodnight and went upstairs. She gave him an hour, and then crept into his room. The sight of him asleep, suddenly young and vulnerable-looking, was almost her undoing, but she forced herself to turn her back on him, go down the stairs and slip out of the door. Mounting her bicycle, she found herself trembling but managed to get it onto the track and freewheeled down the slight hill to the road. All she had to do was exchange the painting for cash.

★

In the train, she wept. She couldn't stop. If this was freedom, where was the exhilaration she had looked for? All she could think of was a wounded man, alone, who needed her, and herself, alone, back in her room at home, the room she had always wanted to escape from and thought she would never return to again.

★

Ginny saw, straightaway, what Conrad meant. The apparent serenity, the prettiness, of the painting did not fool her for a moment. It looked peaceful, innocuous, but she thought the hand that painted it might have trembled. Effort was there, an absolute determination to remain calm. Someone's breath was being held. And the sense of waiting, the anticipation of someone's arrival, was painful. Conrad, charmed though he had been, could not see this. She was, he said, reading into a simple scene a variety of ridiculous complications. 'Accept it for what it is, for heaven's sake,' he urged her. 'Don't make a drama out of a little painting.'

But it felt like a drama to Ginny. Again and again she would

201

look at the painting and feel puzzled. She thought perhaps that the sense of mystery about it might be due merely to how it had come to her. This man who was reputed to have found it on a junk stall in London, what was he like? And Stella herself, fleeing from him, but why? All these questions attached to the painting, giving it a significance it might not otherwise have had. But then Ginny thought maybe what bothered her was not how the painting had been come by, but the echoes she sensed every time she saw it. It reminded her, surely, of a painting she had seen, but by whom? It was a long time since she had been to any exhibitions, other than those held in Cornwall, and she was quite sure that no artist she knew had painted this. Who, then?

She wondered if perhaps she was simply thinking of some famous painting. Vermeer, maybe, or one of the Dutch masters, though the similarity was only in the simplicity and the subject matter, nothing else. And then, after several weeks of pondering every time she looked at it, a memory came to her of the last time she'd been in Paris, in 1906, when she was twenty-six and had gone to stay with her uncle. He'd taken her to an exhibition at the Salon d' Automne and she had seen a painting called *La Mansarde* (she'd had to ask her uncle what the word meant and was told 'the attic'). It was nothing like the painting she now owned but there was some curious similarity. And she had another vague memory, of being taken on that same visit to an exhibition of Bonnard's paintings. They were boldly coloured, unlike this one, but they too included simple interiors, she was sure.

It frightened her a little to think that she might possess a painting of value, but then she told herself she was getting carried away. One day, when she could get to London, she would take it with her and have it looked at. Its provenance was unimportant, and so was its monetary worth. She loved it. It enriched her life. It made her feel dreamy and content, better able to put up with Conrad's philandering and the exhaustion of looking after her two young sons.

It even made her want to paint again.

★

The cottage was on the edge of the New Forest, roughly a mile from Fordingbridge. Stella would never have thought of living there, so far from the hospital with a long bus journey there and back, had it not been presented to her as a possibility by the matron, whose brother owned the cottage. It might do, the matron said (disturbed that the new nurse had nowhere to go other than the hostel and was clearly not happy there, among girls much younger than herself), until she got settled. Stella had no intention of becoming settled, but she did want somewhere of her own to live and the rent for Yew Tree Cottage was cheap. Alan would never be able to trace her. If he tried to, he would think only of her mother's house in Tenby.

Returning to nursing was not easy, nor was it something she had intended to do, but it meant that she immediately earned money and had some sense of direction, even if it was one in which she did not want to go. She did not go home to the cottage every night – she had volunteered for night shifts – but when she was there she was soothed by the place. It was in poor condition, and with only one fireplace for heat, but it was completely peaceful there. The garden was overgrown but had a pretty border of fir trees round it and she used the fir cones to light the fire. People did not trouble her there. The only house nearby was a large one, Fryern Court, but it was not inhabited at the moment, or so she had been told. She'd walked round the outside of it on her first day off and had been rather charmed with the whitewashed courtyard at the rear, where a beautiful fig tree grew, and what looked like well-maintained stables though no horses. The lawn had a pond in the middle, and an avenue of yew trees led away from it. It needed, Stella thought, a large family living there.

For the first few months her main feeling was one of relief. She felt as if she had been running very hard and had only just stopped to draw breath. But then, as she relaxed into a routine governed by her hours of work, she began to recover and to become more confident that she could move on. She had escaped, she'd got out of the trap she had caught herself in, she was no longer intensely needed by anyone. She could be herself, break out from the cycle of caring and need – the care she gave now was restricted to nursing. It was enough. Outside the hospital she had no one to consider except herself. The freedom made her want to paint again. She'd been foolish to imagine that because art, or the pursuit of art, could not be her whole life she had no right to indulge herself. Pleasure might be enough. So she bought some water-colours – oils were too expensive, though she would have preferred them – and some paper and she set to, painting first the fir trees in her garden. It was something to come home for.

When the landlord came to tell her he was putting Yew Tree Cottage up for sale, she wished so much that she could buy it, but there was not the faintest possibility of her doing so. He gave her three months' notice, which was generous of him. It was when she was looking for somewhere else to live that Stella saw the advertisement. She was ready.

A new beginning, thousands of miles away.

LUCASTA

THE DAWN LIGHT was weak, a mere leaking of a lighter grey around the rim of the horizon, but it showed that the trees were beginning to shed their leaves, which fell slowly, singly, in swirling balletic movements quite mesmerising to watch. There was a mist hugging the land but it dispersed quickly, leaving the ruts of the ploughed fields rising sharply in their rigid rows. Lucasta herself had worked the field she was crossing. Yesterday she had managed the three-furrow plough expertly. The farmer, Skelton Wood, a man not given to praise, had grudgingly acknowledged her skill. 'Not bad,' he'd said, 'not bad at all.' She was going to tackle another field today, after she'd helped milk the cows. There was plenty of work all day, every day, and not much time for thought. That was the blessing – no time to think, no chance of daydreaming, with all the tough physical work and the exhaustion that came with it.

But she did notice the beauty. Her limbs might be aching, her eyes tight with fatigue, but she always looked about her and saw the changes in the light and the patterns in the clouds, she always felt breathless at the rise of a skylark and the flash of a fox racing for cover. She didn't comment on anything to the other girls, just silently tucked such sights away, saved them to gloat over later when she was back in the farmhouse trying to sleep. She'd fall asleep immediately, they all did, worn out, but then she'd wake, around one in the morning, and remember, and that was when she needed to play the comforting images of the day in front of her eyes again. It helped. It kept memories of her parents away for a while and worries about her brothers were briefly stilled.

Her breeches were uncomfortable. The corduroy rubbed against her thighs where they did not fit properly and they were still slightly damp from the soaking they'd had the day before. Her canvas leggings were stiff with mud she hadn't succeeded in scraping off, and her felt hat had shrunk a little in the rain and now constricted her head, but with the wind so bitter and strong it had to be worn. What a sight she looked, they all looked. Her mother would have groaned. No velvet skirts and bohemian silk dresses for her, no gorgeous-coloured fabrics to dress in such as Ginny had worn. Her own breeches were brown, her jacket khaki, her pullovers grey – everything old and utilitarian, nothing new or pretty. She looked like one of the better-dressed scarecrows, bundled together for warmth in ugly garments tied with string (and today she did have a piece of string round her jacket, having lost the belt the day before, and needing to wrap it close to her body so that the wind would not get underneath).

She was hungry, but what passed for breakfast wasn't for another hour, after milking. Mrs Wood fed them as well as she could but they all knew how tough it was for her to satisfy her own family never mind six Land Girls. Bread, potatoes, turnips – these were the staples. Breakfast was porridge, usually lumpy but with good creamy milk to help it down, and a slice of bacon or a sausage, if they were lucky, and tea. It wasn't much to get through a four-teen-hour day on, but there were sandwiches at midday (though never anything tasty in them), and in the evening soup and stews which they were almost too tired to eat. 'You're better off than the boys out there fighting for us,' Mrs Wood would say, if anyone complained. They knew it was true. They were safe, or as safe as anyone in the country. Not many planes flew over them, but when they did the girls worked in pairs with one eye on the sky, so that they could warn each other if a battle began. The noise of the tractors was so loud, this was the only way to guard against such dangers.

Two of the girls were going home today. They'd worked their six months and were entitled to a week off, with a free travel pass. Lucasta didn't envy them, though she envied the fact that they had homes to go to. She tried not to think about having no home. Plenty of people were in the same boat, and what might at other times have been thought a tragedy was no longer one. War changed everything. In a way, she was grateful for this. She didn't want to stand out, be an object of pity. The pottery had been demolished, literally razed to the ground, then the land sold. It turned out that it had never belonged to her father, he'd only rented it, and when he died after months in the sanatorium, Ginny couldn't afford the rent. They'd had to move, to the cottage, just as war was declared.

The cowshed was not warm, but with the breath of the cows and the girls it was not as cold as outside and there was a pleasantly illusory feeling of warmth as they all huddled together. Lucasta was good at milking, and liked doing it. In fact, she liked doing most things on the farm, except for rat-catching. When the sheaves were lifted, the men used sticks and forks to kill as many as possible, and Skelton Wood made the Land Girls hold the sacks and take turns to pick up the dead rats and put them inside, counting them as they went. It was a disgusting job, worse than muck-spreading or ditching, and made her feel sick. Once, she'd almost fainted but managed to conceal her distress until she recovered. It was something to write to Sam and Tom about, mocking her own distaste, though writing about any sort of killing seemed wrong. She couldn't bear the thought of either of them dying and tried to blank out all thoughts of it. Her brothers were all she had left, even if she had never been really close to them.

The girls next to her were talking about what they were going to do when they got home. They were both from Exeter, not so far away, and could count on their family homes not having been bombed. Hot baths and comfortable beds awaited them and they relished the idea of being spoiled. Lucasta listened, but said nothing. They knew about her circumstances, and were kind, but it didn't stop them talking about their parents and homes, and she didn't expect it to. Sally, the older one, had invited her home once, saying her mother would make her very welcome, but she hadn't wanted to accept. Here, on Skelton Wood's farm, she could hold herself together, just. She wasn't sure she would be able to without the hard physical work.

Sam and Tom hadn't been able to come home for their mother's funeral. They were too far away, Tom in Australia, Sam in the Far East. It hadn't been much of a funeral, no church service, no funeral tea, only two other relatives, and she could have done without their so-called support. Aunt Phyllis and Aunt Barbara, whom she had not seen in years. One was Ginny's cousin (so not an aunt at all) and the other, Barbara, her father's sister. It was Barbara who asked if there was a will. Surprisingly, there was, made when Conrad died, though there hadn't been much to leave. Barbara said that Conrad had always promised she could have some of the family heirlooms when he died. What heirlooms? Lucasta was baffled. She told Barbara she didn't know what she meant. 'The grandfather clock, Uncle John's,' Barbara said, 'and the mirror, Aunt Jessie's, and the small bureau that belonged to our grandmother.' The clock had gone, sold, but she invited her aunt to take the mirror and bureau from the cottage, and Barbara promptly did so. Lucasta didn't care.

She still had the cottage. The rent was low and she earned just enough to pay it. On her days off, she went there. It wasn't home, it never had been and never would be. She and Ginny had lived there for only two years, after Conrad's death, and the atmosphere was grief-laden. But it was a place to go, away from the farm. It was freezing cold inside, and there was a musty, airless smell. She'd light a fire and sit in front of it, a blanket over her shoulders and a hot-water bottle under her feet, and try to banish memories of Ginny's illness and her death. Crying about it was no good. She didn't weep any more. Instead, she tried to cheer herself by thinking of 'after the war', the game they all played. Sam would return, he *would*, and she would move from this miserable cottage and have a different life. She'd go to art college. She'd promised Ginny she would. 'Don't go to pieces, darling,' her mother had pleaded. 'Use your gift, when all this is over.'

Did she have 'a gift'? How could she know? There seemed no place for art in her present life. She never even thought of lifting a pencil or a paintbrush. Her hands, rough and covered in cuts, did other things. They might have forgotten how to draw or paint. Art was just a dream, a myth; it had no importance in her world.

★

His mother died on 3 December, but Sam didn't know about it until Christmas Day. The 3rd December was the day his battalion left the barracks and went to their jungle stations and pillboxes along the east coast of Singapore. They had only the guns they'd used in training. The new, far more efficient ones, were still wrapped in wax and greaseproof paper. They'd eyed them, in their boxes, as a child eyes sweets.

The camp was built inside a rubber plantation, set in five acres. There was a barbed wire fence round the perimeter and every two hundred yards there were machine-gun posts. Sam manned one of them. It was just a hole in the ground, about five feet deep and with a radius of around ten. He worked out later that at the time his mother died he was grubbing about in the dirt checking that his hole was clear of debris, and building up his firing step, where the Thompson machine-gun would be set. Then he'd settled down for his eight-hour shift. He knew he'd thought of his mother and his sister. All the troops thought of their families, of home. He'd felt guilty, he remembered that. He'd joined up straightaway, and he hadn't had to do so. His mother had begged him not to, not yet, not till he was called up. She needed him, she'd said. She didn't feel well, and it was so soon after his father's death. Tom had already gone, but he'd been gone anyway, working in Australia when Conrad died. Sam had told his mother that Lucasta would look after her, he couldn't wait, he had to volunteer. Yes, he'd felt like a hero in the making; his naivety astonished him now.

Lucasta wrote every week even when she had nothing much to say, and Ginny added little drawings sometimes, nearly always of her cats. And his little sister had been so good, so unselfish, never telling him how ill their mother was, never alarming him, and always insisting that she was managing well. She'd risen to the occasion magnificently, and he'd been surprised. But then he hardly knew her. It took hours of being stuck in a hole to teach

211

him that, hours of going over and over his childhood, sifting image after image of his growing up, overwhelmed by a nostalgia so strong it made his eyes smart. Lucasta had been such a frail child. She was only four and a half pounds at birth, and they'd had to rush her to hospital and put her in an incubator, and he had a distinct recollection that she was not expected to survive. There had been tears and hushed voices and his mother never seemed to be at home. His father retreated to his pottery, and he and Tom had been left pretty much to themselves when they were not at school. Then, when the new baby came home, they had been instructed not to touch her at first, in case she got an infection; and had peered at her, in her cradle, rather afraid of the tiny creature. That was how things had continued for the first few years, until Lucasta (and he and Tom had not liked her funny name, wanting to call her Daisy) began school, when suddenly she seemed to grow stronger. By then, it was too late to change the way they treated her. He and Tom always felt they had to be wary of her.

Whatever the reasons, Sam had felt remote from his sister. Protective, yes, where other people, who might threaten her, were concerned, but not lovingly close. It didn't aid intimacy that Lucasta was a self-contained child, quiet, shy, whereas he and Tom were boisterous and sociable. Often, when his friends came, Sam was embarrassed at Lucasta's attitude to them – she wasn't friendly, she watched them from round corners and looked blank when direct overtures were made. She wasn't pretty, either. He and Tom had inherited their mother's dark good looks, and were strongly built like their father, but Lucasta, up to the age of twelve or so, was thin, with a pale, waif-like face, wispy fair hair, and grey, catlike eyes that were disconcerting. They never seemed to blink. She would stare and stare, holding any returning stare until it was the other person who blinked. The truth was, that from a very early age Lucasta made people feel uncomfortable and this made her brothers nervous; they felt they had to apologise for her. But their mother took pride in her daughter's qualities, constantly admiring her reserve, her habit of weighing everything up before committing herself. It had made Sam jealous. Once he was grown-up, it was obvious that jealousy lay at the root of his far from satisfactory relationship with his sister – a jealousy that had begun with her birth ('At last,' his mother had said, 'a girl!'), continued through her delicate early childhood, when she'd been the focus of so much attention, and finally become pretty unbearable when it turned out that Lucasta had inherited the talents of both parents. Neither he nor Tom could draw or paint, they had no artistic leanings whatsoever. Sam was athletic, excelling at sport and wanting only some future where he could earn a living by his physical prowess, and Tom, who was clever and had a mechanical aptitude, wanted to be an engineer.

When the news of his mother's death finally reached him, Sam told no one. He couldn't quite take it in, though the message was clear enough and had been delivered with sympathy. There was a camp cinema, and for the Christmas and New Year period it was showing *All Quiet on the Western Front*. He sat through it twice, repeating to himself the words 'Sorry to have to tell you . . .' over and over, out loud. Then he got drunk, and slept, and woke to hear the same refrain: 'Sorry to have to tell you . . .' He got out all Lucasta's letters and read them, looking for the clues that were there and which he'd missed. The bombing, when it started, was a relief. Now that the Japanese were not far away, there was a sense of panic, but Sam didn't feel it. He felt calm, half dead already. There was plenty to do. All the time he was carrying out orders he was writing to Lucasta in his head, struggling to find appropriate words. When he finally got the chance to put pencil to very dirty, torn paper all he managed to write was 'Dear Lucasta – Devastated to hear of Mum's death. Hang on, you've been great, will be home soon.' The inadequacy of this pathetic scrawl shamed him. He hadn't even managed to convey his grief never mind concern for his sister.

He promised himself that after this war he would take care of Lucasta. He saw in his mind's eye the two of them walking hand in hand on the cliff path, the fields behind them bathed in sunlight and the sea an unlikely blue. He'd support her, encourage her to paint, help her talent flourish. He would redeem his neglect. Vowing this, he felt better, until there flashed into his mind a memory of his mother once telling him he was full of promises he never kept. But this was one which, if he survived, he was determined to honour.

★

Lucasta took the churns of milk to the road in the cart, handling the reins of the carthorse with care. He was temperamental and resented anyone but the farmer driving him. Each plod of his gigantic hooves shattered the icy puddles along the half-mile of track. They cracked like pistol shots, scaring the rabbits dashing through the undergrowth. At the road, Lucasta got down and, tying the reins to the gatepost, lowered the tailboard. She could just about lift the churns off and put them in the right place. Turning the horse round was harder. When he wouldn't be turned, she sat patiently, waiting. She was as good at waiting as he was. She took a cigarette out of her pocket and smoked it. Mrs Wood wouldn't let them smoke in the farmhouse – she fined them threepence if she caught them. The tiny trail of smoke wreathed its way over the horse's head, and he suddenly turned and began lumbering home without any encouragement.

There might be a letter when she got back. Since their mother died, Tom had written one long letter and Sam had written twice, odd little notes, telling her nothing much but full of concern for her. He wanted to know what she'd done with all their mother's things, had she kept everything? He said he remembered how much stuff there had been and wondered how it all fitted into the cottage they'd moved to. The answer was that it hadn't. Ginny had collected masses of furniture, so much that every room had been jammed full. Most of it had had to go, even Ginny had realised that. She'd only kept the best bits, but this 'best' looked poor in the cottage. Sam would be able to visualise the cottage where she lived. It had been a feature of their childhood, the spooky place, he would recall, where the recluse lived. They'd been scared of him. If he came out of the cottage, they hid, frightened by his burned face and his limp.

214

At night, when on her days off she was there alone, Lucasta would find herself wondering about the recluse, now dead. Her mother used to say he was a sad man, that he'd suffered a great deal, and then his wife left him suddenly. When the boys were gone and they'd rented the place, there hadn't been much in it to clear out, no clues at all as to its previous owner's life. The hut in the garden was more revealing. The estate agent said it was an unsafe structure, they should not go into it, but they had disobeyed him and nothing dramatic had happened. It was full of painting equipment, though most of the paints had dried up and were beyond rescue. Before Ginny became ill, they had begun to clean the place and she was going to use it as a studio – but she never did. She didn't paint again. If she had the energy, on good days, she sketched pictures of her cat, or portraits of Lucasta. Lucasta herself felt no desire, during that time, to draw at all.

It was strange the way the need to express herself in art had left her. She didn't know if it would come back but it didn't worry her. Sometimes, sitting in front of the fire in the cottage, Lucasta would look up at the mantelpiece where her mother's drawings were now propped up, the best of her sketches all in a row. Ginny had been content when she did them, smiling. 'But I never tried hard enough,' she'd said once, though without any apparent real regret. 'I never really put myself into anything,' she'd added, 'like a real artist does, like your father did, like you will.' Lucasta protested that she wasn't like her father and could never be obsessed, but Ginny had said, 'You have it in you, you'll see.' So far, there was nothing to see, but then death and the war could conveniently be blamed.

Ginny's room upstairs was still untouched. Lucasta supposed that one day she would have to sort through the drawers and the cupboard and deal with the contents, but they would wait. She did air the room occasionally, though, just went in if it was a fine day and opened the window. She liked to lean out, for a glimpse of the sea, and the little harbour with boats tossing up and down. The scene etched itself into her mind and comforted her, made her feel somehow philosophical: life went on, some things didn't change. Turning back from the window, she was always surprised by the single picture on the wall, a quiet painting of the corner of an attic room. Conrad had given it to his wife on her fortieth birthday. He'd bought it from someone, but not from the artist, who was unknown. Ginny had loved it. Till recently, Lucasta hadn't known if she even liked it. But lately, she realised that she was looking at the painting in a new way. It seemed now to represent peace, and peace was something to be longed for. The state of mind represented in that attic was enviable, not dreary. She felt a curiosity she had never felt before. She was ready to pull back the lace curtain, put on the coat lying on the chair, take up the parasol. The drawer in the table fascinated her. She wanted to open it and find – what? Writing materials? Cutlery? It was tantalising not to know. Her gaze wandered over the floor, which she judged newly scrubbed, the tiles still warm from the hot soapy water, and took in for the first time the shadow along the wall behind the chair. What was it? Merely a different wallpaper from the rest, or wood? She wanted to touch it.

One day, she took the painting off the wall and studied it carefully, in daylight, outside. Her mother would have known how the subdued effect had been achieved, but she did not. Not yet. She would learn when she went to art college, when she took up her deferred place, if she did. Her life would not be on hold for ever. But something would have to change before she could learn to be the kind of artist her mother thought she could be. There was something lacking in her that true artists had to have, some kind of commitment, and passion.

Passion was also something, she realised, she knew nothing about.

★

The next time she went to the cottage, there was a letter lying inside on the mat. It wasn't addressed to her, but to a Mr Alan Stone. And it was not a circular, but an interesting-looking envelope, and from America. The stamps fascinated her as did the handwriting, firm and bold. She had no right to open it, but she knew that Stone had been the name of the recluse who had lived

216

here, and that he was dead. There was no relative that she knew of to whom it could be forwarded, and no sender's address on the back to which she could return it. She opened it, taking care to slit the envelope along the top edge.

There was only one sheet of paper inside, together with a photograph. This small black-and-white snapshot showed a middle-aged woman and a young man whose age was hard to guess – he could be sixteen or twenty-six. The woman had an arm round his shoulders, and was smiling. The man stared straight ahead, his expression impossible to read. On the back of the photograph, someone had written 'with Jack'. There was an address at the top of the letter, so it could be returned after all. The writer, who signed herself Stella, wrote that more than twenty years was too long a time to have elapsed for her now to be writing to him and that she hardly dared do so. She had never, she went on, stopped feeling guilty about the manner in which she had left him and she supposed it was guilt which had kept her from writing. She had never forgotten him, and had hoped and prayed that some happiness had eventually come his way, as it had hers. She had not returned to Tenby, but after several years' nursing in England she had gone to America, to Ohio, and there she had met a doctor whom she'd married and they had had a son. She thought that 'Alan' might be interested to know that she'd taken up painting again soon after she left him, though only as a pastime. If he had forgiven her, and cared to write, she would be so pleased, but would quite understand if he did not wish to renew contact. He had been on her conscience so long and she supposed her letter was a belated attempt, however feeble, to say sorry.

Lucasta felt disgusted. She imagined how Mr Stone would have felt if he'd been alive and received this missive. The tone of it was not truly contrite – it seemed instead to boast about the sender's good luck, what with the doctor husband and good-looking son. How could that possibly have comforted the recluse, with his limp and his burnt face and his wretched life? And why would the abandoned man be interested in hearing that this Stella had resumed painting? Those awful daubs hanging on the cottage walls must have been hers, and the hut hers too. It gave Lucasta a peculiar satisfaction to think how badly the mysterious Stella had painted.

She put the letter back into its envelope, wishing that she had never opened it. How sad to know that Mr Stone had once had a lover and that she had left him. She felt glad he was long dead and did not have to suffer the pain of reading such a letter. Slowly, she took it into the kitchen and found matches and burned it, letting the ashes fall into the sink. It didn't deserve to be returned to the sender. But though she had destroyed the letter, she could not banish the impact of its contents. Hurrying back to the farm afterwards, she imagined Mr Stone all those years ago realising he had been deserted and howling with anguish. But perhaps that was too melodramatic. Perhaps he had simply settled into a bitterness that never left him, an acceptance of defeat, a fading away of any hope of joy ever again . . . No wonder he became a recluse. It made her shiver.

She never wanted to be so solitary and yet feared it might be her destiny. She must not allow it to be. She must try, once the war ended, to change.

★

Once they were prisoners, time seemed not so much to come to a standstill as to operate entirely differently. Sam wondered how he could ever have thought an hour such a short period – suddenly, it was an eternity, and anything longer beyond imagining. They were moved from Kanchanaburi to Chungkai camp in barges, a hundred of them to a barge, each already loaded with sacks of rice, and the journey was terrifying, each minute of it filled with fear that the barges would sink. The current in the river was powerful and they were going against it. He counted to himself, one to sixty, very slowly. The trip took thirty-seven sixties, thirty-seven minutes which felt like thirty-seven hours.

He was in Chungkai for two years. The first months were spent building huts. These were made of bamboo frames, erected in line, with a main roof-beam of bamboo covered in atap. Each hut held four hundred prisoners, from different infantry regiments, all captured when Singapore fell. They all had to get along together and learn how to survive the brutality of the Japanese guards. There were quarrels and fights, attempts to form cliques, rivalry between huts (especially over food) but eventually a kind of solidarity emerged, united as they had to be against their guards, and a routine was slowly established. 'Leisure time' might be a misnomer – there could be no 'leisure' in the sense they had previously known it – but they did have periods of time each day when they were not herded out to labour for the Japanese. They were all exhausted and weak with hunger, so energy was low, but it was astonishing how reserves of strength were found to do things like play simple games. They fashioned a football out of rags and kicked it about – the guards watched closely but didn't interfere – and someone made a bat out of bamboo sticks strapped together to play cricket with. But it was the stronger men who indulged in such exercise – the majority couldn't attempt to join in and occupied themselves differently and often ingeniously.

Sam felt that he had some good luck. The hut he was allocated to was the best one. The men in it were mostly of a quiet disposition, given to card-playing (the cards made out of scraps of paper) and chess (the pieces made out of hardened dirt) and conversation. Early on, one of the officers suggested that they should give talks, on anything at all they knew something about, and the idea caught on. Then there were those who made music, with primitive pipes and whistles made out of bamboo and drums made out of tin cans. And the artists; they had neither paper nor paint. They drew on the earth floor, or on rags, and used sticks sharpened to a point and dipped in solutions made from vegetable matter. Sometimes the results were so impressive it seemed wicked that the ground had to be raked over at the end of the day. The Japanese did not object to the drawings but they wouldn't let them remain – order had to be restored by nightfall. There was one man, a lieutenant in the Cambridgeshire Regiment, who was brilliant. When he decided to draw, a crowd quickly gathered, Sam always among it. One day he attempted a collage of the view from a nearby clifftop where they'd been on a working party. Sam had been in that party too, and had been able to see for miles over the jungle, and below them, a thousand feet or more, the river snaking along, brown and sludge-like. The artist constructed the spot miraculously, using all kinds of materials – stones, shreds of bamboo, bits from the torn soles of boots, laces, leaves – and when he'd finished, everyone clapped. Even the guards, coming to kick it over and make them rake the ground, were admiring.

Sam watched Lieutenant Parker, and saw how much satisfaction his crude artwork gave him. It wasn't just the doing of it, though that was striking enough, because of the way he became so obviously immersed in what he was creating, but the aftermath. Parker would seem relaxed, enjoying the men's pleasure in his little achievement, and altogether calmer than before. He wasn't a strong man, he took beatings badly, and he hadn't made friends easily, but withdrawing into his picture-making seemed to energise him. Sam longed to see what he could do with real paint and canvas, but it turned out that Parker wasn't an artist at all. He was an architect, he said, though he'd been to art college for a while before he began training. Sam showed him Lucasta's letters with their mother's drawings in them. He'd had no new letters since Singapore fell but he'd managed to hide some of those that had come before.

'Nice,' Parker said, but didn't seem very interested.

'I wish I could draw,' Sam said. 'I envy you, you know that? To be able to do what you do. Gives a point to life.'

Parker smiled. 'I'm no artist,' he said. 'Don't exaggerate. Art won't get me through this, that's for sure. Passes time, that's all.'

'Seems to do more than that,' Sam said, and then, 'It did more than that for my father. Nothing else mattered, really. My sister's got his gift, not me.'

'You're tough,' Parker said, 'that's a gift. It'll see you through, you'll be glad of it. Look at you, still plenty of muscle. Look at me. Wasted.'

Sam felt embarrassed. He folded the flimsy letters away and put them carefully into the waterproof pouch he always wore under his vest, tied round his waist. He hadn't meant to make comparisons between himself and Parker. He'd only wanted to try to express his admiration. They lived in such filth and ugliness in the huts and anything that could lift the atmosphere of weariness and despair was so valuable. That was all he'd meant to say.

Parker left the camp towards the end of 1943, taken off in a squad of twenty, no one knew why or where to. The day before he was taken, he and Sam were standing at the door of their hut, ordered to be ready at dawn for some task or other. They could hear frogs croaking and birds chattering and the sun was rising over the jungle, a violent red ball. There was a thin mist, patchy, hugging the tops of the trees, curling up like steam from them. Parker nudged him. 'What?' Sam asked. 'Beautiful,' Parker said, 'look around. Beautiful. In spite of everything.' Sam looked, and tried to see what Parker saw and to benefit from it, but nothing happened. He couldn't see what Parker saw. He couldn't feel what Parker apparently felt.

★

By 1945, there had been no letters from Sam for fifteen months, but Lucasta did not give in to the feelings of dread that threatened to overwhelm her: no news was good news, or so Tom, writing from Australia, assured her. Sam, he reminded her, was tough, and could survive anything. (A bullet? she wanted to ask, but didn't.) Sam was not a letter-writer, and in any case, situated where he was, it was doubtful that letters could be sent – since the fall of Singapore, the post offices would not be functioning. Working day after day on the land, Lucasta made herself so physically exhausted that her brain seemed numb. She took on extra work willingly, laboured away ferociously in all weathers, so much so that Skelton Wood himself noticed and told her to go steady, he didn't want a sick girl on his hands. He told her to take time off, she was entitled, and had twice passed up on her week's leave. 'Don't think I didn't notice,' he said, 'making a martyr of yourself. Does no good.'

She didn't know what to do with a week off. Obliged to go back to the cottage, she managed to sleep for almost twenty-four hours but then woke feeling weak and ill and incapable of doing anything. Sally called, sent by Mrs Wood to see that Lucasta was all right, and suggested that they should go for a night out to Fowey where she knew a pub that was 'lively', where American servicemen, stationed locally, went. But Lucasta didn't want to be 'lively', so Sally went away, telling her to suit herself. But what did suit her? Without work, she didn't know, she was lost. She went and lay on her mother's bed and thought it would be easy to cry and never stop, but she didn't cry, not a single tear. It was spring, a week of hot, sunny days, and it was the weather which dragged her out into the overgrown garden on the third day. Outside, she felt better. Slowly, listlessly, she began weeding, and when she'd cleared a patch of grass she brought an old wicker-work chair out and sat in it, thinking about Sam and about the war. The tide had turned, people said, the war was being won and this year, 1945, would see the end.

With more energy the next day, she tackled the hut, opening the door wide, emptying the whole place and then sweeping the floor. Next she examined the paints. They were not all dried up and useless. She found a whole set of oil paints in a wooden box which were untouched, and an unused set of brushes still in their cellophane packets. But there was no paper, and no canvases. She could paint over the canvases in the cottage, though, which she now knew to be the work of the woman who had left Mr Stone. Her mother had laughed at them but had let them stay on the walls, saying they would serve as an inspiration to do better. The frames were good. Plain wood, unvarnished and simple. Lucasta went back into the cottage and removed the frame from a still life of roses and an apple. She could paint over it without any feelings of vandalism. Still lifes bored her, however brilliantly rendered. They'd bored her father too, but her mother was attracted to them. She'd liked still lifes, and interiors without figures.

Lucasta took the canvas into the hut and began to paint over it. When the roses and apples had been obliterated, she sat and stared at the now primed and prepared blank canvas. She could begin. She waited. It would come, if she waited long enough.

She would feel it, the excitement, the need to turn this blank square into something.

An hour later, she was still sitting there, the canvas still blank, her hands cold.

★

Official notification came the day before VE Day: Sam was a prisoner-of-war in a Japanese camp. He was not dead. The war in the Far East was not over yet, but he had survived so far and, as Tom had reminded her, he was tough enough to last it out. Relief made her so happy she allowed herself to be swept up in the girls' outing to London.

They were to meet at the station, to catch the first train. There was a thunderstorm that night, but the thunder and lightning only seemed a kind of celebration, and afterwards, in the morning, the air was clear and a fine, sunny day was forecast. The train was packed, standing room only, but nobody complained, everyone was laughing and enduring the discomfort happily. Some of the girls in the party were from other farms and Lucasta didn't know them but Sally seemed to, joking with them, and sharing her cigarettes. Watching the ease with which her friend socialised, Lucasta thought how different her life would be if she had been born with Sally's temperament. She felt stiff and awkward in this company, and had to struggle to take part in the repartee, and as always the urge to run away and be by herself pushed her to leave them. But on the train, there was no escape, and once they reached London there would be none either. She'd never been to London, not once. The thought of finding her way about alone terrified her. She had to stay with the crowd, follow it, be part of it. She'd never willingly been part of a crowd in her life.

★

They made it into Whitehall just as all the traffic stopped. Lucasta, with Sally linking her arm uncomfortably tight, her skin hot and damp through the thin material of her dress, saw a mounted policeman wipe the sweat from his brow. Big Ben began to chime and suddenly silence whipped through the crowds like a wind, touching every laugh and shout until it was stilled. The silence

223

was extraordinary and startling. Then, through loudspeakers, they heard Churchill's words and when he'd finished the cheers began, the magic was gone, and the tumult returned.

There seemed no choice about which direction they should take. The press of people was so enormous that several times Lucasta felt her feet literally being lifted off the ground. They were forced into Trafalgar Square, and round it, everyone singing; around Nelson's Column couples were dancing, swaying together to a music of their own. Fireworks were going off though it was not dark, and streamers cascaded from the steps of the National Gallery, hurled by groups of excited schoolchildren. Sally still had hold of her arm but there was no sign of the other girls. Lucasta strained to find them, and in craning her neck to look behind, was pulled in the opposite direction to Sally and suddenly her arm slipped away. She cried out and saw Sally wave, laughing, and then they were parted, all in a moment.

The terror Lucasta felt made tears spring to her eyes and she turned round and round, trying to fight her way through the throng towards the place where she had seen her friend vanish. But she was small and slight and could make no headway. Then she felt her shoulders gripped and she was being steered to one side, guided in and out of the moving figures towards a building on the left. She came to rest in a doorway and turned to find a soldier smiling at her and shouting something. Safe? Was he saying she was safe? She smiled, shakily, and said thank you, but he was gone. The joy in his face had been ecstatic, and here she was, nervous and frightened, completely out of tune with the atmosphere, stranded in a doorway not knowing what to do.

The sequence of events for the rest of that day always remained confused in her mind. How had she got to the station? How had she found Sally? All she clearly remembered was stumbling into the cottage in the early hours of the next morning, and sleeping in her mother's bed. She was back in her proper place, alone, dependent on no one. This was how she would have to remain, unless Sam could make a difference.

★

Arriving back in England wasn't how Sam had imagined it. On board the ship there was a strange silence as it slipped into Southampton. Nobody cheered, nobody seemed to have the energy to be excited. Instead, there was a tension among the broken-down men, a nervousness, which Sam felt part of. He remembered that when they left Singapore a band had played 'There'll Always Be An England', and everyone had sung. There was no band on the dockside now and few people. They were arriving quietly, almost secretly – was someone ashamed of them? – on a cold, dull, wet morning. The disembarking process was slow, but nobody complained. Everyone shuffled along, collecting clothes and money and tickets without any obvious enthusiasm. Most of the men were going to London and then on to different parts of the country, but Sam was going directly west, to Cornwall, to Lucasta, keeping his promise to himself to try to be a better brother. He felt strange in the suit he'd been given, but was glad to be out of uniform. Women liked uniforms but he wasn't looking for a woman for now.

He was preoccupied for the rest of the journey: what was he looking for, now the war was over? Peace. Rest. Comfort. True, but he wanted more, he was greedy for more. Six years of his life had been wasted and they had somehow to be compensated for. He'd been part of a family and had never appreciated what this meant. He'd deliberately left it, and so had Tom, long before the war, gone off and never given them – his parents, his sister – a thought. He'd hardly written, hardly phoned. He didn't understand how he could have been so unaware of what he'd rejected. But then, if the war had never happened, maybe he would have come to value his family and reclaimed his place within it. He'd have grown up, stopped thinking only of himself. Too late now to cherish his mother and father, but not too late to love his sister. Maybe he could live with her in Cornwall. Looking out of the train window, he thought about becoming a farmer. Why not? He'd never wanted to be a farmer, but now it suddenly seemed attractive, satisfying, to work on the land, using his fitness and strength that way. There was a point to it.

Producing food was worthwhile, it was easy to see where all the effort went, and for what. In his post-war state there needed to be a point to things. Maybe he'd always thought that, maybe it was why what his parents did had baffled him when he was growing up. His father's pots were hardly useful; he didn't make many ordinary cups and saucers and plates, but instead turned out weird urns and ornamental bowls. And as for his mother's paintings and drawings, they gave pleasure to some people but it was fairly fleeting. He'd once begun an argument with his brother about art not having any point, while they were still both at home, and clever Tom had come out with some quote from a Russian writer about 'man cannot live by bread alone'. Couldn't he? Sam thought he could. Man could live by bread alone, and would be safer doing so.

The countryside changed when the train crossed the Tamar. Plymouth looked terrible, bombed to bits, and he'd shut his eyes till they were past it, but now there were fields and trees and eventually the sea. There was no sun, but the sky had lightened and the dullness was tinged with silver. There were more stretches of cultivated land than he remembered. He wondered if he and Lucasta together could work a farm. He hadn't a clue what to do, but she would know. Were farms expensive? He owned no land, so he would have to be a tenant farmer. But who would give him a chance? He was only a returning soldier with no experience, and his strength might count for nothing.

Nobody at St Austell Station to greet him, of course, but then he hadn't let Lucasta know when he would arrive. She wasn't expecting him on any particular day and he preferred it that way. He had wanted to surprise her. Now, standing for a moment on the platform, he felt unsure. His mother was dead. There was no family home any more. The reality of this seemed to dawn on him for the first time, and he felt momentarily dizzy, his head spinning with forgotten images rearing up to confront and mock his situation. No real home here to go to, that was it. Slowly, he set off down the road. The way lay towards the sea. He thought of the recluse, the man who had lived in the cottage where his sister now lived, a figure he and Tom had always been intrigued by and slightly afraid of. They'd see him on the cliff path, struggling up the steep bits with his stick, and make up stories about him and his war wounds. How little understanding they'd had of that war and how his wounds had been inflicted. Once, they'd even fired pellets from their airgun at his windows – God knows why – and he'd come out in a fury, screaming and brandishing his stick. Some people said he was mad, a loony. Their mother told them to keep away from him, he had suffered much. Sam distinctly recalled those words – 'he has suffered much' – because they had sounded so odd. He'd had a sense that his mother had not been referring to war wounds. He and Tom had called him Scarface, never thinking what had caused the scars.

He could smell the sea in the air, or thought he could. He closed his eyes and lifted up his face and breathed in deeply. No stench of death, no whiff of decay, just wind-borne salt and a hint of wild herbs. God, it felt good, pure. This was the place, his home terrain, to tuck himself away and start again. He walked slowly in the direction of his sister's rented cottage, remembering all the times he and Tom had cycled down from the pottery to try to cadge a trip on one of the fishing boats. He should write to Tom, find out what he was doing. Nerves made him hesitate when he reached the gate of the cottage. It was broken, hanging on its hinges as it always had been. He wanted so much for everything to be easy but dreaded the awkwardness there would surely be. He hadn't seen his sister for seven years, years during which they had both changed in ways impossible for the other to imagine. He couldn't even be sure exactly how old Lucasta was when he last saw her – sixteen, seventeen? In his memory of that final visit home, when he went to tell his mother he was joining up and had come to say goodbye, Lucasta was only a shadowy presence in the background. It was his mother he remembered, everything about her that day, her tears, her embrace, all the emotion of his leaving. He'd had no time for his sister. It suddenly occurred to him that he might not even recognise her. And his own appearance might scare her. Looking in mirrors wasn't something he'd done much of, lately, but he knew how he looked — battered, hardened, slightly threatening. He'd aged in more ways than mere years, as had most of his contemporaries who'd fought alongside him. They looked like men in their forties not their twenties. He wondered if he now looked like their father, and if this would shock Lucasta, and whether she had turned out like their mother, which would shock him.

The young woman who opened the cottage door, while he was still standing at the gate, was nothing like their mother, but she was instantly recognisable all the same. She stared at him long and hard, but there was no shock in her expression, only the same uncertainty he was himself experiencing. Finally, he pushed open the gate and made his way up the path and she smiled and said his name, but it was not easy to embrace her. She did not relax into his arms, or hold him tight, but instead put her own hands up and held his face, as though to be sure he was who she thought he was.

'Well,' he said, 'an odd place to find you, little sister. Do you remember Scarface?'

She nodded, gestured for him to come in. 'Tea?' she said.

'I'd rather have a drink, if you've got one.'

She shook her head.

'OK, tea, then.' It gave her something to do, and himself time to struggle with his uncertainty.

She was slim, fine-boned, graceful. Her hair was long, tied back on the nape of her neck with a ribbon. No make-up. The eyes still arresting, still watchful, still making him uncomfortable, but then how could he not be uncomfortable after such a long time.

'So,' he said, when he'd been given the tea, 'so, how are you? How have things been?'

She smiled, and sipped her own tea, still standing beside the cooker. 'I'm fine, considering. And you?'

'Fine, considering. Considering quite a lot, eh, for both of us?'

She nodded, came and sat at the table with him, then asked him the obvious questions, about when he'd got back, how bad had things been, and he answered, keeping his answers factual and shrugging off the deeper implications. All the time, he was studying her, trying to grasp what she was like, but he could guess very little about her state of mind. Something was needed to connect them but he couldn't produce it. Then she said, 'Are you here for long?'

'Could be,' he said. 'Depends.' He wanted her to ask, on what, but she didn't, merely giving one of her funny, grave little nods.

'Depends,' he was obliged to repeat, and then add, 'depends on you, really.'

'Me?' She was startled, suddenly wary.

'Well, I thought maybe we could farm together.'

She laughed, and seemed relieved. 'Joke,' she said, smiling.

'No, not a joke, not necessarily. Could be serious, I mean a serious idea. What do you think?'

Now she was frowning. 'You never wanted to be a farmer,' she said, almost accusingly. And then: 'You can't just decide to be a farmer, not like that.'

'Why not?'

'You don't know the first thing about farming.'

'I could learn.'

'It takes years.'

'I've got years, I hope.'

'But where would you start, where would you find a farm? It's not like buying a house.'

'You could help me. We could do it together.'

'But I'm leaving, don't you remember? I'm going to London. I'm taking up my place at art college.'

After that, they were both quiet. Disappointment and a sense of having been clumsy kept Sam silent. It must have showed in his face because Lucasta murmured that she was sorry. It was going to be like this, he thought, coming back from the war, thinking he could walk into people's lives and assume nothing had changed for them when everything had changed for him. He would have to learn not to take anything for granted. Finally, he found his voice again and began asking Lucasta about herself, about how she was managing, whether she had enough money, where she was going to live. He questioned her, too, about who owned the farms around them, who might look favourably on him. She said there was always plenty of work for unskilled labourers, emphasising the unskilled. And suddenly the whole idea seemed ridiculous, and he laughed, and said he must have been mad to entertain it for even the length of a train journey – romantic nonsense, nothing more.

It was uncomfortable that night, being together in the cottage. Both of them were polite and trying desperately to connect with each other. Lucasta asked about the war, but he didn't want to talk about it, or rather he didn't know how to. He'd start a sentence intending to describe some incident and run out of words halfway through it. His head would fill with an image of what he'd been going to tell her but the words wouldn't come, and so he was left stranded, feeling far away, failing entirely to communicate the fear and horror he'd experienced. What he craved was a drink, some alcohol, but she had none and the nearest pub was too far away to walk to just for a drink. He felt tense and unsettled and wanted to leave, but by then it was late and he had nowhere to go.

She took him up to a bedroom, saying it had been their mother's, she hoped he didn't mind, but the bed was longer and wider and more comfortable. He was so tired and dispirited that he didn't object, though he didn't like the idea at all. Should he kiss her goodnight? No. It didn't seem right, she kept her distance. Lying in bed, he found himself wondering if Lucasta had ever kissed anyone. She was attractive, but there was the same off-putting coolness about her that there had been as a child, and no boy would have been daring enough to risk it. But his sister's personal life was none of his business. Though he might fancy he was now *in loco parentis*, he couldn't expect her to accept that in the circumstances. He had to prove himself, but he didn't know how.

Sleep didn't come as quickly as he wanted it to. The bed was fine, but he couldn't bear the thought of his mother's having slept here. He lay there studying the room in the moonlight which shone through the open, uncurtained window. The room was small, with a sloping roof, and flowered wallpaper that in the dim light seemed unsettling, alive. There was a tiny iron fireplace and above the mantelpiece he could see a painting, but he couldn't quite make out what it was of – perhaps it was one of his mother's. He hadn't thought to tell Lucasta that he would like a memento of some sort, though he didn't know what. A painting would do. A small one, that he could hang easily and take with him wherever he went. Maybe this little painting. He would ask Lucasta.

★

Lucasta stayed up after Sam had at last gone to bed. She had nothing she needed to do, but she didn't want to lie awake thinking about him. If she waited, and walked about a bit, and read, then maybe when she did go up she would sleep at once. He looked so old: that had been the first shock. She remembered him when he had last lived at home, so handsome and energetic, with a thick head of black hair, always tanned, always lively and bright. Their mother had been forever shouting at him to sit down, keep still, but he was always on the go, eating meals standing up and dashing off to meet friends, take a girl out. He'd been a whirlwind in the house. But all that seemed to have gone – this man who had turned up was heavier, stronger but also calmer. He'd sat for over an hour, she'd noticed, without once moving, and when he did it was in a cautious, deliberate way. His hair was still black but it was cut brutally short, making his face look squarer and drawing attention to his large ears which she never recalled noticing before. But it was the colour of his skin and the lines on it which made the greatest change. His complexion wasn't tanned, it was a dull beige colour, which made him look ill, and the frown marks on his forehead were deep. Looking at him, she'd felt sad and sorry for him. This colossal change was, she realised, to do with the war and what he had been through; but then she thought of the soldier in Trafalgar Square, and how none of this weariness had been in his face.

But perhaps that man had had a very different war from Sam. She tried to appreciate what it must have been like for him, but though she could imagine the awful, stifling heat, or thought she could, she could not exactly visualise the place where he had been imprisoned. He didn't seem able to describe it, and she saw that struggling to do so upset him. It troubled her that Sam's memories, trapped in his mind, might plague him for the rest of his life. What he needed was someone who could help him deal with them, and she knew she was not that person. She had the desire to be, and she longed to love, and be loved by, her brother in an open, easy, affectionate manner, but she was as frozen as he was when it came to communicating concern. It was as though they were stranded on either side of a river, and that river was the war.

★

The morning was better. Sam woke up refreshed after almost ten hours' sleep. The sun flooded the bedroom and warmed his face where he lay. He closed his eyes and revelled in the warmth and comfort, listening to a song thrush perched somewhere very near his window. If he strained, he thought he could hear the sea in the distance, and something else, the faintest hum, perhaps of a tractor. Peaceful sounds, all of them. He could hear Lucasta moving about downstairs, the gentle clink of a cup, the tap of a spoon, the quiet opening of a cupboard. He should get up, get washed, shave, dress, go down, but it was heaven lying there, he couldn't move. The painting above the mantelpiece, when he did open his eyes, was not as interesting as he'd hoped. He wondered why the artist had bothered to paint the rather dreary corner of a room. There was nothing happening, no drama or bright colours. He didn't think he wanted it, after all.

They had breakfast outside, sitting at a rickety wooden table underneath a pear tree. Lucasta worried that there wasn't much to eat, but to him the brown bread and butter, and a boiled egg, were a feast. It was a Sunday. 'Do you go to church?' he asked her, teasing, guessing she wouldn't. But she said that she did some-times, though she didn't know why, it was just 'somewhere to go if it was raining'. The pathos of this touched him, though he took care to hide his reaction. When she'd cleared the breakfast things away, she suggested a walk on the cliff path and he agreed eagerly.

Walking was good. They would be doing something and the awkwardness between them would seem less heavy. If he remembered correctly, a lot of the cliff walk had to be done in single file and conversation would be impossible.

An hour later, they came back to the cottage much more relaxed with each other and Lucasta asked, 'Sam, can I draw you?'

'What, now, here?'

'Yes. Here, outside. If you just sit where you are, I'll try. It might take a long time.'

'Well, I'm not going anywhere, not yet.'

It took ages to get everything set up, with Lucasta endlessly changing his position until he began to become a little irritable and impatient and had to control the temptation to tell her he'd changed his mind. But finally she was satisfied. He went and stood beside her, looking at what she'd produced. It was not in the least like him, but that pleased him and meant he could speak freely.

'Well,' he said, 'I don't recognise myself, that chap doesn't have much to do with me, but it's striking, that's one thing. Wouldn't like to meet him on a dark night.'

She said nothing, just began quietly putting things away. He didn't know how, but he knew he had upset her. To change the subject, he said, 'Have you heard from Tom recently?' She shook her head. 'I wonder if he'll ever come back?' Sam said, lamely. 'He seems to like it there.'

'He does,' Lucasta agreed. 'He mentioned a woman in his last letter, someone he's getting fond of, an Australian. There's nothing for him to come back for.'

'There's you.'

'Me? Don't be silly. Why should he come back for me?'

'He's your brother, he worries about you, I'm sure.'

'Rubbish. He knows I can look after myself. I'm not his responsibility. Or yours.'

'But he cares about you, as I do.' She frowned. He cleared his throat, and repeated, 'I *do* care about you, that's why I've come.' She was taking everything in the wrong way. It was infuriating.

His concern, so difficult to express, seemed to annoy her and he couldn't understand why. He didn't want to be childish, but it was tempting to take offence and slam out of the cottage. But then she said, 'Sorry,' abruptly, and he saw there were tears in her eyes. The moment she realised he had noticed this, she rushed into the kitchen and began washing dishes noisily, and he didn't dare go after her. Instead, he put a record on the old gramophone in the corner, some sort of jazz. She came back with some sandwiches she'd made, and they sat together, eating and listening to the music. He almost fell asleep but jerked himself upright when the record ended.

'I'll have to go to bed,' he said. 'I get so tired all the time.' He hesitated – it was so exhausting trying to think what to say, how to bridge the gap between them – and then said, 'I'll be leaving tomorrow, going to London. Have to get myself sorted.'

'I went to London last year, on VE Day. It terrified me. I don't know how I'll manage when I start at Chelsea.'

'The college will fix you up. You'll be all right. Send me your address when you get one. I'll send you mine as soon as I'm settled. I'll write to you here till you go to London.'

'You'll write?' She looked incredulous.

'Yeah, why not?'

'You never did, before the war. Mum used to . . .'

'Don't.'

'Sorry. OK, write. I'll write back. If you write.'

'I will. I'm not just saying it. I want to.' He hesitated, longing to say more, to tell her that he wanted to get to know her, to feel that the blood link between them meant something, but as ever the words wouldn't come, they were lurking in his mind but they were too sentimental and mawkish. Instead, he said, 'I'd like something of Mum's to take with me.'

'I'm afraid there isn't much. I did write and ask you if . . .'

'I know. But I couldn't think . . . what about one of her drawings or paintings? Are they stashed away somewhere? That one in my room, where I slept, I thought maybe – though it doesn't really make me think of her . . . or . . .'

'No wonder.'

'What?'

'That the painting in your bedroom doesn't make you think of her, because Mum didn't paint it.'

'Who did?'

'Don't know. A better artist, I think. It was a present, don't you remember? Just before I was born, for her fortieth.'

'God, no, I was only, what, three, four?'

'Anyway, it wasn't hers. I wouldn't have let you have it, even if it had been. It's too precious.'

'You're welcome to it.' He didn't like the way she'd said that. 'How about a cat drawing? There were loads of those.'

He left the next morning with a small black-and-white charcoal drawing of Turpin, the cat they'd had when he was about seven. It fitted easily into the inside pocket of his jacket, it was so small. He liked feeling it there, next to his heart, and kept patting it as he and Lucasta walked to the station. Just as the train was about to come in – they could hear it approaching – Lucasta said, 'I'm glad you came. Thanks.' He was so ridiculously pleased, and managed at last to kiss her and hug her as he'd been wanting to ever since he'd seen her. Her body in his arms felt both fragile and soft. It touched him, made him almost tearful, and he had difficulty keeping his composure. She did not resist his embrace but she did not respond either, except for placing her arms tentatively round his back and allowing herself to be held. It was he who stepped back, releasing her. He wanted to say something but, yet again, the right words would not come. He squeezed her hands as he let her go, then picked up his bag and got on the train. 'Keep in touch,' he said, through the open window of the carriage door, his voice sounding strangely hoarse. 'I'll send an address as soon as I have one, I'll write, I will!' He made a point of continuing to wave until she was no longer even a speck in the distance.

*

The relief Lucasta felt when once more she was alone in the cottage was a physical thing, like a headache lifting, a pain disappearing. It scared her even though she was glad of the sensation. What was to become of her if she could not bear the company of others? And Sam was not 'others'. He was her brother, who cared about her and, in his own way, loved her.

She picked up her portrait of him and scrutinised it carefully. Had she caught something of him? Perhaps she had, after all. It had felt exciting, somehow, at last, to have tried. It was always a strange feeling, the charcoal in her hand having a life of its own as it had swept over the paper guided, it seemed, not by that hand, or her eyes but some other force. It wasn't something she could tell anyone. Too fanciful, too pretentious. But it was true. She hadn't lost the power.

★

Sam wrote short, stilted letters, but he wrote often. The letters didn't arrive regularly every second week or even every month, but their very irregularity could be depended upon. Sometimes the gap would be long, as long as six weeks, and then there would be two letters within days. They came from all over the world, mostly blue airmails. Lucasta could tell that the airmail sheet suited Sam and understood why – one whole side and then the turnover flap, and he was done. It was a space he could manage, it wasn't intimidating. He filled these blue airmails with information. That, to her brother, was obviously the point of a letter – to give the receiver information. He didn't write about thoughts and feelings, fears and hopes, but about where he had been, where he was going, what he had seen and done. They were travelogues and didn't develop their relationship in any way, but Lucasta loved the airmails and was touched that Sam sent them. She saved them all.

Her own letters were not like Sam's. She found them difficult to write, and worried that they might overwhelm Sam in their detail. She tried to follow the pattern of her brother's letters, writing back immediately, and once she was in London, she had plenty to tell him: about art college, and what her timetable was like and what she was learning, and about the other students. Because of the war, most of them were quite a lot older than she was but she liked this: she got on better with older people. They were more serious, less like the average giddy students she had feared. And there was a lot to tell him about London and how she had come to love it, to her own great surprise. What she liked was the very thing she had thought she would hate – its vastness, its complexity. She found it liberating not to be known, to be anonymous in the crowds, where no one looked at her, no one noticed her. Remembering her terror on VE Day, she was embarrassed.

But then, once her education was finished, the letters became easier to write. At first, she rented a bedsitter in the Vale of Health, in Hampstead, which gave her something to tell Sam, and at the same time she got a job in an art gallery.

The owner was a woman, of about sixty (Lucasta thought), called Charlotte Falconer, who had lived in Hampstead all her life. Her gallery was a corridor of a room, at the top of Heath Street, almost at Whitestone Pond. Someone told Lucasta that Miss Falconer was wealthy and belonged to a well-connected family who had owned a large house, somewhere off East Heath Road, now turned into flats. She herself didn't live there but in a tiny flat above her gallery, a very modest space consisting of two rooms and a bathroom. She had apparently inherited her father's art collection, sold some of it, and founded her gallery on the proceeds. She was reputed also to have a private income and had become a patron of young artists. Her speciality was portraits, which was how Lucasta had come to enter the gallery, having seen, through the glass door, portraits hanging on the walls.

Charlotte – she wouldn't hear of being addressed as Miss Falconer – seemed to fill her little gallery, not because she was tall and broad-shouldered, which she was, but through the size of her personality. She had an energy about her, even when sitting still, which made Lucasta feel weak. At first, when Lucasta started working for her, Charlotte's inquisitive nature proved a strain. 'I'm prying,' Charlotte said, as her direct questions about Lucasta's past went unanswered. 'I shouldn't, I'm sorry. Don't take any notice – I can't help wanting to know *everything* about people.' She said this so frankly and cheerfully that one really could not take offence, and as Lucasta confessed in a letter to Sam she felt ashamed of her reluctance to satisfy Charlotte's harmless curiosity. She was not, she realised, devoid of curiosity herself when it came to wondering about her employer. Sometimes, she was surprised and impressed by Charlotte's knowledge. Charlotte didn't lecture Lucasta exactly but there was something of the teacher about her – had she trained, perhaps? – and her lessons were more inform- ative and enjoyable than those Lucasta had been given at college.

It was Charlotte's idea, when Lucasta had worked there for a year, that she should rent the top flat in her old home. The rent she quoted was, Lucasta knew, far below the market value but Charlotte said it was more important to her to have tenants she liked and trusted than to make a lot of money. She took Lucasta to see the flat. 'These had been the maids' rooms, and the attics, when it was our family house,' she said. 'I always liked them. I have a thing for attics, something about the simplicity of them, the way they pare life down.' But there was not much of an attic feeling left about this converted top floor, now that the ceiling levels had been altered and some walls knocked through. Lucasta accepted Charlotte's offer, of course, writing to tell Sam how lucky she felt to have found such a flat. She mentioned in this letter how the normally ebullient Charlotte had seemed unlike herself when she was showing her the flat – quiet, pensive, even a little sad.

Once she had moved in, Lucasta invited Charlotte there for a drink, but Charlotte said that she found it painful being in her old home and that she'd rather meet Lucasta in a café, if she didn't mind. They had a meal at the Cresta, a Polish restaurant near the gallery, instead, and after that occasionally they met for a drink in one of the local pubs. It suited Lucasta perfectly. She never got to know her employer intimately but they were friends. She judged Charlotte to be a contented person, happy with her gallery, and deriving great satisfaction from promoting young portrait painters. She never invited Lucasta to her own flat, which she said was too small to entertain in, but Lucasta thought it was

more that Charlotte wanted to keep it to herself, and she understood this completely. It was odd, with Charlotte being the
outgoing, generous person she was, and with her being well-off,
for her to want to keep the flat to herself, and for it to be so
modest. But Lucasta liked the contradiction.

While Sam travelled the world, Lucasta went on helping
Charlotte, and in her spare time began to paint portraits. Charlotte
commissioned the first, of herself, and was so pleased with the
painting that she displayed it in her gallery. Other commissions
followed, and slowly, over a period of ten years, Lucasta reached
the stage of being able to support herself by painting full-time.
When she was forty, she turned one of her rooms into a studio
and, greatly daring, established a new rule: people who wanted
her to paint their portrait came to her, she did not go to them.
It was a rule which almost proved her undoing, because people
who had the vanity to wish to have their portrait painted were
not the sort of people who were willing to climb stairs to an
attic flat. But she'd made the rule, and persevered, and in time it
came to seem a charming eccentricity, with which sitters interested enough to engage her services were happy to comply. She
made a reasonable living, and was happy in her work, and reported
to Sam that her success was growing. It seemed a little conceited
to say so, but if she didn't who else would tell Sam? He knew
no one in the art world who would pass the word on that his
little sister was reckoned to be a promising portrait painter, a name
to watch.

Once, Sam wrote, very sweetly and shyly, offering her money.
He had sailed a boat via the West Indies to New Zealand and
sold it at an unexpectedly large profit. He could, he wrote, let
her have £100. Such an amount would have been very handy at
the time, when she was still struggling, before she moved into
Charlotte's flat, but Lucasta had declined it, with thanks. Sam's
way of life seemed as precarious as her own, and she thought he
would have more use for it than she did. She was right. The next
boat Sam helped to build and then sailed halfway round the world,
did not fetch much money. It had been damaged in a storm, he

wrote, and his costs were hardly covered. After that experience, he gave up the boat business and became a ski-instructor. How he got into this Lucasta never did find out. It was one of the periods when there was a long gap between his letters and, when one arrived, it was preoccupied with the Alpine scenery in Austria where he was working. He wrote that she should come and visit him, and she almost did, but then her cat was sick and she couldn't leave; and Sam didn't ask her again, clearly thinking a sick cat was just an excuse.

Sometimes, Lucasta wondered if she suffered from agoraphobia, so extreme was her dislike of leaving her flat. She would let herself run out of basic foods – milk, coffee, bread – and then, near the closing times of shops, she would be forced to dash out and get what she needed. Again and again it happened, twenty past five on a Saturday and only ten minutes to dash to the High Street. It was ridiculous. And yet, once out, she enjoyed it and was in no hurry to return (which showed, she felt, that she was not truly agoraphobic, but just had difficulty with departures). She invariably ended up, carrying whatever vital supplies she'd gone for, wandering first up Heath Street and then onto the Heath above the Vale of Health. She'd sit looking down at the Pond, and think, for some reason, of Cornwall and wonder how on earth she had ever managed to leave it when she so hated change and moving and disruption of every sort.

Her rooms pleased her all the time. Over the years, she had lavished such care and attention upon them, striving to have every detail how she wanted it, and she felt she had succeeded – her rooms were her. Her living room, though the furniture was antique, looked modern with its white walls and plain varnished floors and no curtains, only blinds. The blend of the old and new was what gave her most pleasure. She felt it represented something of herself, though writing to Sam she was unable to explain exactly what she meant.

Sometimes in his letters, Sam would mention girlfriends. There was Beatrice for a while, who was replaced by Clare, whom he seemed extremely fond of, until she too vanished without explanation. Tom had married meanwhile – Sam had visited him in Australia – and was very happy, with two children, both boys. In a postscript, after that visit, Sam had commented that he couldn't see himself marrying and asked if she was 'tempted'. Lucasta had replied that there had been no one tempting, and left it at that. There had seemed no point in describing to Sam the kind of fleeting affairs she'd had. None of them had been in the least serious. Sam could never be her confidant. She didn't want to bare her heart to him, or to anyone, preferring to maintain her absolute privacy. Privacy was all. It wrapped itself round her and she hugged it to herself, content to be protected by it. She sometimes felt that her rooms knew her best – if they could have talked, they would have had a great deal to tell which would have surprised listeners. The pleasure she felt, for one thing, every time she came back to her home and closed the door behind her. Something always lightened within her, and she took a while to get used to it. The silence was so soothing. She moved among her things carefully, gliding across the floors with barely a sound, her skirt giving the slightest of whispers. This contentment with her own presence was her strength. Nobody could violate it for long. Those who came to her flat hardly touched its essential calm. They came (by arrangement only), they left, mere ripples on the smooth surface of her life. She was lucky, she thought, to have her own territory and rule it so completely. The room breathed, it held her. The room had power over her, it was not inanimate.

She thought about hanging the little painting over the mantel-piece, but the space was too big. To the right of the fireplace, in the slim space between it and the door, where the light was not strong, she found the perfect spot. It looked right there, the canvas so small but fitting into this place perfectly.

★

Paul Mortimer had not wanted his portrait painted at all, but it had been his wife Ailsa's idea, her present for his fiftieth birthday, and he didn't want to hurt her feelings. However, it was a nuisance to have to go to the artist's studio in Hampstead and toil up those stairs and obey her instructions. She didn't try to charm him or make him feel comfortable but instead was polite, just, but brusque, and didn't offer him refreshment during all the hours he was with her. Once, when he had a dry throat and coughed, she offered him a glass of water. She was so thin herself that she looked as though she never ate or drank. He studied her because there was nothing else to look at, except the easel with her head appearing from behind it, staring at him. It was slightly unnerving and made him fidget. The chair she'd posed him on was a ladder-backed wooden chair, upright and hard, and he sat with his arms crossed, feeling the wooden bars press into him. He knew he was frowning and probably looked bad-tempered. She'd be painting him as an ogre.

The sessions, mercifully, were not quite a full hour. She knew he was uncomfortable, of course. When she selected the damned chair she had told him just to say if he found it too uncomfortable and she'd find another, but he was too proud to admit that he found sitting bolt upright too difficult. So he was stuck with the chair, and with the pose. 'Sit how you want,' she'd told him, 'but be sure you can hold whatever position you choose.' First he'd put his hands on his knees, and then he'd folded them. First he'd had his legs slightly apart, then imagined how this would look, and brought them together, only to settle on crossing them at the ankle. He'd been told to wear what he liked himself in best – an invitation to vanity if ever he'd heard one, and he wasn't going to fall into that trap. He wore a dark suit and a white shirt.

He wondered about the artist. She was not young, about forty, perhaps. He didn't find her attractive, though he supposed some men might like her feline looks. She had good skin, pretty hair and her eyes were arresting not just because of their size and shape but their colour, more green than grey, the irises flecked with some other colour which he couldn't quite decide on – gold? Every other woman in London was wearing a short skirt but Lucasta Jenkinson – an absurdly incongruous mixture of names – had on a long skirt, down to her ankles and tied at the waist with a bow to one side. It was made of some sort of floaty blue material and the top she was wearing matched the shade. Her figure was good, she was slim but her breasts were well rounded and were emphasised by her thin sweater. What struck him most was her extreme neatness and freshness – there was nothing of the messy artist about her. She cared about her appearance, he thought, and her clothes, took time and trouble over both. But for her own benefit, he decided. Certainly not for his.

Was there someone else? If so, all evidence was well hidden. No one lived with her, he was pretty sure. He'd tried, at the beginning, to chat her up, since she was clearly not going to chat him up. She appeared not to hear him. Twice, he'd asked the same question, twice there was neither acknowledgement nor reply. But then he remembered she had told him, on his arrival, that if she were silent during the sitting he must forgive her, it was how she worked. But it made him uneasy to spend nearly an hour without any communication, and being stared at. He was sure his discomfort would show in the finished portrait, and he'd hate it. She wouldn't let him see the work in progress. About that she had been very definite, and he'd accepted that it would perhaps be a kind of unwelcome interference. But he was a curious man and found containing his curiosity frustrating – he wanted a quick glance, no more. But at the end of each sitting, she stood up and thanked him and then waited until he had left the room. She didn't even see him to the door but remained beside her easel, bidding him goodbye, and thanking him, from a distance. He longed for some distraction to take her from the room – a phone call, a parcel being delivered – but though there was one afternoon when the door-bell rang, she ignored it. 'Feel free to answer the door,' he said, trying to hide his eagerness, 'I don't mind.' She said nothing, and then when the bell sounded even more insistently and he fidgeted with anxiety, she said, 'Please keep still, Mr Mortimer. I never interrupt a sitting. The caller will call again,' and he felt reprimanded.

On his way out of the house that day, he found a parcel sitting outside the door at the bottom of her staircase. It was tucked behind a tub of geraniums on the step, safe from all except the most prying eyes, and the postman, or delivery man, had put a note through the letter-box, saying where it was and what time he'd called. Paul hesitated a moment and then picked up the parcel – quite light, quite small, though just too big to go through the letter-box – and went back up the stairs. He climbed them as quietly as he could, hoping to surprise Lucasta Jenkinson, simply to see how she would react when caught unawares. But he didn't catch her unawares. She was waiting for him outside the front door of her flat. 'How kind,' she said, holding out her hand. 'Thank you.' 'Hope it's something interesting,' he said, feeling slightly foolish, because she must have seen him coming up almost on tiptoe. 'The stamps look interesting, anyway,' he added, just for something to say. She smiled, said goodbye again, and went into her flat, closing the door gently. He left thinking how much he disliked aloof, remote, self-contained women who couldn't even bring themselves to engage in pleasantries never mind any more meaningful social contact.

There were six sittings before she said anything to him other than good morning, good afternoon, please make yourself comfortable, goodbye, thank you. By then he was playing her at her own game, entering with a nod of greeting – that trumped her good morning – and settling down quickly on the damned chair. On the seventh, and penultimate occasion, she did not at once take up her own position. Instead, she stood in front of him, quite close, and said, 'I'm having trouble with your tie.'

'My tie?'

'Yes. It looks wrong. There's something about it.'

'You mean the pattern, the stripe?'

'Yes. It doesn't fit. I wonder, could you remove it?'

'You mean, not wear a tie?'

'Yes. Or not that one.'

His hands felt oddly sweaty as he fumbled to take off his tie, letting it drop to the floor.

'Now undo the button,' she said. 'Your top shirt button. Thank you. Much better,' and she went back to her easel.

What was she playing at? All those sittings, and she had said

244

nothing about ties or shirt buttons. Had she only just noticed he was wearing a tie that didn't 'fit'? He would look absurd, a formal suit and white shirt without a tie. If he was to be protrayed in an open-necked shirt he wanted it to be a casual shirt, worn with casual trousers. He should have said so, made his objections clear, but he'd meekly obeyed. It felt better, though, not to be wearing a tie and to have the neck of his shirt open. Was she looking at his throat, or at the gap where his chest hair showed, the beginnings of it, at least a hint? Her move had almost been like a sexual advance and yet she was so unsexual, or did he mean asexual, it couldn't have been that. The words kept repeating themselves in his head – 'I wonder, could you remove it? . . . Now undo the button' – but he was sure that there was no trace of innuendo.

At the end of that particular hour – which felt like an eternity – she actually smiled. 'Thank you,' she said, 'that was much better, getting rid of the tie. It changed things.'

'You should have said earlier.'

'I didn't know earlier. It just occurred to me what a tie was doing to you.'

'I always wear a tie at work. I'm used to ties. They don't *do* anything to me.' He was irritated by her silly assumptions. But she didn't defend herself, merely raised her eyebrows and looked amused and he was shocked to realise he would have liked to slap her.

'One more session, I think?' he said, calmly enough.

She nodded. 'Good, thank you, next Tuesday, then. Would you mind if I took a photograph before you go?'

'Now?'

'No. At the end, before we finish. It might be useful, before I deliver the portrait, to get details right, an *aide-mémoire*.'

'Certainly.'

'Thank you.'

He left her flat in a fury.

★

From the beginning Lucasta had found it hard to conceal her attraction to Paul Mortimer – it had been a shock, to feel what she did the moment he walked into her studio. There had been no preparation for the physical sensations he aroused so immediately, the faint tingling in her limbs, the sudden palpitations, the heat spreading through her body. And yet he was not conventionally handsome, no chiselled features or noble brow or lustrous hair. He had about him something of Sam when he came back from the war, a toughness, a hard look, and a weariness in the lines of his face. He had great confidence, too, striding into her flat, arm outstretched, towering over her and meeting her stare with a measured one of his own. His hand, when she took it, was strong, the skin rough, and he gripped her own a little longer than necessary. It had taken all her self-possession to remain cool and polite, and she had hurried to begin the work. Once she had done so, she felt more in control, and able to explain her reaction as the result of having expected a quite different sort of man.

He was a company director, that was all she'd known. The name of the company had meant nothing to her and she hadn't been curious enough to ask questions. The portrait had been commissioned by his wife, though Lucasta had never met her, for his fiftieth birthday. It had all been fixed up through Charlotte, whose gallery Mrs Mortimer had been taken to by a friend, to look at Lucasta's work. The money was significant and Lucasta accepted the commission without first meeting the sitter or his wife, though she was surprised this had not been insisted upon. She was asked to 'capture the essence of the man', which somehow sounded affected, but she was not so prosperous that she could afford to let this put her off. Once Paul Mortimer came to sit, she saw that she would have no trouble catching his 'essence'. The suit was boring and she decided quite quickly to ignore it. She'd paint him from the shoulders up, concentrating on his face. But she didn't tell him this. On the contrary, she encouraged him to believe that his whole posture was important, right down to the way he positioned his feet, and enjoyed watching him try to make himself comfortable on the upright chair. He failed, but his discomfort translated into a determination to endure which gave him the most aggressive expression. This was what they must have meant about catching his 'essence' – his 'I will not be beaten' attitude. Every time she lifted her eyes from the canvas to study him she was overwhelmed by the power blazing out of him – he could hardly contain himself, he might at any moment spring up and shout at her. For a moment her brush trembled in her hand. She found herself clearing her throat repeatedly with the effort of composing herself.

He'd tried to begin a conversation but, from every point of view, she could not afford to have one, and was telling the truth when she said she had to work in silence. But the deeper reason, in this case, was that she might have given too much away. He would attempt to charm her, she could tell, without being overtly charming. Over and over again, throughout the weeks, she reminded herself that she knew nothing about this man, except that he was an immensely successful company director and that he was married, with children. Her attraction to him was purely physical, chemical almost, or that was how she described it to herself – it was a matter of hormones, leaving her mind disengaged. She neither liked nor disliked him, she did not even know him, but was drawn to him in the most superficial of ways. It was always the same for her. The few affairs she had had were due to sexual attraction, and when that was satisfied there was nothing left. Sometimes she thought she ought to get to know a man properly before indulging her own frank desire for him. But it would mean a level of disturbance she could hardly tolerate. And she did not want people to 'get to know' her, either. Intimacy, true intimacy, involving minds and hearts and emotions, was abhorrent to her. This, she acknowledged, was so abnormal it was better not to mention it. It hurt people, and she had no wish to offend or pain anyone. It was better to pretend that she was busy, or ill – anything to get out of prolonging such encounters.

Paul Mortimer was only one of several men to whom she had been attracted in the same straightforward way, but he was different. Usually, she could tell at once that the object of her attraction was also attracted to her – all she had to do was give a signal. But in his case she warned herself against it. She also warned herself against something else: thinking that *he* was attracted to her. She had spent hours studying him, and saw that he was not. On the contrary, he seemed to regard her with something like disdain, if not actual contempt.

After Paul Mortimer had returned to give her Sam's parcel (a jade necklace, for her birthday) she had difficulty settling down. She stood at her window, watching him march vigorously along the road, then she turned to examine his portrait: it was good, striking, perhaps the best thing she had ever done, though whether he, or his wife, would like it was another matter. If they didn't, she would keep it, and refuse to accept a fee. Hours later, as the light faded outside, she prowled through her rooms, unable to sit down, feeling tense and jumpy, and her cat complained loudly, wanting to curl up on her lap. She never went out at this time of evening, never, but suddenly she grabbed her coat and rushed down the stairs and into the road, cutting across to the Heath and almost running towards the ponds. She kept up the pace all the way down the hill, slowing down only when she reached the path between the ponds, pausing to look at the reflections of the houses in the darkening water. More in control, she continued up the hill ahead until she stood on the top, with all London spread out before her, a mass of lights beginning to appear like a rash across all the buildings. Thousands and thousands of people there, behind those lights, within the walls from which they beamed out, and herself alone, outside all of them, and looking down upon them.

What was wrong with her? She felt irritated with herself, angry that she was behaving like a woman with no dignity. Breathing deeply, she tied her scarf tighter round her neck and began the walk home. She met no one. It was almost dark now, though not pitch black, the way nights like this had been when she was a child in Cornwall. Then if there was no moon and the stars were hidden by clouds, the dark had been frighteningly dense. There were cars on East Heath Road providing yet more light, a constant bathing of the trees with the brightness. She felt exhausted, though with what she could not decide. Everything inside her felt disturbed, agitated. Once back in her flat, she was calmer, as she always felt whenever she returned. Then, glass of wine in hand, she sat in front of the fire and ate her supper, the cat quiet at her feet. There was hardly enough light to see the attic painting in all its sweetness but tonight it did not soothe her, as it had done so many times when she'd been agitated, but on the contrary, it saddened her. She remembered that as a girl, when first she'd noticed her mother's picture, it had seemed a peaceful image, the pretty corner of an attic, but also insipid, unexciting, even soporific. But over the years she had come to see it as triumphant, catching a mood of something gained after great effort, and she had found it uplifting. Now she changed her mind again. It was surely a picture of sadness, a gentle wistfulness, the reflection of an aching heart. She couldn't bear its poignancy. Taking it down, she went and found a piece of clean cloth and wrapped it up. It was ultimately too full of heartbreak and she did not want her heart broken by a painting.

In the morning, the paleness of the square where it had hung stood out. She looked around for something else to put there, but could find nothing the right size. The nail hung empty, accusing her.

★

Paul Mortimer was an observant man. When he was a child, his father had made a game of training him to be what he was himself, a detective, and he had never lost the habit of memorising the contents of a room, the colour of a person's eyes and hair, the names of shops on the bus route to school. He'd enjoyed it. His father would wait until they had left a restaurant and then cross-examine him: how many people had been there, how many tables, who had been sitting to the right and left of them? He was brilliant at it, and had never failed to delight his father even though he had not gone on to join his profession – and his talent had served him well, both in the army and in his later career.

So it was not so remarkable that he should notice, on his last visit to Lucasta Jenkinson's flat, that a painting had been removed. To get to her studio he had to walk through her living room and he knew exactly what it contained right down to the magazines and books (poetry, he noted) on the low glass table in front of the fireplace and the colour of the tall candles in the glass candle-sticks above it. He knew, from the height of these candles, that she had lit them the night before – in a week, he reckoned she burned three-quarters of each candle. Everything in this room was always immaculately tidy and clean, not rigidly so but with a pleasant, artistic feel for colour and arrangement, unlike her studio which was stark and bleak and not at all how he had imagined an artist's studio would be.

He had deduced – deduction was another part of his father's training – from the contrast in the two rooms that Lucasta Jenkinson was two people, as, he had discovered, a great many people were. All he ever saw was the artist, the portrait painter, the worker – someone austere, conscientious, demanding, exact, who required no communication with anyone else. He'd seen her withdraw into her own world, where he was simply an object. But he sensed that there was this other woman who was romantic and interested in others and had tastes far outside her working life. She might also – but this was guesswork, and his father had discouraged guesswork based on nothing but hope – have a sensual side so carefully hidden that it was in danger of being forgotten. When his wife Ailsa had asked him how he was getting on with Miss Jenkinson during the sittings he told her there was no 'getting on', there was no rapport at all between them. Ailsa had frowned, unconvinced, but he felt he was telling the truth.

She was ahead of him, leading him into her studio and his place on the hated chair. To her back, as they passed the fireplace, he said, 'I see you've removed a painting.' He saw her hesitate a fraction before continuing to lead him to his position, and then she said that yes, she had. 'Why?' he asked. 'I thought it pretty, though it was hard to see it properly, hung there.' By now she was at her easel, and he was at the chair, and they were facing each other. She could hardly not reply.

'I'm surprised you noticed it,' she said, and there was a level of sarcasm in her voice which he did not like.

'Oh, I noticed it,' he said quite sharply. 'Twelve inches by ten, I would say, an interior of an attic room, contains a wickerwork chair, with a white cushion on it and a parasol leaning against it, and a small wooden table, in front of a curtained window, with a little bunch of flowers in a jar in the middle of it, the floor . . .' He could tell she was astonished as he paused. '. . . The floor is, I think, tiled?'

'Yes, tiled.'

'But you didn't paint it, did you?'

'No.'

'Who did?'

'I honestly don't know.'

'Why did you remove it?' Would she say it was none of his business? Would she say he should be quiet, she must start work?

'It became too sad,' she said. 'Are you settled? Shall we begin?'

He crossed his arms as usual and stared straight ahead, as he always did, thinking about the possible significance of what she had, so surprisingly, told him. After a few minutes, she put down her paintbrush, and frowned.

'Something's changed,' she said, 'you look different.'

'I'm the same as ever,' he said. 'Same position, same clothes.'

'No, you're not the same. You must be thinking differently.'

'And that can change what you see?'

'Of course, in this case.'

'Well, then, it's your fault.'

'My fault? How?'

'Telling me that the little painting had become too sad to you. It makes me wonder in what way it became sad. Whether you are sad yourself, and if so, why? It's intriguing, worrying even.'

She flushed and turned away from him. 'We must get on, Mr Mortimer. This is the last sitting.'

'I know that. I want to get on. It's up to you. There's nothing I can do about my expression, I'm afraid. Shall we try again?'

He felt he'd taken charge of the situation and it pleased him – she, after all, had been in control up to now, throughout all the sittings. But when, instead of returning to her easel, she walked over to the window and stood with her back to him, her hands flat against the window panes, he began to wonder if he had spoken too abruptly, too harshly. He could see from how taut her body was that she was struggling to compose herself but not all his father's training could help him decide what precisely was wrong. When she returned to work, he saw she was now very pale and unless he was mistaken her hand, the hand holding the paintbrush, was shaking slightly. No more was said, by either of them. Whatever had been wrong with his expression must have righted itself or else she had decided that it did not matter. Gradually, the colour returned to her cheeks, and she seemed absorbed in what she was doing.

It was a little after the usual time when she stopped. 'Finished?' he asked, still holding his position. She nodded. He got up from the chair and stretched his back. 'My fault, I know, for saying the chair was fine. It was torture. That's probably what you saw in my expression.' He was trying to joke, but failed. 'Well,' he said, 'so that's it.'

'I'll deliver it next week.'

'Come to my birthday party, bring it then.'

'Thank you, no.'

'You don't go to parties, is that it? Or you just don't want to come to mine?'

'I don't go to parties.'

'How sad, a pretty woman like you. You might enjoy yourself.'

'I don't think so. You've left your newspaper.' She bent down and picked up his *Times*, and held it out. As he took it, he felt like pulling her towards him with it but instead simply held on to it. So did she. 'I'm sorry,' she said, almost whispering.

He didn't ask for what. 'Don't be,' he said, and let his hand creep along the rolled-up newspaper until it touched her own. She snatched her hand away immediately. The action told him everything.

★

It was not as easy as that. The portrait was delivered and everyone seemed to admire it, though Paul himself thought it alarming and ugly. If what he saw constituted the 'essence' of him, then people must think him cruel, heartless – that was what he saw in it. No, his wife said, not cruel or heartless but 'utterly determined to get what you want, and you always have done'.

What he now wanted, he realised to his own surprise, was Lucasta Jenkinson, whom he was supposed never to see again. That was what he said to her, when he turned up unannounced at her door.

'I am supposed never to see you again,' he told her, 'but I want to. I want to get to know you, to find out why you are sad.'

'I didn't say I was sad, Mr Mortimer.'

'You did, *Miss* Jenkinson. During our last sitting, you were upset about that painting, you said . . .'

'I said the painting had become sad, not that I was sad.'

'But you are, aren't you? You are sad.'

'This is embarrassing . . .'

'Yes, it is. I am embarrassed, but embarrassment won't make me give up. Please, can I at least take you out for lunch, to say thank you for the portrait?'

It took weeks. She refused lunch, but after several phone calls, and great persuasion on his part, she agreed to walk on the Heath with him for half an hour. She looked at her wristwatch constantly but he was determined not to be offended. He did all the talking, managing to catch her interest (he hoped) by telling her about the sort of art he collected. He liked bold, colourful paintings – Matisse, Van Gogh, Derain – and had tried to buy the work of young artists who painted in the style of the great Fauves. She was not impressed. She shrugged, and said she thought Fauvism had serious limitations – it was too crude, too vehement for her taste. Colour was not everything. Nor did she approve of his collecting the work of artists who were essentially imitators. Originality was of more value. He assumed she thought he had been boasting, and so was quiet for the rest of the walk; but at the end, he asked if they could walk again, and perhaps because she felt she had been too harsh (or so he judged), she agreed.

Soon, their weekly walk was established as a regular event. She never asked him a single question about himself, and when once he mentioned his wife and sons she made a gesture indicating that she did not wish to hear more. But gradually he learned a great deal about her background through his own polite but persistent enquiries, carefully made in as oblique and subtle a manner as he could. Sometimes, replying, she smiled slightly, as though to let him know she knew he thought he was being clever. Quite quickly, he was absolutely sure that his instinct on that last day of sitting had been correct: she was attracted to him. They walked side by side, never touching, but her body was alert, sensitive to his own movement – it felt like a dance and increasingly he dictated the rhythm and felt she was responding whether she knew it or not. His confidence, always strong anyway, grew.

He had a flat, which Ailsa his wife knew nothing about, though it sometimes occurred to him that her ignorance was deliberate. The flat was in a mews, behind Devonshire Street, and even when he had no mistress, he liked to go there occasionally, liked the secrecy of it, the feeling that he could hide, become someone else. He took Lucasta there one Thursday, two months after they'd begun their regular walks. He suggested that instead of walking on the Heath they should venture further, to Regent's Park. They took a taxi and began their walk near the Zoo then wandered right round the whole park, coming out at Clarence Gate. She stopped, expecting him to hail a taxi again, to take her home, but he said maybe she would like to see his flat where he sometimes stayed, he could give her a glass of wine there before she went home and afterwards, if she cared to, they could perhaps share a meal. She hesitated a long time, the traffic thundering by, but he did not dare try to persuade her. At last, she nodded, and they crossed the busy road and went to his flat. She was, he thought, wary, but not nervous. He poured her some wine, and they sat together sipping it, both silent. One wrong move and he knew he would never have another chance. But she took the lead. 'Well?' she said, putting down her not quite empty glass, and standing up.

It was a strange sexual experience, like none he had ever experienced before. It bewildered him. He had looked forward to the foreplay, the caressing and stroking, but she did not seem to want this and made it plain that she had an urgent need to progress at once to consummation. Afterwards he felt as though he had in some way been humiliated. He lay beside her feeling confused, even dismayed. Had he not just had what he wanted? What he had planned? But this was not what he had wanted, or not *only* what he wanted. It appeared to be what she wanted, what she was prepared to grant him, and it was nothing like enough. He wanted to know her completely. Lucasta's body was the least of what he wanted. He might have been allowed to invade her body but the rest of her was tight shut.

That first time, neither of them spoke after they had dressed, till she was leaving, when she smiled and said, 'Thank you,' and gave a little nod of approval which he hated. He felt he was being treated as he himself had treated others but before he could overcome his rage, and object, she had gone.

★

They never made love in her flat. The idea, she said, made her shiver. She would not, she said, be able to work there if he had invaded her territory. It made him feel like an animal.

Sometimes, they went away, to Paris, to Florence, to Rome, exploring art galleries. Those were good weekends, when she seemed freer and yet closer to him, and he could begin to believe that the fusing of their hearts and minds which he so desired was going to happen. He'd been with her longer than he had been with any woman except his wife and, far from becoming tired of her, his longing for her intensified. He began to think of what had always been unthinkable: leaving his wife, Ailsa. Once, he hinted at this to Lucasta and was so sharply reprimanded that he was offended. Then he began to notice that Lucasta would make small remarks about how they were spending too much time together. She said her work was suffering, she wasn't single-minded any more and it showed. Twice in one month she failed to turn up at the flat when they had arranged to meet and he was left disconsolate, brooding. An awful fear was growing in him that she was going to fade out of his life as he had faded out of the lives of several women he had known. She was doing what he had prided himself on doing, letting him down lightly, preparing him for desertion. He couldn't stand it.

For a while, several weeks at least, Lucasta wondered if what she felt for Paul was turning into love. It was a word she shied away from, a word she'd always been impatient with, suspicious of its meaning. She had loved her mother, but that had been a love so natural she had never had to question what it meant. It was not so easy to define what she felt for Paul. The physical attraction had been, and remained, powerful, but then came the warmth, the great affection, which surprised her. It was a little like the feeling she had for her absent brother Sam. Not love, but a tenderness towards him, a sense of some connection existing which could not be broken. But there was, she discovered as time went on, another element in what she felt for Paul that was not there with Sam. It was an intimacy which had nothing to do with bodies. She felt increasingly *free* with him. She did not guard her words or shield him from her thoughts. Was this love, then?

The change came while she was working. At first, she hardly noticed it. Her mind wandered a little and she found herself staring at the woman whose portrait she was painting as though she could not see her clearly. She was thinking about Paul, his arms round her that morning, the pleasure of his embrace. It was over in a moment, the distraction. She collected herself, and frowned, and carefully concentrated on painting. But it alarmed her, this interference: it must not happen again. When it did, and more seriously, when images of Paul, echoes of Paul, drifted in front of her work she resented them. Her work suffered. Twice she had to abandon a commission, dissatisfied with what she had turned out. This made her angry, first with herself and then with Paul. She felt she wanted to retreat from him before he took over her mind entirely and stopped her working. But, on the other hand, was he worth it? Worth sacrificing her work for? And was she perhaps mistaken, in blaming her involvement with Paul for a falling-off in her painting which might have happened anyway? The questions were endless and tormented her.

Some of this torment she revealed to Paul – it would have

been impossible to hide when they had become so close. He said he was flattered to have such an influence. She told him he didn't understand the panic she experienced each time she found she could not work properly. He asked if painting mattered more to her than he did, and the way in which he asked this, smiling, happy, made it clear what he expected the answer to be. She didn't reply, but he was so confident he mistook her silence for agreement. 'You know I love you,' he said, 'you know we're in love, meant for each other. Don't fight it.' She wanted to tell him that he had missed the point: it was not love that was in doubt (though she still had some doubt) but what love *did* to her. She was no longer herself, she could no longer immerse herself in painting, and she did not like the result. She was lost, adrift, and he did not anchor her as painting did.

Then he went away, on business, for a month. He bombarded her with phone calls and emails but in spite of all this communication he receded as a force in her life. She worked well again and the relief was enormous. When he returned, everything had altered. His power had gone, and once it had gone it never came back. She was her own person once more, and intended to remain so. If he noticed the difference, he said nothing. He carried on as though nothing had changed.

★

Once she had made her mind up, she thought carefully about what to give Paul as a farewell present. She wanted him to have some token of her regard for him, something that might have a significance when he had got over the hurt. He had made her happy over the months they had been together, or as happy as it was ever in her power to be.

She said, on what she intended to be their last day together, 'Do you remember, you wondered if I was sad? When I was doing your portrait?'

'Yes. You said you weren't.'

'You didn't believe me.'

'I didn't know you. I do now, as much as you'll let me. You're not sad. You weren't sad then, just self-contained.'

'I was sad, actually. And I expect I'll be again. It's part of me, this melancholy. It suits me. I work better.'

'Are you telling me something?'

'Yes. I want to go back to being on my own, Paul. I'm sorry.'

They were walking along the canal. She'd deliberately chosen to tell him while they were outside on the move. But now he stopped abruptly and pulled her, quite roughly, to face him. 'Don't be ridiculous,' he said. 'You do not want to be alone. We're part of each other now, you know we are, it's stupid to deny it. What are you trying to make out this is, some tawdry fling?'

'No. It was good. I told you, you stopped me being sad for a while.' There was a man on a bike trying to get past and Paul had to release her to make way for him. She began walking again, briskly, eyeing the steps a few yards ahead where she could get up onto the road. It had suddenly crossed her mind that he could become violent.

He caught up with her easily, but didn't grab her arm again. He seemed to be breathless and she shot a quick look at him. His face was very red and she could see a thin smear of sweat on his forehead. 'Paul,' she said, touching his hand lightly. 'I want to give you something. Look, it's in my bag. I want you to look at it, and try to understand. Please. Take it.' He took the package but didn't open it. Together they went up the steps. There was a taxi coming down the street and she flagged it and was inside in a great hurry, dreading that he would follow. But he didn't. He stood, clutching the package, looking stunned and incapable now of any action. She knew he would be determined not to let her go. He would phone and write, he would turn up and lay siege to her. There would be no escape. The only thing to do was for her to escape, flee from him, give up her flat and go somewhere else. Sam was back in the country. He had tired of travel, and had returned to Cornwall. She could go there, to begin with. It would all have to be done quickly, without hesitation. She would have to act in a fashion quite foreign to her nature.

But she felt equal to the task.

AILSA

THE JOURNEY was enough to put off all but the most determined, which is what she had intended. Ailsa didn't want
to be checked up on, by those few people who would worry
about her, nor did she wish to be found and lectured on how
selfish she was being or how much better she would feel if she
accepted invitations to be looked after. What she wanted was to
see if she could live by herself, entirely self-sufficient. The very
possibility of managing without other people excited her, but she
could not expect this to be understood. To those who knew her
she was a grieving widow, devastated by the death of her husband:
she must need support and comfort till she could begin to 'get
over' the tragedy. The truth – that Paul's death had not been a
tragedy for her – was impossible to confess.

She had dressed with care for the funeral, dreading that those
gathered together would detect her relief and deduce that she
was not, after all, distraught. Of course, in view of the nature of
Paul's death, a certain amount of relief was permissible. The cliché
'all for the best' had been much used and, by the more tactful,
the opinion that Paul would have wanted his suffering brought
to an end as quickly as possible both for his own and her sake.
They were wrong, but they didn't need to know that. Paul had
wanted every last minute of life, whatever his suffering (and he
said the pain was not so very great). He had known that she
wanted to be free, and that she had not forgiven him for his
betrayal all those years ago. It had soured their marriage even
though it had not broken it, and living with the pretence of
happiness had been a terrible strain. Divorce, however, had been
out of the question. It had not even been suggested, by either of
them.

So she had garbed herself in black, and had worn a hat with a veil, but she had not overdone the weeping. Her head had remained bowed during the Mass, and her hands clasped, penitent fashion, in front of her. Her sons, either side of her, had adopted a similar posture, and one of them, Cameron of course, had squeezed out a few tears, quickly wiped away. She had been quite glad of those tears, they had made the family group authentic somehow, and had helped her remain controlled even when face to face with Lucasta Jenkinson, who, she was sure, had not intended a confrontation in the church – their encounter was accidental, a matter of arriving at the door at the same time – and when it happened the woman had behaved well, inclining her head respectfully and then quickly departing. She had looked old and tired, but Ailsa had taken little pleasure in this. It was all a long time ago, Paul's infatuation, but at the time Lucasta Jenkinson's appearance had puzzled her (though she had only ever had a glimpse of her, when she delivered the portrait). It had made her distress worse that Lucasta was not the sort of woman Paul could normally be expected to be tempted by – not beautiful in any accepted sense; whereas Ailsa, not given to false modesty, knew that she herself was thought to be.

Once she was told of the affair, she had burned the portrait. The humiliation of realising that she herself had brought Paul and this woman together was too painful to bear. She was trembling when she carried the portrait into the garden, right to the far corner beside the brick wall, and poured petrol over it before retreating and hurling a lighted taper at it. The flash that followed, and the blaze of the fire, were immensely satisfying. She watched Paul's face disappear and with it Lucasta Jenkinson's power over him, or so she hoped. The portrait had hung in the house for six months before she had discovered what had been going on and she had felt shamed by her ignorance. The affair went on for another six months after she knew of it, and had burned the painting, but she did not suffer as much – once acknowledged, terms were agreed upon (odd though these were) and she managed to keep her dignity. She hadn't wanted to know when Lucasta

Jenkinson left London to return to Cornwall and it was all over, but Paul had made it his business to inform her. His expression gave nothing away. He was matter-of-fact, cold, dismissive of his now absent mistress. Ailsa was not fooled. Rejection was not something her husband could tolerate easily, and she had seen all the small signs of his fury and then distress and finally his depression. She had even felt sorry for him, though not sorry enough to show any compassion. It was shocking to discover how all the love she had for Paul, over so many years, seemed to have disappeared. She could not understand where it had all gone, and was frightened by the bitterness that had so suddenly taken its place. Their marriage had never flourished again though outwardly remaining intact. If, after Lucasta Jenkinson rejected him, Paul had other affairs, she no longer cared. The 'terms' for continuing as they were remained the same.

And then his illness began. He was fifty-two by then, working harder still now that he was running the company. There were medical investigations of one sort and another – though it had taken him a fatally long time to go to a doctor at all – and then he had several operations and drug treatments. He told her the prognosis before the second operation but she had guessed even after the first. 'Four, five years, if I'm lucky,' he said. In the event, he had seven, though the last eighteen months were of a desperately poor quality. All that time, he remained at home. She nursed him herself, with plenty of help, it was true, but nevertheless she was his prime carer and he did not have to end his days either in a hospice or a hospital. His gratitude was profound and he expressed it often, but her devotion bewildered him. She saw that he cherished the hope that she might still love him, in spite of the Lucasta Jenkinson affair, and she let him think so. It seemed too cruel to tell him that it was pity that motivated her now. Keeping him at home, keeping herself in front of him, made her feel good. She knew this was a dreadful admission but then it was not one which she had to make to anyone but herself.

She had wondered, at one point, whether he would ask her to contact Lucasta Jenkinson and tell her he was dying, and she rehearsed in her head what she would do and say; but he never did, and she was thankful. Once, and once only, during the last six months, they came close to discussing what had happened in a way they never could have done before. He was heavily drugged with morphine and scarcely aware of what he was saying, but he suddenly frowned and motioned her to come near him. 'Do you remember the painting?' he said. She naturally thought he meant the portrait. 'You know I burned it,' she said. 'No, no, the little painting,' he said. She had no idea what he was talking about. 'The little painting,' he repeated, 'the little picture.' She kept silent, letting him ramble. 'Looked at it often,' he murmured. 'I don't know what she meant by giving it to me.' Then he sighed. 'The heartache in it maybe.' There were tears then in his eyes. 'So difficult,' he whispered, 'love, so difficult, isn't it, all the trying, striving, hoping. Empty. Like the room.' Then he slept, and she thought he might be dead, so still did he lie, so imperceptible was his breathing, but she felt his pulse and, though it was faint, he was alive.

Next morning, after a good night, he was temporarily drug-free, and she asked him what he had meant about the 'little picture'. He shook his head, said he must have been rambling. But after he died, she soon discovered the picture. It was in a drawer, in his bedside cabinet, very carefully wrapped up in a piece of cloth. She stared at it, turned it over, and immediately connected it with Lucasta Jenkinson though without any evidence. Lucasta must have painted it and given it to him. Why else would he have hidden it? Rage that he'd thought about it while he was dying and had dared to tell her so made her want to burn it too, but the anger faded quickly and, left holding the painting, she began to study it, looking for what Paul had seen there. His comment made no sense to her. What had the corner of an empty room to do with love? Paul never talked about love. He had never said, in so many words, that he loved her, not even at the beginning. He had said, 'You are lovely,' he had said, 'I adore your eyes,' he had said, 'Your skin, it is so beautiful, it drives me mad to touch it.' Extravagant compliments, which had pleased her at the time. She had believed that they meant that he loved her. But he had never directly said so. Whether he had done so to Lucasta Jenkinson or any other woman she had no means of knowing; but she doubted it. It was not in his character to declare himself so completely. And yet, dying, he had spoken of love, of the difficulty of loving, the striving it involved, and the emptiness at its heart.

She showed the painting to no one. Partly, she was afraid someone would recognise it and tell her that Lucasta Jenkinson was indeed the artist. Though it did not seem likely to her that Paul's mistress had painted this: it was not like what she knew of her work – surely she was a portrait painter? – and she preferred to think it was the work of some other woman (though why a woman, not a man?). At any rate, she wanted no other eye to behold it and tell her more than she wished to know, and so she hid it and when the time came to leave, on impulse she took it with her. It was small, it was light, it fitted easily into the flap of a case.

★

The sea was rough when they crossed, but she found it exhilarating. The ferryboat chugged very slowly through the waves, the noise of its engine tremendous, drowning the great slapping of the sea itself. Ailsa remained on deck, with the spray hurtling over her, until the pier vanished, and then went inside. The boatman did not speak to her – she would have been unable to make out a word anyway – but stared ahead, holding the wheel tight. There were no other passengers. Lots of cargo, but no other people. After half an hour, Ailsa felt the boat slow down, the harsh throb of its engine changing to a steadier rhythm. They were coming into the east of the island, where the harbour lay, sheltered from the fierce winds. The boatman pointed through the glass partition as land came into view, and she nodded and went back on deck for the last few minutes.

The view was almost obliterated by the rain and the thick, black banks of cloud lying sullenly over the whole island. She could barely see the hills which she knew were there, and not a building was visible except for the outline of the old fishing

265

station, where the herring had once been cured. There was a truck parked near the jetty, and as the boat's engine cut out, leaving only the noise of the wind, a man got out and walked to meet them. He and the boatman exchanged words, both of them turning to stare in Ailsa's direction as she struggled to put her rucksack on and pick up her bags. Neither of them said a word to her as she stepped unsteadily onto the jetty, but the man held out his hand to take her luggage and she gave it to him, afraid that she would slip on the wet surface if she tried to carry too much. 'MacPhail,' the man said, and put her things into his truck. '*Tha droch shìde ann,*' she said, to astonish him, but he appeared not to understand her Gaelic, or, if he did, to think it was a state-ment of the obvious: of course the weather was bad, it needed no reply.

★

The weather continued bad, raining ceaselessly, all the first month. It was June, but the rain fell as though it were the middle of winter, great sheets pelting from a leaden sky. Twice a day she went out, twice a day she was soaked in spite of her supposedly waterproof clothing. In the mornings, she walked east, to the furthest extremity of the island in that direction, in the afternoons to the west. There was little to see. Visibility remained so poor that the hills were still hidden and it was only when she reached the sea that there was any change in colour. The sea, for all the dim light, looked silver, a dull metallic sheen, and the white horses crashing on the shingle beach gave the waves a certain grandeur. She liked to stand there, staring at nothing; only the noise stopped the scene from being eerie. Each time she turned and left the sea, the silence closed once more round her and she was aware of her footsteps slicing through the thick wet grass. Then, she did shiver, though not with fright. This is what it meant to be alone, cut off, forced in on oneself. It was not what she had imagined.

The croft offered few comforts. It had been modernised in a minimal way – it had running water, sewage went into a septic tank, and there was a small oil tank in the garden which provided fuel for heating, luxurious by island standards. But the floors were stone and uncarpeted, and the furniture sparse and uncomfortable. There was a bed (single) in the one bedroom; and in the downstairs room, which was both kitchen and living room, a cheap Formica table, with two stools under it. Two battered armchairs stood in front of the fire, and there was no other furniture. No refrigerator, none being thought necessary since there was a larder. There was no colour in the place at all. The walls were stone and remained unpainted – they were not even rendered or plastered. The chairs were leather, the dark brown worn black with age. The table's surface was slate grey. Hardly any light came in through the small window, which had heavy wooden shutters to close over it, but no curtains. The 'garden' had neither flowers nor shrubs, and the lawn was more heather than turf. A fence ran round the half-acre, broken in places, and where a gate had once been there was a gap.

'Do you ken where you're going?' MacPhail had said to her, when finally he had spoken that first day. She'd nodded. Of course she did. She had come here as a child, with her family, she knew both croft and island very well. But she no longer knew the people. Most of the islanders she had got to know, in holiday times, forty years ago, had died or left for the mainland. Once, there had been more than a hundred people living here, but now there were only a dozen. MacPhail was the son of a fisherman who used to take her father out with him, she knew that, but he did not recognise her or her name, though she used her maiden name and had expected him to know it. But it suited her to be thought a stranger and so, when asked, she said only that she knew what the croft was going to be like. MacPhail seemed to doubt this. She saw him watching her closely when they reached it, looking, she was sure, for signs of dismay. She betrayed none. He unloaded her stuff and was gone, to spread the news, she imagined, of the madwoman taking up residence.

Nobody bothered her. Nobody called to see if she needed anything or to invite her to their house. The few people on the island kept themselves to themselves and expected others to do the same. There was no longer a shop or a school, and the tiny chapel had long been abandoned – no service had been held there for a decade. There had never been a hospital, and now there was no doctor either. Anyone who was ill had to take the ferry to the mainland. There was one farm, on the other side of the island from the croft, but she remembered that even years ago it was hardly worthy of the name. The farmer was old and could hardly look after his hens and goats and the plot where he grew vegetables. His wife was dead, his children long since left, and he was stubbornly resisting all attempts to make him join them. No tourists came, there was nothing to see, no historic connections. If any did venture here, they left quickly. Even on a sunny day, it was not a picturesque island, but a barren, windswept outpost with a range of hills as its backbone and no buildings of architectural interest. Indeed, everything man-made was ugly.

She had a routine worked out from the beginning and stuck to it in spite of the atrocious weather. Her mood was not one of melancholy but of hope, though hope of what she couldn't have said. She had energy, and needed to use it, so her walks were long and made at a great pace in spite of the weight of her heavy wellingtons. She went out straight after her breakfast of porridge and long-life milk, and when she returned applied herself to learning not just Gaelic but Italian. She'd brought tapes with her, and books. She was especially determined to master Gaelic, the language of her forefathers, even if hardly anyone spoke it now and she would never be able to practise. Speaking phrases aloud in the croft, she liked the sound; and out on her walks, when she practised talking aloud to herself, the words felt part of the wind. She baked late morning, bread, made with dried yeast, and sometimes cakes like those her mother made, though these used up ingredients too quickly and she did not want to go to the mainland yet to renew her supplies. She made soup, broth, for the evening, enjoying all the chopping and cutting of onions and potatoes and carrots. Only after her second walk did she feel there was a hiatus in her day – she did not quite, at half past four, want to come inside and stay there, but there was no alternative, so she listened to the radio, though the reception was poor, and made the best of those hours. If the rain would only stop, things would be different, but she was not entirely dismayed by its continuation. She felt she was preparing for something and that the weather was forcing her to do so. She couldn't pretend in these circumstances. She had to face things.

Every day, going in and out of the croft, she looked at the little painting she'd brought with her, and wondered if she was getting any nearer to understanding it. It looked incongruous, stuck there on the stone wall, hanging perilously from a nail she'd driven into a crack. Some days, she could hardly see it at all.

★

On 2 July, the rain stopped. Waking early, Ailsa could not at first account for the light – the room was full of it, every dark corner illuminated. Sitting up, she looked towards the small window, where she had left the shutters open, and saw that it was now a square of gold. Getting up, crossing the room and leaning on the deep sill, she peered out, and there was the sun, already risen from behind the hills, the sky all around it a cloudless blue. Colours she had never known existed emerged on the hillsides, slashes of bright green, streaks of white, great expanses of rich brown. It was as if she had been transported to another country. On her walk, she found tiny white flowers in the sodden grass, and when she reached an inland loch, small and dark like a tarn, there were arctic terns on the water and ravens flying above it. The wood surrounding it was full of trees she recognised and which she hadn't thought would grow there, birch and willow, aspen and oak. She sat there for a while, looking towards the mainland and making out what she thought might be Ben Nevis.

All that day she spent outside, glorying in the warmth and brightness. She saw something jump, fifty yards or so from the shore, and knew it was not a fish. It jumped again, further out, and she wondered if it could be a seal. There was no one to tell her. The sea was calm, only the merest ripple disturbing its surface. She lay on the shingle and ran the tiny stones through her fingers, and found herself smiling. Was this happiness? Would it last? Could it last? The trick was to live in the present, hold off memories, refuse to face any future. She wanted to be suspended in time, she wanted her mind to be emptied, and then she would be ready to restock it: it would be under her control.

This was the beginning.

★

It took a while to become accustomed to the change in the weather. She had expected it to be a fluke, and that clouds would soon drift in and the rain start again. But the heatwave went on. She swam in the sea, bitterly cold though it remained, and grew tanned and healthy-looking. One or two people appeared on the beach she went to but did not stay long. She knew she was watched, and wondered about, but beyond the barest of greetings no one troubled her. Inevitably, when her supplies ran out, she had to take the ferry to the mainland and on the boat she saw MacPhail again. He nodded but said nothing, turning away from her for the rest of the trip. But when she had finished shopping, and staggered down to the ferry again with her rucksack full and a large, heavy bag in each hand, he helped her on to the boat. 'You'll want a lift home, with a' that,' he said, matter-of-fact. 'I can walk,' she said. 'I'll take my time, leave a bag on the jetty.' He didn't reply, but after they'd docked he seized the bags and swung them onto his truck. They drove to the croft in silence, he didn't bother her with questions, and she was grateful. 'Thank you,' she said, gathering her bags together. 'Any time,' he said. 'I'm just up the road.' She knew that 'up the road' was at least two miles and round the end of the hills. She'd seen his house, stone-built like the croft, but with a corrugated iron roof, surrounded by an untidy garden full of old cars and bits of cars. She'd seen his wife, too, a wiry little woman who wore a head-scarf and a man's jacket much too big for her. They had a dog, some sort of mongrel, who barked ferociously if anyone came anywhere near the fence, as Ailsa had done on her walks. The woman had come out, when she heard the barking, but at the sight of Ailsa – who waved – she turned and went back in without responding.

The only person who did speak to her was the postmistress.

270

The island no longer had a post office but there was a postbox on the jetty which was emptied twice-weekly and the woman who did this also delivered the mail that came over. She had a moped and chugged round the island in a self-important way, sounding her hooter unnecessarily at every bend. She wouldn't simply leave letters on the doorstep – there was no letter-box in the croft's door – but insisted on knocking and handing them over one by one, commenting on the postmarks. 'Two from London,' she would say. 'One from South Africa, my that's done well, getting to here.' All the time she would stare at Ailsa, quite open about scrutinising her. She was the one who asked, 'Here for long? Or just the summer, maybe?' Ailsa smiled, said she didn't know. 'You wouldn't fancy a winter here,' the postmistress said. 'I don't fancy it myself, and I've had plenty of them.' She, too, said she was 'just up the road' if needed. Her house, Ailsa knew, was a bungalow on the far shore, resplendent with a crazy-paving path and two urns, one either side of the bright red door, her front garden full of some hardy shrub which flowered yellow. Her name was Jeannie, Jeannie McKay. It was the only name Ailsa had been offered, apart from MacPhail's.

The letters Jeannie brought felt like an interruption: calls to duty that troubled her. Both her sons wrote regularly, or rather Cameron wrote and James's wife wrote for him since James was too lazy actually to do so himself. His concern was real, though, or so Melissa said. 'James has sleepless nights worrying about you,' Melissa wrote. Cameron didn't mention sleepless nights but sounded irritated, asking why she had to be so 'awkward', spiriting herself away like that to some godforsaken remote Scottish island. It was, he wrote, 'unnecessary', and Dad would not have wanted her to go there. Well, he was right. 'Dad', Paul, would certainly have poured scorn on this retreat of hers. He wouldn't even have begun to understand what she hoped to gain by coming to the island.

But then Paul's understanding of her had been limited, and it was her own fault. She had allowed him to cast her in a certain mould and never once had she tried to break out of it. She was meant to be content with motherhood and domesticity and to feel no need for any other fulfilment – a common enough expectation, back in 1957, when they had married. In any case, what could she have done? She had no training for anything, marrying Paul as she did when she was eighteen. She'd been meant to go to Edinburgh University, to read Modern Languages, but then she met Paul, and any thoughts of further education vanished. She knew, given her time over again, she would do exactly the same. She became an army wife, without realising it, which meant constant moving from one base to another, and then came the birth of the boys and the frightening realisation that she felt trapped and inadequate. And what had been Paul's response? 'Nonsense, you're just tired, having two babies so close together.'

He was always ambitious and determined, never content to stay still – she couldn't keep up with him. His leaving the army and going into business did not help her feelings of inadequacy, though she benefited from the stability it gave her. Paul was hardly at home, working all hours, leaving her to bring up the boys. When he was there, he was something of a tyrant and she used all her own feeble energies to protect her sons. That, she supposed, is when it began, the dreadful awareness of not being entirely happy. She tried to hide it, and had maybe been too convincing. She never complained to Paul, but instead took pride in playing the part he wanted her to play, because she couldn't see what else she could do. Never once did it enter her head that she could find another life – she was much too afraid of being alone and much too loyal to find anyone else.

From the island, she wrote back to Cameron, and to James and Melissa, feeling bound to. Her letters, she made sure, were cheerful though there was not much content. She told them about how beautiful the barren island had become in the sun, and how well she felt, leading such an outdoor life. But she didn't invite them to visit her, nor did she mention returning to London. They had to be content with that. She didn't, in any case, believe that her sons, or her daughter-in-law, were truly worried about her – they were just going through the motions of concern, and were perhaps also a little embarrassed at her withdrawal. 'You'll be turning to religion next,' Cameron had said, when she'd told him where she was going. But no, she wouldn't. Paul had been the Catholic. She had never had any faith.

Other letters delivered by Jeannie over the weeks were more problematic, and disrupted her days more seriously. There was one, forwarded from London by Cameron (she had made no formal forwarding arrangements), from Lucasta Jenkinson. In a way, Ailsa had been expecting it. The woman had left the church swiftly on the day of the funeral but Ailsa had felt somehow that this would not be the last she would know of her. Her appearance at the funeral had made her angry. This letter made her angrier still. Before reading it, but having opened it and looked at the signature, Ailsa speculated as to its purpose. An apology? She didn't think so. It would not, she thought, be in the character of what she knew about Lucasta Jenkinson to apologise years later for having an affair with someone's husband. What, then, would her letter be about? Something about Paul? Some tribute? Some regrets? When finally she read it, Ailsa was surprised. She ought to have known that this letter had been written because the writer wanted something.

★

Three glorious weeks, and then the clouds came again, but they did not bring rain. There were once more great banks of clouds, every day, filling the sky, greying it over, and then, towards dusk, they raced away and for an hour the sky would clear and the sun set splendidly, a magnificent red. There was a wind most days, coming in from the Atlantic, but it never built up into a storm. Ailsa changed her routine, adapting to the weather. She still went out every morning, to walk, but in the afternoons she turned to studying, Italian now more than Gaelic, and began trying to make something of what passed for a garden. She doubted if anything would grow, but she enjoyed preparing a small patch of ground: the digging and turning of the soil helped her to think better than walking round the island did.

What she was still thinking about was how to reply to Lucasta

Jenkinson's letter. For a while, she thought she would not reply to it at all — why should she? The woman had a cheek; she did not deserve a response. Then she veered towards thinking that it would be more satisfying to send an extremely curt reply: what you have asked is out of the question, please do not bother me again. But that did not seem appropriate either, and the longer Ailsa left it, the harder any letter seemed. She began to become obsessed, dangerously so, by the whole problem — her mind raced with alternative letters and she was near to making herself ill with repressed fury. Again and again, she looked at the little painting Lucasta Jenkinson had had the temerity to ask to be returned to her, and began to hate it. She should destroy it, then write saying she had done so. That would settle the matter. It would be spiteful, mean, the act of a philistine, of a vandal, but why should she care? Yet Paul had spoken of it when he was dying and to destroy something which had had some strange power over him, and that she herself had grown to love, too, would be akin to sacrilegious. She would have to reply.

★

Once she'd posted the letter in the box on the jetty, she realised how unsatisfactory it had been. It had come out more passionate than she had intended, and was far from being the polite, cold little note she had aimed for. Again and again, planning what she would say, she had schooled herself to hold back on emotion, and above all not to reveal how Paul had mentioned the painting as he was dying — that was an entirely personal and precious memory which belonged only to her. She wished, also, that she had not let Lucasta Jenkinson know that she did indeed have the painting. It would have been perfectly easy to say she had no knowledge of it and that all Paul's effects had now been dispersed. But she had admitted to having the painting, and said that she could not possibly part with it. That would have been sufficient, but she had spoiled the dignified effect by adding that she bitterly resented Lucasta Jenkinson's request and thought it cruel of her to make it. 'You spoiled our marriage,' she wrote, 'which is something I cannot, even now, forgive you for.'

This was the sentence that kept coming back to torture her – it was foolish, unfair, childish. Paul had done the 'spoiling' and what had been spoiled had already been far from perfect. It was her pride that was hurt, and, most of all, she had resented the fact that he had told her about his affair – it could have been conducted discreetly as she came to suspect previous liaisons had been. But he had had to confess and by doing so humiliate her, and then on top of that to suggest 'terms', all to do with maintaining appearances. She should have refused his terms, thrown them in his face and told him she wanted a divorce or at least a formal separation. But she was not a woman who could survive alone, or so she believed.

So they had carried on afterwards, for all those years, the marriage never recovering, just the husk of it remaining, solid though it might appear. And she had realised only during Paul's illness that she was stronger than she had ever believed and was more than ready, far too late, to be on her own. She dared to start thinking that she could have a life that had nothing to do with him. She did not want him back from the dead. In her letter to Lucasta Jenkinson she made no mention of this unpalatable truth though she had longed to, and by saying her marriage had been 'spoiled' she knew she had created the opposite impression. The woman would think she had always loved Paul and that her rage was due to the jealousy and resentment she still felt. But it was not – the anger was because she could have stood on her own, left Paul, or made him choose, and she never had done. But there was another source of fury which she had not let creep into her letter, about the painting itself. Lucasta Jenkinson had written that she had given it to Paul to help him understand why she had to be on her own again, but that she had regretted parting with it ever since. The memory of it had haunted her for years now, and she realised she had been wrong to part with it. It had been a present from her father to her mother, and she should never have let it go. Paul, she thought, had probably never understood its significance and she doubted if he had treasured it. If Ailsa could return the painting, hers would be a magnanimous gesture she would greatly appreciate.

But I am not inclined to be magnanimous, Ailsa had decided. She'd grown fond, truly fond, of the painting, and had got into the habit of looking at it each time she left and re-entered the room, as though checking that nothing had changed. The chair was still empty, the posy of flowers still bright, the window still closed and curtained. She'd noticed tiny details never evident to her before – the texture of the floor, the exact pattern of the wickerwork in the chair – but still she felt the atmosphere evaded her. Had Paul really understood anything about his mistress from it? Or was she right, and he had not seen what she had seen? Sometimes, especially during the weeks of rain when she came in soaked, there had been a warmth there, a welcoming glow of serenity from the picture, but other days the sense of some significant absence was overpowering. She wished the canvas were bigger, that she could see more of what was going on in order to make up her mind about whether this was a happy or a sad picture. It was impossible to decide.

Whatever her feelings, she was not going to let Lucasta Jenkinson or anyone else have it. It was hers, to make of it what she wished, almost a test of how she had changed.

★

Thankfully, there were no more letters from Miss Jenkinson. Weeks went by, and nothing came from her, and Ailsa's anger faded. By October, the nights drawing in rapidly, she was almost ready to leave the island. Her tenancy had been for six months, with an option to renew for a year, but she had already decided that she had achieved what she had come for and would go before the winter began. The islanders, she knew, would see this as a defeat, but she didn't care – it was enough that she herself would know that on the contrary it was a victory, over herself. She felt stable and confident, happy to have tested herself and not found herself wanting – the relief of not having needed anyone's help was thrilling. She could have stayed on the island, though perhaps not in the croft, for longer, especially if she had increased her rare trips to the mainland and given herself some distraction. But she was proud that she hadn't needed others, and she knew she had earned a small measure of respect, from those who observed her, for keeping away from the world so successfully.

October was beautiful. The bracken and heather covered the hills in shades of bronze and purple which became startlingly bright in the sun. The constant change in the light towards evening was almost theatrical, as though the shafts shooting from behind clouds were deliberately directed by unseen hands. It was cold and misty in the mornings but the mist, clinging to every bush and shrub, was a home for diamond drops of water glittering along the paths. Never had she been so aware of nature's beauty, and never more in awe. She wanted somehow to acknowledge and celebrate this feast, and what it mean to her, what it had done for her. Slowly, an idea of what she could do was growing in her mind.

★

MacPhail took her stuff to the ferry on the day she left the island. 'Had enough?' he said. She just smiled. 'Knew you'd never last a winter,' he added. She went on smiling – let him have his little victory. 'Back to London?' He was remarkably inquisitive for an islander all of a sudden. She nodded. No need to tell him of her plans – he wanted to label her as a townie, so let him. He put her bags on the boat, and she paid him, but he seemed determined to have a conversation before she left and went on standing there, staring at her and expectant. 'Will you be back?' he asked, as the boat's engine started up. 'Perhaps,' she said, 'one day, if I need to.' He prepared to step onto the quay, then hesitated, and before jumping off the boat as the ropes tying it to the bollards were being released, he said, 'You've done well, mind, managing.'

All the way across to the mainland, she repeated his words to herself: you've done well. How well, she had yet to see.

★

The cab she'd booked to take her to the station was waiting beside the pier. She chose not to sit in the front with the driver, wanting to enjoy the scenery without any distraction. But the man persisted in talking, pointing out things on the road, and she thought how hard it was going to be to adjust to the society of others. She'd lost the knack.

She wished, when they got to the station, that she did not have so much luggage. There were no trolleys at this local station and she had to ask the cab driver to carry the two heavy bags for her while she coped with the rest. He was not very willing – she should, after all, have talked to him – and she had to produce a five-pound note, an extravagant tip, surely. But he put everything on the train for her, and at last she was off, her journey home properly begun. Arriving in Glasgow was alarming. She stood on the platform, surrounded by her belongings, numbed by the noise, nervous of the crowds surging past as a train on the adjacent platform disgorged its passengers. She tried to take deep breaths, telling herself to keep calm, calm, willing herself to conjure up a vision of the island she had left. And then, behind her, a voice said, 'Would you like a hand with all this, maybe?' and she turned to see a young man hovering there, indicating her bags, his smile shy.

He carried almost everything for her all the way to the main concourse – all she took was her shoulder bag and rucksack – and found a trolley for her. He was off even before she had finished thanking him profusely. Her mood was transformed. There was no need to fear returning to city life – among the formidable hordes of strangers there were people like that thoughtful man. Later, she supposed that was when she had begun to relax her guard. She put her shoulder bag and rucksack on top of all the other bags and pushed the trolley towards the platform for the London train. Her progress was slow, with the concourse packed, but she did not mind, there was plenty of time. She hardly saw what happened. All she felt was a bump as someone passed her too close, and then she saw her shoulder bag, whipped off the mound of luggage, in the hand of a boy running very fast. He was gone before she had managed any kind of exclamation. Gasping for breath, she tried to go after him but the weight she was pushing, and the throng she was trying to push her way through, defeated her.

The station policeman was sympathetic. He took her to his

office, leaving her luggage safely in the charge of someone else, and sat her down and gave her a cup of tea. He reassured her that her train would not be departing for another thirty-five minutes. It was only when he asked her to describe her bag and list its contents that Ailsa remembered it contained the painting. Apart from that, only some shells, a few birds' feathers, and a bunch of heather she'd picked that morning. 'So nothing of value, then?' the man asked. 'You have your money, your credit cards, cheque book, keys?' Ailsa patted the zipped purse she had hanging diagonally across her chest and nodded. But then she began to say, 'It's just that the painting . . .' 'Yes?' the man prompted. There was no way she could explain its significance. 'Nothing,' she said, 'it's just a little picture, of sentimental value.' 'Well,' he said, 'that lad is going to be a wee bit disappointed when he opens that bag — I'd like to see his face. He'll likely chuck it away. If we find it, we'll send it on, if you leave your address.'

He saw her onto the London train himself and stowed her luggage away for her. As soon as the train began to move, Ailsa closed her eyes. She told herself she had been lucky. Nothing important had been lost. Yet even as she was assuring herself of this, she felt uneasy. Wasn't the painting important? It certainly had turned out to be important to Lucasta Jenkinson. She had begged for its return. But it was more than that. Over the last few months, Ailsa reflected, it has come to mean something to me, too. What, then? She wasn't sure. It had become somehow symbolic, she decided, of what she had been trying to do on the island, which was to try to live independently and simply, as the painting suggested life should be lived. What would that boy see in it, though? Nothing. Would he throw it away? If so, who would pick it up and treasure it?

Thinking of what might happen distressed her. She warned herself not to become agitated, and tried to settle into the rhythm of the train. She was almost asleep when the ticket collector came to tell her he had had a call from Glasgow Station saying that her bag had been found in a wheelie bin near the buffet, contents apparently intact. It seemed like such a happy omen for the future.

Ailsa smiled, and fell into a deep sleep which lasted all the way to London.

★

Eight people she had had to talk to in the first twenty-four hours. Her sister Fiona, Cameron, James, Melissa, her neighbour Virginia, Virginia's husband Morton, her cleaner Pat and Pat's little boy, Ryan. Eight people, all of them demanding time and concentration and responses, all of them so kindly welcoming her, treating her as if she had recovered after a long illness. Their expressions of relief were various and hopelessly misplaced but all sounded undoubtedly sincere. 'You're back!' they cried, in tones of congratulations, and she found it hard to bear. 'Now you can start again,' they said, and beamed at her. Start what? she wanted to ask, but knew quite well that they meant her life. Her old life. Her life as she had lived it with Paul – only without him.

Fiona, in particular, scrutinised her carefully. She had never liked Paul, who had patronised her and made her feel that her job as a social worker was a waste of time. Sometimes, Ailsa thought Fiona had suspected a little of what had happened to her sister's marriage, but she had never asked outright what was going on and there had never been any temptation to tell her and seek advice or consolation. They were not close enough for that. But now, no longer concerned with keeping up appearances, Ailsa was more prepared to be truthful, so when Fiona commented on how well she was looking and wondered if this was just the result of a healthy, outdoor island life, she said, 'No, actually. It's the result of standing on my own two feet and not falling over.'

'But you're not the independent type,' Fiona said, 'you went straight from Daddy to Paul, looking for another strong man to adore you.'

'That's very bitchy, Fi.'

'No. Just the truth. Men do adore you. They don't adore me.'

'Fiona, don't be so, so . . .'

'Petty? Pathetic?'

'Don't be so self-pitying. I never wanted to be adored, as you put it. I'd rather have what you have. You've got a career, you do

280

something worthwhile, and what have I ever done?'

'Worthwhile? Not what your late husband used to say.'

'Never mind what Paul said, I know it's worthwhile and I admire you.'

'Rubbish. How can you? How can you admire me when I spend my whole time putting what Paul called sticking plasters over gaping wounds and watching them fall off?'

'There's no point in talking to you when you're like this, Fi.'

'No, there isn't, but you've never wanted to talk to me, anyway, have you, not really talk, as sisters should.'

'I don't know about "should". It would be nice if we could.'

'Then why can't we?'

'There are two of us, Fi, it isn't just me.'

'It is. I don't mind being truthful about how I feel – it's you, you won't *share.*'

'Please.'

'There, you see – the distaste on your face.'

'It's just the word . . .'

'Then I'll choose another word. You won't open up, you won't tell me, your only sister, how you're really feeling.'

'I'm feeling fine. Better than for years. There, that's the truth, that's being open and honest.'

'It isn't being open and honest enough. Why did you really go to that island? I don't remember you loving it as a child, neither of us did, it was Daddy who did. You hated being made to go there when you were a teenager. You loved dancing and parties, don't you remember? Why go there, on your own, now? Be open and honest about that, and I might believe you're trying.'

'This is very tiring, Fi.'

'Honesty is tiring, it's a struggle, but it gets easier, once you've got into the habit.'

'And *that's* irritating.'

'So, evasive as usual, too frightened to let me see what worries you, why you're so buttoned up, the perfect little wife and now the noble widow.'

Looking at her sister, Ailsa thought it would be quite easy to say that she hated her and never wanted to see her again. She looked, as she always had done, manic, wild, not at all how a social worker should look – there was nothing calm and capable about her. Taller than Ailsa, heavier, with once red and now thick grey curls overwhelming her narrow features, she was alarming. Paul had said she looked madder than some of her mad clients, and the boys thought she looked like a witch. Her clothes added to this impression, always black or dark navy, always shapeless. She was, Paul had decided very early on in his acquaintance with her, 'one unhappy woman', and he was sorry for her husband. But Ailsa had spoken the truth when she'd said she envied Fiona's career – she did. Whatever her sister herself said, however much Paul had mocked her 'do-gooding'. Ailsa knew Fi was passionate about her job and that she was good at it. Unhappy she might be in her personal life, but she had a sense of direction Ailsa had lacked, and craved to have.

'Maybe, Fi, I'll learn to open up, but not today, some other time, I promise.' Surprisingly, Fiona smiled and said she'd look forward to that, she'd hold her to it.

★

No one else directly challenged her. Her sons never asked a single question about her island life, seeming to regard her months there as an aberration, never to be referred to again. Virginia, who had kept an eye on the house, wanted to know if she had taken any photographs and was disappointed to hear that the answer was no. She'd brought some shells back, though, and gave them to Ryan, who clearly was not impressed, since they were very ordinary shells, not nearly as pretty as those his grandmother had brought back from the Caribbean.

By the time she got rid of them all and went to bed she was exhausted. She'd lost the skill to relate to people and had practically lost the basic skill of conversing at all. Her long silences while she tried to think of how to answer the most straightforward questions puzzled people – she could see them wondering whether she had some kind of illness which made her so slow or whether she was being rude and ignoring them. Every innocent query seemed either too simple or too complicated to respond to. She had a blinding headache just from hearing all the voices, and when one by one they ceased, and her family, and Pat and Ryan, left, she could still hear them in her head, one roaring noise. Even when she was at last alone in her bedroom the silence was not complete, it was not the thick silence of the island. The noise of traffic was muted but it was there, and then there were all kinds of other sounds which once she had never noticed and now seemed so loud. The central heating sent a groan through the radiators at regular intervals which alarmed her, and there was a ticking somewhere, like a clock (but there was no clock), which she could not locate. When the telephone rang the shock made her heart race and she rushed to stop the hideous sound, then afterwards detached the instrument from its socket.

Already, there were decisions to be made and her head had begun to whir with alternatives. Cameron thought she should sell the house. It was, he said, too big for her, and she would get a good price for it and could buy a flat and a cottage in the country and still have money left over. James thought selling the house would be a mistake and that instead she should let it out, for a fortune, something he had wanted her to do when she left for the island. Fiona telephoned, wondering if she would like her to move in with her. Her divorce had been fairly recent, she soon would have nowhere to go because her house was to be sold and the money split with her ex-husband. Ailsa didn't want to have to think about any of this. There was no need. She could take her time, but no one seemed willing to allow her time. It was, she saw, to be the first test of her new self: to tell all these people to leave her alone without offending or alienating them. Thinking about it, she discovered that she did not really care if she did offend them – they, after all, were offending her by being so persistent, so sure that they knew what was best for her.

She hung the painting at the end of her bed, on the wall facing it, where it immediately looked comfortable. This wall was not large – her bedroom was long but not wide and the end walls were narrow – and the pale grey patterned wallpaper suited the

283

quiet picture. It did not look awkward, as it had done in the croft, and the light thrown upon it from the side window was flattering. She liked lying and looking at it in the morning, lit by this natural light, and at night the two lamps positioned either side were equally kind to the painting. She had begun to see the point of there being no overt human presence in that room – people were disturbances. It was only possible to be tranquil if there were no people around. But if that were so, in the opinion of the artist, she wondered how any kind of life could be managed unless one withdrew entirely from society. Not even on the island had she done that. Human contact had been minimal, and never meaningful, and perhaps that was the trick – but if so, was not existence rendered barren, loveless?

In the days that followed her return, days she found a great strain, and each one of which ended with her in a state of turmoil over quite trivial matters, she thought 'loveless' might be the clue. She was not without love, of varying kinds and degrees, and it was love, bringing with it the need to show concern, that robbed her life of the tranquillity she had experienced on the island. She loved her sons. They were grown men who had long ago moved away from her emotionally, but she was still bound to them by love and could not expel them from her life. Cameron, the elder, in particular, exhausted her with his arguments and persuasion and insistence that she should take his advice. He was especially maddening when he brought his dead father into it. 'Dad said I was to look after you,' he told her, 'see you didn't get into any financial mess, and I'm telling you, Mum, you have to be sensible and sell the house and invest some money for your old age. It's the sensible thing to do, trust me.' She wanted to say to him that it was not a question of trust but of his wanting to take her over and command her as his father had done, and she was not going to have it. She was in charge, of herself, of the house, and would do what she thought fit when she was ready. But she couldn't speak like that to him. He would be hurt. He wanted her to regard him as wise and responsible and knowledgeable, the very image of how he had seen his father.

He was nothing like his father. She had known that almost from the beginning – even as a baby, he had lacked that unmistakable vigour which James later displayed. Cameron was a dreamer, like her. He was a child who smiled a lot and seemed to want to please, and his very amiability had worried Paul. With James, it was different. She was a puzzle to him and his bafflement over her behaviour since his father had died had made him uneasy in her company. He kept trying to show concern, and then backing off from the implications if there turned out to be any. 'Are you all right, Mum?' he kept asking, but there was nothing hesitant about the question, and he clearly expected the answer to be yes. And then, insultingly, though she knew he was unaware of the insult, 'Maybe you should talk to Melissa, you know, have a chat with her?' Melissa had done a course in counselling, and James was proud of her caring nature. No, she told him, as gently as possible, she didn't think she needed to have a word with his wife, she was perfectly all right, he need not worry. 'But I do,' he said, in an irritable tone of voice, as though she were being difficult. 'I can't stop worrying about you. Melissa says . . .' She thought how shocked Melissa would be to know just how far she had moved on, just how swiftly she had come to terms with Paul's death. This had to remain unspoken.

But she went so far as to say, 'I'm fine, James. I find I like being on my own.' He patted her hand, and smiled. She was just a little afraid of James. Even his size – he was over six foot, and powerfully built, like his father – intimidated her. He never looked right in her house, seeming to make chairs too small and rooms too full. His marriage, so young, to Melissa had been a surprise but also a relief – she felt that Melissa, American and clever, took the place she had never adequately filled. If, behind his convincingly mature façade, there lurked a more uncertain James, then Melissa could deal with him. Neither of her sons, she knew, could stand in for their father, and she was glad of it.

★

She wasn't sure, that first month back in London, whether it was quite true that she liked being on her own in the family house.

It was, of course, quite different from being alone in the croft on the island. Here, at every turn, there were reminders of that other life, the life she had lived with Paul all those years. Inevitably, they disturbed her. The memories of happier times were sharp and persistent and it puzzled her that they were not also comforting.

The house, which she had always loved, began to get on her nerves. She didn't fit in any more, she wasn't a woman who wanted a large sitting room full of furniture, or a kitchen where family feasts could be accommodated. Cameron was right, she must sell it and find somewhere smaller; much smaller. Then, she could get rid of all the belongings which had begun to haunt her with their history. She could choose new things, uninfluenced by Paul's taste – and everywhere she looked she saw his taste. It always struck people as odd that Paul collected modern art. Such a hobby (though rather more serious and expensive than a hobby) did not fit with his persona as a man of action, ex-army, known to be ruthless in the conduct of business. But Ailsa had seen this other side of Paul from the start and had been convinced it showed the 'real' Paul, the true self he did not wish to reveal to others, in case they thought him soft. Sometimes she had heard him lie, telling people that some painting he'd bought had been his wife's choice. This was especially true if the painting was of a nude woman. She hadn't minded, but she knew that in fact her own influence was absent so far as their paintings were concerned. Her own taste was only evident in the colour of a pair of curtains or the pattern on a rug (a rug Paul had never liked). It could all go, and Paul's art collection too. The boys could have what they wanted and the rest could be sold.

First, though, she had to sort through all the many drawers and cupboards and dispose of personal effects. About this, Melissa was right, she had indeed been in denial. She'd gone off to her island leaving everything just as it was, closing the door especially firmly on the room that had been Paul's study, and into which he had liked to be wheeled even during his last weeks. She thought about asking one of her sons to tackle this room, but feared that what they might find would shatter their image of their father as devoted husband. She had to do it herself, and quickly, in a matter-of-fact way. So one dark November day she took into the room a roll of black bin liners and a few large cardboard boxes and set to, starting with the desk. It had six drawers, all crammed with papers, neatly arranged. She saw that in fact there were little labels on the rims of the drawers – 'Insurance', 'Car', 'Stocks and Shares'. They could go to Paul's accountant, she needn't bother with them. The sixth drawer was locked. She hunted around for a key, but there didn't appear to be one. She doubted very much whether Paul had opened this drawer in the last year – he couldn't have managed to bend down that far, nor had he had the strength in his by then almost useless fingers to turn a key. She would have to force the lock. But standing looking at the desk, she remembered that there was another desk Paul had used before this one which looked very much the same.

It had been moved to Cameron's old room, where he still slept when he stayed with her. Six drawers, exactly the same, and in the sixth, the bottom one, a key was, helpfully, sticking out. She knew it would fit before she even removed it, and returned to Paul's study. The drawer held letters, all still in their envelopes. They were tied in bundles, with ordinary string or elastic bands. Some were from her. The sight of the pale green envelopes (very expensive these had been, lined with a sort of tissue paper) made her feel slightly nauseous. Only twelve of them, written to Paul in the six months before they became engaged when she had gone back home to Scotland to help nurse her dying father. She didn't need to read them to remember the contents. Most of these letters had been full of details about her father's condition, and professions of love for Paul. These had been extravagant, probably embarrassingly so. She'd been so passionately in love, so desperate to be with him, swearing that she couldn't live without him. She thought she'd burn them, late in the afternoon, in the garden. Nobody would see her.

A small collection of letters from the boys, only nine in all, six from Cameron, three from James, written from school. They might like to have them, though the letters were not of much interest. They were addressed to her as well as Paul, but it was Paul who had elected to keep them, which now seemed touching. She was sure that Melissa would read great significance into James's illiterate scribbles. Another bundle, also slim, from his mother, written from the cruises she was so addicted to. And then the last packet. It was sealed. She opened it: two letters. Plain white envelopes, bold writing. They could only be from Lucasta Jenkinson. The Cornish postmarks were clear.

She thought how, a year ago, she would have grabbed these letters feverishly, with shaking hands, and devoured every word in them even while her vision clouded with hate. She would have wanted to know everything, every last thing that this woman had been saying to her husband. Had she been begging Paul to leave, and come to her? But no, it couldn't have been like that, *she* had dumped him. Paul would not have lied about that. So why, if she had rejected him, did she write to him at all? Because he had written to her? The answer would be in these letters, or the clues to the answer. She must surely have been responding to letters from Paul. What had he said? Had he begged her to take him back? Had he said he would leave his wife? Holding these two envelopes in her hands, hot with tension, sweaty with it, Ailsa felt the weight of her decision. Was she strong enough to burn these letters too, without reading them? Was she strong enough to read them first? Was there any need? Was there any benefit to be had?

Paul had kept them. Locked up. Hidden from her.

★

Cameron took charge of selling the house. He assumed she would not want to show people around, or even be in the house when the estate agent did so, but he was wrong. She wanted to see who might be taking her place and said she would always be there whenever a prospective buyer was brought to look round. The estate agent, never mind her son, did not quite like this, but she was firm. All appointments were for the afternoon, except on Saturdays and Sundays when she agreed to almost any hour. The moment the house went on the estate agent's books there were many applicants – six different lots of people came to look round on the very first day, and thereafter never fewer than two in an afternoon.

Ailsa enjoyed it. She didn't feel in the least (as Cameron had warned her she would) 'invaded' by these people. On the contrary, she felt absolutely in control of them and took them round the house as though she herself were the agent (who pattered behind, occasionally pointing out things she'd missed). 'What a lovely house,' everyone said at some point, usually when she led them through to the conservatory and they saw the terrace and the garden. They all enquired how long she had lived here and when she told them almost twenty years they were impressed. They had been told, of course, that she was a widow, and so did not ask any upsetting questions – it was enough that she wanted some-where smaller now that it was understood she was on her own. Offers were quickly made, so quickly that she was advised to hang on and she might very well get more than the asking price. (Property prices were buoyant in the 1980s.) Cameron thought she should wait for a cash buyer who could complete in the minimum time, without waiting to sell their own property, and at the end of the second week one appeared.

She was French, but spoke excellent and almost accentless English. She was married, with three young children, but she came on her own, in the evening. The estate agent brought her but, by mutual agreement, left her to be shown round by Ailsa, who by then had grown used to the inevitable questions about boilers and central heating, and felt she could cope. The woman, a Mme Verlon, Claudette Verlon, didn't ask any of them. She smiled, but was virtually silent as she was taken from room to room. Ailsa saw her eyes darting about, though, and knew she was taking everything in. When the tour was over Ailsa ended up in the kitchen and, on impulse, asked Mme Verlon if she would like a glass of wine while she thought if she wanted to see anything again. The offer was accepted. Ailsa poured two glasses of white wine, and they sat at the table.

It was two weeks before Christmas and dark outside, and had

been since soon after four. The kitchen was not cosy – it was much too big – but it was colourful, with a fine collection of plates on the pine dresser. Mme Verlon admired the plates, recognising several as being from Provence, and ventured the opinion that Ailsa was artistic. Ailsa shook her head. 'No,' she said, 'I have no feeling for art. It was my husband who collected most of the pictures and pottery. He had an eye, though it was untrained.' 'And was it he who bought the little painting in your bedroom, Madame?' Ailsa stared at her in astonishment. They had only been in her bedroom a couple of minutes, with only one lamp switched on, and she had never drawn attention to the attic painting. She had instead mentioned only the large cupboard (because the estate agent was forever telling her to point out such 'features'). Mme Verlon hadn't mentioned the painting either, and she hadn't had time to study it.

'The little painting,' she echoed, 'on my bedroom wall, facing the bed?'

'Yes.'

'Why ever does it interest you? How did you notice it?'

Mme Verlon shrugged, drank some wine. 'I think I recognised it,' she said. 'It is quite valuable, no?'

'Is it? I've no idea. I've never had it valued.'

'Your husband bought it, perhaps?'

Ailsa hesitated, then said, avoiding Mme Verlon's gaze, 'No. It was a gift. To him.'

'How fortunate he was. You have it insured?'

'I don't think so, not on its own, I mean, only as part of the house and contents insurance.'

'You should treasure it, but perhaps you do, or it would not be on your bedroom wall. It means something, yes?'

Again, Ailsa hesitated. She felt herself blush, and said, hurriedly, 'I don't know. I'm never sure. Sometimes it does, sometimes it doesn't. It seems sad, mostly.'

'Oh, I don't think so, no. Though her life was maybe sad.'

'Whose life?'

'The artist's.'

'Tell me!' Ailsa felt suddenly excited, and leaned across the table to touch the other woman's hand. 'I've always wanted to know who painted it, and why. I don't think my husband knew either, or the person who gave it to him.'

'She was English, but lived in Paris. I've seen some of her work. Your painting is like one of her other paintings, almost a copy of it, but I don't think it is a copy. I would have to look at it carefully.'

Ailsa went to fetch the painting.

★

Mme Verlon held the little painting in her hands and studied it closely. 'May I?' she asked, turning it over, poised to take off the frame. Ailsa nodded. The canvas came out of it easily. Mme Verlon turned it over and scrutinised the back of the canvas. 'I believe she rarely signed her work,' she said. 'It is not significant that this bears no signature. But I think it is genuine. I think it is by Gwen John.'

'Is she still alive?'

'No, no. Dead long ago, I don't know exactly when, but before the last war, I think.'

'Did she live in a room like this?'

'I think so. She was poor. Her brother, you know him, Augustus John, was more famous, and much richer.'

'And she was his sister? How odd. Was she married?'

'No.'

'Children?'

'No.'

'So she was lonely, it *is* a sad painting.'

'I don't know. Someone will be able to tell you. But if I am right, it is precious. You must take care of it. I would love to have it, but I cannot afford to buy it, at the moment, if I am to buy your house, which I would like to do, please.'

The sale went through very quickly, without a hitch, and Ailsa had only a month to find somewhere else and to dispose of the furniture and contents. Cameron, delighted at the amount of money the house had raised, thought his mother should come and stay with him, or else rent somewhere, while she looked 'properly' for her future home, but Ailsa had already made her mind up. She was going to travel, and needed only a base until she'd satisfied her wanderlust, so she bought a tiny flat through the estate agency which had handled her house sale – one room, with kitchen and bathroom, in a new block by the river. Her sons couldn't understand her choice, but were bound to admit it was sensible, for a woman her age. There was a lift, and a porter, and it was new so maintenance would be easy. It would do, for the time being, and be easy to sell when their mother was ready to settle down.

They moved her things for her. It was not an arduous job, since she was keeping hardly anything from the family house. Most of what went into her *pied-à-terre* was new – a new (smaller) bed, because her existing one would have filled the room; a new small pine table; two rather uncomfortable cane chairs – and that was it. 'Pretty comfortless, Mum,' James said, 'and what about a fitted carpet?' No, she didn't want the white-tiled floor covered. She would buy a rug, eventually. In spite of its size, the room fortunately had plenty of storage space, cleverly hidden behind a false wall, and all Ailsa's clothes and boxes went into this long, narrow compartment. The kitchen, though there was hardly room to turn round in it (literally) was well and cunningly equipped. So was the bathroom. She had everything, she announced, that she needed.

The walls were white, a brilliant white. Everything in the place was white – kitchen appliances, kitchen floor, bath, bathroom floor. She'd deliberately put a white woven cotton bedspread over her new bed and made white cushions for the chairs. The effect, not surprisingly, was stark and hurt her eyes, she had to admit. There was so much light, with two big windows, both large, double-glazed panes of glass, flooding the room with sun whenever the weather was good and illuminating it strongly when it was not. There were white slatted blinds in place, but she had rolled them up and never intended to use them – no one, except passing seagulls, could see in and she liked the panorama before her. But something would have to be done eventually about the whiteness, to tone it down. She thought she might buy a grey rug, and maybe one comfortable chair, covered in grey linen. She would also have some sort of curtains, even if she would rarely draw them – there was enough space either side of the windows for them to hang and tone down the whiteness of the other walls.

'You need some pictures,' James said. 'Haven't you brought some nice pictures? What's happening to all Dad's pictures?'

'I've brought one,' Ailsa said.

★

There was no one else in the block as yet, though the other flats had all been sold, and unlike being in the croft on the island, Ailsa found the atmosphere eerie. All that emptiness below her made her feel curiously vulnerable, though in fact the porter was there, in residence, and she was quite secure. Going into her flat she felt startled each and every time – she found herself catching her breath at the sight of this unknown space. No memories at all. No reminders of any previous life. All that connected her with the past was the little painting, said to be by a well-respected artist, Gwendoline Mary John. The focus of attention, it now looked lost on the white wall. The eye was drawn to it, in the strong light, and stayed, reluctant to leave the only interruption in all that bright white.

She had not, as Mme Verlon advised, taken the painting to an expert. She was content to accept the Frenchwoman's opinion and had found out from her all that she wanted to know. She hadn't insured it separately either – she didn't want anyone to look at it. The first thing she would have to do when she returned from Italy was to have the wall upon which the picture hung repainted, a beige colour, she thought. It pleased her to think she had this to come back to, the simplicity of it, contrasting so strongly with the complexity of the family house. She wouldn't get overwhelmed ever again – this room was her life now down to the core. She didn't even want her sons to come into it, or not as they once had done. She was quite free of entanglements, at last. The picture, when she locked the door upon it, reassured her that this was true.

Cameron and James had both been left with keys to her flat, though they were not required to do anything. But all the same, eager not just to be dutiful but to see what his mother might have done to the flat between moving in and leaving it to go travelling, Cameron visited it the first weekend after she had gone. He hadn't a great deal to do on Sundays since he and Elspeth, his partner of five years, had split up and he missed the routine. He still slept late, went out for newspapers, bought croissants, took them home and ate and read, but after that there was a dismal gap. He thought he might take up some sport, tennis probably, but had done nothing about it. He could have visited James, but he couldn't stand Melissa who would be sure to offer her interpretation of why he was on his own again: he couldn't, according to his sister-in-law, 'commit'.

He was living in his father's flat, though whether he would stay there he hadn't yet decided. The existence of this flat in the mews off Devonshire Street had been a surprise to all of them. The moment he and James were told of it by the solicitor, they had worried about their mother. Would she guess? Would she be forced to realise what they had suspected for so long, that their father had had other women and that this was where he took them? But she hadn't appeared to be in any way disturbed. She'd simply seemed to think the flat was another of Paul's clever investments, and there had been no need to protect her. Protection was what their mother had always needed – she seemed to them frail, dependent on their father's strength, and sometimes they imagined that this irked him. 'For heaven's sake, Ailsa,' they had heard him say often enough, 'have a mind of your own.'

Going there with the keys for the first time, Cameron had wondered how long it had been empty. He knew, from what the solicitor had told him, that it had been let for several years, during his father's illness, but the place had an air of such abandonment it did not feel as if it had been lived in for a very long time. It did not feel, either, as though it could ever have been anything as vulgar as a love-nest. Everything about it had a clinical precision – the way the furniture was arranged, the austere shades of the fabrics, the extreme tidiness. Who on earth had his father brought here to satisfy his lust? What a sad business it must have been, going into that bare bedroom with its grey-covered bed, the bedspread stretched tight across it. No hint of warmth or colour anywhere, nothing on the walls, no mirror, only smooth-fitting drawers and cupboards along one grey painted wall.

Cameron changed it dramatically, made it colourful and comfortable, hung London Transport posters on the walls, and yet still he could not banish the previous atmosphere, not quite. He was glad his mother had never been there before he had managed to transform it as much as he could – it would have upset her, she would have sensed something. Surely. Going up in the lift, on Sunday afternoon, to his mother's new home, Cameron thought how odd she had become. She hadn't always been odd. She'd been quite conventional in behaviour. He'd always been rather proud of her – she was the best-looking mother of all his friends' mothers, and he'd been glad she'd never had a career. She was always there when he and James were at home from school, a comforting presence. Had they taken her for granted? He supposed so, but she'd seemed happy enough about it. There'd been no problems with his mother, ever. It was with his father there had been difficulties, with his father there were arguments and fights. His mother was the peacemaker, though she hadn't always succeeded. His father had been powerful, dominant, determined to win whatever struggle he was engaged in. He'd quite often hated his father.

The first thing he did was rush to lower the blinds. Why hadn't his mother done that? The light was unbearable with the sun blazing through the plate glass. But she didn't seem to have done anything to the place. The room looked almost exactly as it had done the last time, the only time, he had seen it, when he and James moved her stuff. The word sterile sprang into his mind. It even struck him that it reminded him of his father's secret flat. The very opposite of the home she had left. Well, this pared-down existence appeared to be what she wanted. It was her way, he supposed, of coping with his father's death, however peculiar it seemed.

He sat for a moment on one of the cane chairs. It made him feel more depressed than ever to think of his mother coming back to this – it wasn't what he had envisaged when he'd urged her to sell the house. He'd imagined her in another house, a neat little terraced house in Chelsea maybe, near James and Melissa (and perhaps, soon, grandchildren nearby to occupy her). But maybe she would not come back from this Italian jaunt of hers. Maybe she would meet someone – but that was absurdly unlikely. His mother had adored his father. No one would be able to take his place, she wouldn't want any other man to attempt to.

He was going to leave the blinds down. Securing the cords either side, he turned and stood with his back to the windows for a moment, looking at the room. She'd hung one picture only on the opposite wall. It looked ridiculous, one tiny painting on a largish wall, dead centre, like a target. He peered at it. It wasn't one he recognised. The wall cried out for his father's colourful, dramatic paintings, the ones by someone who painted like Matisse, a series of three he'd bought years ago and cherished. But this picture his mother had selected was a pretty little nothing, almost colourless, quite unable to make an impression hanging where it did. He must ask her why she liked it, why she had chosen it, when she returned. Perhaps it was simply that it was an echo of herself.

★

It wasn't like going to Scotland, to the island. She'd felt nervous enough then, travelling alone, but this was different, this was abroad, with no one to help her, no Paul to organise everything. Reaching Paris was adventure enough – she was exhausted. Managing the language made her head ache and after she'd forced herself out, to look at Notre Dame, she was glad to get back to her hotel. She ate in her room, not up to facing a restaurant, and despised her own cowardice. This would not do. She was meant to be savouring her freedom, rejoicing in her new-found independence, and yet here she was, scurrying about, enjoying nothing. She almost went home.

She tried hard, instead, to analyse what she was afraid of, what made her so uncertain and nervous when, alone on the island, she had felt so strong and sure of herself. It was, she decided, the presence of other people that did it, being one in a crowd – it was the crowd that unnerved her. If people were all around you, especially people speaking a different language from you, then the sense of isolation, of loneliness, intensified. Her mind was like a locked box, so much in it trying to get out, a great store of trivia jamming the works. Walking down a quiet street, or along an empty corridor in the hotel, her own footsteps scared her, emphasising her solitary state. She began to suspect that she was attracting odd looks, as though this inner turmoil was showing on her face and alarming people, and she took to walking with her head down.

Once, in the Luxembourg Gardens, as she wandered aimlessly among the statues and trees, watching an old woman feeding the sparrows, a man spoke to her. He came alongside her and said, in French, but she understood, that he was lost and did she know the way out of the gardens into the Boulevard Saint Michel. She said, in French, that no, she was sorry, she did not. 'Oh,' he said, 'you're English.' He was American, he said, but his grandmother had been British, Welsh actually. He walked with her until they reached the Observatoire and he saw a sign pointing to the boulevard he wanted. He was young, about Cameron's age, from Ohio. She listened politely to his account of why he was in Paris, and when he left her, with 'Been nice talking to you,' she realised she herself had hardly said a word. But the effect of this minimal human contact was extraordinary. She could feel herself more at ease, and she went to sit on a bench and exchanged pleasantries with a young woman holding a child on her knee, teaching it a song. The child, a girl of about four, leaned towards Ailsa and drew her into the song, and she joined in, her accent making both child and mother laugh. It could be done. She would not go home. She would learn how to function as a woman alone, among others.

★

She thought of Paul more than she had expected to, especially on train journeys, as she sat staring out of the windows, half in a trance as the countryside sped past. Had she loved him? Had she really known him? She'd lived with him all those years, in close proximity most of the time, and yet still there were mysterious glitches in his personality which had never been explained, things that did not fit her knowledge of him. Lucasta Jenkinson, her power over him. Sexual? Possibly. So, had she herself failed him in that respect? It irritated her intensely still to be going over and over this sore place, refusing to let it heal even while she was assuring herself that it had done so. She was fifty-four years old, Paul had been dead a year, yet here she was, travelling through Europe, torturing herself with questions which could never be answered. She must look forward, not back. But in struggling to look forward, there was no place in her vision of the future for another man. She did not want another lover or husband, emphatically not. She did not want ever to be taken over again, even if this would bring security and companionship. She had to stick to her resolution made so successfully on the island: to be herself, beholden to no one. It might amount to going against the grain of the woman she was, or the kind of woman that life with Paul had made her, but this was what she wanted.

★

Ailsa had taken the letters with her. They lay at the bottom of her bag and every now and again she took them out, wondering if she was ready to read them (that is, if ever she decided she was going to). Each time, she got only as far as fingering the envelopes and then put them down. She was not ready, not ready in Paris, not ready in Venice, not ready anywhere until she reached Florence. She stayed in a *pensione* she'd been told about, near Fiesole, and there was something so cheerful about the little villa, the attic room she was given there, that she felt a surge of optimism and thought it might be time to lay this ghost to rest.

Sitting on the terrace, among great tubs of brilliant scarlet flowers, she drank her coffee in the morning and took out the letters. Whatever she decided, they were not going back into her bag. She was going to destroy them, read or unread. What was it Paul had said? About love, about how hard it was? She was shocked to find she could no longer exactly remember. It had been something to do with the little painting. He had wanted her to look at it, to understand. She had looked, and not understood.

She opened the first letter and read it, and then left the other unread. It had not hurt her or even angered her, reading Lucasta Jenkinson's words to her now dead husband. The words were nothing. Paul's might have meant more, but those of his mistress did not, at this distance of time, affect her. So far as Ailsa could make out, Lucasta Jenkinson was trying to persuade Paul that they had never really loved each other but had been in the grip of a physical passion which was now spent. He loved his wife, she wrote, couldn't he see that? Apparently, he couldn't, or there would not have been at least one more letter. How sad, Ailsa thought, that Paul must have gone on pleading and Lucasta Jenkinson continued to reject him. If only she had known she was wrong: that Paul had really loved *her* and not his wife.

Well, she, his wife, his widow, did not now care. She put the letters in the stove which even in this weather seemed always to be lit. 'Just paper,' she said to the kitchen girl. Just paper. But she would keep the picture, for ever. Some day, she might understand its significance.

GILLIAN

ALL GILLIAN KNEW was that the quarrel, with its consequences, had been to do with money, or the lack of it. Nobody in the Mortimer family would go into the details of the split between her father Cameron and his brother James, either claiming not to know or to have forgotten. But what she suspected they had not forgotten was the shock, after Ailsa Mortimer was killed, of discovering that she had left more than half of everything she possessed to a bewildering list of Scottish charities involved with protecting the environment. Why she should have done this nobody could work out – it was not in character, and not what Paul Mortimer, whose money and property it all had been, would have wanted. There were suspicions that Ailsa's will must have been made under duress, but exhaustive investigation revealed no such influence. She had been of sound mind, and her will had been drawn up and properly witnessed before she left London for Italy, some six months before she was killed when a car skidded onto a pavement she was walking along in Florence.

Gillian, brought up on this tale, had often wondered about her grandmother. What was she doing in Florence? Nobody seemed to know. 'She went a bit funny after her husband died,' Gillian's mother, Beth, told her (but Beth had never met Ailsa, coming into Cameron's life after the death of his mother). There were photographs, of course, so Gillian was able to see that her grandmother had been strikingly beautiful. When anyone remarked that she had 'a look' of her grandmother, she was pleased and flattered. Her father, however, said she didn't resemble his mother in the least, but this was because, even after all these years, he still felt angry and could hardly bear her name to be mentioned. What puzzled Gillian, trying to understand what had happened, was why her father cared so much, and why he and his brother James had not spoken to each other since their mother's death. She knew her father had not been poor when his mother left him much less than he might have expected. He earned a lot of money himself, as a financial analyst, so that when his mother was killed he was already well set up. But apparently his anger had nothing to do with money. His distress was to do with the insult. It had felt, according to his wife, like 'a slap in the face'. It had carried a message that he had not been loved, not been valued, not been worthy. Gillian had had to accept this, though her father himself had never confided in her.

But the split with her uncle James was harder to understand. James, after all, had also not benefited from his mother's will and might have been expected to share his brother's feelings. Maybe he did, but since she was not allowed to have anything to do with her uncle or his family, Gillian had no means of finding out. Her mother was vague when pressed.

'Oh,' she said, 'it was something to do with a picture.'

This seemed so unlikely – her father wasn't the least bit interested in art – that Gillian couldn't credit it. 'A picture?' she echoed. 'Dad? He doesn't care about pictures.'

Her mother shrugged, said that was what she had been told. There had been a fight, and it was to do with a picture, she was sure.

'A physical fight?' Gillian asked, astonished.

Another shrug. Her mother didn't know. All she knew was that James had wanted the picture and Cameron hadn't wanted him to have it.

'So who got it?' Gillian asked. 'Where is it?'

'Neither of them got it,' her mother said. 'It was sold.'

'Who bought it?' Gillian asked, but her mother had no idea. She'd tried picking good moments to bring the subject up with her father, when he was in a particularly mellow mood, but he nearly always side-stepped her questions. But nevertheless, over the years, in bits and pieces, she had managed to get out of him that his brother had had no right to anything in his mother's flat and that when he, Cameron, had caught James in the act of 'stealing' a picture he had been furious and had demanded the picture back. James had said he wanted the painting as a memento, and had seen no harm in removing it. Cameron had reported what he termed 'the attempted theft' to his mother's lawyer and things had 'turned rather nasty'. The picture, together with all his mother's personal effects, had been sold. When she had asked to whom, he said a Mme Verl–something had bought it, the same woman who had earlier bought the family house. To Gillian, it all seemed a bit unlikely: two brothers parted over a picture neither of them actually cared about?

It also seemed sad. Gillian was an only child, with a longing to be part of a larger family. She knew she had four Mortimer cousins, two of each sex, living not so far away, in Surrey, and had visions of meeting them and becoming part of what she was sure must be one big, noisy, happy group. She fantasised about having holidays with them, sleeping in the same room as the two girls, whispering secrets to each other and having midnight feasts. That was when she was small, seven or eight, and at her loneliest. She boasted, then, about her boy cousins, of how tall and strong they were, capable of defending her against all comers. The fact that she knew only their names, but not even their exact ages, did not put her off. Later, when she had stopped this kind of fantasising she thought more seriously about trying to contact them. Where would the harm be? In her father's disapproval, maybe distress, that's where. And he would undoubtedly find out.

But, though she thought about it, she made no move. Instead, by the time she was applying to an art foundation course, her interest had switched to the famous (or infamous) picture which had caused all the trouble. She longed to know what it was. Her father, still powerful in her life, for financial as well as other reasons, need never know. There was no danger, as there would have been had she contacted her uncle's family, of his discovering she had set out to trace the picture which had caused so much trouble. She didn't tell her mother what she was going to try to do, but then there were a great many things by that stage which she did not tell her mother.

It was easy enough to begin the investigation. Her father had always been proud of his father Paul Mortimer, and would talk about him freely. Easy, once she had prompted him to do so, to ask her father where he himself had lived as a child. 'Chelsea,' he said. 'But exactly where?' And the answer came readily. She went to the square he mentioned and stood in front of what had been her grandfather's house through the 1960s and 1970s. It was rather grand, impressive. Worth, in 2005 terms, a couple of million, she guessed. She had already checked in the telephone directory and knew that a Mr and Mrs Verlon still lived there, some twenty years after buying it from Ailsa Mortimer, but this did not, of course, mean that they still owned the picture. Mrs Verlon had perhaps bought it only to sell, and by now it could be anywhere in the world. But this only added to the mystery and did not put Gillian Mortimer off in the least.

All that concerned her was how she should present herself when she rang the bell of No. 26, as she was about to do.

★

Claudette Verlon was not expecting anyone on that Monday afternoon and very nearly ignored the persistent ringing of the doorbell. There were so many annoying callers these days, people wanting sponsorship, people representing charities (or so they said) selling useless articles, and, lately, beggars, refugees, asking quite openly for money. She had had an intercom fitted and a chain put on the door, and practised extreme caution.

She had never felt like this in Paris. Her husband vowed that the situation in Paris was exactly the same, that there were no areas in any major European city which could be guaranteed absolutely safe, but Claudette did not believe him. He only told her this to persuade her that there was no point in moving back to Paris, which she had wanted to do for a long time. Her children were all living there now, and she wanted to be near them. But Jacques was adamant: next year, he would retire and then she could live wherever she wanted in Paris. He did not fail to remind her, either, that she was the one who had chosen this Chelsea house when he had been moved to London. He himself would have preferred Regent's Park, and had said so.

The house had charmed her then, as had its very beautiful owner, the tragic widow Mortimer. Claudette had convinced herself that the atmosphere in the place was congenial and that it 'spoke' to her. In spite of the comparatively recent death of Mr Mortimer, the house had seemed a happy place, bright and warm and full of evidence of a surely contented family life. She had been won over, and enthusiastic enough about the purchase to rush her husband into it. And for the last twenty years the house had proved comfortable and they had been happy there. As an investment, it could not have been bettered, and so, from being annoyed with her, Jacques had become proud of his wife's acumen and boasted about it to his friends and colleagues. It was he who was now reluctant to sell, when the time came, and move back to Paris, but Claudette was determined. They were going to make a huge profit and she intended to take advantage of the money which would be theirs to buy some exquisite apartment in, possibly, the Ile St Louis area. She did not want another house. With the children gone, she and Jacques needed only a few rooms, elegant and spacious rooms of course, but only, say, four or five of them, preferably conveniently arranged on one floor. They had started married life in two rooms in Montparnasse, and Claudette found herself these days remembering them with more and more affection, though at the time she had yearned for more space.

This nostalgia was part of the reason why all those years ago she had bought what she hoped was a Gwen John painting. Not the most important reason, not by any means, but part of it. The excitement of a true 'find', if the painting were to be authentic, and therefore extremely valuable, justified her buying it, but the sentimental element was there too. She had a strong suspicion that she had paid far less for it than it was worth. A quick call to Christie's and Sotheby's art departments told her that no oil by Gwen John had come on the market in the last fifteen years and that it would be difficult to estimate how much such a picture might fetch. It was not signed, and its provenance was unconvincing, but she was sure that the so-called 'expert' called in by the Mortimer family's solicitor had not known what he was looking at. His verdict had been 'could be . . . is in the style of . . . matches an existing painting of the same interior', but he hesitated to confirm it as a Gwen John. He had wanted to call in other experts – Cecily Langdale had been mentioned – but the family was impatient, and very satisfied with Mme Verlon's cash offer. The deal was done, and she carried home the little picture and hung it back on the wall of the room where she had first seen it. It looked far better than it had done against Mrs Mortimer's décor. Claudette had stripped the walls of their wallpaper and had them painted a distressed pale yellow, the colour of the primroses. She had the carpet lifted and a blond wooden floor laid down, and the furniture in the room was all old pine – good quality, nothing glossy, and all of it almost bleached in colour. No drapes, but a lace curtain in front of the window. No wickerwork chairs, but a comfortable button-backed easy chair upholstered in pink – again, picking up the touch of pink in the flowers in the painting.

Nobody else used the room. It was Claudette's 'boudoir', but she was rarely in it for long, and she liked to think of it quiet and empty, graced by the picture. She walked through it from her bedroom, on the way to the landing, and imagined she felt a soothing breeze as she did so, though there was no window. Jacques used the other door of their bedroom, never trespassing on what he knew was her territory. If she wanted to give a whole room to one tiny painting, then let her: there were enough other rooms in the house for this not to be outrageous. Sometimes, he would find his wife standing looking at the painting, an odd smile on her face, and he would wonder at the power it had over her. Occasionally, when they were quarrelling (which was not often) he would shout at her to calm down and go and worship her wretched painting. She went. The effect was magical.

When the door-bell rang that Monday afternoon, Claudette was on the top floor of the house, looking for a certificate her daughter had asked her to find and send to her. So, when the noise continued and became irritating, it was easy for her to open the window and peer down to see who was standing on the doorstep, without their being aware of being spied upon. All she could see was the top of a head, but it was clearly a woman's head. Claudette waited. She guessed that this caller would eventually descend two or three of the stone steps – there were eight of them – when she gave up ringing the bell, and she would get a better view. The woman, a young woman, neatly dressed, definitely not a refugee, slowly backed away from the front door and then hesitated halfway down the steps. She was wearing a rather chic jacket, of a subtle shade of green, and she had a matching green ribbon tying back her long, black hair. This decided Claudette.

'Hello?' she called out. 'Hello?'

The woman looked up and smiled. 'Hello!' she shouted back. 'I'm so sorry to disturb you, but my family used to live here and I wondered if I might possibly come in for a moment and ask you something. My name is Gillian Mortimer. Are you Mrs, er, Verlon?'

'Wait,' Claudette shouted back, and closed the window. All the way down the many stairs, she was thinking about the widow who had sold the house to her. This young woman looked like her – she had had no need to give her name. It was safe to let her in.

★

The house was quite different from how Gillian had imagined it. Her father had described it as 'a spacious family house' but it seemed grander than that. The staircase alone was impressive, so wide that surely four people could walk abreast up the stairs. She decided immediately that she would not have liked to live here. Mme Verlon was not the sort of woman she had envisaged either. She did not look French in the least, if to be a Frenchwoman of a certain age was to be chic and elegant, impeccably groomed and dressed – Gillian had seen her in her mind's eye, small and slight, wearing a Chanel suit and expensive pearls. But the woman who opened the door was rather stout and a little masculine in appearance. She had short, cropped grey hair, wore no make-up, and was dressed in black, baggy trousers and a loose cream sweater. She was not unattractive but seemed more powerful than sophisticated. Her gaze was very direct, even haughty, and she spoke English with only a trace of accent. She made Gillian nervous.

Mme Verlon took her into a formal drawing room. 'Do sit,' she said, and sat herself, on the very edge of one of the sofas. She had her hands clasped on her knees and a polite, enquiring expression on her face.

Gillian cleared her throat, feeling suddenly embarrassed. It seemed ridiculous to have come at all. 'My father, Cameron Mortimer, lived here, he was born here, it was his home until he was twenty-two.' Mme Verlon inclined her head, encouragingly. 'When my grandmother was widowed and sold the house she took very little of what had been in it – all the furniture and possessions were sold. But she took one of the pictures to the flat she'd bought and later, after she was killed in a car accident, there was a . . . a fight over it, between my father and his brother.'

'A fight?' Mme Verlon looked astonished.

'Yes. I know it sounds weird. My father won't talk about it. But it seems that my uncle was going to take this little painting and my father objected and it was sold and . . . well . . . you bought it.'

'Ah,' Mme Verlon said, 'the Gwen John?'

'Was it really a Gwen John?' Gillian could hardly keep the excitement out of her voice.

There was a pause. For a moment Mme Verlon's face still wore its enquiring expression, but then a frown took its place. Ever since the retrospective of Gwen John's work at the Barbican in 1985, she'd been faintly worried that the Mortimer family would realise that they had surely let a treasure go. She'd thought about them as she looked at the paintings and became more convinced than ever that what she had in her possession was indeed a variant of *The Corner of the Artist's Room in Paris*. Her painting must by now be worth at least twenty times what she had paid for it. She had been astonished, in 1988, to read that a Gwen John oil, *The*

Precious Book, had been sold for £160,000, and this had made her feel nervous about what she possessed. She'd thought about taking it to be authenticated by the organisers of the exhibition but then there would have been questions as to its provenance and she did not want to mention the Mortimers. The painting was hers, and she loved it, and that was enough – she did not need that stamp of authority. She was almost fearful to show the painting to anyone who might recognise it, and last year, after she had visited the latest Gwen and Augustus John exhibition at the Tate Britain, this apprehension had grown. It was beyond doubt that the painting she possessed was also by Gwen John and she felt guilty, as though she had cheated the Mortimers deliberately.

But nevertheless, she nodded, and told the young woman that yes, she was almost certain it was a painting by Gwen John, a variant of the well-known painting of her room in Paris. 'You know her work?' she asked.

'My art teacher took us to the exhibition at the Tate,' Gillian said. 'I loved her paintings. They are so quiet, very simple and pretty.'

'Quiet, simple, perhaps, in effect at least, but pretty? No, I don't think so. It seems the wrong word, if I may say so, a little insulting.'

'Do you still have it? The painting?'

'But of course.'

'I was wondering if you might allow me to look at it?'

They climbed the stairs to the second floor where Gillian was led through a large bedroom into a smaller room, and there on the wall was the painting, looking exactly the same (except for its frame) as the one she had seen in the Tate exhibition. She couldn't help smiling.

'It amuses you?' Mme Verlon asked, seeming surprised.

'It's not that,' Gillian said. 'It's that it is such a modest little painting to have caused so much trouble – I can't quite believe my father could have got so angry about James wanting it.'

'Ah, but it would not be the painting itself which caused the disagreement, I'm sure. In these cases, it is nearly always to do with the significance of what is fought over.'

'Yes, of course, that's right, that's the point. But all the same, it's hard to guess what the significance was. My father doesn't care about art. I wouldn't have thought this painting would have made any impression.'

'It is a beautiful painting,' Mme Verlon sounded offended. 'Even if it were not a Gwen John, though I believe it is.'

'You don't know?'

'I haven't had it examined by an expert.'

'Why not?'

'On the contrary, why? I love it. It means a great deal to me. I would never sell it. I don't need to know, I trust my own judgement.'

'Thank you,' Gillian said, after another few minutes. 'I'm glad to have seen it. I like to think of my grandmother loving it.'

'Did she?'

'What?'

'Love it?'

'I assume so, if it was the only picture she took when she left this house.'

'She did not seem to me exactly to love it. She knew nothing about art. The painting had some history for her which was not, I think, entirely happy.'

'Really?' Gillian couldn't keep the curiosity, the eagerness to know, out of her voice, but Mme Verlon was already leading the way down the stairs and straight to the front door. Clearly, her patience had been exhausted.

Coming level with her, Gillian attempted delaying tactics. 'You were saying you suspected that the painting had an unhappy history for my grandmother?'

Mme Verlon shrugged, her hand on the catch of the door, about to open it. 'It is a long time ago,' she said. 'I was only with Mrs Mortimer once, for an hour. I cannot remember why I had that impression. You must ask your father.'

'Oh, he knows nothing, or if he did he won't tell me.'

'It is private, perhaps, too painful.'

'But she's been dead ages.'

'Family matters can still be painful.' The door had been opened.

'Thank you for letting me see the painting, and the house,' Gillian said.

'You were lucky to come now. Soon this house will be sold and we will move back to Paris.'

'Will the Gwen John go too?'

'But of course.'

Gillian hesitated. She had her camera with her. 'I hardly dare ask,' she said, 'but could I take a picture of the painting?'

Mme Verlon looked annoyed. 'Why did you not make this request when you were looking at the painting?'

'I didn't like to.'

'And now you'd like to?'

'It was hearing that you'll be taking it to Paris.' She blushed, knowing this hardly made sense. 'I'll be very quick. Please?'

Abruptly, Mme Verlon shut the door and pointed up the stairs. 'Two minutes,' she said. 'I am busy, I am going out.'

Gillian raced up the stairs and through the bedroom into the small room where the painting hung. Her hands trembled as she took her camera out of her bag. The light was good and she didn't need a flash. Quickly, she took a dozen shots, one after the other, and then rushed back to the hall, camera still in her hands. Mme Verlon had the door wide open. 'Thank you, thank you,' she said, and got a brief smile in return.

All the way back home, she was thinking of the painting. What had been its power? Why did it have such a hold over her grandmother? How could any single painting have been so significant to her family?

★

The photographs came out well. Gillian had the best one enlarged and then she framed it. The choice of frame was tricky. At first, she'd thought a simple, plain, narrow wooden frame would suit it best, but the simplicity of the frame somehow worked against the subtlety of the painting. She tried a broader frame, still of plain wood, with the same result, then decided on a darker wood. This worked better, though it was not perfect. But it looked convincing, especially from a distance, and it was from a distance that her father was going to see it.

She planned it well. There was a small spare room on the ground floor at the back of their house. A sofa-bed, a small table, and a bookcase – that was all it held. It had a sash-window overlooking the garden, which faced south and let in plenty of light. It was an innocuous room, uncluttered, without personality, and would do very well.

Gillian hung the photograph not on the larger wall opposite the window but on the wall to the right of it. It looked as if it had been there for ever. She stood in the doorway and imagined her father walking in and seeing it – his shock would surely be impossible to hide. Then she would pounce, when he was still reeling, and ask him why his mother had cared so much about this painting. What was the unhappy history Mme Verlon had alluded to? She could hardly wait.

★

Cameron Mortimer had never been entirely happy about his daughter studying art. She was a clever girl, why did she have to do something so lightweight? He didn't see anything to do with art as being a proper career. Nonsense, his wife had said, there were plenty of 'proper' careers following on from studying art. But his disappointment in Gillian's choice was intense. Perhaps if he had had a son, or even another daughter, he would not have cared so much, could have brought himself to look on an art education more indulgently, but Gillian was his only child and bore the brunt of his disappointment.

He loved her, though. There was no doubt about that. He adored her, and not just for her beauty and talents. Everyone else's daughter seemed to him dull and dreary beside Gillian whose vitality sparkled wherever she went. He could remember picking her up from school one day, soon after she'd started, and feeling such an overwhelming sense of joy when he saw her running towards him across the playground, ahead of the other children, making them all look somehow slow and dull. Everything about her seemed so bright – how she looked, the way she spoke. And other parents were aware of it. He saw them admiring her, and he worried that this admiration might turn into resentment. But it didn't. Gillian wasn't a show-off. She rather inclined the other way, adopting a self-deprecating manner quite early in her school life, and Cameron was glad to see it. He didn't want her to be too aware of her own talents.

It had taken him a while to realise how good she was at drawing. 'Look at this,' his wife had said, when Gillian was only six. He'd looked, and seen a picture of a man and a woman, wearing brilliantly coloured clothes, standing in a garden. Their heads were a bit large, he thought, and all their features exaggerated. Beth had been exasperated. She told him that children of six are mostly still drawing stick figures and can't do proper bodies or faces. He'd accepted her word, without thinking his daughter's ability special. But by the time she was ten, even he had realised that she had talent. He watched her draw their cat jumping from the window sill and had been amazed at how she'd caught the swift movement.

But what surprised him more than Gillian's artistic talent was what he could only describe to himself as her happy nature. She didn't get her exuberance from him, nor did it come from her mother. Beth was pleasant, quite sunny-natured, but had none of her daughter's sheer energy. No, it came from Ailsa, he was sure, from Ailsa when she was young. Of course, he had never known his mother when she was young but he had been told about her often enough by his father. 'Your mother,' he used to tell Cameron, 'lit up everything around her when she was a girl, when I first met her. She radiated energy, life-force, call it what you like – marvellous, you have no idea.' Cameron had agreed: he had no idea because by the time he knew his mother the vitality had vanished. To him, she was beautiful but she was quiet, subdued. Where had her energy gone? And why? He hadn't dared ask his father. Beth said she suspected his mother must have been a disappointed, rather sad woman, from what she had been told about her, and he had been offended. 'She wasn't in the least sad, not till Dad died,' he'd said. 'I don't know where you got that idea from. Mum was perfectly content, she had everything she could possibly want.'

But, after she was killed, he realised that he hadn't really known her. If he'd known her, then he'd have understood why that damned painting meant so much to her. He'd have known what she saw, or what she thought she saw, in it. His father might have understood but then he knew about art, not just about his wife. That was where Gillian must get her artistic ability and taste from, genes passed down from her grandfather, having skipped a generation. James had no artistic leanings either, though he had pretended otherwise, caught trying to steal that picture. Caught literally in the act, the painting in his hands, he was putting it into his briefcase, not a bit ashamed. Asked what he thought he was doing, he'd claimed he was just taking a memento. Cameron had grabbed the briefcase and emptied it onto the table: six spoons (a gift to his parents, he knew, from a silversmith friend), a paperweight, a small clock, and a writing case.

'They're just personal bits,' James had protested. 'I'll pay for them, if it bothers you.'

'You can't help yourself to anything,' Cameron had shouted. 'Mum left all her personal effects to be sold and the money given to those potty Scottish charities.'

'You're being ridiculous,' James yelled back. 'Typically petty. What do a few odds and ends matter, for God's sake! No one will ever know. Give me my case back.'

Cameron handed it back, empty. 'We'll have these things valued,' he snapped, 'and then you can buy them.'

'I'm not buying them.'

'You just said you would.'

'I never thought you meant it. I can't believe this.'

'Well, I do. It's the principle of the thing. She made that will. It's going to be carried out, to the letter.'

He didn't know what possessed him. Anger, he supposed, with his mother, not with his brother. James had tried to snatch the painting back, and Cameron pushed his brother unnecessarily hard so that he'd fallen and cut his head on the corner of the table.

'Bastard!' James shouted, scrambling up, and Cameron had felt a moment of regret, so he'd muttered, 'Sorry.'

'You can stick your "sorry",' James said, 'I never want to see you again,' and he had crashed out of the flat.

Left alone there, Cameron felt utterly wretched. Even picking up the painting and the other articles James had been going to take was painful. What, as his brother had said, would it have mattered? There was nothing he wanted himself. He didn't want the spoons or the paperweight (though he remembered it on his mother's little writing desk) and as for the painting, he hated it. It was the cause of trouble. He associated it now with his mother becoming odd, and it was that which had led to her death. She ought to have stayed safely at home, enjoying a calm and peaceful old age.

He had almost put his fist through the canvas there and then, but was deterred by the thought that James would find out when it did not appear on the list of things to be sold. Instead, he wrapped it in the newspaper he was carrying and took it straight to the solicitors. The rest of the stuff he left in the flat. It was, he hoped, the last time he would ever see the troublesome painting.

★

Excitement was making her nervous. She'd hung the 'painting' the night before and all day she'd been imagining the denouement when she took her father to see it. Exactly how, she hadn't decided – whether to lead him into the room, pretending he was to see something of hers, or whether to say nothing, just ask him to come with her. Should she blindfold him, or was that too melodramatic? This wasn't meant to be a game – it was serious. She must calm down, be offhand, casual, or he would become annoyed and she'd get nothing out of him.

He was later than usual and came in frowning, furious with the Friday night traffic. But he was pleased to see her, and enjoyed being fussed over, though it aroused his suspicions.

'What is this in aid of?' he asked, accepting the glass of wine. One taste, and he knew how cheap it was, but he drank it.

317

'The weekend,' Gillian said, 'and your darling daughter staying in, to have the pleasure of your company.'

'Seems an extravagant sort of rejoicing for such an ordinary event,' he said, drily.

'Ordinary?' protested Gillian. 'I haven't stayed in on a Friday night for months. It's special.'

'And to what do we owe this honour, then?'

'I want to show you something.'

'Oh, if it's one of your art efforts it'll be wasted on me, darling, you know I can't tell a good painting from a bad one and I don't understand any of yours, all squiggles and dots and splodges. God knows, I've tried.'

'It isn't my work. It's something else. Come on.'

She got up and held out her hand. Reluctantly, he took it, groaning exaggeratedly as he raised himself up. She was such a pretty girl, especially tonight, wearing a dress instead of those trousers he hated. Her hair looked properly brushed and hung smooth and thick round her face instead of being caught up in one messy bunch on top of her head. Unless he was very much mistaken, she was wearing a little make-up, and looked groomed instead of wild. He couldn't help smiling as he let himself be led from the room and there wasn't an anxious thought in his head. Whatever she was going to show him, he was convinced it would be something silly and amusing.

He couldn't see anything. 'What?' he said, staring round the small spare room. 'What? I can't see anything. What's the joke?'

'Look,' Gillian said.

'I *am* looking. It looks the same. It's just an ordinary room. What am I supposed to see? Is it a new sofa? Why ever should you want me to look at a new sofa?'

'Dad. On the wall?'

Even then it took a while. He looked, as instructed, at the walls of the room until his gaze fell on the only picture. A small picture. It wasn't one of Gillian's, that was for sure, but then she'd said she wasn't showing him anything of hers. Whose, then? He peered, went closer. He felt a strange sensation of discomfort and yet this picture was innocuous, an empty corner of a room . . . He had seen it before, but couldn't recall how or when. It made him irritable and the feeling of discomfort grew. 'Well?' he said. 'What's the point? I'm lost.'

'Don't you recognise it?'

'No.'

'Oh, Dad!'

'Give me a clue.'

'It was Grandmother's, the only one she took with her from the family house.'

Instantly, he was alert. He glared at his daughter. 'What are you up to?'

'I want to know.'

'Know what?'

'About the painting and the quarrel with your brother and why the picture had an unhappy history, and . . .'

'It can't be the painting, it was sold.'

'It's a photograph of it. I went back to the house and . . .'

'You did what?'

'I wanted to see it.'

'What a damned cheek.'

'Mme Verlon didn't think so. She was really helpful. She said she thought the painting had some sort of significance for your mother, something sad.'

'I haven't the faintest idea of what you're talking about or what that Frenchwoman meant.'

'But the sight of the painting upsets you.'

'It certainly does not!'

The room went quiet. Gillian, standing in the doorway, didn't speak again. It struck her, observing her father, that she had only the glimmer of understanding about his reaction to the painting. Clearly, what upset him was the connection with his mother, but it was more than that, something deeper, some other memory perhaps. So she waited, unusually patient, until her father sighed and said, 'Let's go and sit down, Gillian.' They went back to the sitting room and sat down. Her father looked exhausted. 'I honestly

319

don't know,' he said, 'why you've made such a thing over that painting. You've built it up into something it isn't, some mystery that never existed. Why on earth are you so bothered about it? It's nothing to you, it's nothing to me.'

'It was something to your mother.'

'My mother is dead. She's been dead for twenty-odd years.'

'And you still haven't forgiven her.'

'Don't be absurd. You're letting your imagination carry you away. You're making things up.'

'Tell me the truth then, tell me what really happened, put me right.'

'Gillian, please, there's nothing to tell. My mother was killed in an accident, she left almost everything to some strange Scottish charities, including that dreary little picture.'

'And Uncle James?'

'For heaven's sake!'

'Your only brother, and you don't speak to him, and it was something to do with the painting.'

'History. James was going to take it and he wasn't entitled to it and I told him so. I wish I'd never seen the damned picture.'

'It's by Gwen John. Probably.'

'I don't care who it's by, it's meaningless to me.'

'But it wasn't to my grandmother.'

'Who knows what the hell it meant to her.'

'I think,' Gillian said, slowly, aware that her father was still disturbed and angry, 'I think my grandmother wanted to be the woman in that room.'

'Woman? There's no woman in it. The room's empty.'

'It only looks empty. It's full, though: it has a presence, someone serene and contented and maybe in love.'

'What rubbish!'

'Not to me, not to my grandmother. If the painting could talk . . .'

'Well, it can't, which is a relief. It might come out with the sort of nonsense you're talking. It's just a picture of an empty room.'

320

'It depends who looks, how they look.'

'Let's stop now, Gillian. You're being fanciful, silly. I've no patience with you like this. You're spoiling what promised to be a pleasant evening. What time is your mother back?'

'Soon.'

'Good. Now, can I read my newspaper?'

'Yes, Dad. Read it.'

Quietly, Gillian slipped into the back room and took the photograph down.

★

Gillian's A-level results were excellent: four As. Her father was delighted, his pride in her achievement almost embarrassing – 'Dad, please,' Gillian protested when he even told the plumber who had come to fix a new sink. Once the celebrations were over – an extravagant dinner in a restaurant – Cameron made one last try to persuade his daughter to go to university. But she was adamant. She wanted to take up her foundation course place in September 2006 and before then spend some time in Paris. The idea alarmed him – she was, he said, much too young and pretty to be let loose in Paris – but she pleaded with him, saying she'd work first at Starbuck's, or somewhere, for six months, to earn the money to support herself and he wouldn't have to contribute much. Money, Cameron said, was not the point. It was her safety he was concerned about. But her mother supported Gillian and eventually, with the greatest reluctance, he gave way, on condition that he himself should arrange where she would stay and vet the establishment where she wanted to study.

Paris, when Gillian finally arrived there, was not quite as she had imagined it, not as exotic as she had wanted it to be. Dismayed, she looked round the room she found herself in and thought she might be in any city in England. There was almost nothing about it that looked foreign, no piece of furniture which seemed intriguingly different and strange. Even the window had curtains which would have looked perfectly in place in her parents' house and the carpet was surely an exact copy of the carpet in her bedroom there. There wasn't the faintest whiff of garlic. Instead she could swear there was a smell of frying bacon drifting up the stairs.

But she reminded herself that a city was on the outside of rooms, not in them (though she wasn't quite convinced of this), and that she was bound to be disappointed, arriving at this address late on a wet evening. She had heard French being spoken all around her at the station, and the walk from the Metro to this apartment block had been further evidence that she was in Paris, not London. But she had had her head down, battling against the wind and rain, and, encumbered with her bags and portfolio, had taken little in. When she rang the bell, the landlady opened the door and spoke to her in English, a welcoming little speech but not quite what she anticipated.

Her father had fixed up the digs – that's what he'd called them, 'digs' – through someone he knew at work who had a friend in Paris running a kind of *pension*. Gillian had imagined a flat, shared with two or three other art students – but this would do for the time being until she made friends. She reckoned she would be out of this room within a month. By then, she would know Paris, as well as other students, and would be laughing at the memory of having been forced to land here.

If only it were a garret, empty and romantic. She wouldn't have minded if it were freezing cold (the room she was in even had central heating). There would have been a view of rooftops, and the faint scent of Gauloise cigarettes would have hung about it. Opening the window here was a struggle – there were all kinds of locks – and when she'd managed to force it half open there was not much to see except the block opposite, as new and ugly as the one she was in. She wanted to be in Montmartre, or perhaps on the Ile St Louis, instead of almost in the suburbs. There was no romance here, and she felt disappointed to think that she had swapped one safe berth for another. But she went to bed repeating to herself, 'I am in Paris, I am in Paris.'

★

Madame Verlon, on the other hand, felt like a foreigner in her own city. Twenty-three years since she had lived in Paris, but she had visited often and those years did not explain the unnerving sense of dislocation she now experienced. She had expected to slip back easily into her former life but this was not happening. Maybe, she thought, she was simply suffering from exhaustion after the upheaval of the last month when the London house was vacated – it had been far more upsetting than she had anticipated even though she had done little of the packing up herself. Twenty-three happy years, vanishing before her eyes. Her husband did not know what she was so distressed about. It was she who for so long had wanted to return to Paris, was it not? Yet again and again he found her in tears, standing in the middle of one room or another, and was exasperated. His own excitement at returning to Paris, though initially he had not been keen, could not be concealed, and he was irritated that she was the one who had become such an Anglophile. Claudette said her distress had nothing to do with her liking for the English or for London. It was to do with leaving the house, her home. Houses had souls, she believed, and rooms had an awful power. Until she had re-created another home she would feel bereft.

After a great deal of searching, the apartment they finally bought was not on the Ile St Louis but in the Rue de Rivoli. It was almost exactly what she had envisaged, in spite of the location (Jacques's preference) and she was pleased with it, but there was a lot yet to be done in the way of decoration and refurbishment – it would be a year, she estimated, before she had the place looking as she wanted and could feel she belonged. She had vowed to take her time but already the sight of the hideous tiles in the bathroom made her want to have them ripped out imme-diately, and she could not stand the vile green paint in the kitchen one day longer. In London, she had had at her fingertips the tele-phone numbers of all kinds of workmen and services she had used over the years, but in Paris she was having to start again. Having money did not seem to help. It seemed you had to know the right people, have the right contacts here.

Everything was uncomfortable and she did not seem to be able to sort it out. Packing cases were everywhere, all neatly and effi-ciently labelled, but she could not bring herself to begin the unpacking. Her daughter came to help, but they ended up going out together for lunch and nothing got done. Huguette seemed delighted to have her in Paris, and there was something relaxing about hearing her own language all around. But Huguette did not think her mother was relaxed.

'What's wrong, Maman?' she asked. 'You're all tense. Aren't you glad to be home?'

'I don't know. I feel a foreigner in my own city.'

Instead of fading, the feeling grew; the sense of being displaced made her irritable and moody. Had she felt this when she moved to England? She had no recollection of having done so. All she could remember was falling in love instantly with the Chelsea house, and being endlessly busy settling the children into their new schools and routines.

It was a relief that there was a small room in the apartment which she had been able to claim straightaway as her own. It had once been an annexe to the kitchen, perhaps even a walk-in pantry, but there was a window in one wall, quite large, and out of proportion to the dimensions of the room itself. She hung her favourite painting here, in solitary state. She did not even furnish the room – when she came to look at her painting, she would stand in front of it. The room was more like a tiny chapel than a boudoir.

Looking at the painting here she concluded that for many years she had been misinterpreting it. Casting aside all her complicated theories as to the significance of the empty chair, the parasol, the flowers, she decided that all it said to her eyes now was 'Let life be simple'. Let everything go, all the striving, all the tension, keep the world away. Eat, drink, exercise, be grateful to live and breathe. When she was alone with the painting, this seemed to make sense, but when she was not there, it could sound banal. Her life now *was* simple. Very little was required of her. She had nothing to do except see that her husband was taken care of, and that was not difficult. He was happy, back in Paris; he had forgotten that he hadn't wanted to return. He had taken up with his old friends and pastimes and required little of her.

But she thought the painting lied. She knew that because she had tried to do it once, a long time ago. She was very young, only eighteen, and desperate to get away from home where all she seemed to do was have violent rows with her father who criticised her relentlessly – her appearance, her alleged laziness, her impertinence, all enraged him. Her mother never took her side. She wept during the arguments and said it was like living in a madhouse. Claudette thought this an accurate description – her father, she was sure, was mad. There was no other explanation for his belligerent, aggressive behaviour (though her mother was forever blaming his ill-health and money worries).

So Claudette left. She wanted to sever all connection with her parents, at least for the immediate future. She answered an advert in a newspaper for a job as a general help to an elderly lady who lived in a remote part of Corsica. It was a mistake. She knew that very quickly. Her employer hardly left the house and expected Claudette to stay by her side except for a weekly trip to the nearest village for provisions, in a cart pulled by an ancient horse that barely moved. Claudette made an effort to appreciate the intense silence and the wildness of the landscape, which she tried to draw, but the lack of human contact depressed her. It wasn't the answer, to withdraw from the world. All she had wanted to do was withdraw from her father and the feeling of being trapped. But in Corsica she was in another kind of trap. Her life was peaceful and simple but it was also sterile. She needed people. She needed to love and be loved. She needed a real life. The simple life was not enough. The world could not be kept away, not entirely, if one wished to be happy.

★

It happened more or less as Gillian had anticipated. She did make friends, she did move into an apartment with them (not telling her father until she'd done so), and she did find the Paris she had hoped for. Her text messages to friends in London filled them in on the various attempts to pick her up, but in her letters and phone calls home she concentrated on the exploring she was doing, the long walks along the Seine and down the Champs

Elysées and through the Bois de Boulogne. She tried to get across how she felt she fitted in, in a way she had never expected – 'There must have been something Parisian about me all along,' she wrote. People spoke to her in French because they assumed she was French, and if she could get away with it she tried to keep the illusion intact, communicating in smiles and nods and hand gestures. She loved the flea markets, especially the slightly seedy ones, and picked up there all kinds of unusual objects she planned to use in still lifes. She was quite happy, at first, to be on her own, except for sharing the odd espresso or *citron pressé* with young men who came and sat at her table, but then she made some real friends.

These friends were unexpected ones, though. None of them was an art student. Carole was Australian, doing the Aussie thing of working her way round Europe, and Gillian had met her on a boat going down the Seine. Gillian had been sketching the river-bank near Meudon and Carole admired her drawing – an encounter as simple as that, which led to others. Françoise was French, working as an attendant in the Louvre (where Gillian went regularly) before beginning at the Sorbonne in the autumn; and Gérard was her boyfriend. What he did remained mysterious to Gillian, but it was he who found the apartment in Rue Froide-vaux and suggested that the three of them should share it. But even split between three, the rent was too much and so they needed a fourth, which was where Carole came in.

There were three bedrooms and a living room, with an alcove which pretended to be a kitchen. Since none of them had any intention of serious cooking, this did not matter. The unsatisfactory bathroom mattered more, but they put up with the ridiculously small tub and the lack of a shower because everything else was so pleasing. The living room was huge and virtually empty and had a magnificent view (they were on the fourth floor) over rooftops, just as Gillian had imagined. Françoise and Gérard shared one room, and she and Carole had a room each. Carole took the smallest room, saying it didn't matter to her, it was just such heaven to get out of the hostel she'd been in, and Gillian had the one next to it, a much more attractive room overlooking the leafy cemetery opposite.

Gérard, whatever he did, was rarely there. He often did not come back at night, but this did not seem to upset Françoise, who shrugged and said, 'He's busy.' All their hours of work or study were different, so Gillian was often alone in the apartment and had plenty of time and space and privacy to paint. She tried to paint the living room, with its high ceiling, long windows, superb light. There were two sofas, old pieces of furniture, made of a dark wood with carved arms and high backs. They had cushions of dark crimson velvet which gave off small puffs of dust when anyone sat down. The sun coming through the unshaded windows one day onto the red of the sofas' cushions excited Gillian – it was like a fire burning amid the cool grey of the walls and the black wood of the floor. She set her easel up at the far end of the room. Naturally, the others when they were at home wanted to look at what she was doing, and she had to let them. They were silent after inspecting her work, except for Gérard. He contemplated her canvas day after day – her progress was slow – and eventually commented.

'The spirit of the room, huh?'

She nodded. Exactly.

'You think rooms have spirits?' he asked.

'This one does,' she said.

'So, what do you think has happened in it?'

'Happened?'

'To give it its spirit. These sofas, eh, what have they seen? Who has sat upon them? Who chose them?'

'It doesn't matter.'

'It doesn't?'

'No. That's not what I mean. It isn't about the history of the room, it's about now, just about the feel of the room now, what it makes me feel, and think.'

Maybe she spoke too quickly, maybe her French was not up to what she wanted to say, but Gérard made no other comment. A week or so later, when he came home unexpectedly in the middle of the afternoon, he stood once more and looked at what she was painting.

'You are an Impressionist, then,' he said. 'I didn't expect it.' She made no reply, hoping he didn't need a response. He went on staring until his attention began to irritate her. Abruptly, she stopped, and began cleaning her brushes. He sat on one of the sofas and smoked and went on watching her clear up. 'How old are you, Gillian?' he asked. 'Eighteen? Nineteen? Twenty?'

'Nineteen.'

'And never in love, huh? Today, that is rare, very sweet.'

She frowned, feeling that he was inviting either protests or confessions, so she turned away from him and busied herself with tidying up.

'And now I have offended you, no?'

'No.'

'Good. It's your painting, it shows feelings, just as you wanted it to, but maybe not the feelings you thought it would, eh?'

'I don't know what you're talking about, Gérard, sorry, you've lost me.'

'Paintings,' Gérard said, slowly, 'are feelings. It doesn't matter what the eye sees, the heart must feel, or it is useless.'

'Very profound,' muttered Gillian. She badly wanted to laugh, but his expression was so solemn she didn't dare.

He was staring at her, quite openly, waiting for some reaction she couldn't provide. She began to whistle, to show her lack of concern, and knew she was disappointing him by failing to engage in any discussion. She couldn't imagine what pretty Françoise saw in him.

*

Two months after their return to Paris, Mme Verlon's husband died. An apparently fit, healthy sixty-six-year-old man, who did not smoke, or drink too much, he had a heart attack one night shortly after dinner with some friends. Mme Verlon was not with him. The friends were old colleagues of his, the dinner at their dining-club. She was called, at 11 p.m., by one of them and told that he had been rushed to hospital. What shocked and appalled her was her own reaction. She did not scream or weep but neither was she rendered speechless. 'How dreadful,' she said, quietly, and 'Where is he?' She went to the hospital where he had been taken and met her daughter there. Huguette was distraught enough for the two of them. Her elder son arrived half an hour later, white-faced, and embraced her, offering words of comfort he was more in need of himself. Her younger son was in America, on busi-ness, and had not yet been contacted. So there they were, a group of three, standing in the bare little hospital room, looking down at the dead body. It was Mme Verlon who said, eventually, 'Shall we go?'

That night, lying in bed unable to sleep, Mme Verlon for some reason found herself thinking of the widow from whom she had bought the Chelsea house all those years ago. She remembered having the distinct impression that Mrs Mortimer was not exactly grief-stricken about her husband's death, or that she had recov-ered remarkably quickly. She had thought how odd that must feel, not to be intensely sad when it was expected of one, and she had known, then, that she would not have been able to bear life without her husband. But now, when he had been taken from her, she understood Mrs Mortimer better. Grief could, it seemed, come in strange forms. She was sure that she was full of grief, because she had loved her husband and they had had almost forty years together, but that it was buried and had not yet surfaced in any acceptable form. She felt too calm, too clear-headed (but that could be shock). She did not for one moment imagine that she could not go on with her life – her husband's had come to an abrupt end; hers had not.

What she supposed no one had realised, not even their chil-dren, was how, over the last few years, their lives had become separate within what was, and always had been, a happy marriage. They had not really seen a great deal of each other during the day, though every night, or almost every night, they had slept in the same bed; and their sex life had continued, though it bore no comparison to what it had once been – how could it, after so many years together and considering their age, with such a loss of energy? But what had increasingly struck Claudette as odd was how remote she had become from Jacques, in spirit, that is. She had often wanted to ask him if he felt strangely remote, and yet still close, but had never done so. This was another thing that had changed. Feelings were assumed but not expressed. She had felt incapable of communicating all sorts of fears and hopes (more fears than hopes) and had told herself that this was because there was no point in worrying Jacques.

And there were often trivial things, which she no longer told him. Once, she would have enjoyed telling him about Gillian Mortimer's visit, would have made an entertaining story out of it, and Jacques would have shared her interest in the girl and the connection with her grandmother and her Gwen John painting. But she had not mentioned the unexpected visitor. Her silence was more remarkable, considering that she now had rather empty days, with little to recount. She just, somehow, could not be bothered. Maybe Jacques had experienced the same ennui about such ordinary matters. They had each become locked into their own spheres, and yet, peculiarly, were not uncomfortable with this situation. But it had meant that when death came, there was not the same terror there would have been even five years before. It was as if she had already served a long apprenticeship, and she was almost grateful for it.

She could not speak about any of this. There was the funeral to get through, and the messages of condolence to deal with. She was dutiful, replying to every single letter herself. Huguette stayed with her but was more hindrance than help, crying at regular intervals and full of remorse for not having appreciated her father enough. Claudette found it a strain having to be endlessly sympathetic and reassuring, but successfully hid this. Her sons – the younger one had returned for the funeral – suffered no such qualms of guilt and tried their best to be useful. They dealt with the solicitor over their father's straightforward will and handled other practical matters. Their mother was pleased with them. The younger son, clearly influenced by his time in America, assured her one day that 'It's all right to cry, you know, Maman.' She said she knew that, but liked to keep her tears private. That seemed to satisfy him.

When everything had settled down, which is to say that all three children had gone back to their respective lives and she was alone, Mme Verlon toyed with the notion of returning to London. But, obviously, she could not go back to the beloved Chelsea house, and it was too daunting to think of finding a suitable place. Besides, her children would be upset, and she was touched by their concern for her. She had never been emotionally demonstrative with them – she was not that sort of woman – but she cared about them and enjoyed their company, so it would have been foolish to deprive herself of it. Her elder son's wife was expecting a baby and she was surprisingly (she surprised herself) interested in becoming a grand-mother. No, she could not return to London.

But the apartment she now lived in was not the place for a woman on her own. It was too spacious, almost too grand, with its huge rooms and high ceilings. She kept wanting to retreat into the kitchen and the little room off it, to hide and pretend the rest of the apartment did not exist. It was not like her to want to do this – she had always liked and needed generous spaces to live in – but she concluded with relief that it was a sign of missing her husband. He had been such a loud, convivial man that being in small rooms with him would have been oppressive. When, very occasionally, he had joined her when she was looking at her painting, she had been eager for him to leave her alone. His pres-ence overwhelmed the picture.

She wanted to move, but where? She still wished to be in central Paris . . . near to art galleries and all the other cultural centres which were her chief source of pleasure; but she wanted peace and quiet too. She needed advice, and turned to one of her late husband's friends who owned a rather grand estate agency. He came to see her to get a clearer idea of what exactly she was looking for, what kind of apartment, though he thought he had grasped the sort of location, central but quiet, etc. She took him into the little room off the kitchen and, to his bewilderment, showed him the painting.

'There,' she said, 'I want a room like that.'

'An *attic*?' asked Bernard, horrified. 'You want to give this up to live in an attic?'

'No,' Mme Verlon said, 'I don't want to move into an attic but into an apartment with an attic as part of it. I want what this painting shows, the life it represents.'

Bernard stared. 'But, Claudette, there *is* no life there, that I can see. There is an absence of life, no?'

'Then maybe I want a place where there is an absence.'

Embarrassed, Bernard said no more. Mme Verlon could see that he thought grief had unhinged her. But he did his best to be co-operative. He would get one of his employees on the job straight-away. There were plenty such attics in Paris, and there might be just the thing in a *bijou* apartment on the Ile Saint Louis. He would send round Gérard Maritain to talk to her the next day. Gérard was an artist himself, but, in the way of so many artists, had had to turn to business to support himself. He would find what she wanted, she could rest assured.

★

Their meeting was entirely by chance, if one believed in chance, which Mme Verlon was not entirely convinced that she did. Was life random? There was enough evidence to suggest so, but it went against her own orderly nature to credit this. Some co-incidences were so extraordinary that they unavoidably had about them that feeling of having been 'meant'.

So, it was chance, a coincidence, that as she went into the Louvre, Gillian Mortimer was coming out. That day, there were no crowds. It was raining torrentially. Mme Verlon stepped from a taxi, umbrella at the ready, and made a dash across the court-yard. She paused at the entrance to shake and then fold up her umbrella just as Gillian, coming out, stopped to zip up her jacket and put the sketches she had been doing in her bag. They each recognised the other at the same moment. Of the two, Gillian was by far the most surprised and found herself saying, 'Mme Verlon, isn't it? You're in Paris now?' which afterwards she thought a bit ridiculous. Mme Verlon said yes, she was, she'd been living here a few months. 'And you?' she asked, 'you are studying here?' Gillian said yes, she was, she was on a short course, and had been copying Murillo's *The Young Beggar* as part of her homework. 'I remember such homework well,' said Mme Verlon.

After that, what was there to say? Mme Verlon felt that she must take the lead. 'Perhaps,' she said, 'you would care to visit me and take a glass of wine?' Gillian said she would be delighted, it would be such a pleasure, and Mme Verlon produced a card with her address on, suggesting an evening, the following Friday, when she would be at home. The moment the girl had taken the card, and said goodbye, Claudette wondered what she had done. She had done no entertaining since her husband died, with the exception of giving Bernard coffee when he came, and she had no real desire to make the effort. But she had issued the invitation, and since she had not asked for Gillian's address she could not cancel it. All the time she was in the Louvre, she felt distracted. She didn't know why she had come. Boredom with being at home. A boredom, a pointlessness to her days, which was growing and about which something would have to be done. Drifting around the Louvre, or any other museum, was not enough. The immense building depressed her, its grandeur overwhelmed her, and whereas once, as a student, she had leapt up the various staircases, eager to get where she was going, now her legs ached and her feet needed persuasion to carry on. What was she looking for? Comfort? Distraction? Neither. She wanted, she thought, to be uplifted in some way, to feel her spirits rise, as once they had done when she stood in front of those paintings.

She herself hadn't painted for years. Years and years. The longing, the urge had simply disappeared, round about the time Huguette was born. It wasn't something, then, that she had missed. It was Jacques who had commented upon her lack of productivity, and at first she made excuses – she had no time, with the baby, it was impossible to settle down, to concentrate. But she knew this was not the case. Lack of time had had nothing to do with it. She had simply felt no desire to be painting. She was content. And so it had gone on, with the birth of the boys. It didn't make her sad no longer to think of herself as an artist, so perhaps she never had been one. All she'd done was amuse herself with the little talent she had shown. She didn't feel that maternity had robbed her of the chance to exercise this talent but that rather she had discovered another which satisfied her more. There was no resentment in her.

But now, there was a new need in her. Could she start to paint again? The idea seemed almost embarrassing, but as the first cautious thoughts entered her mind she felt a little surge of excitement and wondered if they were telling her something she rather wanted to hear.

★

Gillian felt she should take a present, but it was difficult to think of one when Mme Verlon was so obviously rich and had everything. Flowers were always safe, but she wanted to be more original. She wondered if she dared take one of her own paintings, or whether that would be like boasting. She'd done some small oils, studies of a jug she had found in a flea market, and they had turned out well. But she didn't have the confidence to present one to a connoisseur and so she fell back on flowers after all. She was particular about them, though, searching everywhere until she found primroses and then buying six little bunches of them and having them tied with white ribbon. The effect was pretty.

Mme Verlon's apartment was in what had once been an hotel – and was quite alarmingly luxurious, situated as it was in the Rue de Rivoli with its views over the Jardin des Tuileries. Gillian was awed by the grandeur of the building. There was a concierge in uniform who seemed doubtful about letting her go up in the lift at all and insisted on ringing Mme Verlon to see if she was expected. Alone in the lift – fitted out like a room, with a carpet on the floor and two chairs – Gillian thought how impersonal and formal this place felt, but when she was welcomed into Mme Verlon's apartment she was surprised to find it not in the least stiff or opulent. She admired the room she was taken into, but Mme Verlon said it was not finished – she meant the furnishing – and now never would be because she was moving soon. 'My husband died, you know, soon after we came here.' Gillian said how sorry she was, but Mme Verlon made a dismissive gesture, indicating that she didn't want to discuss it. 'I want somewhere smaller, somewhere more interesting,' she said.

There was an uneasy silence which Gillian could not think how to break, or whether indeed she should be the one – the visitor, the younger – who should break it. Mme Verlon sat on the edge of the sofa, straight-backed, hands clasped in her lap, dignified and a little forbidding, just as she had been in the Chelsea house. She seemed to be waiting, but what for? Gillian asked if she was glad to be back in Paris and was told that in some ways she was, but not in others, which led on to a stilted conversation about the rival merits of London. Then she was offered wine, and left alone while her hostess went to get it. Mme Verlon brought in olives, too, glistening in an oddly shaped pottery bowl, which Gillian admired. Mme Verlon said she had made it herself, many years ago, when she was an art student; Gillian asked where she had trained; and that in turn brought Mme Verlon to enquire about Gillian's present education . . . it was all very polite, very awkward. The sooner it was over, the better, Gillian thought. The glass of wine, she was relieved to see, was quite small. Two or three gulps, and it would be drunk and she could start to leave.

But Mme Verlon surprised her, by asking if she would like to see the painting again. Gillian knew at once which painting she meant. 'Where is it?' she asked. Mme Verlon got up and led the way through another room into a kitchen and then to a small room opening off it. They stood side by side, as they had done in the Chelsea house, looking at the painting.

'So it's back where it started,' Gillian said. 'If you're right, if Gwen John painted it in Paris.'

'Yes, but this is not the Paris she knew, I am sure. She would not like to think of it *here*, in this apartment.'

'How many years is it,' Gillian asked, 'since it was painted?'

Mme Verlon shrugged. 'Perhaps nearly a hundred, something like that.'

'A long time. Will you keep it?'

'I will keep it, yes, of course, how could I not? I try to live by it. But I do not intend to leave it to my children. They would not appreciate it: it means nothing to them.'

'So where will it go? To a gallery or a museum?'

'Perhaps. It might be best, it might be right.'

'It would look lost, hanging on the wall of a museum.'

'There is that to think about. Yes, it would not be happy on such a wall, it would be diminished, I think. There would be no time for those who see it to gain from it. They would look, they would pass on, they would think it pretty but insipid, rather dull. It would be a pity.'

'But why not leave it to your daughter? It needs to go from woman to woman, to be part of their lives, affecting them every day.'

Mme Verlon looked at Gillian with astonishment and a new interest. 'That is well put,' she said. 'It has a power all its own. I have felt it. But you are young, it cannot have the same meaning to you. You are young, beautiful, happy – it has nothing yet, perhaps never, to do with you. It is just a painting you like, you admire.'

'No,' Gillian said, 'it has a history. I don't know what it is, not even my grandmother's part in it, but something is there, more than the paint on the canvas. Don't you think so? Don't artists want to put more than the paint on the canvas?'

After Gillian had gone, Mme Verlon felt quite stunned. The girl had articulated what she felt herself. She had expressed exactly her feelings about the painting, and now that they were out in the open, as it were, they made her decision as to its future harder. A museum of modern art would not do. The painting needed to go, as Gillian had said, from woman to woman. But how could she make sure that it did? She would leave it to Huguette, but then what? Huguette would not sell it, if instructed that it must not be sold, but who knew what she would feel about it? And who would she pass it on to? Maybe she ought just to let the painting take its chance, as it had been obliged to do when it left the artist's hands. Maybe she should leave instructions in her will that it was to be sold, on condition it was not sold to an institution but to an individual woman who would keep it in her home. Impossible to enforce such a condition, perhaps, but it would be fun to try.

Meanwhile, she had it to herself. She would take it with her, wherever she ended up going, and it would be part of her life still, as it had been part of the lives of others, and she would benefit from it. Had that not been its purpose? To keep the world away, for a few precious moments at least, every time it was looked at?

★

Gillian walked the long way home very slowly, back down the Rue de Rivoli, past the Louvre, over the Pont Neuf and into the Rue Dauphine which led, via two streets she did not know the names of, into the Luxembourg Gardens and through them, finally, into Montparnasse and the Rue Froide-vaux. She would not see Mme Verlon again, unless they had another accidental encounter. There had been no rapport between them – their only point of contact was the painting, and that was not enough to give them a future as friends.

It was a beautiful evening, and now at last she appreciated Paris and relished its difference from London. Her French was still halting, but she was picking up the slang fast and she understood most of what she heard. There were subtle advantages, she was learning, in being a foreigner in a city, a matter of seeing things differently from the way the resident population saw them. She felt the shock of the new every time she turned a corner she did not know and was surprised. Her mind filled with sudden glimpses of people and places which fed into her imagination and sparked off ideas. This excited her and made her want to paint more than ever, to let this thrill run down her brush and onto canvas. She had meant what she had said to Mme Verlon: she wanted to put more than paint onto her canvases, something that could always be felt if the onlooker knew how to identify it.

All the way up to her apartment, she was hoping none of the others would be there so that she could set to work immediately.

★

It was easy enough to arrange. Mme Verlon made an appointment with her solicitor and her will was put in order. She bequeathed the painting described as 'oil painting, untitled, possibly by Gwen John, of the corner of an attic' to Gillian Mortimer, with the wish that she in turn should bequeath it to another woman of her choice who would appreciate it. The solicitor thought the painting ought first to be authenticated, since if it was by the alleged artist it would be of serious monetary as well as artistic value, but Mme Verlon declined to have this done. She had told her children whom she was leaving the painting to, and they had no objections, whatever its value – they were all very well provided for already.

It pleased Mme Verlon every day after that, simply to think of how the painting would carry on its life, with women who would respond to its simplicity and yet who would not be fooled into imagining there was neither passion nor longing within it.

The artist would think that enough. She had painted it to keep the world away. If it helped others to do the same, her purpose was fulfilled.

Acknowledgements

Gwen John, Mary Taubman (Scolar Press, Aldershot, 1985).

Augustus John, Michael Holroyd, revised edition (Vintage, London 1997).

Gwen John, Alicia Foster (British Artists series, Tate Publishing, London, 1999).

Gwen John: A life, Sue Roe (Chatto & Windus, London, 2001).

Gwen and Augustus John, catalogue for the 2004 Exhibition, ed. David Fraser Jenkins and Chris Stephens (Tate Publishing, London, 2004).

Gwen John: Letters and Notebooks, ed. Ceridwen Lloyd-Morgan (Tate Publishing, London, 2004).